DOPPELGANGSTER

DOPPELGANGSTER

Laura Resnick

DAW BOOKS, INC.

DONALD A. WOLLHEIM, FOUNDER
375 Hudson Street, New York, NY 10014
ELIZABETH R. WOLLHEIM
SHEILA E. GILBERT
PUBLISHERS
www.dawbooks.com

First Paperback Printing, January 2010.

1 2 3 4 5 6 7 8 9 10

For Mom & Dad
(the only existing versions of themselves)
who liked the title

DOPPELGANGSTER

PROLOGUE

The fact that I had killed a man was really putting a crimp in my love life.

Well, okay, to be strictly accurate, *I* hadn't killed him. But I had helped. And I had watched enough of the Emmy Award–winning cops-and-lawyers drama *Crime and Punishment* on TV to know that cops weren't very understanding about that sort of thing. I had even auditioned for the role of a murderess in a *C&P* episode the previous year, but I didn't get the part. So, since I had never even played a killer, actually *being* one now was something of a novelty.

It was also rather awkward, since I was dating a cop. Or at least trying to date one. And he was a straight-arrow cop who didn't look the other way when it came to breaking and entering and vandalism (two more awkward secrets I was keeping from him), never mind murder.

Which is not to say that I had done anything wrong. On the contrary. I stand by my actions. I was fighting Evil.

And if that sounds absurd to you, well, that's understandable. It sounds pretty damn absurd to me, too.

The man I had helped kill—and I'm using the word "man" in its broadest possible sense—was a demented sorcerer's apprentice who tried to take over New York City by summoning a virgin-raping, people-eating demon.

You probably think I'm kidding.

In a series of events that I was trying hard not to think about now that they were over, I had helped Dr. Maximillian Zadok, Manhattan's resident sorcerer and local representative of the Magnum Collegium—a secret organization whose worldwide mission is to confront Evil—track the villain to his underground lair. There we had faced the demon Avolapek (an individual about whom the words "biliously repellant" are far too kind), had defeated him in what might loosely be termed combat, and had slain his maniacal creator, the rogue apprentice Hieronymus.

I am not making this up.

How Max had eliminated Hieronymus was not entirely clear to me. *Most* things about Max were not entirely clear to me. He and a fellow mage, a man named Lysander—whose day job is keeping Altoona, Pennsylvania, safe from Evil (yes, really)—had done some chanting in another language, and Hieronymus had vanished. According to Max, this was dissolution, which he described to me as "something remarkably similar to death." Since it was a permanent, all-dimensions solution to the problem of Hieronymus and his evil plans, I had no objection. But I also had a feeling that a jury might consider any legal difference (if one existed) between murder and dissolution to be so piddling as to make no difference at all in our conviction and sentencing, should these events ever come to light.

By the time Max arrived at Hieronymus' secret lair to save me from becoming demon dinner, I had already beaten Hieronymus to a pulp with a candelabra and then thrown him as a decoy at the virgin-raping Avolapek (who did not refuse a free meal, so to speak). So a jury might reasonably conclude that I had actively assisted in the evil apprentice's demise—or at least softened him up for it. I figured Max and I could both be in big trouble over those events—unless a jury *also* believed the part about Hieronymus summoning a demon and trying to kill a bunch of people (including me) at the very moment we snuffed out his life.

I pictured myself saying in a court of law, "Well, Your Honor, there was this evil sorcerer's apprentice and a flesh-eating, power-granting demon he summoned from a primordial dimension . . ."

Even I couldn't see a way to make that script work.

Which was why I felt it was imperative that Detective Lopez, who'd dogged our steps on that case, should never find out what had happened that fateful night. Happily, no one was pressing charges about the breaking and entering and vandalism that Max and I had previously committed (hey, we were trying to prevent more innocents from getting hurt, okay?), and Lopez had dropped that particular subject by now. He was, however, still perplexed about what had happened the night that Max and I, along with several missing persons (Hieronymus' victims, whom we rescued when we defeated him), suddenly turned up at an obscure Morningside Heights magic club without explanation, all looking (and smelling) as if we'd been to hell and back. There was also a white Bengal tiger with us—but I digress.

The problem was . . . I really liked Lopez. He liked me, too. But I was jumpy about any topic that might lead to his asking about that night. He sensed I was hiding things, and that raised his cop hackles. So our first couple of dates hadn't gone that well. Nevertheless, he asked me out a third time. Obviously, it would have been smart for me to say no. From the beginning, actually. It would have been wise to avoid Lopez altogether, to stay off his radar.

But, come on, I'm a single woman in New York City. It takes more than a morbid fear of doing life in prison for homicide to make me turn down a date with an employed, attractive, single, heterosexual man who has nice table manners, listens when I talk, and knows how to kiss.

So I said yes to a third date.

We both worked nights, so we'd met for lunch on our previous two dates. This time, Lopez wanted to take me out for dinner. He said he had something to celebrate. He was a detective in the Sixth Precinct and usually worked second shift, getting off around midnight. I was doing eight shows per week as a chorus nymph and unrewarded understudy in the new off-Broadway musical *Sorcerer!* So Lopez traded shifts with another cop so he would be free on Sunday, the one night I wasn't working.

Unfortunately, it turned out to be a bad night for me. Also for my love life. And things soon got worse. Before long, someone was trying to kill me. And Lopez.

So maybe he'd have been better off if he'd never asked me out a third time.

1

The good-looking man standing in my doorway wanted to have sex with me.

That much was apparent just from the way he was dressed. I wasn't born yesterday. (In point of fact, I was born twenty-seven years ago.) A man who goes to that much trouble to look sexy has got definite plans in mind when he arrives at a woman's door.

Lopez wore a sophisticated, well-cut black jacket and trousers with a black silk shirt. Open at the neck, the shirt exposed the smooth, dark golden skin of his throat. Even in my current state of panic and depression, I noticed how tempting this was. But only briefly.

The dim light in the hallway glinted off his straight black hair as he held out a single red rose to me.

I frowned. "What are you doing here?"

He looked a little surprised by this reception, but quickly regrouped. "We have a date tonight."

"We do?"

"Yes, Esther." The hand holding the rose dropped to his side. "Sunday night. Dinner. I wanted to . . ." Thick black lashes lowered over blue eyes as his gaze flickered over me. "You're not exactly dressed for celebrating," he noted.

"Celebrating?" I snapped. "*Celebrating?* Are you insane?"

He blinked. "Did something happen?"

"Ohmigod!" I suddenly realized what he was doing there. "We have a date tonight!"

He lifted one brow. "Do you want to close the door? I could knock on it, and we could start all over again."

"You look nice," I said, hoping to make up for my earlier behavior.

"Can I come in?" he asked patiently.

"Oh! Of course." I moved aside and gestured for him to enter my home.

I live in a good apartment for a struggling actress in New York City. It's a second-floor walk-up in the West Thirties, near Ninth Avenue. The neighborhood is about as elegant as the floor of a public bathroom, and the apartment is old and falling apart. But my place is spacious (by Manhattan standards) and rent-controlled, and I have it all to myself.

However, even with rent control, I was currently worried about how I'd keep a roof over my head.

I closed the door behind Lopez and turned to face him as he stood in my living room. I realized he looked better than nice, he looked traffic-stopping. I suddenly regretted that I was greeting him with messy, unwashed hair, wearing old sweatpants and a T-shirt from the Actor's Studio, with a half-eaten pint of Ben and Jerry's ice cream in my hand.

Prince Charming meets the Bag Lady.

Except that Detective Connor Lopez didn't look innocuous enough to be Prince Charming. (He also didn't look like a Connor.) Thirty-one years old, he had inherited exotic dark looks from his Cuban father and lively blue eyes from his Irish American mother. Average height, with a slim, athletic build, he looked like a man who'd want more than a chaste kiss in exchange for rescuing the sleeping princess. Especially dressed the way he was tonight.

I'm 5 foot 6 and in decent enough condition to do eight performances of a song-and-dance musical in skimpy clothes every week, but I'm not skinny enough to work in Hollywood. I've got brown eyes, brown shoulder-length hair, and fair skin. My looks are versatile, and I can play heroines onstage, but my face, like my figure, doesn't meet Hollywood leading-lady standards. However, when he chose, Lopez had a way of looking at me that made me feel like a sexy movie-star vamp.

That wasn't the look he was giving me right now, though.

Eyeing my not-ready-for-dinner appearance, he said, "I can wait while you change. Er, *shower* and change."

"I can't go out!" Seeing his expression, I said more calmly, "I'm sorry. I just can't. Not tonight."

Now he looked concerned. "Are you okay?"

"No." My stomach roiled. "I think I'm going to be sick."

"Maybe eating half a pint of ice cream before dinner wasn't such a good idea?"

I shook my head. "It's not that." As my stomach churned noisily, I said, "Well, maybe that didn't help."

"Have a rose." He held out the flower again. As I accepted it from him, he added, "And tell me what's wrong."

"*Sorcerer!* is closing." I wanted to cry.

Both brows rose this time. "That's unexpected, I take it?" When I nodded, he said, "When did you find out?"

"About two hours ago." I had come back from yoga class, done two loads of laundry, cleaned the apartment, and was just about to step into the shower when I got the call informing me I was out of work. I'd been in a blue funk ever since.

"So . . . just like that? The show's over?"

I nodded morosely and sat down on my couch. I gently laid the rose on my coffee table, then I took another bite of ice cream. Lopez sat down next to me and took my free hand. Then he looked down at our joined hands, frowning a little.

"Sorry," I said. My hand was sticky. "It's the Turtle Soup."

"The what?"

I waggled my Ben and Jerry's carton at him. "The ice cream. Lots of caramel."

"Oh." When I tried to pull my hand away, he held fast and said, "No, it's okay."

"In times of stress, I need ice cream," I explained.

"Of course." He smiled. "Give me a bite."

I scooped some out of the carton in my lap and brought the spoon up to his mouth. His lips were full and, I knew from experience, felt lush when he kissed.

Our eyes met as I spooned caramel-laced ice cream into his mouth. When I started to pull my hand away, he held it in place so he could lick the spoon. I also knew from experience that he knew just what to do with his tongue when he kissed.

"Mmm," he said, still looking at me.

It should have felt sexy to feed him ice cream. Normally, it would. As previously noted, I wasn't dating him because it was the smart thing to do; I just couldn't keep away from him. And the way he looked tonight, with his thick black hair falling over his forehead and his open collar showing off his smooth throat . . .

I sighed dispiritedly. I was just too upset to feel sexy. I was also too unkempt and dirty. Some other time, when I felt better, I'd regret that I had wasted this moment. But right now, even Lopez couldn't stir my hormones. That's how bad I felt.

Evidently realizing that *all* he'd get out of this moment was a bite of ice cream, he let me lower the spoon. "That's pretty good. But I'm still a Cherry Garcia guy."

"Heath Bar Crunch is my usual poison." I sighed. "But this was all I had in the freezer when I got the call."

Since I'm an actress, I need to watch my weight. Especially while working in *Sorcerer!*, where my tight costumes left a lot of skin bare (albeit covered in green body paint and glitter). So I try to limit my ice cream consumption to special occasions and dire circumstances; since life is full of both of these, I always keep a pint or two on hand, just in case.

"So does this mean you're . . ." Lopez shrugged, not quite sure how to phrase it. "Out of work?"

I nodded. "Out of work."

"That was fast."

"Welcome to my world." I ate another spoonful of the Turtle Soup.

"What happened?"

I knew that to a normal, salaried person—even to a cop, who sees everything—the sudden, unexpected shift from employment to unemployment that's a normal part of an actor's life looks pretty dizzying. In fact, it makes actors dizzy, too. Right now, my head was reeling.

"Well, you know, reviews haven't been so good," I said. *Sorcerer!* was a tepid musical built entirely around the (rather mediocre) magician who was the producer's husband. After sitting through a performance, Lopez had said that only the chance to see me scamper around stage half-naked for two hours had made it a good evening. Although this sort of comment is flattering coming from my date, it's alarming coming from an audience member. I continued, "So our houses haven't been good."

"Your houses aren't good?" he repeated with a puzzled expression. "You mean, audiences don't applaud?"

"I mean, they don't come. Ticket sales are weak," I clarified.

"Ah. Yeah, I noticed that the night I came to see you. A lot of empty seats."

I nodded morosely. "That's a bad house—one with a lot of empty seats. And *Sorcerer!* is an expensive show. Golly Gee's salary alone ..." I trailed off, since I'd just accidentally stepped into territory I tried to avoid when I was with Lopez.

Golly Gee was the surgically-enhanced, B-list pop star who played the female lead in *Sorcerer*! I was a chorus nymph and her understudy. My involvement in fighting Evil with Maximillian Zadok had begun after Golly had vanished one night during the show's disappearing act. I mean, *really* vanished.

Lopez knew from interviewing us during the course of that investigation that Max and I both believed Golly had vanished magically. (Which was indeed the case.) He thought this was crazy, which Max assured me is a very common reaction to paranormal events. I understood Lopez's point of view, since it was initially my reaction, too. Only overwhelming evidence to the contrary, right before my eyes, had convinced me to believe in things now that I knew Lopez still did not believe in.

And any attempt to convince Lopez of what had really happened would no doubt wind up leading, in the end, to admitting that Max and I had killed Hieronymus. Or sort of killed him. (The fact that any such explanation would also convince Lopez I was nutty as a fruit-cake concerned me, too, since I didn't want him to stop asking me out.) True, we had saved Golly Gee and the other disappearees, but Lopez would insist on knowing how. And he was good at questioning people and putting together scattered details until he figured things out. I knew that if I let the subject be opened, there was no chance that Lopez would let it be closed until he knew everything.

So, having foolishly lowered my guard enough to mention Golly, I tried to backtrack. "Anyhow, musicals are very expensive, and without enough revenue coming in, they've decided to close the show."

"It probably hurt the budget a lot when Golly, er, disappeared for more than a week?" Lopez said, watching me with cop eyes now instead of potential-lover eyes. This was exactly the sort of thing that had made our first two dates a tad awkward.

"Yes. Keeping the theater dark for that long was expensive." I had refused to go on in Golly's place and do the disappearing act without knowing what had happened to her. It was the only time in my entire life I had let a show down. And it's a good thing I did! If I had performed, I would have become one of Hieronymus' victims. The show only resumed ten days later, when the evil apprentice was dead (or dissolved) and Golly was back where she belonged. "Losing all that income hurt us." I took a bite of my ice cream.

"Golly has never been very clear about where she went." When I didn't reply, Lopez added, "You haven't, either."

"Oh, it's all over now," I said, scooping up another bite of ice cream and offering it to him. "So I don't see why—"

He pushed the spoon aside as he said, "Because filing a false report with the police is illegal."

"No one filed any false reports!" I put the spoon back in the carton.

"And now Golly's explanation—like *yours*, Esther—is vague, contradictory, and makes no sense."

"I haven't given you an explanation!" I snapped.

"That's right. You really haven't." His expression said he was waiting for one now.

Oops.

I decided to change the subject. "Can we please focus on *my* crisis for a minute? I'm out of work!"

He had the grace to look a little contrite. "Okay. Fair enough. Are you—"

"Worried about bills? Yes! I'm also worried about paying rent! Worried about when I'll get another acting job! And trying to find a way to earn a living until then."

He let go of my sticky hand and put his arm around me. "I'm really sorry this happened," he said soothingly. "I know you were hoping the show would run a while, maybe even move to Broadway."

I leaned into his arm. I'm not prickly, I like being comforted. I admitted, "I guess I wasn't being realistic. We never really got off the ground, and an expensive show needs to come out of the gate like gangbusters to succeed these days." I sighed wearily. "But I did think we'd at least make it through summer. So now it's May and I have no prospects for a summer job. I'll have to find a way to make some money."

Lopez had spent enough time with me by now to know that actors differentiate between a real job, which means acting, and just earning money—which means waiting tables, office temping, and other between-job gigs that keep us from starving. In New York, an actor who is "resting" is usually working fifty hours per week somewhere to pay exorbitant rent on an apartment the size of a phone booth. I was lucky, at least, in that I could reduce my expenses by getting a roommate for the second bedroom in my rent-controlled apartment. Although what qualified as a "second bedroom" in Manhattan would scarcely have passed as a small walk-in closet in most other cities.

However, I really liked my space and my privacy; and I also hoped Lopez might start coming over more often. So I'd rather work for a change in my fortunes than let someone move into my apartment. Especially since this city (brace yourself for a shock) is full of weirdos.

"Look," Lopez said, giving my shoulders a gentle squeeze, "why don't you change—um, *shower* and change—and I'll take you out for a nice dinner. Maybe it'll cheer you up a little, and we can come up with some ideas for—"

"I can't," I said apologetically. "I've spent the past two hours making phone calls, and now—"

"I thought you spent two hours being depressed and forgetting I was coming over," he said.

"I did that, too. I'm a multitasker." I shrugged. "I'm freaking out right now, but this kind of thing is a standard part of my profession. When you're suddenly thrown out of work, you have to get on the phone right away to start looking for another job and figure out how to keep paying the bills. No delays, no moping. Even if you're flat on your back and crawling into a pint of Ben and Jerry's at the exact same time you're making those calls."

"So you were on the phone looking for work today?" he said in surprise. "On Sunday?"

"It's a twenty-four-seven city. A cop ought to know that."

"Good point." He took the spoon from me and helped himself to another bite of ice cream as he asked, "Any luck yet?"

"I don't know. I had to leave messages with everyone."

"So bring your cell phone to dinner," he suggested, "and let's go out."

It was a generous offer. I'd have been tempted to strangle a date who spent half the evening on the cell phone, but he was evidently willing to put up with it under special circumstances.

I considered it briefly, but I thought of the effort it would take to shower, get dressed, and primp for a nice evening out with a well-dressed man, and I felt exhausted. Then my stomach churned again, reminding me that eating a lot of ice cream when you're upset isn't always such a good idea.

"I'm really sorry," I said. "I just don't feel up to it right now."

He looked disappointed but said, "Okay. I can understand that."

I felt terrible. A man who didn't sulk under such circumstances was worth more than rubies. "I'll make it up to you," I promised. "But I'd be rotten company tonight. Now that I've made all my calls . . . *now* I just want to lie on my couch moping."

"So you're saying sex is also off the menu tonight," he guessed.

I jumped a little, startled. It was the most direct he'd ever been about wanting to get me into bed.

The blue of his eyes suddenly looked darker. "I had plans."

"And you dressed for the occasion," I noted.

His gaze dropped to my mouth. "I didn't do that for you. I did that for the hostess at Raoul's. I hear she's hot."

"You were going to take me to Raoul's?" It was a pricey restaurant in Soho with a reputation for good food and a romantic ambience. I felt even worse about canceling our date when I recalled, "Oh! You said you had something to celebrate tonight?"

"Yeah." He removed his arm from my shoulders. Leaning back against the cushions, he said, "But I see it's not a good night for a celebration. So we'll do it next time."

"Did you make reservations?"

"I'll cancel."

"But—"

"Don't worry about it," he said. "You didn't know you'd lose your job today."

I rose to my feet. "I'll get dressed. Er, shower and get dressed. And we'll—"

"Suddenly you're feeling better?"

"Well, no," I admitted. "But I don't want to spoil—"

"Then let's save it for a night when you're in the mood." He smiled and added, "For everything."

"I'm sorry. I feel terrible about this."

He waved aside my comment. "Forget it. Raoul's is

the wrong place to take a woman who isn't hungry. If I'm going to pay that much for dinner, we have to eat every bite."

I smiled. "Spoken like a man on a cop's salary."

The phone rang. I grabbed the receiver . . . but then I just stared at it without pressing the TALK button. I felt a sudden sense of looming dread.

"Aren't you going to answer it?" Lopez asked.

"I'm afraid it's my mother," I said.

"She calls on Sundays?"

"No, she calls whenever things are going badly."

As the phone continued ringing, he said, "Don't you want to talk to her?"

"No, of course not."

"She's not one of the people you called today?" he asked.

"Good God, no!"

He blinked at my tone. "Then how does she know things are going badly?"

"I've never figured that out," I said. "She just has this uncanny sixth sense. Whenever things are at their lowest, she calls me. And within minutes, she manages to make me feel even worse."

"I see."

"It's her gift."

"Maybe you should get a phone with caller ID."

"I can't buy a new phone, I'm out of work." I'm an actress, my budget is tight. My current phone would remain in use until it died. "I should never have given my home number to my mother!"

I knew even from our short acquaintance that Lopez was much closer to his parents than I was to mine. However, since his mother pestered him often by phone, perhaps he sympathized with my problem.

"Here, I'll answer it," he said. "If it's your mom, I'll tell her you're in the shower."

"You can't do that!" I clung to the cordless receiver

when he reached for it. "I'll have to explain what a strange man was doing in my apartment while I was showering!"

"I'm not that strange," he said. "Besides, she must realize you date. I mean, if *my* mom realizes that *I* date, then surely—"

"Dating and being naked in the next room are not synonymous in my family. Anyhow, then she'd fight with me about dating someone who's not Jewish."

"How would she know I'm not Jewish on the *phone?*"

There are things that Gentiles just don't understand about Jewish mothers.

Realizing that any caller who was *not* my mother would give up in another ring or two, I girded my loins and answered the ringing phone. "Hello?"

"Esther! Esther Diamond! Sweetie! It's Stella," boomed a robust female voice in a strong Queens accent.

"Oh, Stella," I said with relief. "Thanks for returning my call so soon."

I met Lopez's eyes and smiled. He took the ice cream carton from my lap and ate another spoonful.

"Are you kidding?" Stella said. "I called back as soon as I got your message. Of course we can use you around here! A good voice, sturdy feet, and a strong back? There's always a place for you at Stella's, sweetie. You wanna start this week?"

"I'll be there tomorrow." We made arrangements, and then I said, "Thanks, Stella."

"No problem, sweetie."

When I hung up, Lopez noted my relief and asked, "An audition? A job?"

"Well, I won't starve or lose the apartment. I got my old day job back. The one I had right before *Sorcerer!* Waiting tables. Though 'day job' isn't quite accurate. I usually get off work around two o'clock in the morning at Stella's."

"Stella's?"

"It's a restaurant called Bella Stella in Little Italy."

He frowned. "On Mulberry Street."

"You know it?" That didn't surprise me. It was a pretty famous place.

"Of course I know it, Esther. There've been two mob hits there in the past five years, and Stella Butera launders money for the Gambello crime family."

Okay, so it was notorious as well as famous.

Bella Stella was a Mafia hangout, particularly popular with the Gambellos. This notoriety, of course, also made it a hot tourist spot, as well as a stomping ground for certain celebrities. Stella perpetually claimed to be thirty-nine, which was probably a dozen years younger than her true age. The restaurant had been given to her long ago by Handsome Joey Gambello, who'd been her lover for more than twenty years—right up until the night he was assassinated in the restaurant's bathroom five years ago.

Lopez said, "Look, I know this is only our third date—sort of—but I don't want you working there. It's not safe."

"Oh, come on," I said. "Nobody there is going to kill *me*. I'm just an actress. Er, waitress."

"When somebody sprays a sawed-off shotgun across the room, the bullets don't go out of their way to avoid law-abiding citizens," he pointed out.

"No innocent bystander—or waitress—has ever been harmed at Stella's." I'm no fool, I had checked before the first time I started working there.

"Not yet," he said. "That would be bad for business, and if there's one things wiseguys love, it's making money. They've been careful at Stella's so far. But sooner or later, it'll happen. A waiter or tourist will get killed in the cross fire."

Since his expression implored me to take him seriously, I did. "I read up on those hits," I said. "There was no spraying of shotguns."

"No," he agreed, "Handsome Joey Gambello was whacked five years ago with a twenty-two caliber, two shots straight into the head. Very professional. Then two years ago, Frankie Mastiglione got shivved while gorging on *pasta al forno*, and no one realized he was dead until he fell facedown into his dinner after the hitter had already left."

So Lopez had evidently read up on the murders at Stella's, too.

"Cops know all sorts of interesting things," I said.

He continued, "But all it takes is one bullet, Esther. Or one hitter who thinks you may remember his face."

"I suppose so," I admitted. "But, then, all it takes is one cab that runs a red light or one lunatic on the subway, right?" Or one sorcerer's apprentice run amok.

"Spending all your nights at Bella Stella raises the odds of dying young," Lopez insisted. "The Gambellos have been at war on-and-off with the Corvino family for decades. Things are quiet between them these days, but it wouldn't take much to trigger another war. And that could make Stella's a dangerous place to work."

"How do you know so much about this?" Before he could answer, I said, "Never mind, I get it. You're a cop, and they're criminals. Of course you know."

"Actually—"

"Look, as day jobs go, this is a good one for me. Wiseguys tip well. I make better money at Stella's than anywhere else, and that's important."

"And I want you to live long enough to spend whatever you make."

"Plus, since we're all, you know, *singing* waiters—" This was a special feature of Stella's; the waiters and waitresses performed on request. "—Stella treats us like actors. She makes it easy for me to get time off for an audition or a quick job, like one day of filming on a soap opera. Most restaurants make that sort of thing a real headache for me. I even got fired from two other places because of it."

"My point is—"

"I understand your point," I said. "I do. But working at Bella Stella is a good between-jobs gig for me. And I can start earning right away, too. So I'm not going to give it up."

"Esther . . ." Lopez let his breath out, sagged back against the couch cushions, and looked at the ceiling. "I just *had* to get interested in a starving actress." He glanced at me and added, "One with no sense of self-preservation."

I protested, "I have plenty of—"

"Still hanging out with Max?" he asked abruptly.

Another awkward subject. "Sometimes."

Apart from enduring Golly Gee's sour temper at work, I hadn't encountered much Evil since we had eliminated Hieronymus, but I had become fond of Max. So I'd seen him a few times since then. Since Max was nearly 350 years old (though he didn't look a day over 70), he was certainly not a rival for Lopez. But Lopez thought he was crazy and probably dangerous, and he didn't like me having anything to do with him.

"Well," Lopez said after a long moment, "at least I can keep an eye on you at Stella's."

I frowned. "You suddenly have time on your hands? Has the crime rate plummeted in the Sixth Precinct, or something?"

He blinked. "Oh. I didn't tell you, did I?"

"Tell me what?"

"That's what I wanted to celebrate tonight. My transfer to OCCB finally came through."

"It did? Good!" I knew he'd been waiting for it for a while. "But . . . I can't remember what OCCB means," I admitted.

"Organized Crime Control Bureau."

"*Oh.* I guess that's how you know so much about Bella Stella and the Gambellos. Organized crime. You've been studying up for your new post."

"What happens at Stella's is pretty common knowledge. But, yeah, I take an interest." He eyed me. "Anyhow, since I'll be keeping an eye on the Gambellos, I should be able to keep an eye on you while you're working at Stella's."

"I don't need anyone to keep an eye on me." But I smiled at him. I kind of liked that he felt protective of me. I wasn't used to that, and it made the Big Apple seem a little cozier.

"All the same . . ." He smiled at me, too.

"As soon as I get a night off, maybe we could take another shot at going out and celebrating?" I suggested.

"Not for a couple of weeks," he said with regret. "Tomorrow I've got to go out to Long Island for two weeks of training. I'll be working long hours, so I'm going to stay with a cousin out there. And I'm going to Nyack next weekend."

"You do lead a life of glamour." Nyack was a suburb across the Hudson. Lopez had grown up there.

"It's my dad's birthday," he said. "I thought about asking you to come with me . . ."

"I'm nowhere near ready to meet your parents," I said firmly.

"Yeah, I thought that's what you'd say."

"So you were planning to wine and dine me tonight, get me into bed, and then abandon me for two weeks?"

"That was the plan," he admitted.

"I'm pretty sure that makes you a cad," I told him.

He grinned. "I'm coming back. I just wanted to mark my territory before I go."

"Mark your *territory?"*

"A woman who could forget I was coming over tonight might forget me completely in two weeks," he said innocently. "Unless I make a strong enough impression."

"You're pretty confident about the effect of marking your territory," I noted.

"I just don't want some other guy stepping in while I'm off training to be a more effective officer of the peace."

"I'm going to be on my feet ten hours a day at Stella's while you're gone," I pointed out. "The only man likely to get my attention is a foot masseur."

"I give a pretty good foot massage," he said.

"Yeah?"

He lowered his lashes and nudged my foot with his. "We can start with that when I get back ... and see where it leads."

Heat crept through me as I looked at him and felt the gentle pressure of his foot against mine. Securing an income a few minutes ago had revived me a little. I was just about to reconsider the possibility of taking a shower when the phone rang again.

Feeling optimistic now, I said, "That could be my agent."

I answered the phone. Then I realized my mistake.

"Hi, Mom," I said morosely.

That sense of looming dread I'd felt when Stella called had been accurate, just a little ahead of schedule.

"Oh, I'm okay," I lied in response to my mother's opening question.

Lopez rose to his feet and made leaving motions.

"Just a second, Mom." I rose to my feet, too, put my hand over the receiver, and said to Lopez, "Two weeks?"

He nodded. "Foot massage."

"Maybe I'll massage something of yours, too," I said.

He grinned. "I'll show you my favorite places."

As he headed for the door, I said, "You're not even going to kiss me good night?"

"With your mom practically in the room? No way."

"But—"

"Two weeks from now," he said. "Kisses and . . . whatever else you ask for nicely."

As I watched my handsome date leave my apartment without a backward glance at my bedraggled self, my mother said, loud and clear, "How's the show going, Esther?"

2

"**Y**ou and me, honey, we should go out sometime."

"I'm flattered." I placed the dinner check on the table and hoped my answer wouldn't affect the size of my tip. "But I can't."

Chubby Charlie Chiccante, a three-hundred-pound capo in the Gambello family, squinted at me as he reached for his wallet. "I'll show you a good time," he promised. "Let me tell you something. In the sack, I'm fuckin' spectacular. Ask anyone."

I said loudly over my shoulder to Lucky Battistuzzi, who ate here at Bella Stella almost every night, "Lucky, is Charlie spectacular in bed?"

Lucky nodded his grizzled head. "The earth moved for me."

Four male acquaintances of Charlie's sitting at a nearby table heard this and guffawed. A predictable round of jokes ensued. I knew from staff gossip that those four guys weren't Gambellos, they were soldiers in the Buonarotti family. It would be exaggerating to say the Buonarottis were on cordial terms with the Gambellos, but there was enough absence of animosity between the families that Buonarotti wiseguys could dine at Bella Stella, a stronghold of the Gambellos, without bloodshed. Well, as long as they didn't irritate any Gambello soldiers.

Whereas Corvino wiseguys knew better than to come near Stella's. As Lopez had pointed out to me, there was a lot of bad blood between *those* two families.

Chubby Charlie rolled his small eyes at the crude jokes the Buonarottis were making, then pulled a red silk handkerchief out of the breast pocket of his suit and patted his shiny face with it. Like Lucky, he was a regular at Stella's. And Charlie, who was in his late fifties, was notorious among the staff; he always ate two full entrees, sweated while he ate, and propositioned his waitress.

Whether Charlie tipped well depended on whether he liked your voice. He always wanted a song with his dinner. If he enjoyed the performance, he left a generous tip. If he didn't, he stiffed you. And no server at Stella's chose to argue about this with a man who was rumored to have killed at least seven people (mostly members of the Corvino crime family). Tonight, he had demanded to be seated in my section, and he'd requested a rendition of "That's Amore." As always, I'd sung to the accompaniment of our accordion-playing bartender.

Now, as Charlie stuffed his red handkerchief back into his breast pocket, he said to me, "So why won't you go out with me? You got a fuckin' boyfriend?"

Lucky put down the newspaper he'd been reading after finishing his dinner and said to Charlie, "Hey, watch your language, *paesano*. You're speaking to a lady."

I smiled at him. Alberto "Lucky Bastard" Battistuzzi had acquired his nickname due to surviving two attempts on his life as a young man, *both* times because an attacker's gun jammed. He had spent almost forty years as a hit man for the Gambellos, but he was reputedly retired now. Or semiretired. He'd once quoted another "Lucky" wiseguy to me, the famous Charles Luciano, saying the only way out of his business was "in a box." According to kitchen gossip, he had probably killed more people than anyone else who ate at Stella's. But despite his profession, he always behaved like a gentleman toward me.

"Hey, I'm just askin' her out," Chubby Charlie protested. "What's your fuckin' problem?"

"You know want to know what my problem is?" Lucky retorted.

"*Yeah*, I want to know what your fuckin' problem is," Charlie riposted.

"You're asking what my problem is?"

"*Yeah*, I'm askin' your fuckin' problem."

"*I* ain't the one with the problem," Lucky said.

"No?"

"No!"

"So who's the one with the fuckin' problem?" Charlie bristled. "*Huh?* Come on, wise ass! Tell me!"

I'd worked long enough at Bella Stella to know that this was typical dinner-table talk among wiseguys, so I just accepted the cash that Charlie handed me for his dinner while he was arguing with Lucky, and I interrupted only to ask him if he wanted change. When he said no, I gave him a big smile and tucked a flapping edge of his bright red handkerchief more securely into his breast pocket; he had tipped me very well. I must have been in good voice that evening.

"*You'll* be the one with the problem," Lucky advised him, "if you don't show some respect. Esther's dating a cop."

Chubby Charlie went rigid and looked at me with an appalled expression. "You date a *cop?*"

I nodded. I hadn't seen Lopez since he'd left my apartment that Sunday night nearly two weeks ago, and we'd only talked once briefly by phone since then. But we were planning to have another date after he got back from Long Island. Meanwhile, telling customers that I was dating a cop was a quick-fix solution to men like Charlie Chiccante.

"A *cop?*" Charlie repeated.

"A detective," I said helpfully.

Lucky said to him, "You want that a cop should hear you've been hitting on his girlfriend?"

"Jesus." Charlie looked at me as if I'd nearly given him a case of the clap. "Dates a fuckin' *cop.*"

"And he's very possessive," I said. "Wouldn't like it if he found out you'd even flirted with me." I smiled at him again. "But I was flattered."

(Yes, I was hoping to encourage more good tips. I had bills to pay.)

Charlie's shiny face got quite pink as he heaved himself to his feet. He dropped his napkin on the floor and said, "I was just being charming, you know? Didn't mean nothin' by it. Wouldn't hit on a cop's girl."

"Of course not," I said.

He gave a big belch and patted his massive belly. "Oof! I'm stuffed! I think I fuckin' ate too much."

"Oh, really?" Lucky muttered.

Charlie said to me, "Tell Stella the *pasta arrabbiata* was fuckin' out of this world tonight." He brought his hand to his mouth to kiss his fingers in an eloquent gesture of appreciation, then fastened his suit coat over his enormous stomach. The buttons looked strained. Charlie considered himself a snazzy dresser and often (misguidedly, in my opinion) called attention to his appearance. He dressed more formally than most wiseguys, almost always arriving at Bella Stella wearing a suit and matching accessories (socks, tie, and handkerchief).

After taking a satisfied glance in the mirror on the nearby wall, Charlie wished me good night and left the restaurant.

"What a schmuck," Lucky said.

"Thanks for stepping in," I said.

"I don't like guys who try to take advantage."

"Me, neither."

"When's your cop coming back, anyhow?"

"Friday." I had told Lucky that Lopez was out of town, though I hadn't said more than that. He was working this weekend (and so was I), so I wouldn't see him then, but I hoped we could get together soon. I was looking forward to that foot massage. Or maybe I'd feed him some ice cream again, only this time . . .

"Friday?" Lucky said. "You mean tomorrow?"

Startled out of a very private reverie, I nodded. "Yes."

Lucky said, "Well, good. It's about time. He's takin' a risk, leaving a pretty young woman unattended for so long."

I smiled and asked, "And how is it that *you're* still unattended, Lucky?" Like most wiseguys, Lucky had married and had children. But Mrs. Battistuzzi had died a few years ago, and Lucky never brought a date to dinner. "Do you like bachelorhood?"

He shrugged. "A man gets lonely."

"So you think you might settle down with someone again?" I asked as I started clearing Chubby Charlie's table.

"Well, actually . . ."

When I glanced at Lucky, he lowered his eyes. I thought he might be . . . *blushing*.

"Hey, Esther, I got that." Angelo, one of the busboys, came over to Charlie's table and started clearing it. "Stella says it's slow tonight, you can leave early."

I nodded, then asked, "Lucky, can I get you anything else before I go?"

He waved me away. "Nah, I'm fine. Get out of here, kid."

"This fuckin' job," Angelo said. "Such bullshit."

Angelo Falcone was an aspiring young wiseguy. He had the social skills of a rabid squirrel, and he made sure the rest of us knew that working in a restaurant was *way* beneath him. When he wasn't bussing tables, he was doing everything he could to make himself useful to the

Gambello family, in hopes of achieving a full-time career change. Since I didn't want to know anything about my coworker's life of crime, I had told him, too, that I was dating a cop. (Though absent, Lopez sure was coming in handy lately.) And since Angelo wasn't very bright, I had to *keep* reminding him about my cop "boyfriend" to make him shut up.

Glad that Charlie had tipped me so well on such a slow night, I went into the staff room, took off my apron, clocked out, and divvied up the bartender's and busboy's portions of my tips. Then I grabbed my sweater and purse, and I headed out of the restaurant. As soon as I was out on the street, where my cell phone got better reception, I checked my voice mail. I was hoping for a message from my agent telling me I had an audition. But no such luck. I snapped the phone shut and sighed.

"Did your date let you down?" said a voice behind me.

I turned to see Chubby Charlie approaching the restaurant. He was smiling flirtatiously (as he no doubt imagined it) at me.

Wondering why he was back, I said, "Did you forget something?"

"Yeah." He grinned. "I forgot to ask you out last time I was here, honey. You're one of Stella's girls, right?"

"Um, I'm one of the servers here, yes. But you *did* ask me—"

"I thought so! You're the one with the good voice, yeah? You sang 'Beyond the Sea' last time I was here." He patted his heart. "Got me right here."

The gesture drew my unwilling attention to his chest. "Did your handkerchief fall out of your pocket?" Although I had tucked it in for him a few minutes ago, I saw that it was missing now.

"Huh?"

"Your red handkerchief," I said.

"Hey, you remember it?" Looking pleased, he slapped

the empty pocket. "I fuckin' lost it. Can you believe that? Probably some prick stole it."

"That was fast." I wondered who on this street would be reckless enough to pick the pocket of a Gambello killer.

"It matched this tie so great, too," he said sadly.

"Uh-huh." I tried to push past him. "Good night, Charlie."

"Hey, where you goin', cutie? I want to hear you sing tonight."

"Your memory's slipping, Charlie," I said. "I *did* sing tonight."

"Well, I ain't fuckin' been inside tonight yet, have I?" Then Charlie noticed my sweater and purse. "So you're leavin'? I guess I won't get to hear you sing tonight. Shit. Well, next time, huh? I'd fuckin' love to hear you do 'That's Amore.' It's what I was gonna ask you to sing."

"But . . ." He *had* asked me to sing it. Tonight. Wondering if he was having some sort of ministroke, I asked, "Are you okay?"

"No! I'm starving to death! I got stuck in traffic. And now, I swear, I could eat the fuckin' table!"

"But you just ate—"

"Maybe you should join me," he said. "You look a little dizzy."

"I . . . I . . ."

"Got a date? Got a boyfriend? Got a fuckin' dental appointment? What?" he prodded.

"You asked about my boyfriend," I said, studying him for signs of a mental breakdown. "Do you remember?"

"Yeah, I asked two fuckin' seconds ago. What the fuck is the matter with you?"

"No, you asked *earlier* tonight," I said. "I'm dating a cop. A detective. Remember?"

Charlie fell back a step, an appalled expression on his face. "You date a *cop*?"

"Yes."

"A *cop?*"

Or maybe *I* was the one having a mental breakdown.

"Jesus." He shook his head and muttered, "Dates a fuckin' cop."

"We *had* this conversation," I said.

"When did we fuckin' have this conversation?"

"Fifteen minutes ago."

He squinted at me. "Does Stella know you're doing drugs?"

"I'm *not* doing—"

"'Cuz she runs a clean place. If she finds out you're into that stuff, she'll can your ass. And I don't fuckin' blame her." He wagged a fat finger at me. "If you want a good job at a nice place like this, you should keep your fuckin' nose clean."

This was just what I needed: to be lectured by a foul-mouthed killer.

"I'm going inside now," Charlie said. "I'm fuckin' starving. I could kill for some *pasta arrabbiata.*" At the door to Stella's, he paused and looked at me. "You're still a great singer, though. Even if you are all fucked up."

"Such a tribute," I muttered.

Lucky Battistuzzi exited the restaurant as Charlie entered it. When he saw me standing there, staring after Charlie with a frown, Lucky asked, "Was he bothering you again?"

"Not exactly. But I think something's wrong with him."

"*Yeah*, something's wrong with him. He's a schmuck."

"Besides that." I recounted the conversation to Lucky. "Isn't that strange?"

"Hmm. Like the evening was erased from his memory?"

"Yes," I said. "Including the massive dinner he just packed away."

"You'd think even a screwball like Charlie would re-member that he just ate," Lucky said, shaking his head.

"Especially since he said just a few minutes ago that he was stuffed."

"He didn't even remember you singing?" Lucky asked.

"No."

"And he seemed to love that. You sounded great, by the way."

"Maybe he's having a ministroke?" I wondered if we should call a doctor before Chubby Charlie keeled over in the middle of Bella Stella.

"Maybe he was caught in a time warp or something," Lucky suggested.

I blinked. "You've been watching too much SyFy Channel. I was thinking of something more prosaic. Could a myocardial infarction cause this behavior?"

"*What* kind of infection?"

"Um, a problem with his heart," I said. "So that maybe his brain isn't getting enough oxygen."

"You think something's wrong with his brain?" Lucky snorted. "I'd say *that's* a given."

"He's a hundred pounds overweight, and he packed away enough food at dinner to kill a wildebeest," I said. "I thought he looked a little red-faced when he left."

"Red-faced? Well, sure." Lucky shrugged. "He just found out he was makin' the moves on a cop's girlfriend."

"I'm wondering if his behavior is a warning sign." Chubby Charlie was a repulsive human being, but I'd nonetheless feel bad about just letting him drop dead tonight, maybe from a stroke or heart attack.

"Ah, Charlie's always been strange, kid. Moody. Forget it."

"But—"

"Look, if you're worried about him," Lucky said, "why not come to church with me?"

"Because I'm Jewish."

"God don't care about that. You could light a candle and pray for Charlie's good health."

"I was thinking of doing something more practical than that," I said. "Like maybe warning Stella or calling a doctor."

"What makes you think lighting a candle ain't practical?"

"Spoken like a good Catholic."

Lucky put his face against the restaurant's window and peered inside. "Charlie's already sitting down and yacking at his waitress. Seems perfectly normal to me. Have a look, Esther."

Following his example, I spotted Chubby Charlie just in time to see him pinch his waitress' bottom. "Perfectly normal," I agreed.

"See? No reason to worry."

"I don't know, Lucky. What could explain his behavior?"

"Maybe he was pulling your leg," Lucky suggested. "Havin' some fun with you."

"And eating dinner twice in a row tonight?" I said skeptically.

As we continued peering through the window, Charlie looked up and noticed us. He gave us the finger.

That's when I decided it wasn't my problem if he was having a major medical incident. Okay, so I'm not as compassionate and selfless as I could be.

Lucky scowled and stepped away from the window. *"Stronzo,"* he muttered. "Is that any way to treat a young lady?"

I looked at Lucky. "I think you're right. He was pulling my leg. And his digestive system defies all norms of human physiology."

He nodded in agreement. "Okay, then, I'm heading to St. Monica's."

It was a church around the corner, between Mulberry and Mott streets, that some of our customers frequented. "Evening Mass?" I asked.

"I might stay for that, depending."

"Depending on what?"

He lowered his head and shuffled his feet. I thought he might be ... *blushing* again. "Well, uh ... um ..."

"So if you don't go for Mass, what do you do there?"

"I light candles for all the dead guys I know. Especially the ones I liked. And, well, there's, um ..."

"Have you lost many people?" I asked sympathetically.

"I didn't *lose* 'em, I whacked 'em." Lucky shrugged and added, "But the ones I liked, I'm sure they knew it was strictly business."

Since I couldn't think of any response to that, I said, "Well, good night, Lucky."

"You don't want to come with me? It's good for the soul."

"I want to go home. My feet hurt," I said truthfully.

"There's a weeping saint at my church," he coaxed. "Well, sometimes, anyhow."

"A weeping saint? Do you mean there's a good person crying at your church?"

"*Was* a good person. Long time ago. Now it's a statue. Saint Monica."

"A weeping Saint Monica? I thought it was the Madonna that always weeps."

"At our church, it's the saint." He shrugged. "It's still a miracle, y'know, either way."

"Little Italy is full of the strange and the wonderful." Thinking of Charlie again, I said, "Especially the strange."

"Well, maybe next time," Lucky said.

"Maybe next time," I agreed, realizing he was a little lonely.

As I walked toward the subway station, I opened my cell phone again and dialed my agent's phone number.

I *needed* an audition.

Two days later, Chubby Charlie Chiccante wasn't very hungry, and he didn't want a song.

After requesting a table in a secluded alcove at the back of the restaurant, he only ordered one plate of food for dinner. And when I put his meal in front of him, he just picked at it. Dressed in a tight brown suit, accented by a bright green tie, bright green handkerchief, and (yes, I checked) bright green socks, he looked distracted as he pushed his *spaghetti Bolognese* around his plate with his fork for ten minutes.

This was so unprecedented that, despite his rudeness the other night, I felt I had to ask if he was all right.

"Er, Charlie?"

"Argh!"

I fell back a step in surprise as he flinched, cried out, and knocked over his water glass. A few diners glanced our way, then went back to shouting and laughing as they indulged in generous quantities of house wine.

Red-faced and breathing hard, Charlie snapped at me, "*Don't* sneak up on me like that!"

I frowned at him. I had simply walked up to his table. No sneaking involved. "You seem a little tense," I observed.

"Goddamn right, I'm a little fuckin' tense!"

I pulled a cloth out of my apron pocket and started mopping up the mess he'd made. "What's the matter with you?" I said irritably.

"What the *matter* with me? I'll tell you what the fuck's the matter with me!" He looked around, his eyes rolling a little wildly, then leaned toward me and lowered his voice. "I been cursed."

"You mean someone used bad language? And that bothered *you*?"

"What? *No*." He scowled at me. "I been *cursed*. You know—someone's put the evil eye on me! I'm under a cloud. Cursed!"

That clinched it. "Okay, you really do need to see a doctor."

"I don't need no doctor, you moron! I need a . . . a . . ." He waved his arms around. "I dunno. Maybe a *priest?* Could a priest help me, do ya think?"

"I think an e*mergency room* could help you," I said. "I'm calling an ambulance."

"I ain't sick!"

"I think you may be having a stroke," I said. "Or mini-strokes. You need a doctor."

"No!"

"Or maybe you need a psychiatrist."

"I ain't crazy! This is for real! I saw it! I saw it with my own eyes! I *spoke* to it, Estelle!"

"Esther," I corrected.

"And *it* spoke to *me*," he said in rising hysteria. "I'm telling you, it's real! I didn't imagine it!"

"*What's* real?" I asked, still wiping up the spilled water on his table.

He grabbed my arm with clutching fingers and pulled me closer to his red, sweating face as he said hoarsely, "My double."

"Your what?"

"My double! My perfect double!"

I tried to pull away from him. His grip tightened ruthlessly on my arm.

Hoping to distract him enough to free myself, I said, "What are you talking about?"

His eyes wide and anxious, he croaked, "I looked into my own face. My own eyes looked back at me."

"That's called a mirror, Charlie." I started trying to pry his fingers off my arm.

"No, this was a real thing! My double, I'm telling you, my *double*."

"You mean someone who looks like you?" I had to agree it was a distressing prospect in Charlie's case.

"No! He was *me*. He *is* me," Charlie raved. "Ain't you never heard of this?"

"Heard of what?" I asked as I looked around for help.

Charlie needed an ambulance and, I now suspected, restraints. And I needed my left arm back.

"La mia propria faccia nel viso di un altro!" he cried, lapsing into Italian. I'd noticed before that some of the older wiseguys did this in moments of high drama. *"La faccia della morte! La morte!"*

"What?" I was still looking around.

"Are you paying attention?" Charlie shook my arm. "To look into the face of this thing is to be cursed with death!"

There was no help in sight at the moment. Lucky Battistuzzi hadn't arrived for dinner yet, and the other two tables in this section of the restaurant were too noisy and boisterous to pay any attention to me and Charlie. We were in a quiet alcove, but I nonetheless hoped another staff member would notice my problem before I had to make a scene and possibly push Charlie over the brink into a heart attack—or a violent psychotic episode. Meanwhile, I kept trying to loosen his grip on me.

"Death? Oh, *'la morte'*—okay, now I get it," I said. "Charlie, you're hurting—"

"Okay? It's not okay, you stupid broad! Don't you get it? I'm a dead man!"

"You will be if we don't get you to a hospital," I agreed.

"A hospital can't change what's going to happen to me!"

I had a sudden bright idea. "But you said maybe a priest could? St. Monica's is just around the corner. Why don't we go see the priest there, Charlie?"

"You mean Father Gabriel?" he asked with a frown.

I had no idea who I meant, but since the suggestion had created a pause in Charlie's ranting about death and a double, I said, "Yes. Father Gabriel. Let's talk to him. Maybe he can help you."

"You think there's an exorcism for *un doppio?*"

"A dope?" I asked in confusion.

"A *double*. Don't they teach your people nothin'?" He suddenly let go of me and made an exasperated gesture. I staggered backward and rubbed my left forearm as Charlie said, "Ain't Jews got this, too? From the old country? Wherever that was for you guys."

"Got *what?*" I asked.

"You see your perfect double, a thing that looks and walks and talks and dresses exactly like you . . . And it means you're gonna die by nightfall."

I stared at him, surprised and perplexed. "You're telling me you've seen—"

"Ain't that what I been *saying?*" A look of dark fear contorted his fat features. "I seen my perfect double today. I been cursed. I'm marked for death."

"Charlie, you saw someone who looks like you," I said. "Or maybe you're having some heart trouble. That's why I think we should go to the hospital—"

"No!"

"—or to St. Monica's," I said quickly. "To see Father Gabriel. We'll go right now." And while the priest was talking to the gangster, I'd call 911. "We'll tell Father Gabriel what you've seen, and we'll ask him what it means."

"I *know* what it means." Charlie shook his head and added with a haunted expression, "I just don't know who sent it."

I heard the tinkling of breaking glass, a sharp whistling sound, and a soft thud. I looked around for a second, wondering what it was. Seeing nothing out of the ordinary, I said, "So do you want to go now?" No answer. He just sat there with a stunned expression on his face. "Charlie?" Still no answer. "Charlie?"

That was when I saw the huge red stain blossoming on his chest.

"Charlie!" I screamed.

Without even blinking, he slid out of his chair, fell to the floor, and lay there dead.

3

It was a confusing crime scene, because all the wise-guys who'd been at Bella Stella when Chubby Charlie got shot had immediately fled, while others arrived for dinner afterward—and decided to hang around on the street to annoy the cops.

I was sitting in a corner of the restaurant, dizzy with shock. Stella Butera, a voluptuous woman, sat next to me, holding my hand and occasionally patting my back.

Stella's hair, an improbable shade of gold, was teased and curled into a dramatic fall of riotous waves. She wore heavy mascara, her pink fingernails were very long, and her clothes were usually tight and always shiny. Ever since her lover, Handsome Joey Gambello, had gotten killed here five years ago, she'd had plenty of offers for nocturnal companionship, but she'd reputedly remained faithful to his memory. (In fact, she was having a quiet affair with her accountant, but the public pretense of un-touchable celibacy suited her complicated relationship with the volatile Gambellos, several of whom perpetu-ally competed to take over Joey's side of her bed.)

"I can't believe Charlie was killed in front of me," I said. "Right in *front* of me!"

I hadn't liked him, but I certainly hadn't wanted to watch him *die*.

"There, there, sweetie." Stella patted my back.

I stared with dazed eyes at Charlie's corpse, which still lay on the floor. A police photographer was taking pictures of everything, while a veritable army of Crime Scene Unit personnel moved purposefully around the restaurant, gathering evidence. A young patrolman with an awkward expression on his face was watching over me, and two detectives were standing nearby, talking into their cell phones.

"Can't I leave now?" I said plaintively to the patrolman.

"Just a minute, ma'am." He went over to speak to the detectives.

I had given my statement to this patrolman, then to another patrolman, and then to the two detectives. Now I just wanted to go home, pull the covers over my head, and try to forget what I had seen.

Above all, I wanted to get out of the restaurant and away from Charlie's staring corpse.

"I feel like he's looking at me," I said to Stella. "I should have listened to him! He *said* he was marked for death!"

"Of course he was, honey," said Stella. "He was a Gambello capo. Living to a ripe old age ain't a standard part of their benefits package."

The patrolman returned to my side. "I'm sorry, ma'am, you're going to have to give another statement."

"Another?" I said, fighting tears of exhaustion, revulsion, and guilt.

Stella stepped in. "What's the matter with you people? Can't you see she's had enough?" she bellowed.

"Er, Detective?" the patrolman said anxiously, backing away from Stella.

One of the detectives glanced out the restaurant window and said to the patrolman, "OCCB just arrived. They've got to talk to her."

The young patrolman said to me, "Sorry, ma'am."

"Don't call me that," I snapped.

"Yes, ma'am. Er, sorry . . ."

Two more cops entered the restaurant. I jumped to my feet as soon as I recognized one of them.

"Esther," Lopez said, his features creased with concern. "Jesus, I was hoping you weren't here when it happened."

I went straight into his arms and clung to him.

"You're the witness?" he said against my hair.

I nodded.

"Shit." His arms tightened around me.

"Hey, sweetie!" Stella said jovially. "This must be the guy, huh? The cop everyone's been talking about?"

I didn't answer. I just burrowed. Lopez felt wonderful. Strong and safe. I wanted to stay in his arms the rest of the night.

But not in the same room with Charlie's dead body.

"Can we please go outside?" I mumbled against Lopez's jacket. "I can't look at Charlie anymore."

"Sure," he said. "Come on." With one arm still around me, he turned so that I wouldn't see Charlie again as we made our exit.

The cop who had come in with him said, "This is our witness?"

"Yeah," Lopez replied. "I know her."

"So I gathered," was the dry response.

"Esther, this is Detective Peter Napoli," Lopez said. "He's going to be lead investigator on this case."

"Uh-huh," I said.

Lopez told Napoli, "I'll get her statement."

"I'll get it," said Napoli.

Lopez nodded but didn't loosen his hold on me. I was relieved he wasn't just going to abandon me to Napoli. If I had to repeat *again* what it was like to watch Charlie Chiccante die, I'd at least like a comforting face to look

at while I did it. And, as I glanced at Napoli, I didn't
think he looked at all comforting. A pale, brown-eyed
man who was mostly bald, he had a sardonic, suspicious
expression.

As soon as we got outside, where it was nighttime
by now, a familiar voice called, "*Esther!* Are you okay,
kid?"

I looked around. "Lucky?"

Bright lights blinked briefly in my face. I was confused for a moment, until I realized it was flash photog-
raphy. I held a hand up to shade my eyes and squinted.
I saw two photographers in the crowd. Not cops. Media.
Taking pictures of me.

"Miss Diamond!" one of them shouted. "Hey, over
here, Esther!"

"Great, they know your name already," Lopez
muttered.

I ducked my head, suddenly depressed. I dreamed of
being photographed as a successful actress at the Tony
Awards, not as a waitress who'd witnessed a mob hit in
Little Italy.

"Esther!" Lucky called.

I lifted my head again. "Lucky! Where are you?"

"Don't, Esther," Lopez said. "This is a zoo. We'd better take you to—"

Another flash went off in my face. I saw spots and
stumbled. Only Lopez's supporting arm kept me from
falling.

A hand from the milling crowd reached for me. I
flinched, but then I saw Lucky's face and returned his
grip.

"*Grazie a Dio!*" Lucky tore me out of Lopez's grasp
to hug me. "Thank God you're all right, kid! They
wouldn't let me inside, and no one knew for sure if you
was okay!"

I hugged him back and babbled, "Chubby Charlie's

dead! He was shot right in front of me! I thought he was having some kind of stroke or psychotic fit, but then ... Oh, Lucky!"

Napoli snapped at Lopez, "Can't you keep your witness quiet?"

Lopez said, "Esther—"

"Hey, buddy, back off!" Lucky warned him, sweeping me to his side and stepping between us. "Her boyfriend's a *cop*."

"*I'm* a cop," Lopez said, trying to retrieve me. "And I'm her ... I mean ..."

Our eyes met.

I said, "I thought I'd have a chance to explain to you, before you heard about it from someone else, that, um, I've been telling the guys around here—"

"Lucky, relax!" said Stella, who'd followed us outside. "This *is* Esther's boyfriend."

"Oh? *Oh.* Hey!" Lucky turned friendly. "You're the boyfriend?"

Napoli said to Lopez, "Whoa! The witness is your *girlfriend?*"

Lopez looked at me, as if thinking I might know the right answer to this question.

I said, "It may seem as if things between us moved forward without you actually *being* here, but I—"

"Well, *okay*, then, pal! Glad to meet you!" Lucky grabbed Lopez's hand and pumped it in greeting. "Any friend of Esther's is a friend of mine!"

Lopez said to me, "You're *friends* with Lucky Battistuzzi?"

"Hey, you know me?" Lucky sounded pleased.

"Only by reputation."

Napoli said, "Good God, you're dating a mob girl?"

"*No,*" Lopez said.

"Wait a minute!" Lucky bristled. "Are you sayin' you're breaking up with Esther, you bozo? *Now?* Tonight? After the poor kid just saw Chubby Charlie get whacked? What kind of a man are you?"

"I'm not breaking up with her," Lopez said, starting to look like his head hurt.

"No? Well. Okay, then." Restored to good humor by this news, Lucky gestured to a few of the wiseguys in the crowd. "Hey! Guys! Esther's boyfriend just got back to town! Come say hello! Tommy! Freddie! This is Esther's fella."

Tommy Two Toes said, "Yo!"

Freddie the Hermit said, "Hey!"

Lopez said to me, "I can see that you and I have a lot to talk about."

"I can explain this," I assured him.

"So you *are* dating a Gambello girl?" Napoli said coldly.

Lopez said, "Esther, I doubt *anyone* can explain this."

Jimmy "Legs" Brabancaccio came over and extended a beefy hand to Lopez. "So you're the guy who stole our Esther's heart, huh?"

"'Our' Esther?" Lopez repeated darkly.

"Your girl's got a great voice," Jimmy Legs said. "Golden pipes. She's gonna be a big star someday. Her name in lights on the Great White Way."

"Uh-huh."

"Hey, Ronnie! Come over here and say hello to Esther's fiancé," Jimmy urged.

"We're getting *married*?" Lopez said.

"I never said *that*," I told him. "I swear."

Ronnie Romano folded his arms and shook his head. "I ain't makin' the acquaintance of no cop. Not unless what he's got a warrant for my arrest and I can't in no ways avoid the association."

"Aw, come on, don't be like that," said Jimmy. "You'll hurt Esther's feelings."

"Then she shouldn'ta got mixed up with no cop," Ronnie said with a scowl. "Shoulda found herself a nice rib-eye or somethin'."

"Rabbi," I corrected automatically.

"Esther!" someone shouted, pushing through the crowd.

"Now what?" Lopez muttered.

"Angelo," I said, recognizing the busboy who worked a lot of the same shifts I did.

"Angelo Falcone," Napoli said quietly to Lopez. "Busboy and wannabe."

"You okay?" Angelo asked me. "I heard you was with Charlie when he bought it."

"Yeah, I'm okay," I said.

"And *you*," Angelo said, turning on Lopez and Napoli. "You can't pin this on me!"

"We weren't planning to, Angelo," said Napoli.

"No *way* you can pin this hit on *me,* man!"

"Okay," said Lopez.

"I got an alibi!" Angelo said, puffing out his skinny chest.

"Okay, you can go now," Napoli said.

"I got witnesses!"

"Good to know," Napoli said.

Angelo scowled at them. "I'll call my lawyer!"

"Go do that," said Lopez.

"Now?"

"Now would be good," Lopez said.

"Yeah? Okay." Angelo added, clearly relishing the phrase, "He'll eat you for breakfast!"

"Okay," Napoli said absently, checking something in his notebook.

As Angelo departed, Lucky noted, "He's very ambitious."

"Indeed," said Lopez.

Another flash went off.

"We've got to get your girlfriend—er, the witness—out of here," Napoli said to Lopez.

"Who called the photographers?" I asked, annoyed by the flashing lights.

"No one. They're like vultures, they just *know*," Napoli said.

"They monitor police radio communications," Lopez told me. "And flock to the scene of anything that sounds juicy."

"Especially when it's a mob killing," Napoli added irritably. "That's sexy."

"Come on." Lopez took my elbow and tried to guide me away from Lucky. "Let's go."

"Where are we going?" I asked.

Napoli said, "We're taking you into protective custody."

"What? No!" I pulled away from Lopez. "You can't do that! I haven't done anything!"

Lopez put his hands on my shoulders, trying to calm me. "We know that, Esther. But you're a material witness in a mob hit. And the tabloids have already got your name. So you're in danger now."

"But I didn't see anything!" I protested.

"Yeah, like everybody else here," Napoli said in disgust. "Six cops have been canvassing for almost an hour, and nobody saw anything. Of course."

"But I really didn't!" I cried.

"Esther—"

"No! Listen to me!" I jerked myself out of Lopez's grasp and backed away.

When he reached for me again, Lucky stepped between us. "I don't care if you are her boyfriend, that don't give you the right to manhandle her!"

"I'm *not* manhan . . ." Lopez paused for a moment, then evidently decided to change course. "Esther, we need to go somewhere sane and take your statement."

"I've given my statement three times already!" I said, still agitated by the word "custody."

"I know, and I'm sorry," Lopez said soothingly. "But we've got to go over every detail—"

"There are no details!" I insisted. "I didn't see the killer! I didn't see how it happened! All I saw was Chubby Charlie suddenly die right in front of me! After he'd asked me to help him! Or sort of asked me . . . Or . . . I'd *offered,* anyhow, and now he's dead!"

The whole ton of bricks came crashing down on me then. Stress, tension, anxiety, confusion, fear, guilt. All of it. I started crying.

"Now look what you done!" Lucky snarled at Lopez. The old wiseguy put his arm around me and handed me a clean, white hanky. "She's an actress. She's very sensitive!"

"*I* know that," Lopez snapped. "I date her. Now get your hands off her."

"Whoa, he's got a pair, your boy," Lucky said to me. "I like that in a person."

"Both of you, stop," I said wearily. "*Everyone,* please stop." I wiped my eyes and gave a watery sigh.

Lopez looked like he wanted to apologize to me, but he said nothing. Napoli looked ready to arrest everyone on Mulberry Street.

"I'm not going into custody," I said.

"All right," Lopez said, ignoring a scathing look from Napoli. "We'll just talk about what happened. And *then* we'll talk about your safety."

"Okay." I took a breath and got a hold of myself. "I was looking at Charlie," I said. "Talking to him. He seemed hysterical. I was trying to calm him down." I described the tinkling sound of breaking glass I'd heard, and the sharp whistling sound followed by the soft thud, and I explained what I had seen. "And that's *all* I saw. Charlie, with that horrible look of surprise on his face and the blood spreading on his chest. I didn't see or hear anything else. Or any*one* else. He fell to the floor, and I started screaming."

"Who was in the restaurant when it happened?" Napoli asked.

"I'm not sure."

"Come on, Esther," Napoli said.

"*You* can call me 'Miss Diamond,' " I said coldly.

Lopez closed his eyes, as if praying that none of this was really happening.

"You didn't recognize *any* of the customers?" Napoli prodded. "You expect me to believe that?"

"Charlie was sitting off in an alcove, and he came in a little early tonight. Most of the regulars hadn't shown up yet. I didn't know any of the customers who were sitting near him, and I don't remember who else was in the restaurant." Mostly I just remembered Charlie keeling over dead.

"And you didn't hear a car pull up outside?"

"No."

"You didn't see the shooter on the other side of the window?"

"No, of course not," I said. "Charlie wasn't sitting anywhere near the—"

"Detectives, we have a big problem," one of the CSU cops said, interrupting us.

"What?" Napoli asked.

"Come inside and have a look."

"We're a little busy here," Napoli said tersely.

"You need to see this," the CSU cop insisted. "Both of you."

Napoli gave an irritable sigh. "All right." He signaled to two patrolmen to join us. He pointed at me and said to them, "This woman is a material witness in this homicide. You are to keep an eye on her and keep her under control. Do not—I repeat, do *not*—let her move from this spot until we get back." Then he turned and followed the CSU cop back into the restaurant.

Lopez hesitated, giving me a look of mingled concern and exasperation. "Are you okay?"

"I want to go home." I felt exhausted and emotional. "Can't you take me?"

"Not yet. We need more informa—"

"I've told you everything I saw." I put my hand on his chest, wishing he would put his arms around me again. "Please make Napoli let me go."

"That's not how this works, Esther." His voice was firm, but his gaze softened as he brushed my hair behind my ear. "You're not—"

"Lopez!" Napoli shouted, having stuck his head out of the door of Bella Stella.

I glared at the bald detective.

Lopez raised a hand in acknowledgment but kept his eyes on me. "I have to go inside to see what CSU's problem is," he said, stepping away from me. "Don't do anything but stand here and wait for me to come back. Okay?"

I shrugged. "Okay."

He looked at me for another moment, his expression suggesting he wasn't sure I'd comply, then turned and went into the restaurant.

This was not exactly the reunion that I had been picturing for us. I doubted it was what he'd imagined, either.

"Not seein' nothing," Lucky said, distracting me from my morose musings about my love life. "Always the smart choice."

"Huh?"

"It's a good policy, kid. I'd stick with that story. Even if your boyfriend *is* a cop who needs his button."

"So to speak."

I knew that getting your "button" was one of the ways wiseguys referred to becoming "made" men or getting inducted into a crime family. Lopez was new at OCCB and wanted to make a good impression, of course. To

belong, to move up the ladder. I was well aware that tonight was a setback for him, and that I was the cause.

"But I really *didn't* see anything, Lucky," I said. "I
mean, how could I? As I was trying to tell Detective
Charm a few minutes ago, Charlie wasn't sitting anywhere near . . . Oh, my God!" I clutched Lucky's arm as
I realized what I was saying.

"What's wrong?"

"Charlie was sitting in that little alcove at the back of
the restaurant!"

"He couldn'ta been," Lucky said, shaking his head.
"They're saying the shot that killed him was fired
through the front window."

"I know. But I was standing right next to him, and he
was back in that alcove when he was shot."

"But you can't even see the alcove from the
window."

"And since when do bullets go around corners?" I
said.

Lucky whistled. "No wonder the cops got a
problem."

We both turned our gazes to the restaurant. Inside,
through the restaurant's front window—which bore
a hole from the shot fired tonight—I could see Lopez
talking to a CSU cop. They'd figured out the problem, all
right. Lopez made a smooth motion with his right hand
while he backed away from the window, still talking to
the other cop. After a moment, he shook his head and
went back to the window with a frown on his face.

Lucky said, "Your boyfriend's trying to follow the
trajectory. And it don't work."

I frowned, thinking about various episodes of *Crime
and Punishment* that I'd seen. "Could Charlie have been
hit by a ricochet?"

Lucky thought it was over for a moment, then shook
his head. "Not where he was sitting. Not if that bullet

came through the front window." After another moment, of watching Lopez talk with the CSU cop, he added, "Betcha that's what they're saying right now, too."

"So how could that bullet have hit Charlie?"

"And who the hell fired it?" Lucky glanced dismissively at the two patrolmen and added, "Everyone outside is actually telling the truth, Esther. No one saw nothing."

"Really?" It hadn't occurred to me that anyone but me was telling the truth.

"Yeah. Put it all together, and it don't make no sense." Lucky shook his head, frowning like Lopez now. "I'm telling you, it's like Charlie got popped by a ghost."

4

Detective Napoli and a patrol officer took me to the OCCB's charmless headquarters to get my statement. Lopez, whom Napoli obviously didn't want anywhere near me, stayed at Stella's to keep working on the problem the cops were having with the crime scene.

I figured they were looking for evidence of a second gun. Or at least a second bullet. Because the shot fired from the street, through the front window, couldn't have been the shot that killed Chubby Charlie. But it was still the only one the cops knew about by the time I left the scene. And unless the killer could see through walls and program his bullets to turn corners, there was no way the shot that came through the window could have killed the mobster.

If I hadn't been hysterical after watching Charlie die, I might have realized this right away. Or maybe not. I'm an actress, not an assassin. My familiarity with guns, bullets, and firing trajectories is limited to what I see on *Crime and Punishment*.

But Lucky, whose knowledge of such things seemed to be encyclopedic, was baffled.

The cops seemed to be baffled, too. In between bouts of questioning me, Napoli had several exasperated phone conversations with CSU personnel back at Stella's, and one *very* exasperated conversation with Lopez.

At least, I assumed it was Lopez, since there was one point at which Napoli snapped at his caller, "Miss Diamond is *fine*. Now keep your mind on your job, goddamn it!" I doubted that any other cop at Bella Stella was asking after my well-being.

Napoli asked me a lot of questions about myself, about that evening at Stella's, and about Charlie. He didn't ask how I knew Lopez, though. He didn't even allude to the acquaintance. But I had a feeling he'd be asking Lopez *plenty* about it, once they were done processing the crime scene.

"You seem very tight with the Gambellos," Napoli observed, handing me a diet soda after we'd been talking for a while.

"No." I shook my head. "I'm just a waitress. I've been working at Stella's on and off since last year, but only when I don't have a real job—an acting job. I'm not an insider there, and I don't socialize with anyone there. I like the place because Stella is a good employer and the customers tip well."

"Oh?" Napoli affected casual surprise. "I thought Stella and a number of her customers seemed very fond of you tonight. Protective, too."

"I think they were mostly trying to annoy the cops."

Actually, I did have warm relationships with Stella and Lucky. And since a number of the restaurant's regulars liked the way I sang, they often asked to sit in my section and I was on cordial terms with them. But I definitely wanted to quash Napoli's attempt to suggest that I was cozy with the Mafia.

He persisted, "I thought they seemed to count you as one of their own."

"I'm not Italian," I said. "And I think you know, Detective *Napoli*, that people in that walk of life would never think of me as one of the family. So to speak."

"Meyer Lansky was Jewish, but he and Lucky Luciano were like brothers."

"Meyer Lansky was a gangster. I'm an actress waiting tables in between roles."

"But you see a lot at Stella's, I'll bet."

"I keep my head down and mind my own business," I said firmly. "For the most part, I'm not even sure which of Stella's customers is or isn't a Gambello. They don't carry business cards or wear matching shirts, you know. I realize there are real mobsters at Stella's, and I know who the more famous ones are. That's all."

"Famous? Like Chubby Charlie Chiccante?" Napoli prodded.

I nodded. "Charlie has been in the news too many times for me not to know who he is. Er, was."

I was, I admit, prevaricating a little. I didn't like Napoli, and I was uneasy about his evident conviction that I knew a lot more than I did.

A number of the wiseguys who hung out at Stella's, like Tommy Two Toes and Jimmy Legs, had also been in the news, so I knew about them. And wiseguys aren't discreet. The reputations of guys like Lucky Battistuzzi, Frankie the Hermit, and Ronnie Romano were openly acknowledged by the customers at Stella's, as well as by the staff.

But in cases where I didn't know someone's reputation, his status was usually easy to guess. If a man was always in the company of made guys and seemed to be working with them, it was a safe bet that he was also a made guy, a "button man," someone who'd gotten "straightened out." If someone seemed welcome on the fringes of those tight circles but obviously wasn't an insider, he was "connected," an "associate," or a "friend of ours." These were all terms I'd heard wiseguys use to describe various shady men and tough guys who had friendly relations with the Gambello crime family or who wanted to become part of it.

And then there were the Buonarottis. None of them were really regulars, but a few members of that crime family showed up every week. The Buonarottis were less powerful than the Gambellos and so, with the brashness born of insecurity, they liked to make sure Stella's servers knew who they were—made guys, button men, Buonarotti soldiers. Guys with "juice"—power, influence, clout.

We also had many customers who shared the mannerisms and unfortunate fashion sense of wiseguys (loud shirts, shiny shoes, gold jewelry, and an ill-advised fondness for colorful sweat suits), but who weren't criminals. Sometimes it was easy to tell them apart from the mobsters, but not always.

"So, besides Charlie, who else dines at Bella Stella who's a Gambello?" Napoli asked me. "You must have some ideas. Some guesses?"

I blinked. "*You're* a lead investigator at the Organized Crime Control Bureau. Don't *you* know?"

"I'd like to hear your take on it."

"Why?"

"You seem like an intelligent woman."

"You don't think that," I said irritably. "You think I'm a ditz! You're hoping I'm so eager to feel important that I'll show off by trying to lecture you about stuff you already know—or damn well *should* know, since it's your job to know! And in the course of rambling on about life at Stella's, maybe I'll let some important information slip. Except that I don't *have* any important information, Napoli!"

"Then tell me the truth about Charlie's death!"

"I *have* told you the truth!"

"It doesn't work, Miss Diamond. Based on the only possible trajectory of the bullet that killed Charlie, you *had* to have seen the killer."

I blinked. "What?"

"If you were near Charlie when he got shot, then you saw who killed him. There's no way you didn't."

"That's what this is all about? You don't believe me?"

He shook his head. "Your story doesn't hold up against the evidence, Esther."

"I'd prefer that you keep calling me 'Miss Diamond.' "

"So I'm wondering why you're lying."

"I'm telling the truth," I said wearily, beginning to suspect there was no way I'd ever convince him of this.

"Are you trying to protect the killer?"

"Do I *look* like I'd protect a killer?" These questions were getting on my nerves. "Do I look like someone whose protection a Mafia hit man would *want*?"

"So Charlie was killed by a Mafia hit man?" he pounced.

I rolled my eyes. "I'm going to go out on a limb and guess that's the case, Detective."

Napoli suddenly switched tactics, making an attempt to look concerned and sound sympathetic. "So maybe you're afraid of what the Gambellos will do if you tell the truth about what you saw. I can understand that."

"You don't do 'good cop' well," I said. "It just doesn't work for you."

He scowled. "Are you afraid of the killer, then?"

"Generally? Of course! Because the killer is, you know, a *killer*. But specifically? No. Because the killer must know I didn't see him. I mean, if he thought I did, wouldn't he have shot me, too?"

Napoli changed the line of attack again. "Maybe you're trying to avoid trouble with the Gambellos? Maybe you *knew* they wanted Charlie dead, and you're afraid to talk about it."

I frowned. "*Did* the Gambellos want him dead? I thought he was a good earner."

"So you *do* hear them talk business!"

"No. Charlie told every waitress in the place that he was a good earner. He also told us he was good in bed."

"Or maybe *you* wanted him dead," Napoli suggested.

"No, he tipped me well." After a moment, I said, "That came out wrong."

Coplike, he changed the subject without warning. "Did Charlie ever talk about the Corvino family?"

"Not to me."

"To who, then?"

"I don't know. Sometimes I'd be passing his table and I'd hear him say something like, 'Those fucking Corvinos.' I don't remember anything more specific than that."

"Does anyone else at the restaurant ever mention the Corvinos?"

"Yes."

"Who?"

"Almost everyone."

"What do they say?"

"About five times a night, they say, 'Those fucking Corvinos.'" I had not observed much originality of expression among the wiseguys at Stella's.

"Did anyone mention the Corvinos after Charlie got shot?"

"Not that I remember. Mostly, I screamed a lot, then there was a stampede of departing wiseguys and screaming tourists, then Stella screamed a lot, then cops showed up . . . I don't remember much conversation, and certainly nothing about who might have killed Charlie."

"So you think they already *knew* who did it?"

"'They,' who? There was me, Stella, three freaked-out waiters, our accordion-playing bartender, and a couple of tourists from Colorado who didn't see a thing but thought they should wait for the police, even so. No one else stayed inside the restaurant with the corpse before the cops arrived."

"You know more than you're saying."

"You're wrong."

"What aren't you telling me?"

"That I don't like your shirt. Tan isn't your color."

"By lying to me about what you saw," Napoli said, "you put yourself in more danger, Esther, not less."

"What's the *matter* with you? This is the third gangland murder at Bella Stella in five years! Why is it so hard for you to believe I'm just a law-abiding waitress who was unlucky enough to see the latest killing while working there?"

"Because your story doesn't fit the evidence," Napoli said.

"That does it." I rose to my feet. "I'm going home."

"I advise against that, Miss Diamond." He rose, too. "You're a material witness in a mob hit. You're in danger now. I want to take you into protective—"

"No."

Everyone on Mulberry Street must know by now that I had insisted over and over to Lopez and Napoli—as well as to Lucky—that I hadn't seen a thing. And whoever the killer was, he must know, too, that I hadn't seen him. So I didn't believe I was in danger of being permanently silenced if I went about my normal life. But I *did* believe my normal life would get screwed up beyond recognition if I went into protective custody. For one thing, the killer might wonder if he was wrong and I *had* seen something, and that was precisely what I *didn't* want him to start thinking.

More to the point, how was I going to go to auditions while in protective custody? Or earn money to keep paying my rent? And how long would protective custody last? A week? A month? Six months? Until the city ran out of money for guarding me? The rest of my life?

None of those prospects sounded good to me.

"I have nothing to do with whatever business got Charlie killed, and I saw nothing," I said to Napoli. "So the last thing I want is to be treated as if I *am* involved or run my life as if I *did* see something."

"You're making a mistake," Napoli said.

"I'm a witness, not a suspect, and I'm tired. I've told you everything I know, it's late, so I'm *leaving*."

"You're not a suspect *yet*," he said ominously. "But your behavior isn't helping your situation. And don't think that your personal involvement with Detective Lopez will protect you from the law, either."

"I don't need protection from the law," I snapped.

I slung my purse over my shoulder and stomped out of the squad room, wishing a bad case of shingles on Napoli.

It took me hours to fall asleep that night.

In my mind's eye, I kept seeing Charlie's shocked expression as he keeled over dead. I also kept remembering his ranting about how he was marked for death and nothing could change that.

He *knew* he was going to be killed.

I hated imagining what that must be like. Charlie had been a loathsome specimen, but I recalled his terror in his final minutes of life, and I felt sorry for him.

I also recalled Napoli's parting comment to me, and I wondered what Lopez was thinking right now, if he was still awake (which seemed likely—I suspected the cops would be working the case most of the night).

Napoli would be hard on him, I had no doubt about that. But did Lopez also think I was lying, since there was a discrepancy between what the cops thought had happened and what I had actually seen?

Oy. He and I really did have a lot to talk about. And, despite how much I had looked forward to his return, I wasn't looking forward to the conversation we were going to have.

It was very late by the time I fell asleep. And it was very early when the shrill ring of the phone startled me awake. I flinched, choked, rolled over, reached toward my nightstand, and grabbed the phone.

"Hello?" I croaked.

"Were you asleep?"

"Who is this?"

"It's me! Lucky!" His tone suggested this should be self-evident.

I glanced at my alarm clock. "Lucky? It's six thirty in the morning. On a *Sunday*."

"I know. We need to get there early."

"Where?" I asked, my eyes stinging from lack of sleep.

"St. Monica's."

"The church?"

"It's a safe place to talk," Lucky said. "But we gotta get there before people start piling in for the first Mass."

"I don't want to talk, I want to sleep."

"Time enough for sleep in the grave," he said.

"Ohmigod!" His mentioning the grave made me remember what had happened last night. *"Charlie."*

"Yep, that's what we gotta talk about. Can you be there in thirty minutes?"

"What? *Why?*" Then I remembered the cops' conviction that I was in danger. I sat bolt upright, suddenly wide awake as a terrible fear flooded me. I was being lured to my death! "Lucky . . . do you have orders to bump me off?"

"What?"

"Are you— Is this—" I couldn't force out the words.

"Jesus," Lucky said. "Those cops really did a number on you, huh?"

"I-I—" I panted a little.

"Calm down, kid. Breathe. *Breathe*."

Feeling the first trickle of relief, I said, "You're not going to kill me?"

"Madre di Dio, of course not!"

"I didn't see anything," I assured him.

"No one saw anything," Lucky said. "It don't make no sense. I been instructed to find out what happened.

Before the cops find out. That gives me some time, obviously, because they're idiots. But I still need to see you right away. You're the last person who talked to Charlie before he got whacked."

"I'm not sure about Napoli, he might be an idiot," I conceded. "But Lopez is very sharp. You don't want to underestimate him."

"Then I guess I got less time than I thought," Lucky said. "Be at the church in twenty, instead of thirty."

"But—" I heard him hang up.

When a notorious hit man—even a semiretired one— tells you to get up, get dressed, and get downtown in twenty minutes, it's amazing how fast you can comply, even on only a few hours of sleep.

I entered the hushed, shadowy sanctuary of St. Monica's only twenty-five minutes after talking to Lucky.

The church was not very big or fancy, but it had a hallowed, sacred feel. The dawning sun shone through the stained glass windows lining the high walls. The tidy rows of dark wooden pews gleamed softly as the muted morning rays bathed them with ribbons of light. My footsteps on the stone tiles echoed and bounced off the vaulted ceiling as I walked down the center aisle of the empty church in search of Lucky.

I found him kneeling before an altar nestled in the apse on the north side of the church. With his hands folded and his head lowered, he was praying. A painting of the Virgin Mary—improbably blonde and blue-eyed and wearing seventeenth-century European clothing— looked down at him, a benevolent smile on her pretty, plump face. There were about thirty candles flickering gently on the altar. I wondered if Lucky had lighted them . . . for all the guys he'd whacked, especially the ones he'd liked.

I cleared my throat.

Lucky glanced up at me. "You're late."

"Is there any coffee?" The deli on my block wasn't open this early on a Sunday.

"This ain't no suburban ecumenical bullshit," Lucky said, frowning at me. "This here's a *real* church."

"So you're saying there's no coffee?"

He turned his attention back to the Virgin without answering me, made the sign of the Cross, and then rose stiffly to his feet. When he turned to me, I saw that his face was heavily lined this morning, and there were bags under his eyes. His short-cropped, gray hair needed combing, and he was still wearing the clothes he'd worn last night.

"You haven't been to bed," I said.

He shrugged. "After you got dragged off by Napoli, I got ordered to come in."

I knew from my sojourn at the restaurant that this phrase meant he'd been summoned to see the boss. The capo of his *famiglia*. The don of the Gambellos. Wise-guys never spoke his name, at least not in such a public place as Stella's; they always just used the phrase "the boss." But it was common knowledge that Victor Gambello, the Shy Don, was head of the family. He'd earned the nickname because the stutter he'd had as a child had left him with a lifelong habit of speaking softly, only when necessary, and preferably only in private. He was eighty years old now and in very frail health, so he almost never left his house in Forest Hills anymore. I realized Lucky must have been out to Queens and back since I'd seen him last night.

However, just as I was about to comment on how tired he looked, his face suddenly brightened with energy and lively interest.

Wondering what caused this transition, I looked over my shoulder in the direction he was looking.

A beautiful woman was entering the church. She was tall, slim-waisted, and curvaceous. Her black hair was mostly covered by a lacy black veil. Dramatically arching brows framed long-lashed dark eyes. Her skin was almost the same rich, golden olive color as Lopez's. She wore a black dress and no makeup. An ornate cross hung from her neck, and she carried a small handbag. I thought she looked about forty-five, but might even be in her late fifties. Good bone structure, good posture, and good skin made it hard to tell.

Lucky made a hasty attempt to straighten his rumpled hair, stepped forward, smiled, and said, "Good morning, Elena."

She gave him a cold glance and walked right past us.

"She doesn't seem to like you," I murmured to Lucky.

"She'll come around. I just need to be give her time."

When I glanced at him, he looked down and shuffled his feet a little.

Ah. So this was the cause of the blushing I had noticed the other night. Lucky was sweet on a parishioner at St. Monica's.

I said, "I gather you don't come here just to save your soul and pray for the dead?"

"I come here for that, too," he said defensively.

The woman kept walking until she reached the other end of the church. Then she genuflected before a marble figure of a berobed woman, lit three candles near the statue's feet, and knelt to pray.

"Who is she?" I asked Lucky.

"The Widow Giacalona." He nodded to where she was praying. "She's very devout. Prays twice a day to Saint Monica."

I looked at the statue. "That's your weeping saint?" When he nodded, I asked, "Have you seen it weep?"

"Not yet. Only Elena has seen it so far."

"Oh." So much for miracles. "Who is Saint Monica?"

"Patron saint of widows and wives."

"I see." Probably a fitting saint for a neighborhood that had seen decades of mob war between men in the

Corvino and Gambello organizations. After a moment I asked, "Why does Elena light *three* candles?"

"Widowed three times."

"She's lost three husbands?" I said.

"Uh-huh."

"Three?"

"It's very unfortunate," Lucky said sadly.

"Are you sure *she's* not killing them?" I thought three dead husbands might indicate something more proactive than mere misfortune.

"Of course I'm sure!" Lucky looked offended. "You got a nasty mind."

I shrugged. "Well, if her luck's really that bad, I can understand why she might be reluctant to marry again."

"I'm a patient man. She'll come around."

"Maybe. But if she's lost three husbands, are you sure you *want* to be number four? Your marriage could be the death of you."

"I'll be fine." He grinned at me. "I'm lucky, after all."

"If you say so."

He watched her with a lovesick expression for a long moment, then took my elbow and said, "Let's take a walk."

"Can we go find a coffee shop?" I suggested hopefully.

"No, we gotta talk here."

"But you just said we're going for a walk."

"'Take a walk' means we're gonna discuss some business in a place where the Feds can't overhear us," he said patiently. "In this case, we're already there."

"So we can't go get coffee?" I asked in disappointment.

"No. We gotta do this where I'm sure we ain't being bugged."

"But a random coffee shop wouldn't be—"

"You never know," he said.

"What about the widow?" I asked.

"Keep your voice down and she won't hear nothing."

"And what about the priest?" I said, as one emerged from a side door and came toward us.

Lucky looked over his shoulder. "Oh, good morning, Father Gabriel."

The priest smiled. "Hello, Lucky!"

Ah, so *this* was Father Gabriel, I thought, recalling that Charlie had mentioned his name when I suggested going to St. Monica's.

The priest was about thirty and very attractive. He had dark hair, soulful brown eyes, a sensitive face, a nice build, and a warm, friendly manner that was instantly apparent.

He said to Lucky, "We don't usually see you here so early on a Sunday. Everything all right?"

"Just getting my worshipping in early today, Father."

The priest glanced at me, still smiling, and said to Lucky, "I see you brought . . . a friend? A relation?"

"Uh, yeah," Lucky said. "My niece."

"Esther Diamond," I said.

"My Jewish niece," Lucky added. "On my sister's side. We don't really talk about it."

"Welcome, Esther," Father Gabriel said without missing a beat. "We're happy to have you here today."

"Thanks." I smiled back. "What time is the service?"

"Not for another half hour," Father Gabriel said.

"I'm looking forward to it," I said.

"Lucky can show you around the church while I prepare," the priest replied. "If you'll excuse me?"

"Of course." I smiled at him again. He was a hunk, this priest.

He went up to the altar to get something, then exited the church through the same side door he had used to enter. Going back to his study, I supposed, or whatever kind of room priests used to get ready for Mass. Vestry? Crypt? Dressing room?

Maybe I'd ask the Catholic guy I was dating.

If he was still dating *me,* that was.

"Flirting with a priest," Lucky muttered. "You ought to be ashamed of yourself."

"I wasn't flirting," I said.

"Oh, then what was that great big smile you gave him?"

"Well, maybe I was flirting a *little,*" I admitted. "That's one cute priest."

Lucky looked shocked. "There'll be none of that here, young lady. Besides, ain't you got a boyfriend? A possessive one, as I recall?"

"Do I?" I wondered morosely. "I hope so."

"Well, he ain't gonna like hearing you flirted with a priest," Lucky warned.

"Then he'd better *not* hear it," I replied.

"Hmph. Come on. Let's sit down. We're wasting time."

Lucky walked me to the center aisle of the church, genuflected next to a pew that was about five rows from the front, and gestured for me to take a seat.

Then he sat down next to me and said in a low voice, "The word from the top is, we can't have someone feeling free to whack a made guy without permission or warning. Especially not a good earner like Charlie."

"So Charlie was telling the truth about being a good earner?" I mused.

I chose not to dwell on whether Charlie had also been telling the truth about being great in bed. It seemed too improbable, and the images invoked by such pondering wouldn't be good for my mental health.

"So I gotta find who hit Charlie, and I gotta whack him," Lucky said matter-of-factly.

"I don't think we should be talking about whacking in church," I said uneasily.

"What do you care? You ain't even Catholic."

"Even so, it doesn't seem appropriate."

"Hey, this is the place where we confess our sins," Lucky said. "So we might as well plan 'em here, too."

"There's a certain warped logic to that," I admitted. "But I don't want to be involved in planning a retaliatory homicide."

"Huh?"

"Er, I don't want to help you whack someone."

"You think I'd take a girl along on business?" Lucky said dismissively. "You're just gonna help me figure out who done it, so I can make sure he don't do it again."

"I think we should leave this to the cops," I said firmly.

"Until when? Until *you* get whacked out?"

I flinched. "What makes you think I'll get whacked out?"

"Cops think you saw something, don't they?"

"But I didn't!" I insisted.

"*You* know you didn't. But if the cops keep saying you did, how long do you figure it'll take the hitter to decide he should tidy up his loose ends, just in case?" Lucky said.

"Tidy up . . . You mean, kill *me*?"

"A lot of these young guys . . ." Lucky shook his head. "No patience. No self-control. It's disgusting, the things they'll do when they get a little nervous."

I started rethinking my position on protective custody.

Lucky said, "So it's best if you tell me whatever you can, kid. Did Charlie say anything to you before he got whacked?"

I nodded. This, at least, was a subject that I didn't think would make me a potential accessory to homicide. "In fact, he said a lot."

"He had problems? He knew something was up?"

"He knew he was going to die." I added, "But Charlie sounded crazy, Lucky."

"It wouldn't be the first time," Lucky said. "What did he say to you?"

"He said he'd been cursed, he'd been marked for death."

"Hmm. Marked for death?" Lucky nodded. "Go on."

"He talked about *la morte*—"

"He talked Italian?" Lucky stiffened, as if the use of Italian made the situation doubly serious.

"A little. *La morte* was the only part I understood. Oh, and something about a dope."

"A dope?"

"Um . . . a *doppio*?"

"*Doppio.*" Lucky frowned, puzzled. "A double?"

"Yes! He kept babbling about a double."

I'd told Napoli about this, too, but he had dismissed it—just as I had dismissed it when Charlie was clutching my arm and raving about it. Napoli went over and over some parts of that conversation with me, though, since he found it noteworthy that Charlie believed he was going to die. The detective obviously thought that, somewhere in that ranting, Charlie had made a revealing statement about the anticipated homicide that I'd either missed, forgotten, or was deliberately concealing.

Lucky asked me, "What *about* a double?"

I thought back. At the time, I'd been convinced Charlie was having a medical or psychotic episode, and I'd been more concerned with trying to get help than with listening to him.

"He said something about the evil eye," I said.

Lucky clutched the pew in front of us. "The evil eye?"

"I thought it sounded silly, but he—"

"Hah! Don't mock the evil eye, kid."

"He said he'd seen his perfect double. That it looked, walked, and talked like him. I thought he had looked at a mirror and had a hallucination, but he insisted it was real. He said that he'd looked into its eyes, that it had spoken to him, and so now he was marked for death. I know it sounds crazy . . ." I spread my hands.

Lucky rubbed his jaw as he thought it over. I noticed he needed a shave. "But *is* it crazy?"

"Well, something was certainly affecting his brain," I said. "Remember how strangely he behaved the other night? The night he came back to the restaurant and acted . . ." The memory suddenly hit me in a completely different light. "Acted as if . . ."

Our eyes met.

"As if," Lucky said, "he hadn't been to dinner yet."

"Hadn't asked me to sing for him," I said. "Hadn't been inside the restaurant at all yet."

"As if he was . . ."

A chill crept through me. "A different Charlie."

"A *second* Charlie," Lucky said.

"Charlie's perfect double." It took me a moment to realize my jaw was hanging open. "My God, Lucky, we *saw* him! It? Er, the double."

He nodded. "The same night we saw Charlie."

"So which one of them was the *real* Charlie?" I wondered. "And which was the double?"

"I dunno. They both looked like Charlie to me."

"And they both behaved exactly like Charlie," I said.

"But one was a fake. A ringer."

"Why?" I wondered. "And *how*?"

"And where the hell did it come from?"

"That was the last thing Charlie said before he died," I recalled. "That he didn't know who had sent it."

Lucky thought it over. "So did Charlie's *double* whack him?"

"Wouldn't someone have seen it? Charlie's double was every bit as big as Charlie, after all."

"Yeah, that's another problem we got. If the double was the hitter, did it become invisible or something?"

"Has anything like this ever happened before?"

Lucky shook his head. "I been in the business more than forty years, kid. I never seen or heard of nothin' like this. It's *weird*. I got no idea what to do about it."

Wondering just how big a can of worms I was opening, I said, "I know someone we should talk to about this."

"Not your boyfriend," Lucky said firmly.

"No," I said. "Definitely not him." Lopez might have me locked up in a padded cell if he knew what I was planning to do. "Lucky, I'd like to introduce you to Max."

5

Zadok's Rare and Used Books was a cozy shop in an old, ivy-covered townhouse in a quiet street in the West Village. The discreet exterior meant that few window shoppers or casual browsers ever entered the bookstore. But since the shop specialized in rare and expensive occult books, many of them written in ancient languages, it wasn't really a foot-traffic kind of business, anyhow.

"Your friend's a bookseller?" Lucky said as we approached the shop. "Our problem don't seem to me like a *book* problem, kid."

"Max has special expertise that we may need. He just sells books to show the Internal Revenue Service a visible means of support," I explained.

"Ah," Lucky said, nodding. "You mean the store is his perfectly legitimate business interest."

In a sense, that was exactly what I meant.

"I just don't know if he'll be awake this early," I said. We had come by foot, cutting over to Hudson and heading north, since it was an easy walk and since I thought Max might be more coherent if I let him sleep as long as possible, instead of dashing here from Little Italy in a cab by dawn's early light. "He often works late into the night, and—"

A muffled explosion coming from the depths of the bookstore made me flinch.

"What the hell was that?" Lucky demanded.

"I don't know, but it came from below the shop!" Worried about Max, I headed toward his door.

"Wait a minute, Esther!"

"He might be hurt!" Though he was a skilled sorcerer, not all of Max's alchemy experiments went smoothly.

When I opened the door of the shop, Lucky said, "It's not locked? There's something fishy about this."

In fact, it *was* locked. Magically. Max couldn't keep track of the key, so he used a spell that kept out strangers when the shop was closed but allowed him access at all times. I had become a regular enough visitor since Golly Gee's disappearance (and subsequent reappearance) that Max had modified the spell so that I, too, could enter the shop at will.

But this was no time for an explanation that would require even more explanations. So I just said, "No, it's fine."

I entered the bookshop and quickly headed to the back of the building. There was a little cul-de-sac there with some storage shelves, a utilities closet, a bathroom, and a door marked PRIVATE. I opened that door onto a narrow, creaky stairway.

One set of steps led down to the cellar, where Max's laboratory was. The other steps led up to the second floor, where he slept. There was also an apartment on the top floor. Hieronymus had lived up there, and I assumed Max's next assistant would, too. It had been empty for several weeks now. Apparently, finding a decent sorcerer's apprentice wasn't easy. Especially after recent experience had convinced Max to add "must harbor no evil ambitions whatsoever" to his list of requirements for prospective candidates.

"Whoa!" Lucky said behind me. "Weird."

I assumed he meant the method of lighting the stairwell: there was a burning torch stuck in a sconce on the wall. Like the front door lock, it functioned via mystical means.

I smelled something foul floating up from the laboratory, a putrid, acrid odor mixed with smoke, incense, and ... wet dog fur?

"Max?" I called.

The only response was a menacing sound—like a hungry demon's stomach growling.

"Max! Are you all right?" I called, my voice sharp with anxiety.

Lucky elbowed me aside to peer down the steep, dark stairway that was filling up with foul-smelling smoke. "You ain't saying he's down *there*?"

I faintly heard some coughing from below.

"Max?" I shouted.

The growling sound turned into a roar.

Then I heard a man scream in terror. *"Argh!"*

"Max!" I started down the steep, narrow stairs, holding tightly to the railing so I wouldn't stumble.

"Esther, *no*." Lucky made a grab for my arm, but I slipped away, too scared for Max to pay attention. "*I'll* go. You stay—goddamn it!" I heard the thud of his footsteps behind me as he started descending after me.

The roaring sound from the laboratory got louder, bouncing off the narrow walls of the stairwell.

I choked on the smoke, covered my nose and mouth with my hand, and shouted over my shoulder, "Watch your step! These stairs are uneven!"

"No shit!" Lucky shouted back.

I knew the bad language—so common among wiseguys, but so rare for Lucky to use in a woman's presence—was a sign of how perturbed he was.

Understandable. As the roaring reached a pitch that seemed to make the stairs shake, fear ran through me hot and fast. I reached the landing and burst into the laboratory.

At first glance, I thought Max was being attacked by a demonic hellhound. I stared in shock, peering through the smoke-filled room.

Max, a small and slightly plump man, was rolling around on the floor, grunting and crying out in protest. His long white hair was disheveled and tangling with his beard as he tried to ward off his attacker.

An immense, tan canine beast was jumping up and down on top of him as it barked noisily. Its teeth were bared, its pink tongue lolling and its big ears flopping around. The huge creature's paws batted playfully at Max as its tail wagged . . .

Its tail was *wagging*?

I said, "What the hell—"

"Esther, get down!" Lucky shouted. "I'm gonna blow it away!"

I turned around to find myself facing the barrel of a gun. I gasped and staggered backward.

I stepped on Max, who howled in pain. Startled, I lost my footing. I tried to regain it, but I instead did an involuntary barrel vault over the dog. I landed on my head and lay there in a helpless daze as an immense pink tongue started washing my face.

The beast's breath smelled exactly the way you'd expect a hell-spawned canine-demon's breath to smell.

"Esther?" Max said.

The disgusting facial was interrupted by a paw, which was the size and density of a baseball bat, poking me for signs of life. The creature's nails needed cutting.

"Get down!" Lucky shouted—presumably at Max, since I was flat on my back with a massive paw giving me a dermabrasion treatment.

There was an explosion of noise so loud I thought my skull would shatter.

Lucky had fired. The shot missed the dog and instead hit a jar full of dried animal organs. The jar exploded, sending a spray of organs and organ dust all over me.

This revived me enough to sit bolt upright and scream. Then I gagged on the acrid smoke and dust I inhaled.

Another shot convinced the now terrified dog to try to hide, and I nearly smothered when it chose my lap as the handiest refuge. Pinned down by the beast's weight, I was unable to escape when Lucky's next wild shot shattered a beaker that spilled some sticky blue substance all over me and the animal.

"Don't shoot!" I screamed, shoving at the dog and trying to see Lucky through the gradually clearing smoke.

If his next shot came closer to the dog, he might kill *me*, since the creature was huddled on top of me, whining and drooling in my hair.

Max shouted something in another language as he pointed at Lucky. Suddenly the mobster's gun flew out of his hand and turned into a bat—the nocturnal kind with creepy looking wings. The bat hovered over Lucky for a few moments, as if contemplating biting him.

Lucky's eyes got as big as golf balls. He fell to his knees and crossed himself.

Then the bat flew toward me. I don't like bats, so I screamed again and covered my head with my arms. The dog thought I was trying to play and, recovered from the emotional crisis inspired by Lucky's gunshots, it started jumping up and down on top of me.

"Max! Help!" I cried.

"To the rescue!" A moment later, Max grabbed the dog around the neck and heaved backward with all his body weight.

The dog resisted for a moment, then decided to play with Max instead of me. The two of them flew backward together and landed with a thud. The dog got up and wagged its tail, looking from me to Max, who lay prone and motionless.

I sat up, trying to catch my breath as I looked around warily for the bat. I saw it sinking to the floor on the far side of the room. To my relief, it was dissolving and oozing back into its original shape, the inanimate weapon which had given it such brief life. Moments later, Lucky's gun lay on the floor where the bat had been.

I glanced at Lucky. His eyes were squeezed shut, and he was praying fervently in Italian.

"Max? Are you conscious?" I asked hoarsely.

"More or less," came the faint answer. After a moment, Max sat up slowly, disheveled and panting. He rubbed his shoulder as he asked me, "Are you all right, Esther?"

"Sort of." I coughed again and waved smoke away from my face. "How about you?"

"I think I'm being robbed," he said, eyeing Lucky anxiously.

"Oh! No, no," I said, "he came with me."

Max looked confused. "Are *you* being robbed?"

"I didn't know he had a gun with him. I swear." But I supposed it should have occurred to me that a notorious hit man—even a semiretired one—probably never left home without his piece. "He's a friend of mine, Max. The gunfire was, um, a misunderstanding."

"Well . . ." Max watched Lucky praying. "At least he seems repentant."

After the smoke cleared and we felt strong enough to haul ourselves off the floor, it took us some time to convince Lucky to stop praying and have a seat while we restored order to Max's laboratory. It took even longer to clean up the mess.

The room was cavernous, windowless, and shadowy. The walls were decorated with charts covered in strange symbols and maps of places with unfamiliar names. Bottles of powders, vials of potions, and dried plants jostled for space on the cluttered shelves. Beakers, implements, and tools lay tumbled and jumbled on the heavy, dark furniture. Today there was also a lot of shattered glass to clean up, as well as crumbling pieces of dried animal

parts and a sticky blue liquid that was staining everything it touched, including me and the dog.

"Max, is this stuff ever going to come off?" I asked,
rubbing at my arm.

Lucky, who still seemed dazed, muttered, "There's
some on your face, too."

"Damn," I said.

Jars of herbs, spices, minerals, amulets, and neatly as-
sorted claws and teeth sat on densely packed shelves
and in dusty cabinets. There were antique weapons,
some urns and boxes and vases, several Tarot decks,
some runes, two gargoyles squatting in a corner, icons
and idols, a scattering of old bones, and a Tibetan prayer
bowl. An enormous bookcase was packed to overflowing
with many leather-bound volumes, as well as unbound
manuscripts, scrolls, and even a few clay tablets.

For weeks, there had also been piles of feathers all
over the lab. Today, for the first time since I'd met Max,
the feathers were all gone.

"You solved your feather problem?" I asked as I
swept the floor.

Max paused in his efforts to clean up the sticky blue
ooze and gestured to the massive dog, who lay on the
floor assiduously licking a blue-stained paw. "As you
see," he said.

"I see a dog," I said. The huge animal had short,
smooth, tan-colored hair, with a darker face and paws,
and a long, square-jawed head. "Part Great Dane, I
think?"

Max's baby blue eyes widened beneath bushy white
brows. "Oh, *no,* Esther. No. This isn't a *dog.*" He glanced
anxiously at the beast, as if fearful my comment had
caused offense. "I have conjured a familiar!"

I looked at the dog. It looked back at me. Despite its
immense size, its floppy ears were too big for its head.
Its long pink tongue hung out of its mouth as it panted
cheerfully at me.

"*This* is a familiar?" I said.

The dog burped.

"Yes." Max beamed at me.

I supposed this explained (somehow or other) the wet dog fur odor I'd smelled floating up from the cellar when Max first confronted his conjured companion down here. And the explosion Lucky and I had heard must have signaled the creature's arrival. Magic sure was noisy.

"What's its name?" I asked.

"She has chosen to be known in this dimension as Nelli," Max said, his flawless English bearing only the faintest trace of his origins in eastern Europe centuries ago.

"Your familiar is named *Nelli?*"

He nodded. "I believe it's an homage to the great Fulcanelli."

"Who was that?"

Max look surprised at my ignorance. "An early twentieth-century alchemist of great renown. Author of *The Mystery of the Cathedrals*. Fulcanelli's writings influenced my thinking on transmutation, the phonetic cabala of Gothic architecture, and sacred geometry."

"I guess it's always good to keep learning," I said.

"Alas we never met. But no doubt Nelli chose her name because she shares my feelings of affinity with the great Fulcanelli's work."

"No doubt," I said, glancing at the drooling dog. "But you seemed sort of, um, disconcerted by Nelli when I arrived."

"I had not expected quite so *large* a canine," Max confessed. "For a few moments, I thought I had made a dreadful mistake and conjured some sort of . . ."

"Hellhound?"

"Precisely."

I looked at Max's familiar again. As we exchanged gazes, Nelli began wagging her tail. It was long and thick, and its wagging carried enough force to knock over a floor lamp.

I caught the lamp before it fell. "But, Max, I thought familiars were always, you know, black cats or something."

"Cats *can* be familiars," Max said, "but it's not as prevalent as people think. That was mostly a rumor started in the sixteenth century by men who resented widows who preferred acquiring a good mouser to acquiring a second husband."

"So a dog can be a familiar?"

"A familiar can take any animal form it chooses," Max explained. "My difficulty in summoning this one was— Well, in point of fact, my *first* mistake was in assigning the task to Hieronymus, as you may recall."

"I don't think he was making the effort he told you he was making."

"Indeed, no. And since his dissolution—"

"Let's not use that word," I suggested, thinking anxiously about Lopez, various episodes of *Crime and Punishment,* and my desire to stay out of prison. "Let's get into the habit of saying since he *left*. Okay?"

"Of course, Esther. If that will make you more comfortable."

"It will."

"Since Hieronymus left, I have found the demands of protecting New York City from Evil to be a little overwhelming on my own, so I've been increasingly anxious to find a familiar to support my efforts until the Magnum Collegium can send me another assistant." He added a little bitterly, "Preferably one who doesn't want to take over New York by demonic means and, in the process, kill most of its citizens."

"So you kept trying to summon a familiar after Hieronymus left?" I finished my sweeping and poured a dustpan's worth of disgusting substances into the urn that served as a garbage can.

"Yes, but I mistakenly interpreted the spirit I was summoning as avian in nature when, in fact, it found the canine lifestyle more congenial." He shook his head. "I've been distracted by my various duties, as well as by a summons from the Internal Revenue Service, or else I'd have realized sooner that I was able to conjure nothing but feathers because the familiar offering its services to me wanted a different corporeal form."

"So a familiar, er, *applies* for the job?" I said.

"It would be more precise to say that a particular entity chose to answer my summons," Max said. "An entity that deemed itself equal to the task of helping me protect New York from Evil."

Nelli rolled over onto her back. Her tongue dangled sideways out of her mouth. Her paws flailed as she wriggled to scratch her back against the floor.

Lucky, who had been sitting immobile in a chair with a dazed expression on his face, suddenly became alert. "Did you say the IRS is bothering you?"

Max said to me, "Ah! I think your friend is feeling better."

"'Cuz, you know, I can maybe help you with that," Lucky said. "Discourage unnecessary inquiries into your perfectly legitimate business interests. As a favor. For a friend of Esther's."

I was glad that the very first thing I had thrown into the garbage urn was Lucky's gun. I didn't think he had noticed its rematerialization, and I thought everyone would be safer if he didn't get his hands on it again.

I said firmly, "I don't want anything bad to happen to a civil servant, Lucky. On behalf of me *or* Max."

He shrugged. "If you change your mind . . ."

Despite some misgivings, I decided it was time to make introductions. "Lucky, this is Dr. Maximillian Zadok. He's sort of a specialist in strange events."

"Yeah," said Lucky. "I think I get that. How do ya do, Doc?"

"How do you do, Mr. . . . ."

"Lucky Battistuzzi," was the reply. "I'm a hitter for the Gambellos."

"A hitter?" Maxed asked with a puzzled expression.

Lucky waved aside the question. "Mostly retired. I just come out now and then when something special needs doing. Like this problem we got here."

"Ah, a problem!" Max looked interested now. "I suppose that explains why you're here so late, Esther?"

"Late?" I glanced at my watch. "Max, it's not even nine o'clock in the morning."

"It's Saturday morning?" he asked in surprise.

"*Sunday* morning. Just how long have you been in the lab?"

"Good heavens! I really did lose track of time." He explained to Lucky, "Conjuring a familiar is most absorbing work. Not to mention time consuming."

"Are you talkin', like, a sorcerer's familiar?" Lucky asked.

"Precisely."

"*That's* your familiar?" Lucky asked, pointing at the dog.

"Yes."

"That *dog*?"

"Yes, but—"

"It's *your* familiar?"

"Yes."

Lucky took a long look at Nelli. She looked back at him. After a long moment, the gangster said, "In that case, Doc, I'm real sorry I tried to whack it."

"Hmm." Max tugged absently on his beard as he considered what we had told him about Chubby Charlie's death. "Interesting. Very, very interesting."

"Yes, but is it *supernatural*?" I asked.

I immediately realized my mistake. Max started lecturing. The gist of it was, there is no such thing as "supernatural," that's a false construct; almost everything (though not *quite* everything) in the universe is natural, but some things are mystical or magical, and some are not.

Lucky summed up my feelings perfectly by interrupting Max's monologue to say, "Whatever. Who cares? The point is, Doc, do you got any idea what the hell is going on here?"

We had left the laboratory and were upstairs in the bookstore, sitting in comfortable, prettily upholstered chairs in the reading area set up around the fireplace. The shop had well-worn hardwood floors, a broad-beamed ceiling, dusky rose walls, and a soothing atmosphere.

I had gratefully helped myself to coffee at the small refreshments station that Max kept stocked for his customers. It sat near a large, careworn walnut table with books, papers, an abacus, writing implements, and other paraphernalia on it.

Max didn't bother opening the store for business yet. No one but us was awake this early on a Sunday in the West Village.

Nelli was busy exploring the shop, getting acquainted with her new home by sniffing row after row of bookcases, snuffling at modern books on the occult, and sneezing at ancient leather-bound volumes that needed dusting.

"Well," Max said, "I hesitate to theorize about poor Chubby Charlie's death without more information, but it sounds to me as if he may have seen his doppelgänger."

"His doppelgänger?" I repeated. "I've heard the word, but . . ." I shrugged to indicate that my familiarity with it stopped there.

"Understandable," said Max. "It's a very rare phenomenon, and the study of German mythology doesn't seem to have deeply absorbed your generation in the New World."

"Kids these days," Lucky said, shaking his head. "If it ain't on MTV, it don't exist."

"Indeed," said Max. "Plus 'doppelgänger' is hard to spell."

"So what does a doppelgänger do?" I asked.

"It doesn't really *do* anything," Max said. "It's traditionally a portent or omen rather than a proactive agent."

"Huh?" said Lucky.

"A doppelgänger is an apparition," Max elaborated. "Loosely translated, the term means 'double walker' or 'double goer.' It's a second physical version of a person. A perfect double."

I noted, "That's exactly what Charlie said. That he'd seen his perfect double."

"In some cultures," Max continued, "it's believed to be a reflection of a person's soul; in others, it's considered an entirely separate entity from him. In any case, it is a seemingly exact replica of a living person."

Lucky said, "So are you saying this thing, this dopp . . . dopp . . ."

"Doppelgänger," Max supplied.

"This doppelgangster—do you think it could've done a smooth hit?" Lucky asked. "Because if it was a replica of Charlie, well, he had a lot of experience at that."

"A smooth hit?" Max repeated, puzzled.

I explained, "Lucky's asking if the doppelgangst . . . er, doppelgänger could have killed Chubby Charlie."

"Ah! I see. A 'smooth hit'? What an interesting expression."

"It was very clean," Lucky said. "Very professional. One shot to the heart, instant death, no muss, no fuss. And no witnesses."

"And no logical explanation for how it happened," I said. "At least, not so far."

"So what I'm wondering is, did this doppelgangster whack Charlie?" Lucky said.

"Whack?"

"Hit," Lucky clarified.

"You think the creature *struck* him?" Max asked.

I said, "Lucky's asking if the doppelgangster killed Charlie."

"Interesting!" Max said to Lucky, "Your dialect fascinates me. May I ask where you learned it?"

Lucky shrugged. "I'm from Brooklyn."

"I see."

"To return to the question, Max," I said. "Could the double have shot Charlie?"

"It seems unlikely," he said. "The appearance of a doppelgänger is associated with the imminent death of the person replicated—"

"So *that*'s why Charlie was so sure that seeing his perfect double meant he was going to die," I mused.

"—but the doppelgänger merely portends death, it doesn't actually kill the replicated individual."

"How you *pretend* death?" Lucky asked.

"Er, I mean the doppelgänger is a warning of death," Max explained. "It's a sign. As Chubby Charlie seems to have known, seeing your doppelgänger traditionally means you're going to die by nightfall."

"But does it mean you're going to get whacked out by a hitter no one saw and a bullet that traveled around corners?" Lucky asked.

"Not as far as I know," Max said.

"So do you think a doppelgangster could do a hit like that?" Lucky asked.

"I'm afraid I don't know enough about doppelgangsters—er, doppelgängers—to postulate a response to that at this juncture," Max said. "I'm not familiar enough with the phenomenon. Did I mention that it's very rare? I'm going to need to do some research on this."

Feeling very tired, I looked around the store without enthusiasm. "Does that mean we have to start reading?"

"Unfortunately," Max said, "the Germanic portion of my library is very thin. I will need to summon assistance."

"Will there be more smoke and explosions involved in this summoning?" I asked anxiously.

"No, no. I mean to say, I'll need to make some telephone calls to see if I can locate some useful material."

"What do you need Germanic books for?" Lucky asked. "Charlie was Italian. His enemies are all Italian. It don't make sense that a German would be involved in this."

"He had enemies?" Max asked with interest.

"Oh, yeah," Lucky said.

"*Deadly* enemies?"

"Yep."

"Hmm. In that case, we can probably rule out my second theory."

"Which is?" I asked.

"That Chubby Charlie merely imagined seeing his double, and his violent death on the same night of these delusions was pure coincidence."

"So you think there really was a double?" Lucky said. "A *doppio*? A doppelgangster?"

"A man with deadly enemies who sees his perfect double and then dies by nightfall? Absolutely," Max said. "But the manner of the killing ... Hmm, clearly there's something here that we don't understand yet. I must get some Germanic texts."

Lucky objected, "But like I just told you—"

"Yes, I understand, my dear fellow," Max said. "But the great German thinkers wrote about doppelgängers in more depth than anyone else, as far as I know, so my research must delve into their works if I am to gain sufficient knowledge of this rare phenomenon."

We heard a sudden, piercing wail come from the far side of the shop, followed by Nelli barking. Then we heard the slapping and slamming of rapidly closing doors and drawers.

"What's *that*?" Lucky jumped to his feet and automatically reached for his gun. I was glad he didn't have it.

"Oh, dear. That thing is *such* a trial to me," Max said.

"I think it's scared your dog," I said. "Er, your familiar."

We rose to our feet, too, walked past several bookcases, and found Nelli barking in fear at a massive, dark, very old wooden cupboard that stood against the far wall. It had a profusion of drawers and doors, and it was about six feet tall and at least that wide. As near as I understand these things, the cupboard was enchanted by Max's predecessor, and the effects seemed to be permanent. It could be dormant and inert for weeks at a time, but then suddenly, without warning, it would act up again. Apparently Nelli's curious sniffing had stirred it up.

Its drawers and cabinets were opening and closing rapidly, slamming shut with a violence that seemed downright irritable. As we watched, flames started pouring out of some of the drawers.

"That's *dangerous*," said Lucky, wide-eyed and disapproving.

"It's a . . ." I tried to think of a way to explain it to Lucky. "It's a sort of . . ."

"It's a possessed cupboard, right?" he said.

"Er, right."

"My grandmother's family had one, back in Sicily."

"I see."

"I keep trying to neutralize its energy," Max said wearily, "but I don't know how it got this way, and my predecessor cannot be reached for consultation."

This sort of confusion seemed to be rather common among Max and his colleagues. In fact, Max was 350 years old because he'd unwittingly drunk a life-prolonging elixir in his youth (back in the seventeenth century) that no one could replicate, no matter how many times they tried. He had imbibed it *so* unwittingly that he was in his fifties before he realized that he was aging at an unusually slow rate.

He wasn't immortal, but it seemed likely he'd be around for another century or so. Unless Evil got him first.

Unnerved by the aggressive, flaming, drawer-slamming cupboard, Nelli gave up barking at it and instead opted for hiding behind us and whining.

My head was starting to pound, and I decided what I needed most of all was a few more hours of sleep.

"I'm going home," I said to my companions. "I'm tired."

"I'll contact you after I've learned something more about this phenomenon," Max promised, looking pretty tired himself after spending the weekend summoning his whining familiar.

"Wait, Esther, there's one more thing we gotta talk about." Lucky turned to Max and said, "She saw the hit. Do you think she's in any danger?"

Max frowned with concern as he considered this, but finally said, "I doubt it. I really do. A man with deadly enemies saw a portent of his own death. I think it very likely this was an isolated incident that will not recur, let alone involve Esther any further."

At the time, it was a reasonable supposition. We had no way of knowing then just how wrong he was.

6

CHORUS GIRL WITNESSES MOB HIT! was the first head-line I saw on my walk home from the subway station.

"Chorus girl," I muttered unhappily as I picked up the tabloid and read the caption beneath a photo of "alleged Gambello hitman" Lucky Battistuzzi embracing me outside of Bella Stella last night.

I tried to resist looking at the other tabloids, but there's a certain ghoulish fascination to seeing yourself demeaned in semiliterate prose at the local newsstand.

CHUBBY CHARLIE CHECKS OUT! announced *The New York Post*.

ACTRESS ALMOST AXED? asked the *Insider*. This "news story" reported that a "confidential source" claimed *I* might be the intended victim of last night's hit, and Charlie Chiccante just an innocent bystander. Since the story below this one reported that Donald Trump had been dead for a decade and an impersonator had been running his empire all this time, I didn't worry too much that Charlie had actually died because of me.

BELLA MORTE? quipped another headline. The article noted that this was the third violent death at Bella Stella in five years.

"Hmph." I put the tabloid back down after reading

a few lines. Then I saw that holding it for thirty seconds had been long enough to stain my hands with ink.

"Hey, ain't this a picture of *you* on the cover of the *Exposé?*" asked the guy who ran the newsstand. He'd sold me my weekly copy of *Backstage* for several years, as well as various newspapers, magazines, and the occasional candy bar, but we'd never chatted before.

I took a good look and saw he was reading a copy of the *Exposé* that had my picture in it. I was not flattered that he'd been able to identify me from this shot: I was squinting and hunched over, trying to avoid the glare of the flash, and my mouth was gaping open in surprise. Lopez, whose arm was around me, had mostly been cropped out of the photo.

"*That's* the photo they decided to use?" I said. "What did I ever do to them?"

The news seller frowned as he looked at me. "You got blue stuff on your face now."

"I know." The blue substance that had spilled on me in Max's laboratory was on my arm, too, thanks to Lucky shooting up the place.

After looking at the photo again, the news seller said, "Well, at least your cheekbones look good."

"My cheekbones always look good," I said grumpily. "They're my best feature." Actors learn to be pragmatic about our looks. We need to know what casting directors see when they look at us.

The news seller studied me for another moment, then concluded, "Yeah, I'll go along with that. Good cheekbones." He waved the tabloid at me. "It's a bad photo, no denying that. But the headline—SINGING SERVER SEES SLAYING!—that's some lovely alliteration, don't you think?"

"Lovely. In fact, I hope it's what they put on my tombstone." I turned my back on him, eager to go home.

"Hey, don't you want any of these papers?" the news

seller called after me. "This is your fifteen minutes of fame!"

I felt depressed.

As I was walking home, my cell phone rang. I saw that the call was from Lopez, and I flipped open the phone. "Hello?"

"It's me," he said. "Where are you? Are you okay?"

"I'm fine." I was surprised at the urgency in his voice. "Why?"

There was a pause. "I guess I got a little ... I'm outside your apartment—"

"You are?" I was less than a block from there, so I started walking faster.

Lopez said, "When you didn't answer your buzzer or your home phone ... Well, I couldn't think of where else you'd be this morning. I got worried."

"You thought I might be sleeping with the fishes?"

"That's not funny." He sounded exhausted. "Where are you?"

I rounded the corner and could see him sitting on the steps of my building. "Look to your right," I said.

He did—and I saw his whole body sag with relief when he spotted me. I realized then how seriously he believed that witnessing Charlie's death had put me in danger.

He folded his cell phone and put it in his pocket as he stood up. He had removed his tie, and he held his jacket slung over his shoulder. I dropped my cell phone into my purse and met him in front of my building. He had dark circles under his eyes, and he looked tense and tired.

His gaze roamed over my face, and he reached up to touch my cheek. I thought it was a gesture of affection until he frowned and asked, "Why are you all blue and scratched?"

"Oh! That damn dog." I turned my head and brushed self-consciously at my face.

"What dog?" He took my chin and gently lifted it so he could see the scratches Nelli had left on my cheek and forehead.

"Max got a dog. So to speak." I was longing for my bed by now.

Lopez went very still for a moment, then dropped his hand. I realized belatedly that I should have guarded my words.

"You've been to see Max?" His voice was flat.

"Yes." I didn't want to argue about it, so I pulled my keys out of my pocket and started up the steps of my building. "And his dog pummeled me."

He followed me. As we entered the building, he said, "Max got a vicious dog?"

"No, just a big one. Nelli is, um, exuberant."

"Why did you go to see him?" Lopez asked tersely, following me upstairs to the second floor.

"I needed to ask him something."

"About last night?" He was trudging heavily up the steps behind me.

"Yes." I got to the door of my apartment and unlocked it.

"Esther." The exasperation in his voice got on my last nerve.

"What?" I snapped. I turned around and confronted him as he followed me inside and closed the door. When he didn't answer, I said, "Well, *what?*"

He hesitated, evidently realizing I was in no mood to be told how to choose my friends. As I held his gaze, I realized that his eyes were bloodshot.

I took a breath and said in a more mild tone, "You haven't had any sleep, have you?"

"Not yet," he grumbled. "I came straight here from work."

"That was quite a long shift," I said, realizing he must be running on fumes.

"Yeah." He rubbed a hand over his face.

"Does Napoli know where you are?"

"What do you think?" he said irritably.

"I think he grilled you about how we know each other—"

"'Grilled' is too nice a word for it."

"—and would handcuff you to your desk if he knew you were here right now."

"Good guess." He tossed his jacket on the couch and said to me, "We have to talk."

I was sure that would be a big mistake, in more ways than one. I was tired and slow-witted, and he was exhausted and cranky. So I said, "No. Not now."

"Yes, *now*."

"Later," I said, reaching for his hand.

He frowned. "This can't wait, Esther." But he followed me as I tugged him across the floor and out of the living room.

When we got to the door of my bedroom, though, he balked. "What are you doing?"

"Going to bed," I said wearily, pulling him into my bedroom—and not at all flattered by the way he dragged his heels and tried to tug out of my grasp.

"Whoa! Even if this were a good idea right now, which it's *not*, I am honestly in no condition to—"

"Yes, that much is obvious," I said. "You look like last week's leftovers."

"Oh." He blinked. "I suppose I do."

"And I feel like I've been dragged behind a subway train." I pushed him toward my bed. "My head is pounding. My stomach hurts." I pushed him again, and he sat down abruptly as his legs encountered the mattress. "And I don't think I had as much as three hours sleep last night."

"I'm sorry," he said, his expression softening. "I should've realized you wouldn't be able to sleep after what you saw."

"So I refuse to talk about *anything* until I've had a

nap." I kicked off my shoes while he watched, and then I crawled onto the mattress beside him. "What you do is up to you, but I think you should get some shut-eye before you take another step. You look ready to drop. And there's room for both of us." I plumped up a pillow and lay down. "Either way, I'm going to sleep now."

I closed my eyes and sighed, nestling into my bed. After a moment of stillness, Lopez shifted his weight to kick off his shoes, which hit the floor with a couple of soft thuds. Then I heard the click of his belt buckle and the whisper of the leather sliding through his belt loops as he took it off.

I opened one eye and saw him removing his gun and holster. He set them on the bedside table, along with his wallet. Then he lay back on the mattress, sighing as his head sank into the pillow next to mine. He closed his eyes for a moment, then turned his head to meet my one-eyed gaze.

"I've been fantasizing for weeks about getting into your bed," he said, his voice more relaxed than it had been before. "In my head, it was never quite like this."

I snuggled against him and murmured, "This'll do for now."

"Yeah." He slid his arm around me and rested his cheek on my hair. "It will."

A minute later, he broke the contented silence. "Esther?"

"Hmm?"

"How did the dog get your face all blue?"

"Shhh," I said.

Within minutes, the even sound of his breathing soothed me to sleep.

A shrill ringing woke me up.

I sat bolt upright, looking around the room in a bleary daze.

Another shrill ring!

Hoping to stifle the noise, I reached for the alarm clock. Clumsy in my sleepiness, I missed it and knocked over the lamp on my nightstand. It fell to the floor with a clatter, which was when Lopez sat bolt upright, too, looking around in obvious confusion before he realized where he was.

The ringing continued, so I reached for the bedside phone next. When I picked up the receiver, all I heard was a dial tone. So then I picked up the silent alarm clock and stared at it stupidly.

Lopez lay back down and squinted at me in the afternoon light sliding through the Venetian blinds. "What are you *doing*?" he asked sleepily.

"Did we set the alarm?" I asked in a scratchy voice, not remembering why he was there, but not that surprised to find him in my bed. I had, after all, thought often about him being there.

"Huh?" He rubbed his eyes as the shrill ringing continued. "Oh, wait . . ." A five o'clock shadow darkened his jaw. "Sorry." Still lying prone, he fumbled in his pockets. After a moment, he held up his cell phone. "I turned the . . ." He cleared his throat. "I turned the ringer way up last night so I could hear Napoli and my captain phoning me. The crime scene was so noisy . . ."

"Answer your phone," I said tersely as it rang again.

"Huh? Oh. Right." Still half asleep, he flipped open the phone and mumbled, "Hello?" He stiffened and looked a little more wakeful as he said, "Hi, Mom."

I stiffened, too. We were both fully clothed and had done nothing in this bed but *sleep*. Even so, I started straightening my clothing and trying to smooth my hair.

Lopez glanced at me and started to smile. "Yeah, I was taking a nap."

Feeling groggy, I was about to rub my hands over my face but then I noticed they were dirty with tabloid ink.

"Because I was tired," he said into the receiver. "I worked a long shift last night." After another moment,

"I'm not sure. I lost count after I'd been on the clock for fourteen hours . . . I'm fine. Just tired."

When I started to slide off the bed, he grabbed my arm and pulled me down into the pillows. I looked pointedly at the phone in his hand and shook my head. He grinned and, despite my squirming, pulled me closer while he listened to his mother's next question.

"No, I didn't have time," he said. "Okay, I'll go to Mass later. Yes, I promise." He slid his arm around my waist and continued, "Yeah, it was the shooting at Bella Stella. We were on it all night." He nuzzled my neck, his hair tickling my cheek. "Mom, I need to go, can I call you back la . . . What?" He froze in midcuddle and his tone changed. "The tabloids?"

Startled, I stopped wriggling.

He shifted position so that our gazes met, and he said to his mom, "Yeah, that would be the same Esther Diamond."

Great.

Resisting the urge to curl up into a fetal position, I sighed and rolled away from Lopez. He didn't wrestle me when I slid out of bed this time.

I looked over my shoulder at him and whispered, "I'll make coffee." He nodded and sat up. I headed for the bedroom door.

On my way out of the room, I heard him make a brief, doomed effort to go on the offensive. "Never mind that! What are *you* doing reading *tabloids,* Mom?"

It wouldn't work, of course. I went into the kitchen and started brewing some strong coffee.

I knew Lopez had told his parents he was interested in someone, but I didn't know he had told them my name. I wondered if they had dragged the information out of him during his father's birthday weekend, or if he had told them voluntarily at some point. I knew he was close to his family. He might roll his eyes when his mom phoned, but he spoke with her often, and they seemed to have a very open, frank relationship and lots to talk about. And his affection for his father was obvious when he spoke about him. He was also clearly fond of his brothers.

By contrast, I only talked to my parents in Wisconsin about once a month, and I talked to Ruth, my married sister in Chicago, much less than that. There was no hostility between me and my family, we just didn't have that much to say to each other. None of them had ever *disapproved* of my becoming an actress and moving to New York, but they didn't understand it, and I knew they thought of it as a madcap phase I'd recover from when I matured.

One of the many things I liked about Lopez was that he wasn't an actor. (I like working with actors, but dating them is an exercise in masochism.) But something else I really liked about him was that he seemed to understand that acting was my vocation, it was who I was and always would be. In the same way that I could see that being a cop was more than just a job to him—it was who he was.

I frowned as I thought about Max's doppelgänger theory and wondered how much to say to Lopez about last night.

"*No,* I'm not going to stop seeing her." I heard his raised voice in the bedroom as he got exasperated with his mother. "Oh, really? Well, then maybe you shouldn't have brought me up on all those stories about how you defied the family to date Pop!" After a moment, he said, "*I* don't see how it's different . . . Yeah? And what makes you so sure I'm *not* going to marry her and raise three ungrateful sons who won't give me grandchildren?"

"Oh, I was *so* right not to attend his father's birthday party," I muttered in the kitchen.

I gathered from Lopez that the desire for grandchildren had dominated his parents' agenda lately. His two brothers had each come up with creative ways of getting their folks off their backs. The eldest had told his parents he was gay, and the middle brother announced he was becoming a priest. They were both lying, but it took the subject of marriage off the table for a while.

And Lopez, the youngest, had told his parents he was interested in an unstable Jewish woman with unsavory friends (i.e. Max).

I didn't doubt that Lopez's attraction to me was sincere. He was a dedicated cop and it was clear that dating me wasn't good for his career at the moment, so I didn't think that being in my apartment today was a casual choice for him. But I knew it was nonetheless convenient for him that he was seeing a woman whom his mother wouldn't want him to marry. And just in case she decided she could cope with a daughter-in-law who wasn't Catholic, he'd been holding back the shocking news that I was an actress. He was saving that tidbit for an "emergency," he'd told me.

Well, it looked like the cat was out of the bag now. According to today's tabloids, I was a chorus girl with ties to the Mafia. (And since there was a sense in which this was perfectly true, I felt depressed again.) So now Lopez was getting an earful in my bedroom about his taste in women.

"All right, *enough*," I heard him say wearily to his mother. "Give it a rest, would you? Look, I have to go . . . Because I have things to do . . . Of *course* I'm trying to get you off the phone. Is it going to work?"

"Last year, I played Kate in *The Taming of the Shrew* in summer stock," I grumbled to myself. "But do the tabloids mention that? *Nooooo.*"

The scent of fresh-brewed coffee was filling the apartment when Lopez finally came out of the bedroom, looking sheepish.

"Sorry about that," he said.

"I'm just glad it wasn't *my* mother who called," I said sincerely.

"I never suspected her of reading tabloids." Lopez frowned. "I wonder if my dad knows?"

"I guess everyone's got a dark secret."

He sniffed the air and asked hopefully, "Is the coffee ready?"

I realized I didn't know how he took it. We were still so new to each other. I held up the milk and sugar, and I raised my eyebrows in silent query.

He shook his head. "Just black."

"Look on the bright side," I said, handing him a full mug. "It seems certain that as long as we're dating, she'll *never* suggest you think about getting married."

"Good point."

That led me to something I wanted to get off my chest. "Look, I'm sorry I told everyone at Stella's that you're my boyfriend. And, um, that they think we're engaged. It's just that I needed—"

"Oh, I don't care about that." He waved away my apology. "I mean, I know why you said it."

"You do?"

"Sure. A place full of heavily armed wiseguys pinching you, hitting on you, and getting too pushy after they've had a few drinks?" He shrugged. "A cop boyfriend probably comes in handy pretty often at Stella's."

I nodded. "In a nutshell."

"And since I don't *want* those guys pinching you, hitting on you, and so on," he added, "I'm glad you told them about me."

"Oh." I smiled. "Okay."

He smiled, too, then sat down at my kitchen table, half of which was in my living room. That's a Manhattan apartment for you.

After a moment, though, his expression turned serious. "We have to talk about last night."

I slid into the chair next to him. "I told you exactly what I saw. I'm not lying to you."

"Then I need to find out what you're leaving out."

"Here we go," I muttered.

He reached over to me, slid his hand into my hair, and gently pulled my head closer to his. "Look, I shouldn't even be here. And I *definitely* shouldn't have just spent three hours in your bed."

"We didn't do anything," I reminded him.

He kissed me. All of a sudden, without preamble. His mouth was hot, and his tongue was silky, and it was a really long, intense, leading-straight-to-steamy-sex kind of kiss. He needed a shave, but his jaw was just rough enough to feel sexy, not uncomfortable.

When he was finally done, I was dizzy and couldn't speak or move or catch my breath. I just sat there waiting for him to do it again. I think I whimpered a little.

"I didn't do anything," he whispered, breathing hard, "because I was just too damn tired."

"How can you kiss a woman like that . . ." I panted for air, ". . . right after talking to your *mother?*"

He blinked. "Okay, when you put it that way, I suddenly feel too tired again."

"Forget I mentioned it." I leaned forward to kiss him again.

"No, listen to me," he whispered, putting his hands on my face to make me hold still.

"Ow." I winced. "Nelli's scratches."

"Oh!" He brushed his fingertips over my cheek, feather light, to soothe my skin. "Sorry."

"You could kiss it and make it better," I suggested.

He shook his head. "We have to talk."

"I don't feel like talking," I said pointedly.

"Neither do I." He shied away from my mouth again, his eyes heavy-lidded and his breath still coming fast. "But we have to."

"*You're* the one who—"

"I know." His puff of laughter brushed across my face. "I was just making a point. It backfired on me, though."

"Hmph." I sat back in my chair. "Okay, fine. Have it your way. Let's talk."

"We need to go over . . ." He paused, looking distracted, then said, "Wait. First, just tell me. Why is your face blue?"

"Oh, I forgot about that!" I looked down at my blue arm. "Wow, I must be hot, if you can kiss me like that when my face is blue."

"Well, as you may remember, you were green all over the first time I ever saw you. I guess I find you sexy in different colors."

We had met the night Lopez questioned the cast of *Sorcerer!* backstage after Golly Gee disappeared; I was in lots of body make-up and hardly any costume as a green forest nymph.

He asked, "So how did you get so blue today?"

I considered the ramifications of lying and decided to just tell him the truth.

7

"Nelli scared Lucky," I said. "Lucky shot up Max's place. Some weird blue stuff in a beaker fell on me."

It seemed simple enough.

But when Lopez planted his elbows on the table and buried his face in his hands, I decided that maybe honesty wasn't the best policy after all.

"*What* were you doing with Lucky Battistuzzi this morning?" he asked, head still in hands. "No, wait, that's not my first question. My *first* question is, what was Lucky doing at *Max's?* No, wait—" He lifted his head and scowled at me. "What were *you* doing at Max's?"

"On a scale of one to ten," I said, "how important are these questions?"

"*What?*" he snapped.

"I mean, what did you come here this morning to talk to me about?"

He looked dumbfounded. "You drop a bombshell like *that*—telling me you spent the morning watching a notorious Gambello hit man shooting up the home of a guy who you *know* I think is crazy and probably a danger to you—"

"Max isn't crazy," I said patiently. "And he's certainly not dangerous."

"—and you expect me to remember what I came here to talk about?"

"It's been a weird twenty-four hours," I admitted.

"Esther." He seemed at a loss for words.

"I didn't realize the truth would upset you this much," I said.

"Max is bad enough," he said in appalled tones, "but *Lucky Battistuzzi?* Don't you realize how dangerous it is to hang out with him?"

"Don't worry, I took away his gun," I said, thinking this would soothe my concerned suitor.

Lopez's eyes bulged. *"You took away Lucky Battistuzzi's gun?"*

"Actually, I guess Max took it away," I said, recalling the spell which had briefly transformed it into a winged bat. I decided not to mention the details. "But I hid it. So Lucky doesn't have it anymore.

"He has plenty more of them," Lopez said tersely. He shook his head as if trying to clear it. "Why were you with him in the first place?"

"He wanted to know what I could remember about Charlie's death."

"You shouldn't be talking to him about that!" Lopez exploded. "It's a police matter!"

"I know," I said, "but Lucky and Charlie were ... Well, I guess 'friends' would be a wild exaggeration."

"For all you know, Lucky was questioning you on behalf of the killer!" Lopez said in exasperation. "To see if they need to get rid of you!"

"You think Lucky is involved in Charlie's death?"

"Actually, I think the Corvinos killed Charlie," he said irritably. "I think they've probably just fired the first shot in a brand new war with the Gambello family. But right now, that's only a theory, Esther. Without more facts, I have to keep in mind the possibility that Lucky could be involved and might have a motive to eliminate you!"

"That did occur to me," I admitted.

"And you met with him anyhow?" Lopez shouted.

"Only after I decided it was safe!"

"What convinced you it was safe?" he demanded.

At the moment, I couldn't actually remember. So I said, "The point is, it *was* safe, and—"

"No, the *point* is you should not be running off to meet with wiseguys at Max's place!" A horrible expression crossed his face. "Oh, my God. Wait a minute. You're saying . . . *Max* is involved in this?"

"Um . . ." This wasn't going well. I stared silently at Lopez, wondering what to say now.

Looking like he wanted to shout at me again, he closed his eyes and rubbed his forehead. "What is it about Max, Esther? Why do you hang out with him?"

Despite feeling very conscious of the need to stay far, far away from the fact that I had helped Max kill Hieronymus, I said, "He saved my life. Max is odd, I admit, but he's got his reasons. And he's someone I trust. Someone I can count on."

Still looking like his head hurt, Lopez said, "Look, I know that you . . . hear a different drummer. And I *like* that about you."

"I hear a 'but' coming."

"But this is dangerous, Esther. It's also skirting the edge of the law. I don't think you're stupid or a thrill seeker." He made a vague gesture and shook his head. "But you don't know what you're getting into, hanging out with guys like Lucky and Max."

I was startled into laughter. Lopez's dark expression made it clear that my levity only confirmed his fears. But hearing Max and Lucky lumped into the same category struck me as comical.

"You're being naive," Lopez said.

I again tried to think of what to say. Lucky wanted to find Charlie's killer before the cops did so he could whack him. Of course Lopez would oppose my helping with that, and I agreed with him. I hadn't initially intended to help. But Chubby Charlie had seen his perfect double before dying and had talked about a curse. No one could figure out how the murder had been committed, and Max had a theory about a doppelgänger. So I suspected this crime might be something that a smart cop like Lopez just wasn't equipped to solve.

It was the sort of situation I would have thought was insane before getting to know Max and the nature of his work. And I had a fair idea of how insane it would sound to Lopez if I tried to explain it. So I just stared at him in silence, wondering what to say.

"I want to take you into protective custody," he said firmly, putting his hand over mine. "I'm afraid your life is in danger."

"From Lucky?" I shook my head.

"More likely from the Corvinos." He added, "But it's not as if the Gambellos appreciate witnesses, even in a case where the victim is one of their own."

I thought about it. If Max was right about the doppelgänger, I doubted the cops were equipped to protect me. And if Max was indeed right, then the assassin, whether a Corvino mobster or someone else, was no ordinary hoodlum who'd whack me on nervous impulse, as Lucky had initially implied and as Lopez obviously feared.

So I said, "If I agreed I was in potential danger—"

"Esther . . ." He looked impatient, realizing I intended to refuse.

"—I'd go along with this. But . . ."

The strange logistics of the homicide made me suspect Max was right.

And if Max was wrong, well, I hadn't seen anything revelatory last night—but I *had* seen enough movies to suspect protective custody would be unpleasant and not even all that protective.

"I don't think it's the best thing for me," I said.

"Esther, you're—"

"I'll reserve the right to change my mind." Just in case Lopez was right. "How's that?"

"Not good enough," he said.

"But it's the only answer I'm going to give you," I said. "At least for now. So let's not keep arguing about it."

He looked like he really wanted to argue, but he evidently realized it wouldn't accomplish anything. So he said, "All right. I'll let it go for now. But you keep your cell phone with you at all times, and you keep my number on speed dial. *Promise* me."

"Okay." I nodded. "That's a good plan. I promise." When he didn't say anything else, just sat there looking glum, I asked, "So that's the talk? I mean, it's what you came here to say?"

"Huh? Oh. No. Not entirely."

I sighed. "Well?"

"I want to go over everything you saw last night. Until I figure out what the missing piece is."

I groaned as I folded my arms on the table and rested my head on them.

"We need to do this," he said, sounding tired again. "Right now, you're suspected of obstruction, at the very least. And my captain would ream me a new one just for coming here to talk to you alone, never mind sleeping with you."

"We didn't *do* any—"

"It doesn't matter. I can't be involved with someone who's a suspect in an open investigation."

That statement certainly had a sobering effect. We'd been in this situation before. During his investigation of Golly Gee and the other disappearees.

"Then why did you even come here this morning?" I grumbled.

"Because I don't want this thing to go bad for you." After a moment, he added, "Or for us—you and me, I mean."

With my head still on my arms, I waited for him to continue.

He said, "Napoli wants to get a material witness warrant for you."

"What?" I sat up. "Why? All he has to do is ask me to come in again. I haven't refused to answer his questions."

"He says you did. He says you refused to keep talking last night and you walked out."

"Well, of course I did! At the time, I mean. It was late, I was tired, and he was just saying the same idiotic, accusatory crap over and over!"

"That's what cops do. We wear you down until we get the whole story."

"He *had* it," I insisted. "I was fed up. That doesn't mean I'm an uncooperative witness! Even a saint would have walked out by then. Napoli's a jerk."

"He's good cop, though."

"He's a *jerk*."

"Okay, I don't like him either," Lopez admitted. "Not that he'd be heartbroken by that, since I think he loathes me. And I've only been assigned to his team since yesterday," he added morosely. "So the new job's off to a rocky start."

"Look, I'm sorry last night was embarrassing for you. I *am*. But it's not my fault," I said. "I didn't plan to witness a mob hit!"

"I know," he said soothingly. "But now we have to straighten this out before it gets any more complicated."

"I told you everything I saw."

"Then I need to figure out what you haven't remembered or don't realize was significant. That's why Napoli was going over and over this until you wanted to throttle him. He was trying to decide whether you were lying or just not remembering something."

"Well, all he did was piss me off."

"As long as he thinks you may be lying, we've got a problem, Esther," Lopez said.

"And what do *you* think?"

"Like I've already told Napoli two dozen times, I think that seeing someone killed right in front of you really shook you up," he said. "So there's something important that you just don't recall yet."

I frowned again. "Like what?"

"I'm not sure. But the crime scene doesn't add up. Not at all."

"I know. Napoli said so. While accusing me of lying."

"Someone must have moved something. Or changed something. Or lied about something."

"I haven't li—"

"I believe you," he assured me. "Okay? But I think what happened was traumatic for you, so what you're saying isn't accurate, it's just what you can remember right now."

"Well, I can't argue about it being traumatic," I admitted with a shudder as I remembered watching Charlie die.

"The only thing we know for sure," Lopez said, "is that the shot fired through the window couldn't have killed Charlie. Based on where he was sitting and where he fell, the trajectory is impossible. But that's still the only shot we can account for."

"It's the only one I heard," I insisted.

"I'm sorry to do this to you, Esther, but we have to go over it again. And again. Until I figure out what your memory is leaving out."

"I am *so* tired of talking about this," I told him.

"I know," he said gently. "But it's important."

I sighed and looked at the ceiling. "And I guess my only way of avoiding another dance with Napoli is if you bring him something that satisfies him."

"That's right."

I eyed Lopez. "But then you'd have to tell him you were here."

"Yeah, but if he realizes I was here to question you effectively, he'll get over it. And he'll get off your back. Mine, too." He shrugged. "Everybody wins. And then I can do something in your bed more fun than *sleeping* without worrying about a conflict of interest or a breach of ethics or getting suspended."

"Oh." I blinked. "Okay." I sat up a little. "When you put it that way, I guess I can muster up the energy to talk about last night. *Again.*"

He smiled. "Glad you see it my way."

Unfortunately, though, it didn't do any good. I was positive that my consistent description of Charlie's murder was complete and accurate; Lopez was positive it wasn't, but none of his questions produced any new information or potential leads.

After almost an hour of this, he rubbed his hands over his unshaven face and then sat staring silently into thin air, frowning as he considered the puzzle.

Wondering if I should risk bringing up Max's theory, I tested the waters by asking, "What about Charlie's fears that he'd been cursed?"

"Huh?" Lopez looked startled, almost as if he'd forgotten I was in the room. "Oh. All that babbling about seeing his perfect double and being marked for death?"

"Yes. Do you think there could be something to that?"

"I think it sounds like he was off his meds," Lopez said absently.

"What?"

He looked at me. "Charlie was bipolar. It sounds to me like he was having a weird manic episode. That's what Napoli thinks, too."

"Bipolar?" I was startled. "Charlie was manic-depressive?"

"Yeah."

"Lucky said Charlie had always been strange. Moody."
I now remembered that when I'd told Lucky that Charlie had sounded crazy right before he died, the old gangster had replied that it wouldn't be the first time. "But he never mentioned bipolar disorder."

Lopez was still frowning in thought as he replied, "I doubt Lucky knows. It's the sort of thing Charlie would keep secret. Not good for business. Not socially acceptable among his cronies."

"If he kept it a secret, then how do *you* know?"

"Hmm? Oh. About a decade ago, Charlie did time for income tax evasion." Lopez shook his head in disgust. "He probably committed enough violent felonies to get sentenced to two hundred years in maximum security. But the only thing anyone ever caught him at was cheating on his taxes." He shrugged. "So Charlie's medical condition wound up on his summer camp forms."

"His what?"

"Uh, all his records from the detention facility he was in for nonviolent criminals," Lopez clarified. "Which is how we know he was manic-depressive. And if he went off his medication recently . . ."

"Then his delusions about seeing his own perfect double and being cursed might have been some sort of manic episode?"

"That's my guess. But maybe *your* guess was right," Lopez added.

I blinked. "*My* guess?"

"Napoli says you thought Charlie was having a ministroke, or maybe not getting enough oxygen to his brain."

"Oh! Right. Yes. That was my guess." I decided to keep silent about the doppelgänger theory.

He shrugged again. "Maybe the autopsy will reveal that the murderer was just one step ahead of Mother Nature when it came to taking Charlie's life."

"Hmm." Now *I* stared off into space.

If Charlie had stopped taking his psych meds and was having a manic delusion about seeing his perfect double, then Max was wrong, and Charlie's death was an ordinary Mafia hit—albeit a very puzzling one. Could mental illness also explain his behavior a few nights ago? Maybe Lucky and I hadn't seen Charlie's perfect double that night after all. Maybe we just saw a gangster whose psych disorder was out of control . . .

While I was pondering this in silence, Lopez glanced at his watch and muttered, "I have to go." When I looked at him in silent query, he said, "Home, shower, shave, Mass, work."

"You have to work this evening? After the shift you just pulled?"

"I'm the new guy," he said by way of explanation. "But if nothing new turns up, I'm going to leave early. I been rode hard and put away wet."

He finished his second cup of coffee in a long gulp, and went into the bedroom for his shoes, wallet, gun, and belt. Then he came back into the living room for his jacket.

"I'm going to tell Napoli that we talked," he said.

I looked at him. "Are you sure you want to do that? You *are* the new guy, after all. Maybe you shouldn't—"

"It would be easier to convince him I know what I'm doing if I'd already been there a few months," he admitted. "But it's obvious to me that there's no point in Napoli squandering his time, your patience, and my love life by harassing you. You've told us everything you know."

"I hope he agrees," I said morosely.

"I'll be emphatic," Lopez assured me. "And I trust you to tell me if you remember anything else."

"I will," I promised, though I didn't believe there was anything else *to* remember.

"So after I deal with Napoli . . ." He tilted his head. "Want to take another stab at doing this like normal people?"

Still thinking about the problems surrounding Charlie's death, I said, "Huh?"

He smiled. "I've got tomorrow night off. I could put on my black silk shirt again and make a new reservation at Raoul's." Dark lashes lowered over blue eyes as he added, "And maybe you could wear something that gives me sinful ideas . . ."

"Oh!" I smiled, too. "I like this plan."

"Good. I'll pick you up at seven?"

As a recent crime scene, Stella's would still be closed down, and I wouldn't be working. So I nodded. Then I brushed self-consciously at my face and added, "I'll try not to still be blue."

"I like the blue, it flatters your eyes." He stopped by the kitchen table to give me a quick kiss good-bye, then headed for the door. But he paused there and said, "Is there any point in asking you to stay away from Max and Lucky?"

"Will you stay away from Napoli and your mother?" I replied.

"That's what I thought." He left.

8

I got two phone calls late the following afternoon, both of them important.

An old buddy from the Actors Studio called and told me about a role that he'd heard had just unexpectedly opened up after the actress who'd been cast in it had gone parasailing on Saturday and wound up in traction.

Naturally, I phoned my agent.

And while I was on hold on my landline, Lucky called my cell phone.

"We got a big problem, kid," he said. "There's another doppelgangster on the loose."

"What?" I sat down with a thud. "Who? How do you know?"

"We can't talk on the *phone,*" he said. "Don't they teach you nothin' at acting school?"

"But *you* just said there's another dopp—"

"Meet me in an hour at the place we met before."

I frowned. "The place we met bef ... Oh! You mean the church?"

He sighed in exasperation. "Yeah. The church."

"In an hour?" I glanced at the clock and thought about my date this evening. "How long will this take?"

"It'll take as long as it takes." Lucky sounded terse. "And bring your friend."

"My friend?" I said blankly.

"Your friend who's an expert with this kind of problem," he prodded.

"Oh! You mean Max?"

"Jesus, don't use *names* on the phone!" Lucky snapped before he hung up on me.

I closed my cell phone. Then I hung up the landline, figuring I'd call my agent again later. I doubted I'd have time to come back home before my date, so I called Lopez. I got his voice mail.

"I have to go out," I said. "So don't come to my place. I'll meet you at Raoul's."

I was still a bit scratched and blue, so I was thorough about applying makeup. Then I dressed to kill, in a manner of speaking, and styled my hair. Hoping nothing would happen to muss me before my date, I took a cab to Max's.

As soon as I entered the bookshop and called Max's name, Nelli trotted up to me, face and paws stained blue, tongue lolling, tail wagging. I grabbed her shiny new collar so she wouldn't shed on my little black dress while I explained the situation to Max.

"By all means, we must attend this meeting at once!" he agreed. "But, er, although your outfit is very attractive, it's rather, uh . . . I mean to say, are you sure it's suitable for church?"

"It's suitable for a date with the man who's on his way to being my boyfriend," I said. "Which is where I'm headed after this meeting."

"Ah! How *is* Detective Lopez?"

"A little overworked. Come on, Max, I have a cab waiting outside."

He cast a look of undisguised horror toward the street. "A *cab?*"

Max hated modern transportation—cars, trains, planes, elevators, escalators. They all terrified him.

"It'll be fine," I said soothingly. "We're only going to Little Italy."

"We could walk."

"Not in *these* heels," I said. "Anyhow, we'll barely get there in time as it is." Recalling the way I had looked the last few times Lopez saw me, I had put real effort into my appearance today. So now I was running a little behind schedule.

I grabbed Max's sleeve and tugged. "Say an incantation or something, but let's *go*. Come on."

"I'm not sure how long I'll be gone," he said to Nelli as I hauled him out of the bookstore. "Feel free to review some Latin texts if you get restless."

"So how's it going?" I asked as we got into the cab. "With Nelli, I mean?"

"Oh ... there are some communication problems to work out."

"I'll bet." I told our driver where to take us, then asked Max, "Have you found any good source material on our problem yet?"

His face brightened. "Yes! A colleague in Jerusalem is sending me some rare texts. They should be here within a day or two. Federal Express is a most *remarkable* innovation."

"Indeed."

"And my colleague assures me I may keep the volumes as long as I need them," Max said, "since doppelgängerism is not a common problem in the Middle East."

"Well, it's good to know there's at least one problem they don't have there."

I was about to mention the cops' theory that Chubby Charlie had been having a manic episode, but I realized there was no point in talking just now. Max was clutching the door handle in terror and flinching every time the cab swerved. By the time we reached West Houston Street, he was muttering in a language I couldn't identify.

When the cab pulled up outside St. Monica's, I paid

the driver, got out, then opened Max's door and extracted him from the vehicle. His legs buckled briefly, and I clutched him until he seemed steady enough to walk on his own.

"All right?" I said after a moment.

"Yes." He straightened the fedora he usually wore when he left the shop, then adjusted the way his long duster was hanging on his rather short body. The coat had been bequeathed to him by a gunfighter long ago, and he wore it with pride. With his long white hair, white beard, and odd clothing, he made a memorable first impression. Lucky Battistuzzi, however, had seemed quick to recognize the expertise that lay beneath the eccentricity.

Max gestured to the door of the church, which was open to the warm May breeze. "After you, my dear."

I preceded him into the serene and hallowed interior of the old church. It seemed very dark compared to the bright afternoon sunshine outside. I blinked a few times, waiting for my eyes to adjust.

Somewhere in the soft, dim shadows, a woman screamed horribly.

Moving vehicles are just about the only kind of danger Max shrinks from. He responded immediately to the woman's screams by rushing down the center aisle toward the sound of her voice. I dashed after him like a lemming. But my high heels were made for seduction, not sprinting, and I still couldn't see that well. Predictably, within a few steps, I fell down.

"Agh!" I hit the stone floor of the church with a *splat* that knocked the wind out of me.

I lay there for a moment, stunned and gasping for air. By the time I hauled myself laboriously to my feet, leaning on a pew for balance, I realized that the screams I heard were not, as I had thought at first, cries of pain or terror.

Elena Giacalona was enraged, not scared or hurt.

I could see her now that my eyes had adjusted to the dim light. And I could see her companions, too: Lucky, Father Gabriel, and a well-dressed, middle-aged man whom I didn't recognize.

"Stay away from me!" she shouted at Lucky. "How many times must I tell you? How dare you even *speak* to me! Have you no shame?"

"I'm sorry, I didn't mean to upset you," said Lucky.

"You're still speaking!" the Widow Giacalona shrieked.

I glanced around and saw Max then. He, too, had realized that the lady didn't need his help, and he was hanging back now, obviously reluctant to intrude on this scene.

Lucky said, "But, Elena—"

"Are you *deaf*?" said the man whom I didn't recognize. "She don't want nothin' to do with you, you jerk."

"You stay out of this!" snapped Lucky.

As Lucky's body language got menacing, Father Gabriel tried to intercede. "Now, gentlemen," the priest said, "let's all remember where we are."

"Harassing a woman in church is where you are, you piece of garbage!" Lucky snarled at the stranger.

"Sticking your nose where it don't belong is where you are, *cretino*!" shot back the other man.

"If I ever catch you bothering her again ..." Lucky warned.

"Look who's talking!" was the smirking reply.

"*Madonna!* Can't I even pray in peace?" Elena screeched.

She turned on her heel and stormed down the aisle of the church, stalking past Max without even a glance. Her stride was so brisk that the ornate cross around her neck was bouncing.

Since I had met her before, in a manner of speaking, and since she seemed very upset, I felt an obligation to say something as her hurried steps brought her closer to me.

"Are you all right?" I asked.

The intense, long-lashed eyes met mine. "Men are such pigs!"

The thrice-widowed woman stalked past me and exited the church.

Lucky and the other man had already turned on each other, uttering standard masculine threats, the gist of which was that each of them wanted the other to stay away from the Widow Giacalona.

Father Gabriel tried several times, without success, to calm them down.

Finally, the other man capped the escalating exchange of insults by saying, "What makes you think she'd even waste saliva by spitting on you, asshole? You killed her husband, for chrissake!"

"Don't take the Savior's name in vain in *here,* you putz!" Lucky shouted back.

"You killed her husband?" I blurted.

All three men spun around to look in my direction with identical expressions of surprise on their faces.

"Esther!" Lucky said. "Why didn't you say something? I didn't know you was here. You're late."

No wonder he was so sure, when I had asked about it, that Elena wasn't killing off her own husbands.

"You *killed* her *husband?*" I repeated.

He shrugged. "Just the second one."

"Gee, Lucky," I said, "do you think maybe *that's* why she doesn't like you?"

"She got over it," he said defensively. "She remarried."

"Who the fuck are *you*?" said the other man. He turned to Father Gabriel. "Who the fuck is she? Oh! Excuse me, Father. I mean, who is the young lady?"

"It's a pleasure to see you again, Esther." Father

Gabriel smiled at me, then gestured to Max. "Did this gentleman come with you?"

"Yes, Father." I wobbled toward the men, wincing a little. I had turned my ankle when I fell. Max removed his fedora and gave a courteous little bow as I made the introductions. "Dr. Maximillian Zadok, Father Gabriel." I looked at the stranger. "And I'm Esther—"

"Hey, I just got it!" The man snapped his fingers. "I seen your face in the *Exposé*. You're the chorus girl who saw Charlie Chiccante get whacked."

"*Chorus girl,* you schmuck?" Lucky said. "I'll have you know, this young lady is a fine classical actress who also happens to sing like an angel, which is why Stella gives her a job whenever her talents don't happen to be in immediate demand on the stage."

I beamed at Lucky. Maybe the Widow Giacalona should cut him some slack.

"And you, sir?" Max said politely to the stranger. "May we know your name?"

"Sure." The man stepped forward to offer Max a handshake. "Buonarotti. Michael Buonarotti." He smiled and added, "No relation."

"To Lucky?" I said.

Buonarotti scowled. "Jesus, no."

"Watch your mouth," Lucky said. "We're in chu—"

"I mean," Buonarotti said, "no relation to *the* Buonarotti."

I frowned. "To the don of the Buonarotti family?"

"I *am* the don," Michael Buonarotti snapped. "Don't you know nothin'?"

"Then who—"

"I believe he means Michelangelo Buonarotti," Max said.

I was still confused. "Michelan ... Oh! *That* Buonarotti?"

"No, no, really," said the don modestly. "No relation, I assure you."

"Fine," I said. "Whatever. Lucky? We need to talk."

Lucky was frowning at me. "What are you wearing? You can't come into church dressed like that!"

"I have a date," I said tersely. "Anyhow, there's nothing wrong with the way I'm dressed." I was wearing a sleeveless black dress with a beaded bodice that showed some cleavage, complimented by a silky, translucent wrap that was currently slung over my arm. It was my sexiest dress, and it had been too long since I'd had occasion to wear it. Okay, it wasn't what I would choose to wear to temple, on the two occasions per year that I go so that my mother won't nag me, but it certainly wasn't indecent.

"Of course there's nothing wrong with it," said Father Gabriel. "I think you look lovely, Esther. Your date is a lucky man."

"Thank you." I smiled at the handsome priest. Lucky frowned at me and stepped on my foot.

"Nothing wrong at all," Buonarotti agreed. "You look classy. A real eyeful."

"Ain't you got nothin' else to do with your time?" Lucky said, glaring at Buonarotti.

"Oh, I guess I can find something to occupy me elsewhere." Buonarotti rolled his eyes. "After all, I wouldn't wanna intrude on you and your doctor and your fine classical actress, now would I?" He chuckled at his own wry wit. "No, definitely not. So I guess I'll be leaving." He turned to the priest. "Always a pleasure to see you, Father."

"You're always welcome here, Michael."

"Now get lost," said Lucky.

"Someday, Lucky," Buonarotti said with a cold look, "you'll go too far."

"You can count on it."

Buonarotti's glare grew threatening. Then with a suddenness that I found chilling, he banished the look and turned a cheerful smile on me and Max. "Miss Diamond. Dr. Zadok. A pleasure to meet you both."

As we watched Don Michael Buonarotti leave, Max murmured doubtfully, "That man comes here to pray?"

Lucky snorted. "He comes here to hit on the widow. Ever since his wife got sick of his skirt chasing and dumped him."

"The Widow Giacalona doesn't exactly strike me as a 'skirt,'" I said.

"Of course, she ain't! But Buonarotti wants a new wife," Lucky said with a dark scowl. "In addition to his skirts."

"And he's pursuing her in church?" I said.

"I don't question why people enter the house of God," Father Gabriel said. "I just give thanks that they *do*. Especially in this neighborhood, where there has been so much bloodshed over the years. Such as the other night." He took my hand and gazed at me with concern. "I can only imagine how distressing the events at Bella Stella must have been for you, Esther."

Those events were worse for Charlie, obviously, but I nodded and said, "I was very upset."

"To see a man killed in cold blood right in front of you . . ." The priest shook his head. "How dreadful for you."

I didn't want to keep reviewing Charlie's murder, so I changed the subject. "Lucky says there's a weeping saint here?"

Taking my cue, the priest smiled and gestured to the stone statue of Saint Monica. "Yes, we're very proud of it. Of course, only Elena Giacalona has seen the saint's tears so far. She's very devout, you know."

"Prays to Monica twice a day, every day, I gather," I said.

"Elena's life has been plagued by tragedy and loss," the priest said sadly.

I glanced at Lucky. "Indeed."

"She's had three husbands," the hit man muttered. "I only killed *one*."

"All the same, Lucky, you don't think it's maybe a doomed courtship?" I said. "And also not in the best possible taste?"

Father Gabriel looked at the ceiling and remained tactfully silent. As did Max, whose two marriages, centuries ago, had left him with a strong preference for bachelorhood. Which was just as well, since, for mystical reasons that weren't entirely clear to me, his vocation encouraged celibacy. Much like Father Gabriel's vocation, I realized.

"Elena will come around," Lucky said. "I just need to give her time. But never mind that now." Glancing from me to Max, he said, "I got someone you need to talk to."

"And I should prepare for vespers," said Father Gabriel. "If you'll excuse me?"

"Of course," I said.

After the priest exited through a side door, Lucky took my arm. "Let's take a walk."

"Oh, good. We're going to sit in the pews?" My feet hurt. I don't usually wear high heels.

"Not this time, kid. We gotta talk in the crypt."

"The crypt?" I tried to pull my arm out of his grasp. "I don't want to go into the *crypt*. Could you possibly suggest a creepier meeting place?"

"A perfectly understandable reaction," said Max, nodding. "An underground vault, with all the inherent fear of suffocation and smothering that such places naturally engender in mankind."

"You're not helping, Max," I said.

"And there's no denying that a crypt is a shadowy and mysterious chamber rife with negative mythology," he added. "Not to mention the atmospheric hint of dark rituals far older than Christianity itself!"

"Nah, it'll be fine," said Lucky prosaically. "They got electricity down there and everything."

"Why can't we talk up here?" I demanded.

"Because whatever's going on, we gotta be discreet," said Lucky. "Or whoever's behind this situation might figure out that we're sniffing him out."

Since this made a certain amount of sense to me, I sighed and agreed to go into the damn crypt.

"Watch your language," Lucky said. "You're in church."

9

St. Monica's was more than one hundred years old, but the crypt was less intimidating than I had imagined. Possibly because there were about one hundred folding chairs stored there, along with a piano and a rack of costumes from the Easter play that the parish children had performed last month. No room looks very murky and mysterious with a dozen pink bunny costumes in it.

The strangest thing in the room, however, was . . .

"An Elvis impersonator?" I said blankly.

"What's an Elvis impersonator?" Max asked.

"I'm *not* an impersonator," said the man seated at the piano. "I can't help the resemblance."

"You could try dressing a bit less like The King in his declining years," I suggested.

The man was overweight and wearing a white leisure suit with silver trim. His red shirt was open halfway down his chest, revealing thick gold chains nestled in black chest hair. The hair on his head was coal black and thick, with long sideburns; I thought it looked like a wig. He wore a pair of rose-tinted glasses over his puffy, lined face.

"Show some respect," Lucky said to me. "This is the boss' nephew."

"Which one?" I asked. The Shy Don had a big family.

"They call me Johnny Be Good," the man said.

I blinked. "You're Johnny Be Good Gambello?"

"You heard of me, huh?" he sounded pleased.

I had never seen him at the restaurant, because Stella had banned him from there years ago. She said Johnny Be Good was a very bad boy. He had notorious problems with drugs, alcohol, and gambling. Wiseguys disapproved of divorce, and he was on his third marriage. He'd even been caught embezzling from the Gambellos. The only reason he was still alive was that he was a nephew of the don himself, so only Victor Gambello could order his death. And the Shy Don, Stella said, had a soft spot for his blood relatives.

"Yeah, I've heard of you," I said.

"But I'm afraid *I* have not had the pleasure of hearing about you," said Max.

"Who's this jerk?" Johnny asked Lucky.

"This is Doc Zadok," said Lucky, "who's got specialized knowledge that might be useful to our situation."

"And the girl? She's the one who saw Charlie go down for the dirt nap?"

"Yep."

"The one who saw his double, along with you?"

"That's right," Lucky said.

Johnny regarded me. "She's a looker. You didn't mention that."

"Did he mention that my boyfriend is a cop?" I said, not liking the oily way Johnny was assessing me.

He flinched. "You date a *cop*?"

"Why are we here?" I asked Lucky wearily.

"Johnny, tell these two people what you told me," Lucky instructed, setting out a couple of the folding chairs for me and Max.

Johnny nodded and cracked his knuckles. As he began his tale, I draped my wrap over the back of a folding chair and sat down. Max sat next to me.

Johnny Be Good began his tale. "I was in a friendly little establishment uptown last night—neutral turf, you understand—enjoying a social game of cards." He eyed us, as if daring us to mention his famously bad luck at all forms of gambling, including poker. "One of the other guys at the table was Danny the Doctor."

"Who's that?" I asked.

"Danny 'the Doctor' Dapezzo," said Lucky. "He's a capo in the Corvino family. Mean son of a bitch."

"And he's a doctor?" Max asked. "Medicine or philosophy?"

"They call him the Doctor," Johnny Be Good said, "because of the surgical way he cuts up bodies into nice, neat little parts. I'm telling you, Danny can get fifty pieces out of one skinny corpse."

I said to Max, "You had to ask."

Lucky said with reluctant admiration, "Yeah, it's very hard for the cops to identify a corpse after Danny gets done with it. They can't find enough parts."

"So you're playing cards with Danny," I said loudly to Johnny. *"And . . ."*

"And Mickey Rosenblum, from Las Vegas, is at the same table, and he's having as great a night as Danny's having a bad one." He paused and added, "You oughta know Mickey. He's Jewish. Same as you." When I didn't say anything, Johnny prodded, "You know him?"

"No."

He looked at Lucky. "Didn't you say she was Jewish? How come she don't know Mickey?"

"So Mickey cleaned out Danny the Doctor?" I prodded.

"Yeah. And Danny, well, he goes away in a real bad mood, pockets empty, bitching about how he don't even have cab fare left to go visit his girlfriend before he goes home to the missus."

"Uh-huh." Who *married* these men, I wondered?

"And two minutes later . . . Guess who enters the club

and sits down at our table, fresh as a daisy? You got it! Danny the Doctor. And his pockets are full of dough! What's even stranger is, he don't remember a thing. He thinks *we're* nuts when we talk about what just happened with him, right at this very table. And us, well, we figure *he's* nuts, going senile or something. But his cash is real." Johnny smirked and added, "And you know what? Mickey Rosenblum cleaned him out all over again!" Johnny guffawed long and loudly, occasionally pausing to repeat this last bit. Several times. "Cleaned him out all over again!"

Max and I looked at each other. Then we both looked at Lucky.

He nodded. "What did I tell you? We got us another doppelgangster somewhere out there. Only this one's a Corvino."

It proved to be impossible to have an intelligent conversation with Johnny Be Good Gambello in the room, so it was a relief when he suddenly asked Lucky to loan him some cash so he could go enjoy himself elsewhere while the night was still young.

After Johnny left, Lucky said to Max, "I put the word out after talkin' with you and Esther yesterday morning. I know you thought Charlie's doppelgangster was a one-time thing, Doc, but my gut told me otherwise."

"And your gut seems to be very wise," Max said respectfully.

"So by this morning, the whole *famiglia* knew to report anything unusual to me. And since Johnny ain't never been able to keep his yap shut," Lucky said, "it didn't take long for me to hear about him seeing two Danny Dapezzos last night. That's when I figured I better get you two together with him in someplace discreet."

"Like the crypt of a church?" I muttered.

"Well done!" Max beamed at Lucky.

"I don't see what's wrong with meeting in an ordinary coffee shop," I said.

"You are *so* naive," Lucky said dismissively.

I decided to shelve that argument and move on to an obvious question, one that I felt sure Lopez would bring up if he were here. "Look, it's no secret that Johnny Be Good has killed a few billion brain cells with booze and narcotics. So why shouldn't we assume that Danny Dapezzo simply went to an ATM and returned to the poker game, and Johnny has fantasized the rest of the incident?"

"Wiseguys don't use ATMs!" Lucky said, looking shocked. "Not for our *own* money, anyhow."

"Okay, so maybe Danny had a stash nearby. Or mugged someone outside the club. Whatever," I said. "And then maybe he pulled Johnny's leg a little when he saw he could get away with it. My point is, how do we know that Johnny's story is accurate?"

"Because after I talked with Johnny, I talked to Mickey Rosenblum," Lucky said. "We grew up in the same neighborhood, I known him all my life. His family is where I learned some Yiddish words."

"Ah," I said.

"Mickey's sharp as a knife," Lucky said. "And his story is exactly the same as Johnny's."

"Why isn't he here?" I asked.

"It's a parole violation for him to be out of Nevada, so he's on his way back to Vegas right now. Before some nosy cop finds out he's been here." Lucky gave me a warning look. "Which I'm sure we can assume won't happen."

"You need to stop telling me things you don't want my boyfriend to know," I said firmly. "I don't like being put in the middle."

"So I gather Mickey Rosenblum is a reliable witness," Max said, "and we can rule out the possibility that Mr. Be Good is speaking out of delusion?"

"That's right," said Lucky.

I said, "So if they both saw Danny the Doctor's doppelgangster . . ." Then Lopez was wrong, I realized. Chubby Charlie had not been having a manic episode. He had really seen own his perfect double. And I had seen it, too.

"This Danny the Doctor," I said to Lucky. "He's an enemy of yours? An enemy of the Gambello family?"

"Yeah. Like all the Corvinos."

"But Chubby Charlie was one of your own," Max mused.

"Which means," said Lucky, "that someone's hiring these doppelgangsters to whack made guys on *both* sides of the street."

"If you're right, if that is what's going on here . . . Then why is someone doing this?" I wondered.

Lucky shook his head. "It don't make no sense."

I thought about Lopez's primary theory. "So you think that whatever is going on, it's not another Gambello-Corvino war?"

Lucky shook his head. "I don't know who killed Charlie, but I *do* know that we haven't put out a contract on Danny Dapezzo. So if his doppelgangster's walking around now cursing him with death, well, it ain't us that ordered the hit. That's a guarantee. So this ain't no Gambello-Corvino thing. We ain't going to the mattresses with them. Not yet, anyhow."

Max frowned. "Going to the mattresses?"

"Going to war with another *famiglia*," I translated. "It involves sleeping in hideouts where your enemies can't find you. So that you won't wake up dead." I'd learned a lot working at Stella's. "Going to sleep on different mattresses, in other words." Often rather unsanitary ones, I gathered, in a grimy flop shared by several soldiers from the same family.

"Fascinating!" Max murmured.

Returning to the point, I said, "So if it's not an inter-family war, could the Corvinos just be doing some housecleaning, so to speak?"

"That's out. They'd know they couldn't whack Charlie without starting a new war with us," Lucky said, shaking his head again. "And Danny's one of their top guys, so he'd have to screw up big to get himself whacked by his own family. I ain't saying it can't happen. I just think it's too big a coincidence that, like Charlie, he's suddenly got a perfect double."

"Coincidence does seem too improbable to consider seriously," Max agreed.

"So could this be personal?" I asked. "Do Charlie and Danny have something in common?"

Lucky shrugged. "Well, they're both assholes."

"Something more specific," I said.

"Like what?"

"I don't know. Max?" I prodded. "What should we be looking for? What does this mean?"

"And what should we do now?" Lucky added.

"Well, first of all," Max said, "I think we should warn Doctor Dapezzo. We must assume that he's been marked for death by whatever entity marked Chubby Charlie for death."

Lucky nodded. "I can't say I'd be sorry to see Danny take the big sleep, but I suppose we gotta warn him. Anybody could be next, after all. Even *me*."

Which was why I wasn't in a cab on my way home right now, wisely washing my hands of this whole business. Without more facts, as Lopez would say, I couldn't assume that these mysterious doppelgangsters would only portend the deaths of violent felons whom I either didn't know or *wished* I didn't know. What if Lucky or Stella got duplicated next?

I was fond of Stella, a nice lady who employed hungry actors. I was even fond of Lucky, though he was a killer and not very wise about women. If Lopez got evidence on Lucky and arrested him, I wouldn't interfere; but I certainly wouldn't just stand by idly while some supernatural *thing* cursed Lucky with death.

If there's one thing I had learned from Max, it's that once Evil comes to the party, everything goes haywire. So you've got to kick its butt out the door and down the street as soon as you encounter it or you'll regret it later.

"In addition to warning Doctor Dapezzo," Max said, "I need to interview him. Actually, what would be most helpful would be if I could interview his doppelgangster. Er, gänger."

"You want to *talk* to the doppelgangster?" Lucky sounded appalled. "Speak with that *thing*?"

"Well, obviously it does talk," Max said reasonably. "And in a sentient, naturalistic fashion. Mr. Be Good does not seem to be the most lucid and insightful of men—"

"Now there's an understatement," I said.

"—but it does seem likely that he'd have noticed if the doppelgangster was puppetlike or transparent."

"And you and I," I said to Lucky, "couldn't tell Charlie apart from his double. So obviously these doppelgangsters are as lifelike as the real thing. At least when seen in limited doses."

"But since they *aren't* the real thing," Max mused, "it's possible that interviewing one of them will help me understand their purpose. Are they self-aware? Or do they actually believe they *are* the individuals whom they're merely mirroring? Are they appearing in an attempt to warn the doomed individuals? Or are they, in fact, assassins?" He tugged on his beard as he added, "Based on what little material I've currently got access to, I do know one thing."

"Which is?"

"The fact that others can see and interact with these entities . . . that is *most* unusual. Traditionally, the person destined to die by nightfall is the only one who sees the perfect double. Whereas in the two cases we're dealing with, other people not only see and interact with the 'double walker,' they even do so before the mirrored individual is aware of the double's existence."

I blinked. "That's right! Whichever Charlie Chiccante was the real one the night I first saw his doppelgangster, he didn't seem to be aware of its existence. Both versions of Charlie were in a normal mood that evening. It was only on the night he died that he was scared, anxious, and talking about his perfect double."

"So Esther and I saw Charlie's double before he did," Lucky said pensively.

"And now we may know about Doctor Dapezzo's double before he does," Max added.

I checked my watch and gasped when I saw the time. "I have to go! I'm going to be late for my date."

"How can you think about your love life at a time like this?" Lucky demanded.

"How can you pursue a woman whose husband you whacked?" I retorted.

"We can't accomplish anything more until we can meet with Doctor Dapezzo," Max said. "And I gather that, based on the enmity between your *famiglie*, that can't be accomplished this very moment?"

"No," Lucky admitted. "It'll take a little time and finesse to arrange a sit-down."

"So Esther might as well go enjoy the evening she has planned with her young man," Max said, rising to his feet and gesturing for us all to leave the crypt.

"The way she's dressed," Lucky muttered as I started up the stairs, "I can *guess* what she has planned."

"He's taking me to an expensive restaurant," I said primly, speaking over my shoulder.

Lucky snorted. "In that case, there ain't no question what *he* has planned."

"As long as it doesn't involve murder or perfect doubles," I said sincerely, "I'm all in favor of it."

At the top of the stairs, I could hear that Father Gabriel had started the evening service, so I shushed my two companions. The church smelled of incense as we entered it and quietly turned down the side aisle to make our exit.

The priest and congregation were chanting liturgical prayers together. I was surprised by how many people were attending a regular Monday twilight service. Then I noticed they were mostly women, and they were almost as dressed up for vespers as I was for a date. They were also gazing at Father Gabriel with expressions of devotion that did not strike me as entirely spiritual.

I glanced at Lucky and couldn't repress an amused smile. Whether or not he knew what I was thinking, he scowled at me and nudged me toward the exit.

Outside on the street, I said, "Rabbis can get married, you know. In fact, they're expected to. But I don't remember ever seeing one as dishy as Father Gabriel."

"You shouldn't talk that way about a priest," Lucky said. "They're above matters of the flesh."

Given what the news headlines and law courts had revealed about priests in recent years, I rolled my eyes. But I wanted to stop short of really offending Lucky, so I dropped the subject and checked my cell phone. I hadn't been able to get a signal in the crypt, and now I saw that I had missed a call from my agent, as well as one from Lopez.

Since I was going to be a few minutes late for our dinner reservation, I decided to call back my date first.

Lopez answered on the second ring. "Esther! Are you okay? Where are you?"

I blinked, realizing that when he'd called without getting an answer, it had made him worry about my safety again. "I'm fine," I assured him. "Are you at the restaurant already?"

"No. Look, I tried to call you a little while ago—"

"I know. I was out of range. I'll be a few minutes late," I said, "but I'm looking for a cab right now."

Actually, Lucky was trying to get me a cab, but

I decided that fell under the heading of Too Much Information.

"That's why I called," Lopez said. "I'm really sorry about this ..."

"What?"

"I have to cancel."

"Oh," I looked down at my sexy dress as my heart sank. "You do?"

"I just got called in to work," he said.

"I could wait for you." A cool evening breeze drifted across my bare shoulders, and I realized I'd left my wrap down in the crypt. "Or meet you somewhere later?"

"I don't want you to do that," he said with obvious regret. "I think this is going to take most of the night."

"What happened?"

"Johnny Be Good Gambello was just found dead."

"What?"

Lucky and Max looked at me.

"Yeah, they just fished him out of the East River," Lopez said. "The initial estimate is that he's been dead for twenty-four hours."

10

"Whaddya mean, an 'operation'?" Lucky demanded.

"Apparition," I corrected, waving my research book at him. "According to this, an apparition can be corporeal even if the person it's replicating is already dead."

"Huh?"

"While I would much rather not hear myself say something like this aloud," I told Lucky, "apparently it's possible for an *apparition* of Johnny to look and sound real while he's already sleeping with the fishes."

"So now we got operations *and* doppelgangsters?"

"Actually, a doppelgangster is a *type* of operation. So, even though he was dead at the time, I think we saw Johnny's perfect double yesterday." I repressed a shudder of revulsion and tried not to think about the way the doppelgangster had eyed me in my little black dress.

"A *type* of operation? How many types do they got?" Lucky demanded.

I consulted the book again, one from a large pile that Max had suggested I peruse when I arrived at his bookstore this morning. He was currently down in the laboratory in search of a rare scroll or something.

After the initial shock of hearing that they had just been talking to a dead man, Max and Lucky both came to

the obvious conclusion as we stood on the sidewalk outside of St. Monica's yesterday evening: The body pulled
from the East River had been incorrectly identified.

They were right, I realized when I calmed down, it
couldn't be Johnny Gambello. It must be some other
Elvis impersonator. An understandable mistake. Lopez
would discover the error once he arrived at the scene.
And apart from the fact that the discovery of the corpse
had ruined my plans for the evening, it had nothing to
do with us or our strange problem.

Naturally, we called Johnny's cell phone, just to assure ourselves that he was alive and kicking. He didn't
answer. This made us uneasy, but Lucky insisted it didn't
mean anything. After all, Johnny was a mook who lost
one cell phone after another. Or maybe he had turned
it off because he'd gone straight from the church to a
poker game. In any case, we had just *seen* Johnny, so we
knew the day-old body in the river was someone else.

Soothed by this sturdy logic, I went home to eat Chinese food alone in my pajamas and fantasize about what
might have been. Lopez spent the night working, as I
later learned from a text message he sent me (not wanting to wake me). Max went home to commune with his
familiar. And Lucky, who never seemed to sleep, woke
me bright and early the following morning to break the
news that the corpse from the East River was indeed
Johnny Be Good Gambello.

Johnny's wife, who hadn't seen him in several days
(which wasn't unusual, I gathered), had identified the
body. The Gambellos were going into mourning. And
the Shy Don was pressuring Lucky to find out who'd
killed the mook.

"So how many types of operations do we need to be
worrying about?" Lucky prodded now, as I continued
peering at the text in my hands with tired eyes.

I said, "An apparition can be a doppelgänger, an alter
ego, a ghost or spirit, a poltergeist, a remnant or rev-

enant, the result of an out-of-body experience, an astral projection, an etheric body, or a . . ." I took a wild guess at the pronunciation. "A *fylgia*—but this last one seems to have more to do with shapeshifting than with what we're seeing."

Lucky let out a low whistle "It's a whole *salumeria* of supernatural soldiers."

"That sounds like an *Exposé* headline." I added, "The Tibetans believe a double can separate from the original physical body either voluntarily or involuntarily. But considering who's been replicated so far, I think we can rule out their theories in this case."

"Why? Max ain't ruling out *German* theories, after all."

"Because in Tibetan tradition," I said, glancing at the text again, "such separation normally occurs as a result of prolonged prayer and meditation."

"Well, Johnny only went to church when he bet big on a longshot," Lucky admitted. "But Charlie went to Mass and Confession every week."

"Among the Tibetans," I added, "a double or apparition is almost always associated with saints, hermits, and holy persons."

"Oh. In that case, yeah," Lucky agreed. "We can rule that out."

Lucky, alas, was not amenable to wading through a stack of books. He mostly paced around the shop and made phone calls while Max and I tried to figure out what was going on.

"It's not like Johnny will be missed," the hit man said, taking a seat at the old wooden table with me. "It's just that it looks so bad. The don's nephew whacked, and we ain't got no idea who done it? It's embarrassing!"

I thought this seemed like a secondary concern compared to the issue that had my skin crawling. "I just thank God that *thing* in the crypt didn't try to shake my hand."

"It shook *my* hand," Lucky said, looking a little queasy.

I thought about this. "So we know the doppel-gangsters can touch people. Was its hand cold or some-how lifeless?"

"No." Lucky gave a brief shake of his head. "Normal temperature. And felt just like Johnny's hand always did—damp palm, weak grip."

"Hmm." After a moment, I said, "Still no reply from Danny Dapezzo?"

"Not yet," he grumbled. "I've left three messages."

We weren't sure what to think now of the story that Johnny's doppelgangster had told us about Danny the Doctor. True, Mickey Rosenblum had confirmed the story. He had also answered Lucky's phone call this morning (which woke him before dawn in Nevada) and talked some more, but we realized we couldn't be sure Lucky wasn't talking to *Mickey's* doppelgangster in Vegas. Did we indeed need to warn Danny Dapezzo that he was marked for death? Or had Johnny's doppel-gangster simply distracted us with misleading bait? Or, in seeking out Danny, were we entering a trap?

After an hour of head banging this morning, we had agreed that we were theorizing in a vacuum and needed to speak to Danny Dapezzo—or to whatever was mas-querading as Danny now. One or the other anyhow.

"And you're sure it was Johnny yesterday?" I asked Lucky. "Er, I mean, you're sure that you were sure at the time?"

"I known that mook since he was in diapers," Lucky said. "It was Johnny all right. Or, I mean, something ex-actly like Johnny."

I shuddered again, creeped out. "What is going *on*?"

Nelli's toenails clicked on the floorboards as she trot-ted around a bookcase and approached us. She held a book clamped between her massive jaws. As I stared at her, she came over and dropped it at my feet, her im-mense floppy ears swinging as her head moved. Then she looked at me expectantly.

"We can't play fetch with Max's books," I said to her. "Bad dog."

She whined at me.

Since Max was still down in the laboratory, I gingerly picked up the book, which had some drool on it, and rose from my seat to reshelve it. Nelli blocked my path and barked at me.

Lucky said, "Hey, I think she wants you to *look* at that book."

"Good God, this is like some warped episode of *Lassie*," I muttered.

"Come on, be a sport," Lucky urged. "Open it."

"I need this advice from a man who hasn't deigned to open a book since we got here this morning?" I said irritably.

"Fine, give it here." Lucky reached over and took the book from my hands.

It was old and ragged, with a plain black cover. Its edges were frayed, and scarcely anything was left of the gold lettering that had once adorned its cover. Lucky opened the book and frowned as he read the title page.

"What's . . . 'bilocate?'" he asked me.

"I don't know."

Nelli nudged Lucky.

"Knock it off," he said. "Your nose is cold."

My cell phone rang. I checked the readout. "Oh, good. It's my agent." I flipped open the phone. "Thack?"

"'Singing Server Sees Slaying'?" quoted Thackeray Shackleton—not his real name, I suspected.

"Huh?"

"It's certainly not how I want to see you packaged," said my agent, "but that's some lovely alliteration, don't you think?"

"Oh!" Surprised, I asked, "You read tabloids?"

"Geraldo does. He left it on my desk this morning, after he recognized your name." Geraldo was Thack's assistant. "He wasn't sure it was you, though, because of the picture. Not a flattering likeness, is it? I keep telling you, your left side is better. When you see a camera, give them the *left* profile, Esther."

"I was a little overwrought at the time," I pointed out tersely.

"Oh, my God. What am I even saying? Of course you were!" He sounded contrite and horrified. "*Esther*. Are you all right?"

I liked Thack because, like me, he was originally from Wisconsin, so he was hardworking and polite. This is a rarity in theatrical agents. Despite his conventional middle-class Milwaukee origins, he was gay and flamboyant in an uptown yuppie way, so he fit in well in his profession here.

"Yes, I'm fine," I said. "Listen—"

"This mobster was killed right in *front* of you?" Thack said.

"Yeah, I saw him get whacked," I said absently. "Look, I called you yesterday because—"

"My God!" he said again. "Are you *okay*? Are you traumatized? Are you going into the Witness Protection Program?"

"What? No, I'm not going anywhere. And I'm fine. Really."

"I can't imagine what you must be going through! Are you able to sleep? Are you able to eat? Have you left your apartment at all? Can you even get out of bed? Do you want me to have Geraldo bring you anything?"

As Thack continued fretting about my well-being, I started to wonder if I was less empathetic and humane than I should be. Although I had indeed been scared and distraught when I saw Chubby Charlie die, I wasn't as traumatized as Lopez supposed, with his theory that I just couldn't remember what I'd really seen; and I *certainly* wasn't as shattered as my agent assumed I was.

"Look, Thack," I interrupted as he continued wondering just *how* devastated I must be. "Chubby Charlie and I weren't close, it was three days ago, and I'm over it. Let's move on."

"What? Oh! *Oh.* You don't want to talk about it, do you? I'm sorry. I'm making it even worse, aren't I? Bringing it all up again. I'll stop now."

"Okay, so what I wanted to talk about is—"

"I just want to know one thing. Are you getting counseling? Taking any medication?"

"What? No, of course not. I don't need counseling or medication."

"That's denial talking, Esther," Thack said.

No, no, I'm just focused on more pressing matters, such as the two deadly doppelgangsters that I've met lately.

"I'm fine," I said firmly, wondering if, in fact, I needed a whole boatload of counseling and medication.

"You can't get through this alone," Thack insisted. "You're an actress. You're sensitive!"

"Let's be frank," I said wearily. "I'm not nearly as sensitive as the men in my life think I should be."

"You need to talk with someone about this. A professional."

"Well, I . . ." I shrugged and said, "I talked to a priest about it yesterday." Sort of. For twenty seconds.

I would actually rather tell my mother that I was described as a "chorus girl with Mafia connections" in the tabloids than tell her how much time I had spent in a church in recent days. But Thack, being neither Jewish nor my mother, was wonderfully oblivious. He simply said, "A priest? Oh, good! *Good.* Yes, that was a wise instinct on your part. Someone who can offer you spiritual comfort, not just pills and analysis."

Recalling the way a bevy of overdressed female parishioners had been gazing at the hunky priest yesterday, I wasn't sure how many people went to see Father Gabriel for *spiritual* reasons. But he had been warm, gracious, and tactful both times we'd met, so maybe he would be a good professional to turn to in a crisis.

I said, "Thack, the reason I've been trying to reach you—"

"I'm sorry, Geraldo wants something. Hang on a second, Esther."

"Hey," Lucky said, "this 'bilocation' stuff? I think we're on to something here."

Nelli barked cheerfully.

"Shh," I said to her. "I'm on the phone."

Thack was still talking to Geraldo, who sounded agitated. I heard Thack say, "Oh, for fuck's sake." Then he said into the phone, "I'm sorry, Esther, I've got to go. I've got a client doing an episode of *Criminal Motive* this week—you know, the 'brainiest' of the *Crime and Punishment* spin-offs? His character gets found hung upside down in a Brooklyn meat locker. Well, you know what sticklers they are for gritty realism on all the *C&P* sets." Thack sighed. "So they had a little mishap. Now they want me to dash over to the hospital and see if my client is planning to sue them. I'll have to talk him out of it, of course—but really, I wouldn't blame him. A series wins a few Emmy Awards, and suddenly it's, 'Hey, how close can we come to *really* killing our guest performers?' I swear, it's enough to make you want to go back to doing Shakespeare in the rain, isn't it?"

"I *do* Shakespeare in the rain," I pointed out. "But, in fact, *Crime and Punishment* is what I wanted to talk to y—"

"Gotta go. Bye!"

"Wait! I wanted to tell you about . . ." I realized I was talking to dead air.

I tossed my phone on the table in frustration and said a bad word.

"Is there a problem?" Lucky asked, eyeing me.

"Sort of. There's this part that's opened up," I said, hearing Max's footsteps approaching us from the cellar.

"A part of what?" Max asked, setting some dusty volumes and two scrolls down on the table.

"An acting part?" Lucky guessed.

I nodded. "On *The Dirty Thirty*."

"Pardon?" said Max.

"It's the newest *Crime and Punishment* spin-off," I said.

"Crime and Punishment?" Max frowned. "Are we talking about Dostoyevsky?"

"She's talkin' about that TV show," Lucky said. "The one that's got a million spin-offs and wins all the Oscars."

"Emmys," I said. "TV shows win Emmy Awards."

"Whatever."

The latest venture in *C&P*'s empire of prestigious law enforcement dramas was its most controversial spin-off to date, a gritty, morally ambivalent show about police corruption in the Thirtieth Precinct, a.k.a. "the dirty Thirty."

After *C&P*'s regular network had rejected the series, afraid its dark subject matter and antihero protagonists would scare away advertisers, the innovative *C&P* producers had sold *D30* (as it was now known to fans) to a cable network. The show had premiered last year, and had become a critically acclaimed cable hit with a steadily growing audience. Some New York City cops condemned and boycotted the program, while others reputedly provided much of the show's material from their own experiences on the force.

"So you're gonna be on TV?" Lucky asked.

"Only if I get the part," I said. "Which can only happen if I get this audition. The actress who was cast in this role isn't in performance condition anymore—not after this weekend—so they'll need to recast. And fast, too, because they start shooting the episode in a few weeks."

"How come they're shooting now?" Lucky asked. "It's May."

"Some cable networks have had success launching new shows in the summer, when the competition mostly consists of reruns. That's what happened with *Dirty Thirty* last year, and it worked well. So the show is launching its second year of episodes this summer, off-season again."

"And your agent called you about this audition?" Lucky asked.

"No, I found out about this from a friend of mine who knows the actress who had to drop out of the show two days ago because she's in traction now. A good agent is a big asset, but actors who keep their ears to the ground and go after opportunities get a lot more work than actors who just sit around at home hoping their agents will call," I explained. "Anyhow, instead of a general call, the casting director will want to choose the replacement fast, from just a small pool of actresses. And I'm trying to talk to Thack about it so he can get me into that audition."

"What's the role?" Max asked.

"I would play a graduate student who's trying to convince the precinct cops to do something about hoodlums hanging around her street." I hadn't seen the script, of course, but I suspected that in the usual pattern of the show's morality tales, the cops would probably do too little, too late, with a gut-wrenching conclusion to the episode.

"Yeah, I can see you doin' a part like that," Lucky said. "Someone smart and respectable ... who nags a lot."

I gave him a look. "Plus," I said, "the casting director for this is someone who liked me last year, on a different *Crime and Punishment* audition. He didn't think I was good casting for the part of the killer—"

"I'd say he's right about that," said Lucky.

"—but I'm pretty sure he'll remember me and I'll have a good shot at this. *If* I can get in for a reading," I added with some frustration. "My agent and I are having a little communication problem."

"Oh, that's because Mercury is in retrograde," Max said absently. "Just give it about two more weeks, though, and things will improve."

"I haven't *got* two more weeks," I said. "I need to get Thack working on this *today*. They're going to have to recast that role soon to keep up with their production schedule."

Lucky put his book down. "You want me to go deal with this agent, kid? Make him show some respect?"

"No!" I said quickly. "No. *I* will deal with my agent."

"I could talk to the casting director," Lucky offered. "Make sure he realizes it's in his best interest for you to get what you want."

I groaned and held my head in my hands. "*No.* I'm very sorry I even brought it up."

"Well, if you change your mind . . ."

"Or it's possible I could assist," Max said. "There's a certain amulet that might render the casting director susceptible to—"

"Do you both have so little faith in my talent?" I demanded. "You think I can only get this role with the help of extortion or magic?"

"What?" Lucky said. "No!"

"*No,*" Max said. "Of course not!"

"I was just tryin' to help."

"I merely hoped to lend you my assistance, as you lend yours to me."

"In that case," I said, "wish me luck, guys. And just stay out of it, otherwise."

"Ah! All right," Max said. "As you wish. Good luck!"

"You shouldn't say that to an actress," Lucky chided Max. "They're very superstitious, these theatrical types. You gotta say, 'Break a leg!' Ain't that right, kid?"

I smiled at Lucky. "That's right. It's the accepted phrase." I added to Max, "But I'm not *that* superstitious, so I accept wishes for good luck in any form. Though the best wishes in the world will be wasted if I can't even get the audition," I grumbled. "I'll have to try calling Thack again later."

I also hoped his other client would agree not to sue the production company, since a lawsuit might put a damper on Thack's ability to get *C&P* auditions for his actors. And I *really* wanted that audition, since my immediate professional future consisted only of waiting tables. I found that so depressing that I resolutely turned my thoughts to something else.

"Did you say there's something in book?" I asked Lucky.

"Hey, that's right! I did."

"Ah, you found something?" Max asked.

"I gotta give credit where credit's due." Lucky gestured to Nelli. "This familiar of yours, Doc? She's workin' out okay."

"She chews things," Max said in an aggrieved tone.

Nelli snorted and gave herself a thorough shake. The propeller-like motion of her enormous ears made me fear I'd get injured if I stood too close to her.

"What's in the book?" I prodded.

Lucky extended his arms to hold the volume well away from his aging gaze as he read aloud, somewhat haltingly, "'A bilocated individual can be in two places at the same time. After replication, the two portions of the human form may become widely separated from one another. The double—that is to say, the duplicate, the replicate—can be seen by others. It frequently speaks in a voice and performs actions identical to those of the real person. The clothes it wears are also replicas of the original clothing.'"

I looked at Nelli. She wagged her tail.

I said to Lucky, "This is the book the *dog* found?"

"Yeah."

"Don't say 'dog'," Max whispered, casting an anxious glance at Nelli.

"I'm impressed," I admitted to Max. "I know you

conjured her and all that, but I really thought she was just a dumb mutt."

Nelli growled at me.

"I apologize," I said quickly. "I think it's the ears. Are you sure you don't want to rethink that part of your look?"

The sudden chiming of bells indicated that someone was entering the shop.

"Dr. Zadok?" a male voice called. "Maximillian Zadok?"

"Yes?" Max rose from the table and went past the surrounding bookcases.

I shifted uncomfortably under Nelli's wounded gaze. "It was just a suggestion. Forget I mentioned it."

"You hurt her feelings," Lucky said critically. "You should be more careful about what you say."

"At least I haven't whacked any of her mates," I snapped.

Lucky grunted and glared at me.

"Federal Express," said the stranger by the door.

"Ah! Excellent!" Max said.

I realized the package must be the delivery of books about doppelgängers that Max was expecting from Jerusalem. Remembering that conversation made me remember the cab ride, which made me remember my ruined evening—which made me remember that I'd left my wrap at the church. After talking to Lopez by phone outside St. Monica's, I'd been so stunned that I'd forgotten all about it until after I got home.

So, while Max was opening his Federal Express package, I found a phone book and called St. Monica's. I told the administrator who answered the phone that I had left an item of clothing in the crypt yesterday evening. She checked the church's lost-and-found box but told me my wrap wasn't there.

"It's probably still in the crypt," I said. "I'll stop by the church for it when I get a chance. Or if you happen to find it before then, would you hold it for me?"

"Of course."

"My name's Esther Diamond," I said. "Father Gabriel knows me."

"I'll tell him you called."

As I hung up, Lucky eyed the large, ornate volumes Max had unpacked, and asked, "Them's the German books you been waiting for?"

"This is marvelous!" Max said. "When I was young, it would have taken a *year* to borrow books from a colleague as far away as the Holy Land!"

"Welcome to the twenty-first century, Max," I said.

Nelli sniffed the books with mild interest, then turned in a circle three times and lay down near Lucky.

I returned to the subject at hand. "So based on what Lucky and I have been reading, I think that what we met with last night was a bilocated apparition."

"It says here," Lucky added, referring to his book, "that this thing 'cannot easily be distinguished from the real individual.'"

"Yes, that does sound like what we're dealing with." Max frowned thoughtfully as he nodded. "A form of bilocated apparitional doppelgängerism."

"Are we still sure it's doppelgängerism?" I asked. "I know that Charlie saw his doppelgangster and took it as a warning of imminent death, but—"

"So did Johnny," said Lucky.

"What?" Max exclaimed.

Max and I gaped at Lucky. He looked pleased with the effect his statement had on us.

The old gangster said, "Johnny Be Good saw his own perfect double before he got whacked."

11

I said, "Johnny saw his doppelgangster before he died?"

"Yep. That was one of the calls I made while you was reading and Max was downstairs. I talked to Johnny's grieving widow." Lucky rolled his eyes, and his ironic tone indicated that Mrs. Gambello wasn't as heartbroken about her husband's death as Johnny Be Good might have wished. "I just didn't want to have to say this twice, so I was waiting for Max to come back upstairs."

"Well?" I prodded.

"Johnny come home the other night, laughing and babbling about how he just seen a guy who looked exactly like himself. He was drunk off his rocker, like always, so his wife ignored him."

"So he *saw* it?" I suddenly felt cold.

Lucky nodded. "The missus says that Johnny claimed the guy he saw was a dead ringer for himself. A perfect double. He told her he could've sent this other guy home to her bed, and she'd never know the difference. Except for . . ." Lucky lowered his eyes and shrugged. "Er, Johnny thought his double would lack his amorous talents and that's how his wife would know the other guy was an imposter. But she says Johnny overestimated himself in that regard, so if the double had any more imagination than a *dog,* that's how she'd know it was a ringer."

When Nelli picked up her head and stared coldly at Lucky, he said to her, "Hey, it's wasn't me. I'm just repeating what Johnny's wife said. And she don't know from dogs, so let it go."

Nelli sighed and put her head back down on her paws.

"And that," Lucky continued, "was the last time Johnny's wife saw him. He left the house at some point the next day, while she was out, and he ain't been home since. Ain't called, neither."

"So Johnny's doppelgangster hasn't visited his home," Max mused.

"Unless that *was* his doppelgangster," I said. "Pretending to have seen itself."

"Huh?" Lucky said.

"I mean—"

"Oh! Never mind, I get it." Lucky added, "Based the estimated time of death, I figure Johnny was whacked sometime after his wife saw him and before Mickey Rosenblum played poker with him."

And according to the morning papers, Johnny was knocked unconscious before being dumped in the river, so his death did indeed seem to be murder.

"So Mr. Rosenblum was playing cards with Johnny's doppelgangster," Max mused.

"If that really *is* Mickey I been talkin' to on the phone." Lucky rubbed a hand over his face. "I hope so. I like Mickey."

"And now we know *both* victims saw their perfect doubles shortly before dying," I said.

"Doppelgängerism." Max's voice held conviction. "Charlie knew he'd been cursed. Johnny Be Good just didn't understand what he was seeing."

"That's easy to believe," muttered Lucky.

"But what is the purpose of these doppelgangsters?" Max wondered.

"At a guess," I said, "murder."

"Yes, but why has such an elaborate phenomenon accompanied the murder of these two individuals?" Max asked. "Were they especially important men? Did they have unique powers?"

Lucky shook his head. "Charlie was a good earner, but he wasn't hard to replace. We moved someone up into his spot by yesterday, and we expect Charlie's, uh, branch of the business to continue running smooth without him. And, God forgive me for speaking ill of the dead, Johnny was a useless *momzer*. It's not like his death is a kick in the nuts for us, even though the boss is upset about it."

"Hey," I said. "Could the guy you promoted to Charlie's spot be behind this?" And then Johnny's murder, I supposed, would be misdirection, an attempt by a rising Gambello mobster to keep suspicion off himself.

Lucky shook his head. "No, he's in Charlie's spot now because we trust him. He was headed for something good anyhow, so he sure didn't have to whack another Gambello to get it. Plus he knows what would happen to him if he did that and we ever found out. And he ain't the doppelgangster-creating type. You can trust me on this."

"So we're back to regarding the Corvinos as the most likely suspects for killing Gambellos?" I said.

"The most likely," Lucky agreed.

"Unless Doctor Dapezzo had indeed been replicated, too," Max pointed out.

"We need to find out for sure," Lucky said, casting an accusatory glare at his silent cell phone.

"And there's something else we need to find out," I said. "Where are Charlie's and Johnny's doppelgangsters *now*?"

Lucky's jaw dropped. "Holy Mother!"

Max's eyes widened. "Of course! Why didn't *I* think of that?"

"Charlie ate dinner a second time at Stella's on Thursday without being aware it was his second visit of the evening. Or so he said. So we can theorize that Lucky and I saw his doppelgangster that evening, though we still have no idea which diner was Charlie and which was the double," I said. "Johnny's doppelgangster was talking to us yesterday. And now, as far as we know, no one has seen either of them since the hits. So where *are* they?"

"Hey! Hey, wait! I got it!" Lucky skimmed his book, and then rested his finger on a particular paragraph. "It says here, 'The bilocate—that is to say, the replica—is always formed of e . . . eph . . . ephemeral substances enchanted through mystical means. While it looks, sounds, feels, and perhaps even smells genuine, its very nature means that it lacks the in . . . intrin . . . intrinsic permanence of normal human matter. This is presumably why every recorded bilocate—of which, it must be admitted, there are very few instances . . .' *Madonna*, this writer is wordy! Uh, every recorded bilocate . . . 'has only been known to exist for a short span of time, and no bilocate has ever been recorded developing an independent existence of its own.'"

"Ah." Max nodded. "Of course."

"Of course, *what*?" I said.

"Don't you see, kid?" said Lucky. "A doppelgangster is created, given the contract, and then vanishes when the hit is completed. The perfect assassin!"

"No, I don't see. Johnny was already dead when we met with his 'bilocate,'" I pointed out.

"Hmph." Lucky frowned in thought.

"Why," Max wondered, "would the entity creating these doppelgangsters want at least one of them to continue masquerading as the victim after he's deceased?"

"Of course!" Lucky jumped up. "I got it!"

Startled, Nelli jumped up, too, tail wagging, tongue lolling as she panted and gazed expectantly at Lucky. Max and I gazed at him expectantly, too.

"Okay, Charlie's death occurred in front of witnesses, no way to hide that," Lucky said. "But Johnny . . . He was found in the river. If you want to get rid of a body quick, that's a good place to put it."

I cleared my throat.

"Apart from getting a corpse out of your car trunk real fast, if you're worried about getting caught with it—er, speaking theoretically, that is," Lucky said.

"Of course," Max said.

"Apart from that, any forensic evidence that was carelessly left on the body deteriorates a lot faster in the water than on land. Plus, you can always hope that something living in the water eats the corpse."

"Do we *have* to go into this much detail?" I asked.

"My point—"

"And you do have one?"

"—is that dumping a body in the river is one way to confuse the trail for the cops. And however the hell Charlie's shooting happened, that's obviously confused the cops, too."

"That's for sure," I said, thinking of Lopez and Napoli.

"And what's gonna confuse 'em even more?" Lucky prodded.

Max and I gazed at Lucky in bewildered silence. His expression suggested that we were disappointing students at a seminar on the Way of the Wiseguy.

"We ain't the only people," Lucky continued, enunciating carefully out of consideration for our slow wits, "who saw that doppelgangster walking around and living Johnny's normal life, even after Johnny was floating face down in the East River."

"Oh." I rubbed my hands over my face as I realized what he was saying. *"Oh."*

"Oh, my goodness," Max said. "That explains it."

"There will be contradictory witness statements about when Johnny was last seen or could have died," I said.

"Exactly!" Lucky was pleased we had finally caught the train.

"But ever since Johnny's body was found, no one has seen or spoken to his double. Including us." I shuddered when I realized, "That . . . that *thing* suddenly decided to leave our meeting in the crypt. Somehow it knew! Knew that its original had just been found dead and its life-span was over."

Lucky nodded. "It sensed that its job was done. That it was time to sink back into whatever eph . . . ephemeral substances it came from."

"But *how* did it know?" I asked. "And how did something that seemed as stupid as Johnny's doppelgangster—"

"A *perfect* replica of Johnny," Lucky muttered.

"—manage to conceal the sudden awareness of Johnny's death from us?"

"I hypothesize," Max said, "that it was created that way. I suspect the creature may not have known that Johnny Be Good's body had been found. It may not even have killed Johnny. We must keep in mind that poor Chubby Charlie saw his perfect double, but *no one* saw who killed Charlie, even though many people were present and the doppelgangster, based on what we know so far, is a visible, tangible phenomenon."

"So if we're not sure the double killed Johnny Be Good, and we're not sure it even knew he was dead . . ." I spread my hands in a helpless gesture.

"Keep in mind the short lifespan that Lucky has mentioned. I suspect the creature was created to last only until the death of the original was discovered," Max said. "At that moment in time, and quite possibly without knowing why, the doppelgangster felt a sudden compulsion to depart. Shortly thereafter, I suspect, it ceased to exist."

"So . . ." Lucky thought it over. "The reason we ain't seen Charlie's doppelgangster since before he got whacked is because there were witnesses to his death."

Max nodded. "There was no interval between Charlie's death and the discovery of his demise. I postulate that his double ceased to exist almost immediately thereafter. But in Johnny Be Good's case . . ."

I said, "The river has damaged the evidence, and there are witnesses who'll confuse the trail considerably because they saw or spoke to 'Johnny' hours after the forensic estimate suggests that he was already dead."

"The police will be forced to conclude," Max said, "that a serious mistake was made in the collection or interpretation of the physical evidence. And they'll never be able to pinpoint what it was."

"So the killer doesn't even need an alibi for the time of the murder," I said. "Because the cops will never be sure when it happened."

"Meanwhile, in between when Johnny's wife last saw him and when he turned up dead, no one was lookin' for him because no one knew he was missing." Lucky said with reluctant admiration, "This is one slippery hitter. The cops'll never figure out who whacked Johnny. Or Charlie."

I looked at Lucky. "And you know who else might never figure this out?"

Lucky let out his breath and nodded. "The Gambello family. The Corvinos found a hitter that can pick us off like wooden ducks at a carnival shooting gallery. And we might never figure out who it is or how he's doing it."

"You've got two deaths in the family, and you're just guessing it's the Corvinos," I said. Lopez was just guessing, too. "But I don't see how that makes sense. Not with a killer as smart as you say this one is. Surely the Corvinos must know you'll suspect them and hit back. So why isn't the killer trying to make these deaths look like an accident?"

Lucky shrugged. "Because in our line of work, one death might be an accident, but two is always a business problem. No matter what it looked like, we'd suspect the Corvinos by the time the second guy bought the farm. So why bother to disguise it? For the Corvinos, the main thing is to keep the cops from nailing them for these hits." As his phone rang, he added, "Betcha they're enjoying this." He glanced at the readout. "It's Danny."

"We need to meet him." Max added firmly, "Without bloodshed."

Lucky answered his phone by saying, "I been tryin' to reach you since last night, you putz."

Max looked at me anxiously.

"Danny won't hang up," I assured him in a low voice. "This is how people in Lucky's profession talk to each other."

"Ah! Another interesting example of their dialect. I see."

Lucky said, "What? Huh? Why should I believe you? Who? When? Get real." After another minute or two of this, he covered the receiver with his hand and said to us, "Danny says the Corvinos been watching the news and are feeling very concerned. They claim they didn't do these two hits on our family, and they want a sit-down to make sure we ain't gonna hit them back, because that would be a terrible injustice."

"Do you think that's Danny talking? Or is it his double?" I asked.

"Don't really matter," Lucky said. "Whichever one it is, Max wants to talk to him. Er, it. Whatever. Right, Doc?"

"Indeed," said Max.

Lucky nodded and said into the receiver, "I'd rather

kiss Osama Bin Laden than have a sit-down with you, you jerk."

Max gasped and reached for the phone. I stopped him, figuring Lucky knew what he was doing. While I struggled with Max, my own phone rang.

Lucky covered his phone while I checked the LCD panel on mine. "Relax, Doc," he said. "Reverse psychology. Let's let Danny think this sit-down was strictly his idea, that we don't even want to come. It'll make our hand stronger when we're face-to-face."

"Oh!" Max relaxed. "I see." He smiled. "My dear fellow, clearly I should leave this in your hands. I apologize!"

My caller was Lopez. I flipped open my phone. "Hello?"

"Hey, it's me. I'm sorry about last night."

Lucky whispered to me, "Should I suggest the bookstore?"

"For what?" I said.

Lopez said, "Uh, for canceling our date."

I covered the phone for a moment so he wouldn't hear me speaking to Lucky again.

Lucky said, "For the sit-down. Do we want to meet here?"

I shook my head. I was disinclined to hold a Mafia sit-down in the place where Max lived and worked.

"Esther?" Lopez said, sounding puzzled. "Are you okay?"

I removed my hand from the receiver and assured Lopez, "I'm fine. Everything's fine. You really don't need to worry so much about me." Then I said to Lucky, "How about Bella Stella? It's closed and empty."

"Oh, please, don't you start on me, too," said Lopez. "Stella Butera is bad enough."

"What?" I said absently into the phone.

Lucky shook his head. "No way will the Corvinos come to Stella's. It's Gambello turf."

Lopez said, "Stella's lawyer is claiming restraint of trade and . . . oh, a bunch of other stuff. I can't keep his jabbering straight after two minutes. And it turns out Stella's got friends in high places. So it looks like we're going to have to let her reopen the restaurant soon."

Lucky said, "Danny's suggesting St. Monica's."

"That's good," I said with a nod to Lucky.

"Not it's not good." Lopez sounded irritable. "Look, I know you like Stella, and I know you want to start earning again—even though I *really* want you to find a safer job—but it's a crime scene, Esther. A crime where we can't even figure out how the crime was committed! So we might need to go over the scene again. But it looks like that's just too damn bad, and Stella will get her way."

Lucky said to me and Max, "Okay, we're on. The sit-down is set for St. Monica's. Tonight at eight o'clock."

"Meanwhile," Lopez continued wearily, "the Shy Don's lawyer—who, by remarkable coincidence, is the same lawyer representing Stella—is pressuring us to release the bodies of Chubby Charlie and Johnny Be Good, so that the family can hold their funerals."

"So release the bodies," I said absently.

Lucky and Max looked at me. I waved a dismissive hand at them.

"It's a *murder* investigation, Esther," Lopez said. "And we're not scheduling our work around the Gambellos' social calendar!"

"Sore subject?" I guessed.

"Sorry. I didn't mean to snap at you." Lopez sighed. "Anyhow, until we sort out the discrepancies between the physical evidence and various witness statements, releasing the bodies to be embalmed isn't our favorite choice."

"I know there are discrepancies," I said. "But I told you exactly what I saw. I told Napoli. I told you *both*. Over and over."

"I didn't mean you," Lopez said soothingly. "Well, not *just* you."

"Oh?"

Nearby, I heard Lucky making the exchange of insults with Danny that signaled they were preparing to say good-bye and get off the phone.

Lopez said to me, "We've got witnesses who say they talked to Johnny Gambello hours after the medical examiner says he was already dead."

"So there's confusion about when Johnny Be Good died?" I asked, a little loudly. When Lucky and Max looked at me again, I nodded.

"We're going to have to reinterview everyone we've talked to," Lopez said, sounding tired.

I prudently decided not to mention that I was one of the people who'd spoken with Johnny after he was dead.

Deciding it was time to change the subject, I said to him, "Never mind dead wiseguys. How are *you?* You've been working ridiculous hours. You haven't even had a day off since coming back from Long Island!"

"Oh, I'm fine. Actually, that's why I called," he said in a lighter tone. "They finally noticed my overtime and ordered me to take a couple of days off. Are you free tonight?"

"Tonight?"

"Yeah."

No, no, no . . . I wanted to drum my heels and cry.

"I *wish* I was free," I said sincerely. "But I have plans I can't change. Uh, too many people involved."

"If it's an orgy, I could come along and be your partner," he suggested.

"I can't bring a date to this," I said truthfully.

"Oh, well. Okay." The fact that he never sulked was fast becoming one of my favorite things about him. He asked, "What about tomorrow? I could come over."

"Yes," I agreed readily. "Absolutely. Let's do something together tomorrow."

"You *know* what I want to do together." His voice was silky now.

I glanced at Max and Lucky, wishing they'd feel a sudden, doppelgangster-like compulsion to depart.

"And I want to cooperate fully with that," I said carefully.

Lucky gave me a wary glance. I shook my head and rolled my eyes, hoping he'd think I was just humoring Lopez about the investigation.

"Well, I was thinking . . ." Lopez said. The tone of his voice made me fantasize about the expression on his face right now. "Since dating has turned out to be too complicated for us to manage, maybe we should backburner this dinner that we keep canceling."

"That's right," I said, realizing. "You've never even bought me dinner!"

"Not for lack of trying," he pointed out.

"The bum!" Lucky said.

"Is there someone with you?" Lopez asked.

"I'm in a shop." Strictly speaking, this was true. "You were saying?"

"Oh, you're shopping? Okay, since you're busy, I'll make this fast. I was thinking I'd come by tomorrow afternoon for a few hours of hot sex—you know, the kind that makes the neighbors complain about the noise. And *then* I'll take you out for dinner. Or maybe we'll just order out. We'll play it by ear after we've exhausted each other. Deal?"

A wave of heat washed over me, and I didn't trust myself to say anything in front of Max and Lucky that wouldn't make the rest of the day extremely awkward for me.

"Still there?" I could hear the smile in Lopez's voice.

"Yes," I said faintly. "It's a deal."

"See you then," he murmured. "Oh, and don't bother dressing up for the occasion. I don't plan to be gentle with whatever you've wearing when I get there."

I made an involuntary sound. Lopez laughed. Max and Lucky looked at me strangely.

"Bye," I choked out.

I gently folded my cell phone shut, then sat there staring at it with a stupid smile, feeling flushed and dizzy . . . and extremely conscious of the two men gazing at me with fatherly expressions. Max looked anxious, Lucky looked annoyed.

"What did the cop want?" Lucky said. "You look all pink and guilty."

"It's under control," I said, continuing my pretense that Lopez had called about the case.

"Don't kid yourself," said Lucky. "Love ain't *never* under control."

I thought of the Widow Giacalona and supposed he was speaking from experience.

"One gathers from your end of the conversation that, as we surmised, the police are indeed struggling with physical evidence that conflicts with eyewitness accounts?" Max said.

"Uh-huh," I said.

"This is a realm in which the mundane forces of law and order, though well-intentioned, are helpless—and possibly even an impediment."

"You mean the cops could get in the way?" Lucky asked.

"Precisely." Max's expression grew concerned. "Or even endanger themselves."

"And you're not looking at me that way because you're worried the charmless Detective Napoli could be in danger," I guessed.

"Well, I feel some concern for Detective Napoli's safety, too, but I know you are not attached to him."

"No, indeed."

"And as you and I have previously seen," Max said gravely, "Detective Lopez is a most dedicated and astute young man. He may pursue this case with more determination that is healthy for him."

Realizing Max had a point, I looked at Lucky.

The old hit man said, "Don't even think about it. I ain't gonna expend energy to watch a cop's back."

"He's my boyfriend," I pointed out. "Or almost."

"You should be more careful about the friends you choose," Lucky grumbled.

"I believe that, in good conscience, we must count Detective Lopez as an innocent under our protection," Max said to Lucky.

Lucky snorted. "I met this guy, and I can guess how he'd like *that* description."

"Max didn't say we should *tell* Lopez we're watching out for him," I said, knowing Lucky was right. Lopez would be appalled to learn how involved in this I was, and he'd be somewhere between amused and insulted that Max and Lucky were thinking of watching his back. "But even so . . ."

"Oh, for God's sake," Lucky said in disgust. "Fine. Whatever. We'll watch your boyfriend's back. But if you think he's going to return the favor and watch *ours*, then you don't know nothin' about cops."

"Thank you, Lucky." I beamed at him. He scowled back at me.

Max said, "Did he press you about our plans?"

"Huh?"

"Did Detective Lopez attempt to ascertain our next move?"

"Oh! Um, no."

"So we can go ahead with the sit-down without worrying the cops will bust in?" Lucky asked.

"Yes." The case had obviously not been Lopez's priority when he called me. I felt hot again. "We're good to go."

"Well, then," Max said brightly, "let's plan our strategy. Er, how *does* one prepare for a meeting of this nature?"

"First rule of a sit-down," Lucky said, "you gotta leave your piece at home."

"My piece?" Max said.

"Your rod. Your peacemaker," Lucky elaborated.

"We don't want to make peace?" Max asked in confusion.

Lucky sighed. "I can see we got a lot of work ahead of us before tonight."

12

Hoping to collect the transparent black wrap I had left behind the night before, I got to St. Monica's half an hour early for the sit-down.

I had just finished talking with Lucky on my cell phone. He wanted to make sure I had followed his advice after leaving the bookstore that afternoon; I assured him that I was now dressed appropriately for the evening. Lucky thought a meeting between the Gambellos and the Corvinos, particularly in the current circumstances, would be tense enough without the presence of outsiders making everyone jumpy. However, since he also thought Max and I needed to be there, he decided the best thing would be for us to try to fit in.

I felt sure I could comply, but we both had our doubts about Max. So while I went home to change clothes, Lucky had remained at the shop, continuing to teach Manhattan's resident mage to blend in with the wiseguys. Lucky had also phoned two of his colleagues and told them to be at the sit-down; Danny would bring two soldiers, too. So now, with a small bunch of violent felons due to arrive soon at St. Monica's to hear (little did they suspect) our theories about apparitional bilocated doppelgängerism, I prayed for good luck—and felt an unprecedented impulse to make the sign of the Cross.

"I've been hanging out in church too much," I muttered to myself.

I glanced around the shadowy, silent interior of St. Monica's, hoping to see Father Gabriel. It was presumably too late in the day for a church administrator to be here, and I had no idea where they stowed lost-and-found items. I supposed I could go into the crypt to see if my wrap was right where I'd left it . . . But the last time I had visited the crypt, I'd met a doppelgangster down there, so I was reluctant to venture back into that subterranean chamber on my own. Even the bunny costumes from the Easter play couldn't make that place seem unthreatening to me now.

My roving gaze settled on the only other person in the church at moment. The Widow Giacalona was kneeling before the altar of Saint Monica, her head bowed in prayer. People weren't exaggerating about her devotion.

I wondered if the widow would go to the crypt with me to look for my wrap.

When she lifted her head, crossed herself, and rose to her feet, I cleared my throat and said, "Hello. Nice to see you again."

She looked over her shoulder at me. The large, dark long-lashed eyes showed no spark of recognition. "Have we met?" she asked with a faint frown.

I realized that by dressing to blend in at the sit-down I had changed my appearance so much that the widow didn't know me.

"I'm Esther Diamond." When this obviously didn't ring a bell, I added, "Lucky Battistuzzi's friend."

You know—a chorus girl with ties to the mob.

"Oh. Yes." A look of disgust crossed her face. "Lucky's *gumata.*"

I knew from conversations I overheard at Bella Stella that *gumata* was a loaded word for a wiseguy's girlfriend; men said it carelessly, and women never used it nicely

However, the widow had lost three husbands and had legitimate grievances against Lucky, so I decided to let the insult pass.

I simply said, "I'm not his—"

"With a pretty young thing like you on his arm," she interrupted, "why won't he leave *me* alone?"

Well, even though I guessed she was at least twenty years older than me, she was beautiful in a rich, earthy way that I thought would make any number of men walk right past me to get a date with her. (Which is okay; talent lasts longer than beauty, and I want to keep getting acting work until the day I shuffle off this mortal coil.) But, though she evidently wasn't vain about her looks, she was way off base about my relationship with Lucky. I wondered if it was my outfit.

"I'm not being euphemistic when I say 'friend,' Elena." She scowled again, and I said, "Er, Mrs. Giacalona. Lucky's like an uncle to me, and he'd be dismayed to learn anyone had other ideas about our friendship." When this, too, failed to warm her expression, I added, "I have a boyfriend. A nice young man."

"Another Gambello?" she said, her voice full of loathing.

"No, he's a cop."

That surprised her. "You date a *cop?*"

I sighed. "Yes. I do. I date a cop."

"You're kidding."

"No, ask anyone," I said, hoping we could get on a roll here, so I could ask her to go into the crypt with me without it sounding too strange. "Half of Stella Butera's customers have met him by now. You know Stella?"

"Yes." The widow glanced at Saint Monica. "Stella lost her man, too."

"Just the one." After a moment, I said, "That came out wrong."

"Stella used to come here. We prayed together sometimes." Elena shook her head. "But like so many, her faith was not enduring. She doesn't pray to the saint anymore."

Rather than seeing it as a sign of weak faith, I figured that Stella had eventually gotten over the death of her longtime lover, Handsome Joey Gambello, who had been killed at the restaurant five years ago. Now she chose to live in the present and look to the future, and that struck me as healthy. However, Stella had indeed lost only one man. I supposed it wasn't surprising that a thrice-bereft woman like Elena Giacalona was keeping regular company with Monica, patron saint of widows and wives.

Seeking a friendly comment to fill the silence, since this still didn't seem quite the right moment to invite Elena into the crypt with me, I said, "Who was Saint Monica? A devout medieval widow?"

"Not medieval." The widow shook her head. "She lived in the fourth century. Monica was married to an abusive pagan husband, and she spent her whole life praying he would convert to Christianity."

"Were her prayers ever answered?" I asked, thinking that sounded like a grim marriage for both spouses.

"Yes. He converted on his deathbed."

"Better late than never, I suppose."

"She was also the mother of Saint Augustine."

"Oh?" I thought it was too bad Max wasn't there to see that I am not quite as uneducated as he thinks. "Author of the *Confessions* and *The City of God*, right?"

The widow seemed to warm to me, smiling a little. "Yes, that's right."

"He's also the guy who said, 'Lord, grant me chastity . . . but not yet.' " I enjoyed a friendly chuckle over this all-too-human plea.

The widow's expression turned cold. Apparently it was not one of her favorite saintly quotes.

Hoping to repair the damage, I said solicitously, "I hear you've seen Saint Monica weeping?"

"Yes." She turned to gaze at the saint's statue and crossed herself. "Yes, I have."

A reverent expression warmed her face, making it even more beautiful. Also a little scary—there was a spark of zealous fervor there that, for a moment, didn't look wholly sane.

She said in a passionate voice, "My devotion has been rewarded with the saint's grace and mercy. She has shed tears for my sorrow."

"That's amazing." Careful to keep my skepticism out of my voice, I asked, "When was this?"

"It's happened several times." The widow clasped her hands in front of her chest and gazed with rapture at Saint Monica. "She feels the pain of the brokenhearted, and she weeps for us."

"'Us'? I thought no one but you had seen her weep."

Turning away from the saint, the widow gave me a cool, dismissive look. "You're not the only one who doesn't believe me."

"I didn't say—"

"Don't patronize me. *I* know what I have seen." Her voice was sharp. "And if you have not suffered enough sorrow in love to see it, too, you should be grateful rather than mock me."

Now I felt bad. "I'm *not* mocking you. I swear." I decided to fall back on a convenient excuse. "I'm Jewish, I don't know from saints and their miracles."

She blinked. "Oh, Diamond. Yes, that's a Jewish name, isn't it?"

"It's certainly not Italian."

"Are you converting?"

"Good God, no!" Seeing her offended expression, I added quickly, "My mother would die."

Her eyes widened and, in what seemed to be a reflexive gesture, she raised her right hand to her neckline to close her fingers around the ornate cross that hung there on a silver chain. "It's bad luck to say such a thing, even in jest."

"Who's jesting?" When the widow frowned and re-moved her hand from her throat, I noticed for the first time how lovely her pendant was. A graceful, old-fash-ioned piece, it consisted of a softly glowing mother-of-pearl cross embedded in a larger, ornate, silver one, and it was delicately decorated with tiny diamonds. "What a beautiful cross," I said, hoping to change the subject. "Where did you get it?"

"It was my mother's," she said tersely.

Since it seemed unlikely she'd ever warm up to me, I decided to cut to the chase. "Look, I left my wrap here—"

"So 'everyone' knows your young man—your *cop*—at Stella's?" she said suddenly, surprising me.

"Well, not everyone, but quite a few of the guys have met him by now."

"So he's a meat eater?"

Wondering why this question made her sneer, I said, "He's not a vegetarian, if that's what you mean."

"What?"

I elaborated, "Lopez likes a good burger." I knew this from our two lunch dates, which now seemed awfully long ago.

"*Idiota!* I said a *meat eater*. Don't you know anything?"

"Huh?

"He takes a boost, right?"

"A boost?" I frowned, confused. "You mean ... a leg up?"

She looked exasperated. "*Bribes*. Kickbacks. Crumbs from the Gambellos' table."

I gasped. "He does *not* take bribes!" I finally got it. "Oh! A 'meat-eater' is a corrupt cop?"

She made a hand gesture that suggested it had taken me a long time to arrive at this realization.

I said, "I hadn't heard that one before."

She stared at me without warmth.

"Lopez is not a corrupt cop," I said firmly. "He's a straight arrow. Very dedicated." As I had good reason to know.

"Then what's Officer Lopez—"

"*Detective* Lopez."

"—doing hanging around Stella's place with all those *goombata?*"

"He doesn't hang around there, and he certainly doesn't hang out with *goombata*. He's investigating Charlie Chiccante's murder. Also Johnny Gambello's murder." I paused. "You did hear they're dead?"

She made a spitting gesture. "Good riddance to them both!"

"Yeah, Lucky said they wouldn't really be missed."

"Lucky killed them?"

"What? No! *No*." Although it was a doomed cause—and a warped one—I made a clumsy effort to improve the widow's opinion of my friend. "Actually, Lucky's working with the good guys on this one."

"Lucky is working with Detective Lopez?" she said in astonishment.

"Uh, not in the strictest sense," I said. "But Lucky's trying to discover who killed Charlie and Johnny."

"Of course he is. They were Gambellos."

"Oh. Right." So much for improving her opinion of Lucky. "And Lopez is trying to find the killer, too."

"I see. What I don't quite see is where *you* ... Oh! *Oh*." She nodded. "Now I recognize you. You're the singing server who saw the slaying, aren't you?"

"Does *everyone* in this town read the tabloids?"

"I'm a widow," she said tersely. "I have a lot of time to fill."

"Yes, I'm the one who saw Charlie get killed," I admitted. "And I ... sort of got dragged into Johnny's death, too, though it's complicated—and pretty disturbing—to explain how."

"Johnny. That *babbo*." She looked me up and down.

"Yes, you look like his type." The remark was clearly not a compliment—which wasn't surprising, given her opinion of Johnny. I'd heard the word *"babbo"* at Stella's often enough to know that it meant someone who was a useless idiot.

I wondered if my costume was overdone. As per Lucky's advice, I had done my best this evening to look like the type of *gumata* I often saw hanging out with the *goombata* at Bella Stella. My hair was teased and curled and sprayed within an inch of its life, I was wearing heavy makeup, berry-colored lipstick, too much mascara, and long, sparkly earrings. My blouse was satin, my skirt was faux leather, and they were both uncomfortably tight—as were my spike-heeled shoes.

I use the tiny spare bedroom in my apartment as my theatrical trunk. When preparing for an audition or rehearsing a new role I've been hired to play, I find it helpful to wear clothes that suit the character rather than my own clothes. So in addition to stocking that back bedroom with some basic props, I keep a huge quantity of costumes, accessories, and makeup there. It's all stuff I pick up for peanuts at thrift shops and rummage sales, and it has come in handy many times.

So when Lucky had suggested I try to look like a Gambello girl tonight, I didn't know exactly what I had in that room that would fit the bill, but I knew there would definitely be something. But the way the widow looked at me when she said I was Johnny's type made me wonder now if I'd done *too* good a job with my costume.

"I was not involved with Johnny," I said emphatically. "In fact, there's a very real sense in which I never even met him."

"You didn't miss a worthwhile experience," she muttered. "His father died in prison, his mother bullied him, and the Shy Don spoiled him. The result was a weak-willed, lying, skirt-chasing loser with a booze-pickled brain."

"It sounds as if you knew Johnny well," I said in surprise.

"No, I haven't talked to him in years."

"But all those details about his upbringing," I said. "And the way he turned out—your description sounds just like the guy Lucky knew, too."

She tilted her head and made a gesture of acquiescence. "I knew him a long time ago. Johnny was young then, but he was already pathetic and self-destructive. I just never thought it was all his own fault."

I frowned. "But he was a Gambello, so how did *you* ..." I met her dark, angry expression, and my jaw dropped. "Oh. You've had *three* husbands." Since Lucky had killed one of them, and since she clearly hated the *famiglia*, I had simply assumed that all of her husbands had been enemies of the Gambellos. But now I realized that Elena's knowledge of Don Victor Gambello's family life during Johnny Be Good's youth must mean that ... "One of them was a Gambello?"

"My first husband," she said curtly.

"But what about your second husband?" I said, stunned. Had Lucky whacked a fellow Gambello to win the widow?

"He was a Corvino," she said brusquely. "Is there anything else you would like to know about my personal tragedies, young woman?"

"What family was your third husband in?" I asked, too ghoulishly fascinated to remember things like tact or courtesy.

"I don't want to talk about my husbands with you!"

"That's understandable," I admitted.

In an apparent effort to regain control of the conversation, she spread her hands and said, "I don't understand—if you're Jewish and you're not converting, then why are you here at St. Monica's? *Again*."

Considering what she had just told me, this didn't seem the right moment to say that I was here tonight for a Corvino-Gambello sit-down. So I blurted, "I need to go into the crypt. Will you come with me?"

"Excuse me?"

"I left something down in the crypt," I explained. "A wrap I was wearing last night. And I'm afraid to go down there alone to get it."

"Why?" she asked, in the same tone she might use with a staggering drunk.

I tried to think of the simplest way to explain it. "I saw an apparition of Johnny Be Good down there."

Her gaze sharpened. "Why would Johnny haunt the crypt of St. Monica's?"

"When you put it that way, maybe you can understand why I'm afraid to go down there alone."

"Johnny Gambello was not devout," the widow said disapprovingly. "Not even mildly faithful. Not to his various wives or his family, and certainly not to God."

"I hear he prayed whenever he bet big on a longshot," I offered. "So he must have come here semiregularly from the sound of it."

"Of all the places he might turn up in the afterlife ... church?" She shook her head. "No, I don't think so."

"Nonetheless, he was in the crypt yesterday."

"Since you say you never even met him, what makes you so sure it was Johnny?"

"Lucky was there. He says it was definitely Johnny."

"So you and Lucky both saw Johnny? *After* he was dead?"

I nodded. "Which is why I don't want to go into the crypt alone."

"Maybe you're mistaken about the timing," she said. "What did this apparition look like?"

"Just like Johnny, but—"

"Did he ask Lucky for money?"

"Well, yes."

"So that explains what Johnny was doing in church,"

she said. "Unless he'd bet on another longshot right before dying."

"But—"

"Obviously, you saw Johnny just *before* he was murdered."

"No, he was murdered well before we saw—"

"Father!" Elena looked over my shoulder and her face brightened.

"Elena!" Father Gabriel called across the church. "You're here late this evening. I missed seeing you at the service today."

"I was sorry to miss it, Father. So I thought I'd meditate in prayer for a while now. *If,*" the widow added with an unfriendly glance at me as I turned to face the priest, "I can find a few moments of peace, that is."

Father Gabriel had entered through a side door. Leaving the dark wooden door ajar behind him, he crossed the floor of the church to the widow. Then he glanced at me and said warmly, "And who is this with you, Elena? A friend? A relative?"

"Neither," she said. "This is Esther Diamond."

Still smiling, Father Gabriel frowned a little in confusion. "No, no, I know Esther, and she's ... er ..." His gaze flickered over my cheekbones, up to my hair, then back to my eyes. *"Esther?"*

"Hello, Father, nice to see you again."

He recovered from the shock of my appearance with admirable speed and grace. "And a great pleasure to see you here again, too. I talked to Lucky today, so I was expecting you, of course. I just didn't quite recognize ... Well, you look very pretty. Again."

I beamed at him. "Thank you, Father."

"If Lucky's coming," grumbled the widow, "*he* can go into the crypt with you."

"Yes, that's what Lucky said," Father Gabriel said.

"Huh?" I said.

"I've set up some chairs, a table, and some refreshments in the crypt for you, as per Lucky's instructions," the priest said cheerfully.

"We're meeting in the crypt? Again?"

The widow gave me another sharp look. "I thought you said Lucky was like an uncle to you."

"He is. Do you really imagine," I said in annoyance, "that I would choose the crypt of a church for my amorous encounters?"

"I thought Lucky chose the place," she retorted.

"We're conducting business down there," I said. "Regarding these murders."

She lifted her brows. "Indeed?"

Father Gabriel said, "And I'm so pleased you and Lucky chose St. Monica's for this meeting. A house of God is certainly the right place to take the first step toward ending this new round of violence and renewing our bonds with each other as brothers and sisters in Christ our Lord." He did a little double take when he looked at me and remembered I wasn't a Christian. "And also certainly the loving bonds of, er, Moses, Abraham, Yahweh . . . Yes, indeed. All very good people, too."

"Whatever," I said. "The point is, there's something Evil going on here, and we need to put a stop to it before anyone else winds up dead."

"The men who have been killed," the widow said, her voice bitter, "men like Johnny and Charlie. Why do you care? Do you know how much misery they caused in their time? Why should you want to prevent the deaths of more men like that?"

"I witnessed one of these deaths, so the cops think the killer may target *me*," I said. "And there's too much about these killings that we don't understand, such as how they were accomplished—"

"The papers say Johnny was hit over the head and dumped in the river," Elena said. "No mystery there."

"—and what the role of these doppelgangsters is."

"Doppelgangsters?" the priest and the widow said together.

"Um, it's complicated," I said. "Anyhow, my point is, these aren't typical mob hits; there's something very strange occurring, and since we don't know why Charlie and Johnny were chosen for these murders, we can't say for sure that the next victim won't be an innocent bystander—like me or Lucky."

"There is nothing *innocent* about Lucky Battistuzzi," the Widow Giacalona spat.

Since she had every reason to feel that way, I didn't argue. Instead, I asked the priest to escort me into the crypt.

"Now?" he said. "You don't want to wait for the others?"

I explained that I had come early in search of my wrap. Seeing his blank expression, I asked, "Didn't the administrator I spoke to on the phone today give you the message?"

He shook his head. "At least, I don't think so. I admit, I can be a bit absentminded. But I was in the crypt earlier, Esther, to set it up for your meeting, and I don't remember seeing an evening wrap there. Of course, I'm not very knowledgeable about ladies' accessories, and I wasn't looking for it. Shall we go and have a look now?"

I nodded and thanked him. He gestured for me to precede him, then encouraged the widow to find solace in her prayers. With Father Gabriel's sturdy footsteps echoing behind me, I went toward the stairs that led down into the crypt.

13

Once Father Gabriel and I were out of earshot of the widow, I said, "I think I made her angry. I didn't mean to."

"Well, it must be admitted that she's prone to anger," Father Gabriel said gently, as we descended the stairs to the crypt. "Especially when the subject of, er, certain families comes up. The Gambellos and Corvinos have given her much to grieve over."

"*Both* families?" I asked curiously.

"Oh, yes. Both families. It's terribly sad. The trials she has been through, the sorrows and injustices . . ."

The lights were already on at the bottom of the brick-lined staircase, as well as inside the crypt. Within the underground chamber, I found no memories of Johnny, thank goodness. Just bunny costumes, chairs, tables, and food. A *lot* of food.

I said, "Wow! When you said refreshments, I thought you meant a pot of coffee and a box of doughnuts."

There was a folding table set up near the far wall, and it was practically groaning beneath the weight of deli foods from, I assumed, one of Little Italy's mouth-watering *salumerie*. Paper-thin slices of prosciutto were delicately rolled and arranged on the same platter with shining slices of fresh mozzarella, creamy-colored provolone, plump purple figs, well-marbled salami, crisp-looking slices of red and green bell pepper, and pale green melon balls. Another tray contained slices of lightly seasoned roasted eggplant and grilled zucchini, four kinds of olives, and marinated mushrooms. There was a basket of Italian bread, and a generous supply of miniature cannoli—crispy tubes of dessert pastry stuffed with sweetened ricotta cheese and tiny bits of dark chocolate, then dusted with powdered sugar. A selection of sodas, fruit juices, and bottled water was chilling on ice, and there was an electric cappuccino maker with a pitcher of milk beside it.

"There's no wine," Father Gabriel said apologetically. "I just thought, you know, a tense meeting about a deadly matter among bitter enemies . . ."

"Ah," I said. "Yes. Alcohol might not be a good idea. They could get tipsy and shoot up the church."

"Or one of us," he said with feeling.

"Good point," I said.

"I hope they won't mind."

"With this spread, I don't see how any reasonable person can have objections." Our eyes met . . . and though we exchanged no words, we shared the same thought at the same moment—and chuckled together. This meeting wasn't for *reasonable* people, of course; it was for wiseguys. I smiled at the priest, liking him. "I'll explain it to Lucky. I'm sure he'll agree and take care of any complaints that arise."

"Thank you."

"Was the collections dish especially full on Sunday, Father? This seems like a pretty expensive refreshments table."

"Lucky said that Danny Dapezzo would reimburse the church."

"Oh." I nodded. "Good."

Since I doubted Lucky had cleared that with Danny, I decided to make sure *someone* repaid the priest. I doubted any of St. Monica's parishioners made their weekly contributions in the belief that their hard-earned cash would be used to feed tasty delicacies to wealthy wiseguys.

Looking around the crypt, Father Gabriel said, "Thinking of the widow's tragic past almost made me forget why we came down here. Do you remember where you left your wrap?"

"Draped over the back of the chair I was sitting on."

Since the room was rearranged, there was no telling which chair had been mine. I didn't see the garment anywhere, so I started looking through the chairs that were folded and stacked against the wall. "Maybe someone put my chair back, and my wrap slid down to the floor?"

"Let's see." The priest started investigating a different stack of chairs.

I couldn't resist asking, "I understand Elena has lost three husbands, Father?"

"Yes, her life has been very difficult. Hmm, no, I don't see a black wrap over here. I'll look at that stack over there," he said. "Elena's losses have brought her closer to her faith, but at great personal cost."

"Her first husband worked for the Gambello family?" I asked, trying not to sound gossipy.

"More than that. He was one of the Shy Don's many nephews."

That surprised me. "Was he a brother of Johnny Gambello?"

"No, Anthony and Johnny were cousins. But they were almost as close as brothers. Anthony was older, and he tried to take Johnny under his wing. Help him, give him some guidance. But that, of course, turned out very bitterly."

"How so?" I asked, looking around the room and wondering where else my wrap might have fallen or been dropped. Among the bunny costumes? It seemed unlikely, but I checked anyhow.

Father Gabriel explained, "About twenty years ago, Johnny had an affair with a lady whom a certain drug lord considered his, er, exclusive companion."

"Okay, I know Johnny wasn't very bright, but why would the woman do something so dumb?" I wondered.

"Well, though his looks were eventually ruined by his indulgences, Johnny was quite a handsome young man. So the woman may have found him irresistible. I remember neighborhood girls my own age swooning over Johnny back then, though we were much younger than he, of course."

"So you grew up around the Gambellos?" I asked.

"Yes. Hmm, I'm afraid I don't see your wrap anywhere, Esther."

"No, I don't, either." But I was more interested in our conversation by now. "You knew Johnny back then?"

"No, I just knew who he was. As everyone did. Well, everyone except the cuckolded drug lord and his thugs."

"They came looking for him?"

Father Gabriel nodded. "But Johnny was not unaware of the risks of wooing that woman, so he had taken a precaution when introducing himself to her. And it's easy to believe that he was too foolish to consider how horribly the jest would backfire, or what it would cost others."

"Oh, my God!" I covered my mouth. "Er, pardon me, Father. I mean . . . You're saying Johnny told the woman he was Anthony?"

The priest nodded. "Precisely. As a result, Anthony's body was found . . . Well, I'll spare you the details, but it was a brutal death. And Elena, just over thirty at the time, became a widow."

"What a terrible story," I said with feeling. "No wonder she hated Johnny. But considering that Johnny had caused his cousin's death, why didn't Don Victor . . ."

"Well, Johnny was *also* a nephew of the don. So he was given a pass."

I'd heard the expression before. At Bella Stella, of course. "And I gather it wouldn't turn out to be the last time, either, that the Shy Don spared Johnny for doing something that would typically be a killing offense."

"No, indeed," the priest agreed.

"But how did Elena wind up married to a Corvino, after that?" I sat in a chair and gestured for the priest to do the same.

"She fell in love," Father Gabriel said simply, taking a seat. "They met here, in fact. I gather she sought support and counsel from Father Stefano, who was the priest here back then. Father Stefano encouraged their love, believing that the union of a Gambello widow and Corvino soldier might end the constant and deadly violence between the two families." Father Gabriel sighed. "He had a good heart and a strong faith, but he was naive about these matters."

"It's a real Romeo and Juliet story, isn't it?"

"With an equally unhappy outcome."

"When the Gambellos found out," I guessed, "the sh . . . er, things hit the fan?"

"Elena married her Corvino lover in secret, then went alone to Don Victor's home to confess the truth, to ask for his forgiveness and blessing. He was so enraged, he tried to kill her."

I gasped, imagining the violence of that confrontation. The frail old man's vitriol and fury, Elena's fear and desperation, and the thugs who were probably just outside the door, prepared to carry out whatever heinous act their boss ordered.

Father Gabriel continued, "But even the don, who had committed so many acts of deadly violence before growing old and turning over the dirty work to his subordinates . . . Even he stopped short of murdering a woman. *Just* short. Elena says she had dark bruises on her throat for a week after that night."

I put my hand up to my own throat, disturbed by the mental image of the Shy Don trying to kill his nephew's remarried widow.

Father Gabriel shrugged. "There is some reluctance among wiseguys to murder a woman."

"I guess that saved Elena's life."

He sighed. "Well, they didn't kill Elena, but as far as the Gambellos were concerned, there was still unfinished business to settle. A Corvino had courted a Gambello widow. He had poached in sacred territory. In their code of honor, they couldn't rest without making an example of him. So Lucky . . . *Oh*. Oh, dear." He looked at me, evidently recalling that I hung out with Lucky. "Never mind."

"So Lucky killed him?" I asked in shock. "For *that*?" I had assumed Lucky's murder of Elena's second husband was "business," not something so personal, so vicious.

"Yes."

"No wonder she hates Lucky so much," I said, appalled.

"Yes," Father Gabriel repeated.

I felt depressed. I was suddenly ashamed to think of Lucky as my friend, as someone I liked.

Lopez had been right, I was naive. I knew Lucky was a killer! Had I really supposed he'd had *good* reasons for murdering people?

"Of course, Elena remarried in time," said Father Gabriel.

"Uh-huh," I said, not really interested now, feeling sick as I thought about the deeds of a man I had described to Elena as my friend only a few minutes ago.

"To another Corvino." The priest shrugged. "Perhaps she was lonely. Or perhaps staying within a powerful family made her feel safer. But, of course, Eddie Giacalona was killed, too. About two years ago."

"By Lucky?"

"No. By another Corvino."

I looked at Father Gabriel in surprise. "They killed one of their own?"

"For betraying the family." He snorted and added, "Not all bosses are as sentimental as the Shy Don."

"So Elena must hate the Corvinos almost as much as she hates the Gambellos."

"It's an obsession with her." He looked even sadder. "She comes here to pray twice a day, almost every day. But her heart has not yet felt God's infinite love and forgiveness."

"That's hardly surprising, is it?" I said.

He suddenly changed his tone and the subject. "But listen to me, gossiping about all this water under the bridge. We still haven't found your wrap, have we? We should look in the lost and found. If you spoke to Mrs. Campanello—that's who was in the office today—she probably came down, found it, and put it there. Why didn't I think of that before? You stay here, Esther, I'll go look."

He was gone only a minute before I discovered that, in my newly dark mood, the silent crypt felt oppressive and Johnny's ghost was everywhere—like the ghosts of Elena's husbands. So I slid out of my chair and climbed the steps back up to the church.

It seemed Elena Giacalona was not destined to pray in peace this evening. There was a man sitting next to her on the church pew, talking to her. I recognized Don Michael ("no relation, I assure you") Buonarotti. His presence didn't seem to agitate her the way Lucky's did. They were speaking together in low voices. The expression on her face was serious and a little tense, but she seemed to be speaking to him in a reasonable way. At one point, she placed a hand over the pendant that hung around her neck. I thought again of the Shy Don trying to strangle her.

Her gaze shifted away from Buonarotti and she saw me. The stiffening of her posture must have warned him they weren't alone; he immediately looked in my direction.

"Miss Diamond." He rose to his feet. "Nice to see to again."

I was surprised he recognized me. No one else had. I supposed Elena must have told him I was here.

"How are you?" I said politely.

"Disappointed," he said. "I'm trying to convince this lovely lady to join me for dinner, but she refuses."

I gestured to our surroundings. "You've chosen an interesting setting for courtship."

He shrugged. "It's where I can count on finding her."

"I think I'll start praying at home," Elena said. "I get more peace there."

"Did you see where Father Gabriel went?" I asked them.

"Through that door." Buonarotti indicated the same door the priest had come through earlier.

I turned to go in search of him, but I stopped when the door opened and he came through it.

"Oh, Esther! I thought you were still downstairs," he said.

I didn't want to tell him that I was afraid to be alone in a well-lighted room full of good food and bunny costumes, so I said, "I thought I'd come help you search the lost and found."

"Oh, it's only a cardboard box under a table," he said with a smile. "No help needed. But I'm afraid I didn't find your wrap there."

"No?" I was disappointed. Also surprised. "Do you think it's been stolen? From a *church*?"

"It wouldn't be the first time," the Widow Giacalona said in disgust. "It's disgraceful, Father!"

"There've been thefts here?" I asked in surprise.

"Yes. Too many lately. And what else would you expect," Elena added darkly, "with all the *goombata* and young thugs who come to this church?"

"Now, now," said Father Gabriel, "they should be respected for attending church, not accused of stealing. Besides a few misplaced items hardly counts as a crime wave."

"If you say so, Father," the widow said grudgingly.

"So do you think my wrap is gone for good?" I asked in dismay.

"Oh, perhaps Mrs. Campanello put it somewhere else and didn't tell me," Father Gabriel said.

"No, it's been stolen," Elena said with dark certainty.

"Well, Father, I understand you've got company coming that I don't particularly want to see," said Buonarotti, "so I'll be on my way. Elena, may I escort you home?"

I thought she would refuse, but Father Gabriel said, "Please do agree to it, Elena. It's later than you usually come here. It would comfort me to know you're not going home alone."

"Very well, Father." As she stood up, she ignored the hand that Buonarotti extended to her. "But I will certainly be *entering* my home alone."

"Hey, did I suggest otherwise?" said Buonarotti, feigning offense. "But . . . maybe we could stop for dinner along the way?"

The widow rolled her eyes and turned away without answering him. But I thought I saw a touch of amusement on her face, and I wondered if she'd give in. Maybe the man was wearing her down. Even if she was understandably reluctant to get involved with yet another wiseguy, she might be flattered by the Don's attentions. And, unlike Lucky, this suitor had not killed any of Elena's husbands.

After Don Michael and the widow left, Father Gabriel went back to the crypt to see if his arrangements needed any finishing touches. I stayed in the church and strolled over to the statue of St. Monica. I studied the saint for signs of weeping. Finding none, I shrugged; the widow's religious fervor was undoubtedly accompanied by wishful thinking, perhaps even by outright hallucination. Then, since it seemed the thing to do, given my surroundings, I put a coin in the donations box and lit a candle, hoping for a successful sit-down. Although only gangsters had been killed so far, that didn't mean that no innocent person would ever be targeted by the powerful entity committing these murders.

While I was wondering if Elena would find love again, this time with Michael Buonarotti, Lucky and Max entered the church.

They brought Nelli with them. She noticed me before they did, and she wagged her tail. Apparently she'd forgiven me for the comment about her ears. Maybe dogs—or familiars—didn't hold grudges.

"So these were straight hits?" Max was asking Lucky as they walked down the aisle of St. Monica's.

"No, no, someone was sending a message with these hits." Lucky stopped in the middle of the church and elaborated. "A straight hit is when no one ever finds the body. Clean and tidy. Bada-beep-bada-bope-bada-boop."

"Oh! Yes, of course. I remember now."

"No evidence. No corpse. No case."

"Understood, dear fellow."

"Don't call me that at the sit-down."

"Yes, of course," Max said.

"And don't say 'of course.' Say 'no shit' or 'whatever' or 'sure.' Got it?"

Max nodded. "Whatever."

"When you risk the cops finding the body, it's because sending a message is important enough to take that chance."

"Sure."

"So what's the message we're supposed to get outta these hits?" Lucky said. "We still don't know."

"No shit."

I blinked at the first vulgarity I had ever heard Max use.

I also blinked at his appearance. He wore a black pin-striped suit with black shirt and a white tie. I looked down and saw he wore shiny black shoes. His unruly white hair was tamed by gel and scraped severely away from his bearded face. The ensemble was topped off by a black fedora with a white hatband.

He looked like a hippy who'd been cast in a *Guys and Dolls* revival.

As Lucky continued talking, Max glanced down the aisle and saw me walking toward him. "Oh, excuse me, miss? We're looking for . . . *Esther?*"

"Max?"

Lucky's jaw dropped. *"Kid?"*

Nelli's tail wagged harder, expressing her happiness at the reunion.

I said to Lucky, "What did you do to Max?"

Lucky preened. "Ain't I a genius?"

"I should never have left the bookstore today," I said with conviction.

"Oh, dear," Max said fretfully. "Do I not look the part?"

Lucky said, "Ignore her. You look perfect. But don't say 'oh, dear.' Say 'fuck.' "

"I can't say that!"

"Then say *'Madonna'* or 'bite me.' "

"It's a lot to remember," Max said, starting to look flustered.

"You'll do fine." Lucky gave me a stern look. "Tell him he'll do fine."

I nodded. "You'll do fine, Max."

"But, Esther, is my ensemble not convincing?" Max asked.

"Well," I said honestly, recovering from my shock, "I am not the expert on what will make these guys take you seriously. Lucky is. So let's go with his judgment on this."

"Exactly," said Lucky. "And may I say, kid, even with-

out my help, you did a great job. You could almost be
Danny's eldest daughter."

"He lets his *daughter* dress like this?"

Lucky asked, "Where's Father Gabriel?"

"In the crypt."

"Everything's all set up?"

"You *are* going to pay him for all that food, aren't
you?"

"Won't have to," Lucky said. "Danny called for the
sit-down, so he'll make a big donation to the church
when he gets here and sees the spread. He's a vicious
bastard, but he knows what's right. At most, I might
have to pay for the wine."

"There is no wine." I explained why not.

Lucky shrugged, then nodded.

Max asked, "So ... we won't need to ask for a
receipt?"

"A receipt?" Lucky said. "At a *sit-down*?"

Suspecting the source of Max's sudden interest in fis-
cal paperwork, I said, "Did you receive another letter
from the IRS today?"

"Yes. It appears to be a litany of dreadful threats. It's
most distressing," Max said morosely. "It also doesn't
really seem to be written in English. That is to say, the
words are English, but they make no sense."

"That sounds normal," Lucky muttered.

"I wonder if this is all because Mercury is in retrograde?" Max mused.

"Okay, what does that mean?" I said.

"It's astronomy," Lucky said.

"Astrology," Max corrected. "When Mercury, the astral body that rules communications, is on the other side
of the sun from Earth, then communications here become confusing and difficult. It happens three times per
calendar year, on average, because Mercury's solar orbit
is so much smaller than Earth's. And while Mercury is in
retrograde, which typically lasts for about three weeks,

letters get lost, messages get garbled, comments get misinterpreted, people have trouble keeping their appointments, and so on."

Lucky looked alarmed. "Let's hope everyone keeps tonight's appointment. We got serious business to discuss!"

I thought about how hard it was for Lopez and me to get together lately, and about my trouble communicating with my agent to get the audition I wanted; I'd left another message on his answering machine late this afternoon. I also thought of my missing evening wrap and the lack of communication about it between Father Gabriel and Mrs. Campanello.

"How much longer did you say will Mercury be in retrograde?" I asked anxiously.

"Oh, another ten days," Max said. "I wonder if the IRS will stop harassing me then? Or at least make more sense?"

"You want I should take care of this little problem for you?" Lucky offered.

"No!" I said sharply, forgetting about my communications problems as I envisioned the implications of Lucky's question. "*I* will look over Max's IRS correspondence when I have time. *You* will stay out of it, Lucky."

Lucky looked annoyed by my tone. "Whatever. Max and I will go downstairs and have a word with Father Gabriel now. Esther, you stay up here and direct all the arrivals to the crypt."

"Of course," I said. "It's how I've always longed to spend a Tuesday evening."

14

After everyone arrived at St. Monica's for the sit-down, I wasted an hour of my life watching wiseguys stuff their faces (and, boy, can wiseguys eat) and listening to them brag about the women they had bedded and the punks to whom they had taught a lesson. Realizing that if I was alive at the age of one hundred, I'd still look back on tonight and regret this squandered hour of my sojourn on this planet, I took Lucky into the stairwell to have a quiet word with him.

"I thought we were here for a sit-down," I whispered.

"This *is* a sit-down," he whispered back.

"No, this is more like a family reunion in hell."

"It's a *process*," Lucky said. "This ain't a meeting between lawyers and accountants, you know. We're blood enemies. You gotta allow time for everyone to get comfortable with each other and get used to makin' eye contact without reaching for their pieces."

"I thought no one brought pieces!" I whispered in alarm.

"Relax, no one did. I searched 'em as they came in. That was a figure of speech."

"Well, it's been an hour. Aren't they comfortable *yet?*"

"It ain't a good idea to rush things," Lucky said. "Anyhow, officially, Danny's the one who called for this sit-down. So protocol is, it's up to him to bring up our mutual business."

"Our 'mutual business'?" I repeated sharply. "You mean the killings, Lucky?"

My tone annoyed him again. "*Madonna*, you're edgy tonight. Maybe you shoulda stayed home."

"No, I'm just wondering how you could have . . ." I bit my lip and reined in my temper. Lucky's ruthless murder of Elena's husband was not a subject to be discussed in whispers in the stairwell and under these circumstances. "Never mind. Let's go back in." I avoided his eyes and brushed past him.

When we reentered the crypt, my gaze sought out Max, who was sitting with Father Gabriel. The priest seemed to be accepted here as a sort of referee. And Lucky had been right to insist that Max and I adjust our appearances. I looked exactly the way the Corvinos (and most other wiseguys) thought a woman should look, so they found me unthreatening and accepted my presence though the avid ogling of the two Corvino soldiers made me feel self-conscious. (The Gambello soldiers, who knew I was dating a cop, averted their eyes from my tight outfit.) Meanwhile, the only comment that Max's appearance inspired was an unabashed compliment from Tommy Two Toes on his snazzy ensemble.

Max and I had been introduced to the others as friends of Lucky's. This was no casual phrase among wiseguys, I knew that much. It meant Lucky was vouching for us, guaranteeing that we were trustworthy people. Mobsters took such a voucher very seriously; if we turned out to be rats, snitches, or trouble, then this introduction could cost Lucky his life. I tried to be touched by his faith in us, but I could only think of him murdering a Corvino for the sin of falling in love and getting married.

While the wiseguys conversed and stuffed their faces

(how could they *still* be hungry?), Max got up and of-fered (yet another) plate of prosciutto and cheese to Nelli, who began gobbling it eagerly as soon as he set it on the floor for her. I suspected her digestive system would make him regret this benevolence around three o'clock in the morning.

The wiseguys were talking about money. That was what wiseguys often talked about at Bella Stella, too. It was their favorite subject.

"So then this *gavone* at the car dealership," Tommy Two Toes said to everyone, winding up for the punchline of the seemingly endless anecdote he had been telling, "says to Little Paulie that he 'knows some people,' and he tries to offer Little Paulie a knockdown loan—from the family!"

Lucky silently crossed the crypt to make himself a cappuccino, but the five other gangsters present, includ-ing Tommy, guffawed loudly. Father Gabriel looked at Max, and Max looked like he wanted to ask what a "knockdown loan" was. Since he didn't, though, I gath-ered that Lucky had advised him not to ask such ques-tions. All I knew was that there were different kinds of loans, with different kinds of outrageously high interest rates (known as "vig" or "vigorish") and different kinds of punishment if the borrower failed to repay on time.

As the laughter died down, Nelli finished eating her prosciutto and walked across the room to gaze longingly at the cannoli tray.

Lucky, who was standing nearby, asked, "Doc Zadok, is it okay if I give her one of those?"

"Hey, you shouldn't oughta give no sugar to a dog," said Jimmy "Legs" Brabancaccio, the other man, besides Tommy, who had joined Lucky here tonight to represent the Gambello crime family. Jimmy had nearly stormed out of the crypt upon learning there was no wine, but Lucky had calmed him down. "Sugar is bad for a dog's pinkies or somethin'."

"I think you mean pancreas," I said absently.

"Pancreas? Yeah, that's it!" Jimmy Legs looked at me with newfound respect.

Lucky shrugged and said to Nelli. "Sorry. We gotta keep you healthy. You got important work to do in this dimension, helping protect the city from Evil."

I realized that Max had *also* explained some traditions during the afternoon he and Lucky had spent together.

Nelli whined and gazed imploringly at Lucky. After a moment, he gave in and slipped her a pastry.

"What are ya doin'?" said Jimmy Legs. "You're gonna make that dog sick."

"Just one won't hurt her," said Lucky. "Everything in moderation. Ain't that right, Danny?"

Danny "the Doctor" Dapezzo's cold, sharklike eyes met Lucky's. "That's right."

Danny had been accompanied here tonight by Mikey Castrucci and Fast Sammy Salerno. They were both thick-necked Corvino soldiers with short dark hair, loud shirts, casual pants, and gold jewelry. Danny, a balding capo who looked about fifty-five, had a trim build, maintained good posture while the others slouched, and was dressed with tidy propriety: brown trousers, a pale shirt, a brown tie, and a tan sport jacket. He ate sparingly, spoke quietly, and lectured the other men at the table about diet and exercise. At a casual glance, he would blend into the woodwork or disappear in a crowd. But after watching those cold eyes for a while, I found it all too easy to believe that he had developed a high skill level at cutting fresh corpses into small pieces.

As the conversation continued, Jimmy Legs passed around a photo of his new love—a snazzy boat he'd recently acquired.(Not bought; acquired.)

Lucky accepted the photo, stretched out his arm to hold it farther away, and squinted at it. "Not bad."

"Not bad?" Jimmy repeated, offended. "She's a beauty!"

"Give it here," Danny the Doctor said, reaching into his pocket for a pair of reading glasses. As he put them on, he said, "You're getting old, Lucky, you should get a pair of these."

Lucky shrugged off the comment and petted Nelli, who burped at him.

Danny studied the photo and said, "Yeah, I used to have a little boat like this, before I upgraded."

Jimmy's predictable response was interrupted by Fast Sammy, who said to Danny, "Hey, ain't those glasses new boss? They look good."

"I hate them," Danny said curtly, handing the photo back to Jimmy. He took off the offending spectacles and gave them a contemptuous glance before putting them back in his pocket. "But my old ones are missing, goddamn it. Those frames were *real* gold, you know."

Mikey Castrucci, speaking with his mouth full, looked at the rack of costumes along the far wall and said, "So what's with all the fuckin' bunny costumes?"

"The children wore them in our Easter play," Father Gabriel said.

"That's fuckin' stupid," said Mikey. "When did you ever see a fuckin' *pink* rabbit? For real, I mean?"

"My six-year-old granddaughter was in that play," Danny said quietly. "And she was adorable, so watch your goddamn language."

Mikey shrugged. "I'm just saying, boss. In nature, there ain't no such thing as a pink bunny, so why—"

"Shut the fuck up," Danny ordered.

Mikey complied.

Although Corvinos and Gambellos rarely ate in the same restaurants, apparently the church was neutral enough turf that members of both families could be parishioners without violence breaking out in the middle of Mass.

"Yo, buddy," said Fast Sammy to Max, who was telling Nelli apologetically that the prosciutto was all gone now. "Uh . . . Doc Zadok, right?"

"Sure."

"What the hell kind of a dog is that, anyhow?"

"Well, she ain't precisely a dog." Max did not sound like a wiseguy. He sounded like Lord Peter Wimsey or Sir Percy Blakeney (a.k.a. the Scarlet Pimpernel)—some fictional historical aristocrat with a man-about-town speech affectation. And his slight Eastern European accent made the overall effect seem almost surreal. "She's actually my fa—"

"She's part Great Dane," I said quickly. "And part, um . . . we're not really sure."

As the men looked my way, Mikey and Fast Sammy gazed lasciviously at my legs. I considered telling them I was dating a cop.

"So she isn't a purebred animal?" asked Danny Dapezzo.

"No," I said.

"I only have purebreds in my house," Danny said fastidiously.

"Whatever," said Max.

Busy enjoying another cannoli that Lucky had just slipped her, Nelli ignored us all.

"Why are parts of her blue?" Tommy Two Toes asked.

"There was a slight accident in Doc Zadok's laboratory a couple of days ago," said Lucky, reddening a little. "The mess ain't worn off the dog yet."

My own blue stains had finally faded. But I washed regularly with soap and water, and I doubted Nelli did.

"You should be more careful where you let your mongrel roam," Danny said to Max.

"Bite me," said Max.

Danny rose to his feet with menace on his cold face. "*What* the fuck did you just say to me, you prick?"

Max looked at Lucky in confusion, obviously wondering why one of his newly-acquired phrases had caused such offense.

"Hey, you insulted the guy's dog," Lucky said to Danny. "You expect Max to just take that from you? With the dog sittin' right *here*?"

Danny glanced from Max to Lucky to Nelli. His eyes were like a snake's, beady and empty of expression. After a long, tense moment, he said to Max, "You overreacted."

"Sure," said Max.

"I'll give you a pass. This time." Danny sat back down and added, "What the fuck did you bring a dog to sit-down for, anyhow?"

"She's necessary for our business tonight," Lucky said.

"How is a *dog* necessary?"

"Are you opening the floor for discussion?"

Danny grunted. "Yeah. Enough of this bullshit. I'm opening the floor." He cleared his throat, glanced at Jimmy Legs and Tommy Two Toes, then looked at Lucky again. "We want to make it clear, before any unnecessary and unjust retribution occurs, we got nothing to do with the unfortunate hits that your family has experienced. As God is my witness, no Corvino had a hand in these deaths." He crossed himself.

Father Gabriel, looking uncertain about the etiquette, crossed himself, too.

"Why should we believe you?" Lucky asked.

"What would we gain from these hits?" Danny challenged.

"One of our capos is dead, and he was a good earner. The don's nephew is dead, so the boss is in mourning."

"Like I said, what do *we* gain from any of that?"

"You think if we get distracted by a few mysterious hits," Lucky said, "there'll be an opening for you to move up and become the number one family in this town."

"We *are* the number one family in this town," Danny shot back.

"In your dreams!" said Tommy Two Toes.

"Watch your mouth, you *babbo*," Mikey Castrucci snapped.

"Whoa, hang on," said Lucky. "Danny and me is senior here, we'll do the talking."

Danny cast an angry glare over the assembled group and said, "Let's stick to the point." He looked at Lucky. "We ain't done these hits, and we ain't seekin' another war with the Gambellos."

"Okay, let's say for a minute that I believe you," said Lucky.

"Really?" blurted Fast Sammy.

Danny hit him in the head. "Go on, Lucky."

"I'm gonna cut right to the chase and ask you a real specific question, Danny."

"I got nothin' to hide."

"Have you seen your own perfect double lately?"

There was a puzzled silence. Then Danny said, "Huh?"

"Although my boss thinks you guys probably did these hits and we should just wipe you off the city map once and for all . . ." Lucky shrugged, ignoring the muttered curses of the three Corvinos at the table. He pulled out a chair and sat down, too. "We got an alternative theory about these hits that we want to discuss. And my friend Doc Zadok is the one who's gotta explain it to you."

Recognizing his cue, Max stood up, straightened his tie and adjusted the rakish angle of his fedora. "Thank you, Lucky." He looked around the room for a moment, then punched his fist into the air and said, "Yo, fellows! Listen up!"

I blinked.

"Oops, I nearly forgot. Before we begin," Max said, "I need to ask: Are any of you Lithuanian?"

"Lithu*what?*" said Jimmy Legs.

"To be clear, I have absolutely nothing against Lithuanians," Max assured them. "Well, not personally. But there are certain professional boundaries which I am honor bound to respect."

Danny the Doctor looked at me. "Are *you* Lithuanian? I know you ain't Italian, anyhow."

"No, the Diamonds came from Russia," I said. "A century ago."

Max had a thing about Lithuanians. It had come up before a few times, and I had meant to ask about it, but it tended to slip my mind when stumbling across, oh, doppelgangsters and evil sorcerer's apprentices. Anyhow, I vaguely had the impression that, for Max, being Lithuanian was sort of like belonging to a different *famiglia*.

"Relax, pal. Everyone here is Italian," said Danny. "Except for Miss Russki, that is."

"Very well, then. Er, I mean to say, sure. Whatever." Max cleared his throat. "Yo, fellows, there's an evil entity in town that's whacking guys on both sides of the street, whether they're Gambellos or Corvinos," he began. "Now look at me. Look right at me. Good. This is not like any other hitter you've ever, um, mattressed against. This hitter's got juice like you ain't never imagined. You had better respect what I'm saying."

Max paused to consult his notes.

I wanted to look away, but I couldn't. There was a kind of excruciating fascination to his performance.

"I'm going to explain what you don't know about these hits," he told the wiseguys. "And then we will talk about, er, some suitable precautions that I strongly feel are advisable."

As Max laid out the facts about Charlie's and Johnny's doppelgangsters, the strange ways the victims had died, and what we believed we understood so far about the doppelgänger phenomenon that was occurring here in the city, the bewildered revulsion on the wiseguys' faces changed to open skepticism.

"Whoa. Whoa. *Whoa*," said Mikey Castrucci. "You're saying you met with Johnny Be Good *after* he was dead?"

"That's right," said Max. "So you can understand why we thought this phenomenon worthy of investigation."

Mikey shoved his chair away from the table. "That's it. I'm outta here."

As the gangster stomped out of the crypt, Max said, "Nelli? If you please."

In a frightening burst of speed for so large a beast, Nelli leaped across the room, jumped on Mikey, and knocked him down to the floor. He screamed in terror. Except for Lucky, everyone in the room jumped to his feet.

Tail wagging, Nelli started sniffing Mikey all over.

Obviously afraid to go near an unpredictable dog that big, Danny demanded, "What the fuck is going on? What is that mutt doing?"

Nelli paused in her task long enough to glance at Danny with open dislike. Then, enormous ears flopping, she went back to examining Mikey.

"Yo, listen up," Max said. "I have instructed Nelli to frisk you guys."

"We *been* frisked!" protested Fast Sammy. "So you know we ain't packin' heat!"

"I ain't looking for your heaters," said Max. "I'm attempting to ascertain if any of you is a doppelgangster."

Nelli finished sniffing Mikey, then turned her back on him and returned to Max's side.

"So," Danny said. "I guess he's not a dopp . . . whatever."

"Doppelgangster," said Max. "No. At least, we hope not. In truth, Nelli's never encountered one, and she's very new to this dimension, so we're not positive she can identify one. But it does seem worth trying, don't you agree?"

Danny guffawed. "You think one of those doppelgangsters is *here?*"

"It's certainly possible," said Max.

"This is bullshit!" Mikey Castrucci hauled himself off the floor, dusted himself off, and stormed out of the crypt, radiating wounded pride.

Lucky looked at Danny, who did not stop his subordinate from departing. "Are *you* staying?"

"Hell, yes," said Danny. "I ain't heard anything this funny since Bob Hope passed away. Hey, make my day and tell me he's been doppelgangstered, too. What I wouldn't give to see him perform again! I *loved* that guy!"

Who would have guessed that Danny the Doctor had a sense of humor?

Fast Sammy said to Danny, "Come on, boss, this Zadok guy is a whack job."

"Shut the fuck up," said Danny. "I'm enjoyin' myself."

Since it wouldn't look good to leave the capo alone at a sit-down with three Gambellos, Fast Sammy grumbled but stayed in his chair.

"Now what?" Danny prodded.

"Now," Max said, "Nelli will frisk everyone here, while I finish what I was saying before that *babbo* created a commotion and left."

"Watch you your mouth," Danny warned.

"Madonna," Max said.

So Nelli walked around the room sniffing everyone, which Danny found quite amusing. And he couldn't contain his hilarity when Max reached the crux of the matter.

"Me? *Me?* A doppelgangster of Johnny told you he'd met a doppelgangster of *me?*" Danny laughed so hard that his beady eyes watered. "Oh, no! Oh, my God! It's too good!"

When Max explained that we'd had some concerns until Nelli examined him, that *he* could be the doppelgangster, I thought Danny would fall off his chair laughing.

"I assure you, my dear fellow . . . er, buddy," said Max, "this is not a laughing matter."

"You're killing me!" Danny cried, pressing his hands over his stomach as if it ached, while he continued to laugh uproariously.

He had not struck me as a mirthful person. I guess you never can tell.

"The only reason we're having a sit-down with you, you *schmendrick*," Lucky said in exasperation, "is that if your doppelgangster *is* out there somewhere, then we're willing to believe you guys ain't behind these hits."

"So we need . . ." Max sighed, sat down, and took off his hat. Since the sit-down was going so far off course anyhow, he evidently decided to abandon his attempts to establish a Mafia persona to make the wiseguys feel more comfortable with him. "Oh, dear. I must not be explaining this crisis with sufficient clarity."

Father Gabriel patted Max on the shoulder. "I can see you're in deadly earnest, Dr. Zadok. But, well, surely you three must realize how absurd this sounds?"

"If we'd had any doubts before," I said, "I think we certainly realize it now."

"I'm telling you, Danny," said Lucky, "this is serious business. We came here tonight to warn you. We think you're marked for death."

Danny sputtered with renewed laughter. "Oh, Lucky! I wish we weren't blood enemies! I'd always heard you was a fun guy, but I had no *idea!*"

Max added, "Please, Mr. Dapezzo, we truly believe your perfect double is roaming the city preparing to curse you."

"Hoo, hoo, haw, haw, mwa-ha-ha-ha-ha-HA!"

Max rubbed his brow. "I'm not communicating this very well."

I said, "You did fine, Max. It's just, er, not being received as we had hoped."

Max sighed, met my gaze, and nodded. "Mercury Retrograde. I should have realized what could happen."

After Danny left, red-faced with mirth and gasping for air, we discovered he had dropped the piece of paper we had given to him with Max's and my phone numbers written on it in case he couldn't reach Lucky at a crucial moment. When we spotted it on the floor, I grabbed it and ran upstairs, hoping to catch Danny. He and Fast Sammy were outside the church and getting into their car—which Mikey Castrucci was driving, and which was waiting curbside for them—when I caught up with Danny.

I pressed the piece of paper with our phone numbers into Danny's hand, reiterated our warning, and urged him to call us if he saw anything unusual.

He cracked up again, and was still laughing as his car rolled away from St. Monica's.

Back down in the crypt, Tommy Two Toes and Jimmy Legs looked like they thought Lucky had lost his mind. However, he was a Gambello and had seniority, so they hadn't contradicted him in front of Danny, and they didn't say anything in front of Max and me, either.

After the two gangsters left, Father Gabriel brought a bottle of wine downstairs—from his personal stash, I supposed—and offered to share it with Lucky, Max, and me. We accepted with gratitude. Lucky was annoyed with the Corvinos, Max was discouraged, and my nerves were frayed. So I enjoyed the mellow warmth of the Sicilian red wine as it slid down my throat and into my belly, soothing me.

"Well, perhaps there was one productive result to the evening," Max said, trying to regain some of his habitual optimism.

"Oh?"

"I thought the Corvinos seemed very sincere in their assurances that they're not behind these murders."

"Of course they seemed sincere, Max. They're wiseguys." I glared at Lucky. "Professional liars."

"What did *I* do?" Lucky snapped.

"We don't have enough time tonight to talk about what you did," I said coldly. I also didn't have the energy right now.

"Huh?" Lucky frowned. "What is with you tonight?"

"Esther does have a point," said Father Gabriel. "Logically, what would the Corvinos do but deny involvement in these hits?"

I said to the priest, "You think they're just stalling? Trying to create a window of time for hitting more Gambellos before there's any retaliation?"

Father Gabriel said, "Doesn't that make more sense than anything else?"

"But it doesn't explain why they—or *someone*—has involved doppelgangsters," said Max.

"Yes, well, as for that ..." Father Gabriel looked apologetic. "I'm sorry. You're intelligent people, and you seem convinced and sincere, but it just sounds so fantastic."

"Oh, really? But transubstantiation," I said testily, "when bread and wine become the body and blood of Christ, while still looking and tasting exactly like bread and wine ... *That* seems perfectly reasonable to you?"

There was an awkward silence, and I realized I'd offended the priest. I was about to apologize, but Father Gabriel smiled awkwardly, rose from his chair, and said, "Pardon me. It's late; I should start closing up the church."

"Nice goin'," Lucky said, as soon as the priest left the room.

"Nerves," I said shortly. "I'll apologize to him."

"I think that was your chance, and you just missed it."

"I need this from *you*," I said, "of all people?"

"Me 'of all people'? What's *that* supposed to mean?"

"Let's not quarrel among ourselves," Max said firmly. "We have enough problems to confront without adding that to the list."

Lucky snorted. "Max is right." He raised his hands in a gesture that indicated he was backing away from the argument.

Calming down, I looked at him curiously. "Why do *you* believe in the doppelgangsters, Lucky?"

"Huh?"

"I don't mean *now*," I clarified. "After all, you were there, too, talking to Johnny after—as we now know—he was already dead. I mean, why did you believe at first, as quickly as I did, that there was something supernatural going on?"

Max said, "As I've noted before, there really is no such thing as 'supernatural,' all phenomena are natural, but some—"

"Not now, Max," Lucky and I said in unison.

I continued, "When I met Max, I was reluctant to believe in this sort of thing until he forced my eyes open and I saw things I couldn't deny or explain any other way.

"But, as Max taught me, most people rationalize phenomena like this according to the conventional wisdom they've been taught. And if such explanations are inconsistent, then they find reasonable excuses for that. Like the Widow Giacalona. She thinks we're mistaken about when we saw Johnny's apparition—it must have been Johnny himself and we're just confused. That's how most people view events like this, and why they have no notion of the world that Max and his colleagues inhabit and the work that they do.

"You, on the other hand . . ." I shook my head. "You were quick to realize something mystical was going on as soon as I told you about Charlie's fears of a perfect double and the evil eye. And when we met Max and you saw what goes on in his laboratory . . . well, you seem faster than most people to accept the unusual for what it really is." Faster than Lopez, certainly.

Lucky shrugged. "Well, I was raised a strict Catholic, and there's a lotta mysticism in the Church, y'know. Like Father Gabriel, for example, I believe in transubstantiation."

"I'm sorry," I said. "I was being testy."

"Yes, you were. But you're Jewish, so you ain't expected to believe in our rituals, just like we ain't expected to believe in yours. I spent a lot of time in Mickey Rosenblum's home when we was growin' up, so I know how superstitious Jews are, too." He shrugged. "Anyhow, more to the point, I was raised by my grandmother, who was a *strega* from Sicily."

"A what?"

"A *strega*. A witch."

"Ah," Max said with interest. "A white witch, I assume?"

"Yeah, sure. But she was willing to put the screws on people she thought were bad. And she raised me with a lotta the knowledge and memories she brought over from Sicily, where this kind of thing was more accepted in her day. So I guess it gave me some insight that not everybody has got."

"Indeed," Max said. "And we're very fortunate to have your expertise and dedication devoted to this matter, my dear fellow."

Lucky sighed. "Didn't help much tonight."

"So what do we do now?" I wondered. "Just hope no one else gets duplicated?"

"Well, I, for one," said Max, "am planning a long night of reading Germanic texts. It should be most invigorating. Especially since my High Middle German isn't what it used to be. I look forward to renewing my acquaintance with the language."

"Doc, you're just a party animal," Lucky said. "There ain't no containing you."

I said, "Maybe I'll just, oh, go home, go to bed, and hope for a full eight hours of sleep for a change."

"Me, too," said Lucky.

"And while wisely preparing for the worst, we should

nonetheless strive for optimism," Max said. "It is possible, after all, that poor Chubby Charlie and Johnny Be Good were the only intended victims of these strange events. Perhaps Johnny's doppelgangster misled us, and there never was a duplicate of Doctor Dapezzo. In which case, his mirth over our fears was well-merited."

It was a comforting thought to go home with.

However, the next day, Danny Dapezzo phoned me in a blind panic, his sense of humor all gone. He had just seen his perfect double, and he knew death was coming for him.

15

I was scrubbed clean, well-rested, and flushed with excitement when Lopez arrived the next day for the afternoon we had planned.

With the sit-down over and no word from Lucky, Max, or anyone else since then, I was hoping to have a whole day and night to myself and the attractive man who was admirably persistent in his efforts to date me.

I had gone shopping that morning and stocked my kitchen with romantic delicacies that I couldn't afford, such as champagne, fresh shrimp, French cheese, juicy strawberries, and Belgian chocolate, so that we wouldn't have to go out when we got hungry. I also bought a jumbo package of condoms; ah, yes, the romance of dating in our era. Then I washed my sheets, plumped my pillows, tidied my bedroom, and chose a pretty outfit that, while not sluttily obvious, wouldn't be too difficult for Lopez to remove in a hurry: a simple knit dress, black and short-sleeved, with low-heeled red shoes.

I was so ready to take a new lover that I was quivering by the time I buzzed him into the building, opened my front door, and listened to his footsteps ascending to my apartment with flattering haste.

When he got to the top of the stairs, I saw he was wearing a crisp, pale shirt tucked into blue jeans, and carrying a big paper bag in one arm. He smiled when he saw me. "Hi."

"Hi!" When he reached my door, I asked, "What's in the bag?"

"Tomorrow's breakfast." He slid his free arm around my waist and drew me close for a kiss. "Lox," he whispered against my lips. "Bagels." He kissed me softly. "Cream cheese." A longer kiss. "Coffee. Do you have a grinder?"

"Huh?" I said dizzily.

"I got beans, not ground," he murmured. "It was all they had."

"Huh?"

"The coffee," he breathed against my neck.

"Um . . ." I'd already forgotten the question.

He backed me into the apartment while kissing me, then kicked the door shut behind him. The bag he was carrying interfered with his attempt to pull me closer, and we both laughed.

"Here," I said, "give that to me." I slipped out of his embrace, took the bag, and carried it a few steps into the kitchen. "I speak from bitter experience when I say we don't want to forget about the lox and leave it sitting out all night."

He folded his arms across his chest and leaned one shoulder against the wall, next to where the kitchen phone hung, and watched me as I unpacked the groceries. "Some other guy was generous enough to bring you lox? And here I hoped I'd be the first."

"It was my bat mitzvah party, not a date." I pulled fresh bagels and a rich-smelling bag of roasted coffee beans out of the paper bag. "And it took days to get the odor out of the house."

"Since I can't eat all that fish alone, I hope you've recovered by now. A bar mitzvah is when you're what, thirteen?"

"Yes." I put the smoked salmon and the cream cheese

in the refrigerator. "But 'bar' is for boys. A girl has a bat mitzvah."

"Ah. You see how much I learn by going out with you?"

His coal black hair was shiny, crisp, and a little ruffled from his trip here. The pale shirt showed off the golden dark color of his skin. His blue eyes were sparkling, and his smile was sexy.

I said, "I guess you're here because you cleaned my slate with Detective Napoli?"

"You *know* why I'm here." His look was sultry. I quivered again. But then he said more matter-of-factly, "But, yeah, I talked to Napoli. Everything's okay now. You're not under suspicion, and there won't be a material witness warrant. He wants to question you again—"

"What?" I said in alarm.

"Hey, you witnessed a hit, Esther. Of course he wants to question you again, if only to get your official statement verifying that you didn't see anything that can help us find the killer."

"Oh. Right."

"But I convinced him that you're not lying or concealing anything. So it won't be a hostile interview. And I'll be in the room, too. Okay?"

I nodded. "Okay." And if we stuck specifically to what I saw and heard at the time of Charlie's death, I could leave Lucky, Max, and doppelgangsters out of my statement, which Lopez would certainly prefer.

I finished putting away the groceries and said, "Was it hard work for you to convince Napoli to ease off?"

"Yes." He tilted his head and looked at me through dark lashes. "So come over here and make it worth my while."

"Ah, so there's a price attached to my freedom?"

"Hey, I got Napoli off your back and I brought you lox," he said. "What more do you want?"

"Actually . . ." It took me only a few steps to come toe to toe with him. "I want *plenty* more."

"Oh?" He slid his arms around me. "So just how long will it take to satisfy you?"

"All night." I wrapped my arms around his neck.

"Damn, and it's still only daytime," he murmured, lowering his head to mine. "I can see there's an awful lot of work ahead of me."

"You bet."

After a few minutes of long, slow, hot kisses, my head was reeling and my legs were shaky. Breathing hard and feeling mindless, I leaned against him while he leaned back against the wall.

"You look so good in this dress," he whispered, his rapid breaths mingling with mine. "Now take it off."

"Don't be so lazy," I whispered back. "*You* take it off."

"Mmmm." He started pulling up the hem, stroking my legs while he tugged at the soft material. I caressed his hair and then started unbuttoning his shirt.

The phone rang.

We both stiffened in surprise for a moment, since the phone ringing on the wall was so close to us, then we went back to kissing feverishly.

By the third ring, though, I realized who might be calling. So I turned a little in Lopez's arms, reaching for the nearby phone.

He pulled my hand back to his body. "Ignore it," he whispered.

"No, I . . ." I moaned a little when he kissed me again. "I have to . . . to . . ." The phone kept ringing. "This'll just take—"

"Not now." He pulled my dress up around my hips.

"It might be my agent," I said, evading another head-spinning kiss. I had left more messages for Thack today. "It's important."

"So is this." He kissed my neck and nuzzled my hair.

"I've been trying to talk to him about— Oh!" I gasped when I felt Lopez's touch in a brand new place. "It's an aud ... aud ... *Mmmm*. An audition." When I reached for the phone again, I accidentally knocked the receiver off the wall and sent it clattering to the floor.

A male voice on the other end of the line squawked, "Hello? Hello! *Hello?*"

Lopez sighed, leaned his head against the wall, and let me go.

"This will be quick," I promised breathlessly, stooping down to pick up the phone.

"Yes, it will," he vowed, sliding his arms around me from behind as I put the receiver to my ear.

He kissed my neck while I said, "Hello?"

"Esther? Esther Diamond? Is that you?"

I frowned, realizing it wasn't Thack. "Yes, this is Esther."

Lopez nibbled on my earlobe and slid his hand slowly across my stomach.

"Did you send this thing after me?" the caller demanded shrilly.

"Huh?"

"Is this *your* doing?"

"What?" I closed my eyes, torn between my caller's obvious distress and what Lopez was doing. "Oooh."

"I saw it! I just saw my perfect double!"

I stiffened and gasped, but not, alas, because of the delicious way Lopez was trying to regain my full attention.

"*What* did you say?" I said, realizing who was on the other end of the line.

"You heard me, you bitch!" shouted Danny the Doctor. "Did *you* send this thing after me?"

Lopez raised his head, having heard the agitated volume, if not the specific words.

"No, of course not," I said. "I tried to warn you. To *help* you."

"In that case, what the fuck do I do now?" Danny shouted.

Well aware of the arms that were still wrapped around me, and the cop ears that I could tell were now listening to my half of the conversation, I said carefully, "Am I the first person you've called?"

"No! You think I'd call a *girl* first?" Danny said contemptuously. "But Lucky's line is busy and the Doc ain't answering his phone!"

Max couldn't hear his phone from his laboratory, which was where he probably was right now.

"All right," I said. "Tell me where you are. I'll meet you there and I'll take you to a safe—"

"I don't want *you*. I want Lucky! No! *No!* I want the weird guy, the one who knows all about this shit! The Doc! And I want to know what the fuck to *do!*"

"The first thing you have to do is calm down," I said sharply. "Get a hold of yourself."

Lopez's arms fell away from me as he realized this was a serious matter. Anxious to avoid his perceptive gaze, I kept my back turned to him as I continued the conversation.

Danny shouted, "You find that weird old guy, and you bring him to me! Do you hear me?"

"Yes."

"You tell him I want protection from that ... that *thing!* That doppelgangster!"

"All right," I agreed. "I need to know where you are."

"Why? So you can have that thing whack me?" He sounded close to hysterics.

"So I can bring—" Remembering that Lopez was standing right behind me, I rephrased what I'd been about to say. "So I can do what you've asked."

"I ain't *asking*, I'm *telling* you!"

Danny seemed intent on making it hard for me to *want* to save his life.

"Understood," I said. "So where can I find you?"

"I'm goin' to the mattresses!"

"And where would *that* be?" I prodded.

"Can that doppelgangster tap phone calls?"

"No." At least, I didn't think so.

"I'm gonna be in my cousin Vinny's ventilated wine vault. Safest place in the world. There's a steel door with a combination lock. Nothing and no one can get to me there."

"Where is it?"

"It's in the cellar of Vinny's wine shop, you dumb broad!"

I scowled. "Which would be *where?*"

He gave me an address in Brooklyn Heights. Since Lopez was watching me, I memorized it rather than writing it down. "Okay, I'll be there as soon as possible."

"You bring the Doc," Danny ordered again.

"Yes. Absolutely." Since I suspected Danny would be heavily armed when we arrived, I added, "And I beg you to stay calm."

"Are you *nuts?*"

"This is no time to panic," I said firmly.

"I just been cursed with death by a doppelgangster! If ever there was a time to panic, it's *now*."

As he slammed the phone down on me, I supposed he had a point.

With a sigh, I hung up the receiver and turned to face my would-be lover. "I'm really sorry about this," I began.

"Something bad has happened," he guessed.

"I have to go. Right now," I said. "I'm so sorry."

"Shh. It's okay. Take a breath." He put his hands on my shoulders. "I'll come with you."

"What? No!" Seeing his surprise at my horrified reaction, I took that breath, as he had advised. Then I tried to pull my scattered thoughts together. "That's not a good idea."

"Let me help you." His face was serious, his gaze earnest, his sex drive forgotten for the moment.

I silently cursed the Evil that was dragging me away from this man right now.

I wanted to avoid lying to Lopez. So, choosing my words carefully, I said, "I can't bring a stranger with me. It wouldn't be appreciated."

"Then I'll wait outside for you, or in a cab or something."

I shook my head. "No, this will take a while."

"Esther—"

I kissed him. After a moment of surprised immobility, he slid his arms around me and kissed me back. I knew it was a dirty trick, kissing him so he'd stop talking about this; but it certainly wasn't as if I didn't want to kiss him. And go right on kissing him. For hours.

While we kissed, I tried to calculate how long it would take me to go get Max, go to Brooklyn, pry Danny Dapezzo out of his cousin Vinny's wine vault, and get him back to the bookstore in the Village. At which point, I would cheerfully abandon Lucky and Max to question Danny about the doppelgangster and come up with a plan of action, while I returned to my interrupted plans with Lopez.

I *tried* to calculate it, but it wasn't possible to think while Lopez was kissing me. Not possible at all.

Trying to regain my breath when he let me go, I settled for saying, "Look, this should only take a few hours. We'll meet here again tonight, okay?"

At that point, I decided, I would have to tell him the truth about where I had gone today—and why. But right now, I was in a hurry and didn't have time for the big argument I knew we'd have. So the truth would have to wait until tonight.

"Okay," Lopez said, "I'll come back tonight. But, look, are you sure I can't even—"

I kissed him again. Quickly this time. "I have to go."

He hesitated for a moment, obviously puzzled and probably wanting to ask if my caller had been Max, but then nodded. "Okay."

"The fact that you never sulk is one of my favorite things about you," I said suddenly.

He smiled and touched my cheek. "You don't sulk, either. And dating a cop isn't easy."

"That much is true."

I picked up my purse and walked through the front door as he held it open for me. I locked the apartment, and we went down the stairs together. Once outside, he put his arm around me as we walked to Tenth Avenue, where he hailed a cab for me. When a taxi stopped next to us, Lopez opened his mouth to give the driver the address of my destination, then realized he didn't know where I was going. He looked at me in silent query.

"I'll see you tonight." I kissed him once more and hopped into the cab. To my relief, it instantly squealed away from the curb, as if fleeing deadly danger.

It took a few minutes to convince Max we'd never find a taxi driver willing to take Nelli to Brooklyn Heights with us, and we must therefore leave her behind. And once the two of us were finally in a cab and heading toward the bridge, we encountered heavy traffic; many of the downtown bars and restaurants were doing their midweek stocking up of food and alcohol for the coming weekend, so the narrow streets were clogged with parked delivery trucks. Then, to top it off, there was an accident in Brooklyn that caused traffic to back up onto the bridge, where we sat for twenty minutes.

After several tries, I finally reached Lucky on his cell phone. He had been in Queens, and now he was on his way to Brooklyn to help Danny. As Max and I sat in traffic, Lucky told me he'd been calling Danny without getting any response.

"Well, he said he was going to lock himself in a vault," I reminded Lucky. "His cell phone probably isn't getting a signal in there."

"Let's hope that's all it is."

"Call me when you get there. We're still stuck on the bridge." After I hung up, I said to Max, "We should have taken the subway, we'd be there by now."

Since we weren't moving at all, Max was fairly calm. "I propose we walk."

I nodded and said to the driver, "We're getting out here."

He gave me a horrified look. "You can't do that!"

I sighed. "I know you were counting on the meter running up to an astronomical sum while we sit here, but this is an emergency. We can't dawdle. A human life is at stake."

"Oh, come on, lady."

"Also," I said, "we'll tip you well."

"Yeah?"

I muttered to Max, "How much cash did you bring?"

"Is one hundred dollars sufficient to cover our obligation?" he asked me.

"That's way too much," I said.

"That's perfect!" The cab driver snatched the hundred dollar bill from Max. "Thanks, buddy! You folks have a nice day."

"Hey!" I said.

"No, Esther, we have more urgent concerns than mere money." Max opened the door, exited the cab, and extended his hand to me.

I didn't know if he had invested wisely over the past three hundred years or if the Magnum Collegium—the secret, ancient, worldwide organization that had sent him here paid him well. Either way, he always seemed to have a healthy cash flow. So since he didn't want to fight with the driver about the money, I let it go.

The wind on the bridge whipped my dress around my legs as we walked above the East River and toward Brooklyn Heights.

"You look very nice, by the way," Max said.

"Thanks," I said morosely, recalling why I had worn this clingy black dress and these pretty red shoes today.

Once we reached Brooklyn, we walked south for a few streets to get away from the traffic jam. Then I hailed another cab.

"Oh, *must* we?" Max said with dread.

"Yes, we must," I replied as a taxi pulled up next to us. "Manhattan is the only borough I know well. I haven't the faintest idea how to find this wine shop on foot."

This cab driver, however, didn't know Brooklyn any better than I did. He also didn't speak English. And Max's Russian was rusty, especially when combined with the stress of being in a moving vehicle. So we drove around for quite some time in search of Vino Vincenzo, the wine shop where Danny was hiding.

"There are days when I really hate New York," I muttered.

Just as we found the right street and turned into it—going the wrong way down a one-way street—my cell phone rang. The caller was Lucky.

"I'm here at the wine shop," he said. "But I'm too late."

"What do you mean?"

"Danny's dead," Lucky said.

Our cab rolled to a stop in front of Vino Vincenzo.

"What?"

"Dead," Lucky repeated. "In the cellar."

I half wondered if the gangster had died of old age while we made our epic journey to this spot.

"Are you sure?" I asked.

"I know what a corpse looks like," Lucky pointed out.

"How was he killed?"

"Shotgun."

"How do you know that?"

"I seen it before," he said patiently. "And it's pretty hard to mistake."

"Oh." My head was reeling. "How long ago?

"About ten minutes," said Lucky. "Where are you now?"

"I'm right outside the wine shop. Max is paying our cab driver." I got out of the cab.

"Don't come downstairs. I'll come up. This is not something you should see."

I absorbed that for a moment. Then Max took my elbow, and I said, "All right. We're coming inside now."

I briefly relayed to Max what Lucky had just told me. Whatever had happened here, it hadn't attracted a crowd. There were only a few people on the street, and they were going about their business. A massive young white man with big muscles and short brown hair was guarding the door of the wine shop, blocking the way.

"We're closed, miss," he said as we approached him.

"We're here to see Lucky," I said.

He looked at Max. "You're the Doc?"

"Yes," Max replied.

"Okay, you can go in." He stepped aside long enough to let us pass, then resumed his position.

As we entered the shop, I said to Max, "He should have been standing there all along. Then maybe this wouldn't have happened."

A shaky voice said, "He *was* standing there all along."

I looked at the tidily dressed balding man who had just spoken. He was pale, sweating, and looked queasy. Something about his beady eyes was familiar. "You must be Danny's cousin?"

He nodded. "Vinny Dapezzo." He looked at Max. "You must be the Doc. I've been expecting you. Danny said you'd know what to do." He gulped and started shaking. "And Lucky said there'd be a young lady with a white beard ..."

"Pardon?" Max said.

"Sorry. I mean ... Um ..." Vinny shook his head, as if trying to clear it. "Lucky got here right after it happened. Thank God. I know he's a Gambello, but ... Well, I was a *mess*. So were Danny's boys. We had no idea what to do. I don't, uh ..." He started wringing his hands.

Lucky emerged from the back of the shop. It was an attractive place, elegantly decorated, very upscale, reflecting the expensive neighborhood and the well-heeled professionals who probably shopped here. Everything seemed to be in perfect order. You'd never guess that a notorious mobster was lying dead in the cellar.

"What happened here?" I asked.

Lucky and Vinny started to speak at the same time. Then Lucky said, "You tell it, Vinny. You were here."

Agitated and wiping his damp brow, Vinny Dapezzo nodded. "Danny showed up here this afternoon carrying two Glock semiautomatics and a big supply of ammo. He said someone was after him. So he was going to lock himself in the vault and wait for the Doc. It's ventilated." Vinny paused. "The vault, I mean."

"So he told me," I said.

"I keep the specialty bottles there. That's why I've got the vault. Because the stock in there is so valuable. We do off-the-street retail business, of course, but my real interest is limited editions, rare vintages, and collector's items. So if you're looking for something very special, miss, or if you want a unique gift for—"

"Vinny," Lucky said.

"Oh, my God, I'm babbling, aren't I? Sorry." Vinny looked like he might cry. "Where was I?"

"The vault," I said helpfully.

"Right. Danny said we shouldn't allow anyone into the cellar. Then he said ..." Vinny started swaying a little. For a moment, I thought he might pass out. "This whole thing is so crazy!"

"Take a steady, deep breath," Max said gently, "and give yourself a moment to put your thoughts in order."

Vinny gave Max a grateful look and nodded. After a few slow, calming breaths, he said, "Okay. I'm telling you exactly what happened, even though it sounds nuts."

Max nodded. "Understood."

"Danny said the killer was crafty, ruthless, and might be disguised—might even look just like *him*. Identical. A perfect double." Vinny shook his head. "He was jumpy and confused, not making much sense. He kept babbling in Italian—"

"He talked Italian," Lucky said pointedly to me.

"So this was serious," I guessed.

Vinny continued, "He said something about a *doppio*—"

"A double," Lucky translated.

"—and then, looking scared out of his wits, he started shouting stuff. It didn't make any sense. Stuff like, *'La mia propria faccia nel viso di un altro!'*"

I drew in a sharp breath. "That sounds exactly like what Charlie said to me!"

Vinny asked, "Who's Charlie?"

"Charlie Chiccante," I said.

"Who?"

Lucky said to me, "Vinny ain't in the family business."

"Oh. And I guess you don't read the tabloids?" I said to Vinny, a little pleased.

"Oh, wait a minute! Charlie Chiccante." Vinny nodded. "Yeah, I read about it. Isn't he that Gambello capo who got whacked on Saturday night by a chorus girl with ties to the mob?"

"I didn't whack him," I snapped. "I just *saw* him get whacked!"

Today was Wednesday. I prayed that by the following weekend, some celebrity scandal would make tabloid fans everywhere forget all about me.

"So . . . I don't understand," Vinny said. "Are you saying that Charlie Chiccante and Danny got done by the same hitter?"

Though not in the family business, he'd obviously grown up with the vocabulary.

"We think so," I said. "Lucky, what does that phrase mean? The one that Charlie and Danny both said before dying? *La mia* . . . whatever."

Lucky said, "'I saw my own face on someone else's face.'"

"Doppelgangster," Max said with a nod. "Like poor Chubby Charlie, Danny understood what he had seen."

"Because we tried to warn him," I said.

Vinny looked bewildered. "So that stuff Danny was babbling, that *means* something to you guys? I thought he was just having a stroke or something."

"Believe me, I know exactly how you feel," I said, "Go on, Vinny, what happened next?"

Vinny wiped his glistening forehead, nodded, and made an obvious effort to collect his thoughts.

"Nathan over there, he works for Danny." Vinny pointed to the young man guarding the door. From this angle, I could see that Nathan had a gun tucked into his belt at the small of his back. "Danny left him and Bobby at the entrance there, with instructions to search everyone who came in. *Everyone*. I didn't like it, and I knew the customers would hate it. But, well, Danny's not really a guy you say no to. And he's the one who bankrolled me to open this shop, after all."

"I see that Nathan's still by the door now," I said. "But where's Bobby?"

"With the body," Vinny said. "It didn't seem fitting to, um, leave it lying alone before the priest gets here."

"You called a priest?" I said.

"It's what you do when a guy dies." Vinny glanced at Lucky. "Even a guy like Danny, I guess."

Max said, "So the two young men guarded the door and searched everyone who came in?"

"Actually, no one came in. Middle of the week, slow day. Nothing happened," Vinny said.

I nodded, recalling that the street outside was almost empty when we got here.

"So about an hour passes," Vinny continued. "I'm stocking the shelves, and then . . . *BOOM!*"

I jumped a little.

"Shotgun blast," Lucky said. "Always loud."

"I didn't know what it was at the time," Vinny said. "I just knew it sounded like a cannon and had come from the cellar. So I told Nathan and Bobby to stay by the door and, if asked, say that a wine casket had exploded in the cellar. It's stupid, but it would get rid of people. And I went downstairs. There's only one way in or out of that cellar, and no one had gone past us. So I figured that one of Danny's Glocks had gone off."

"Semiautomatics can be a little jumpy," Lucky said with a nod.

Vinny continued, "I wanted to make sure Danny hadn't shot himself by accident—or, you know, shot a twelve hundred dollar bottle of wine. I called to him through the door a few times. He didn't answer, but that door is pretty thick."

"It's why Danny chose the place," Lucky said.

"I was getting really worried," Vinny said. "I mean, why didn't Danny open the door and tell me that everything was okay, that he'd just misfired by accident? I suddenly thought maybe he *did* shoot himself. Maybe he needed help! So I keyed in the combination to unlock the door, and I opened it." He added, "And the whole time, I was saying, in a loud voice, 'Don't shoot, Danny. It's me. It's Vinny.' Because he'd been, you know, so jumpy. I was pretty nervous, to be honest."

"That's understandable," I said.

"And when I opened the door . . ." Vinny crossed himself. "As God is my witness, this is the truth. There was no one else in the vault. No one else downstairs . . ." His voice started quavering. "And what was left of Danny was lying there in a pool of blood. His face was all gone, his chest was blown to bits, his brains were splattered all over the bottles and—"

"The lady don't need so many details," Lucky said.

"Oh. No. Sorry, miss. I'm just so shaken up, you know?"

"Of course," I said.

"And his Glocks . . ." Vinny shook his head. "Danny's guns were still in their holsters, fully loaded. Untouched."

I looked at Lucky for confirmation.

"They ain't been fired," Lucky said. "Danny didn't get a shot off."

"I don't understand," I said. "How did the killer get past Vinny, Nathan, and Bobby without being seen and then get through a locked steel door? And then how did he vanish so quickly? With a *shotgun?*"

Shaking like a leaf in high wind, Vinny started weeping. "Sorry. It's nerves. Just nerves." He wiped his streaming eyes. "Danny was my cousin, but to be honest, I didn't like him. Not enough to cry over his body, anyhow. But what the hell is going on here?"

Lucky looked at me. "This doppelgangster business is getting to be a real pain in the ass."

16

I didn't want to cause Lopez any more embarrassment, not after he'd gone out on a limb to get Napoli off my back. This meant I didn't want to get my name on any police reports related to Danny Dapezzo's death, since it might be difficult for Lopez to explain to the Organized Crime Control Bureau what his girlfriend was doing at the scene of yet another mob hit.

Lucky was also in favor of avoiding contact with the cops. In fact, he, Bobby, and Nathan were all opposed to reporting Danny's death to the police. However, Vinny was a respectable businessman who had just, through no fault of his own, discovered a violently murdered man in his cellar. Due to his family connections, he was used to looking the other way, he said, but there were limits, and we had just reached them. So he rejected (somewhat hysterically) the three gangsters' plan to cover up the crime, remove Danny's body by stealth, and dump the corpse somewhere in New Jersey.

Max and I sided with Vinny. As I explained quite firmly to Lucky and the Corvino soldiers, I had no intention of becoming an accomplice in concealing a homicide and destroying evidence.

So Lucky, Max, and I left the scene while Vinny was calling 911 to report the shooting.

The three of us were silent all the way back to Manhattan, not wanting to discuss the case within earshot of our cab driver, but too absorbed by the subject to talk about anything else.

When we got to the bookstore, Nelli greeted us with enthusiasm, then stared intently at Max as he related the details of Danny's death to her. While he talked, she drooled a little.

I walked through the bookshop, followed by Lucky, and sank into a cushioned chair near the fireplace. "You really think they won't slip up and mention to the cops that we were there?" I asked Lucky.

"Vinny, Bobby, and Nathan? No, they'll be fine. And even if they do say something—which they won't, so stop worrying—they don't even know your names, after all."

I doubted the absence of my name would keep Napoli off my trail if he got a description of me, and I knew Lopez would quickly realize who "the Doc" was. So I decided to hope the subject just never came up.

"Well," I said, "at least Vinny's story about Danny's death will sound so crazy, the cops will probably be fully occupied with trying to figure out how he died."

Lucky shook his head. "Nah, it's going to sound like what the cops hear all the time when they're poking their noses into mob hits." In response to my puzzled frown, he said, "Nobody saw nothin'."

"Oh," I said as I realized what he meant. *"Oh."*

"They'll think Vinny's just covering up when he claims that a killer with a shotgun got past him and the Corvino soldiers unseen, blew Danny away, and disappeared without a trace." He shrugged. "Business as usual. And you can bet he won't tell them the vault was closed and locked when Danny died. Anyone raised by the Corvinos will know better than to confuse the cops with unnecessary details."

"Hmm." I saw Lucky's point. The story the cops

heard at Vino Vincenzo would sound much more mundane than one *we* had heard. "Poor Vinny. Either way, I think he's in for a very long interview with Detective Napoli."

"Probably. But even though he's pretty shaken up, he knows the score. He won't mention us to the cops." Lucky sat down by the fireplace, too. "And when I called Father Gabriel, I told him to say that Vinny is the one who asked him to come. So he won't drag me into it, either."

"You called Father Gabriel?" I said. "For a death all the way out in Brooklyn?"

"It's one of the five boroughs," Lucky said. "Not exactly a distant region. Anyhow, he was Danny's priest. That's who you call when a guy kicks the bucket—his own priest."

"Oh, really? When you murdered Elena's second husband, did you call *his* priest?"

"No. You don't call for the priest when you're the one who whacked the deceased," Lucky snapped. "When are you going to get off my back about Sally Fatico?"

"Who?" I said blankly.

"Elena's second husband!"

I frowned. "She married a man named Sally?"

"Salvatore."

"Oh."

Max and Nelli came over to the alcove to join us. Nelli had a large rawhide bone in her mouth. Max was carrying a tray with some cookies and coffee cups on it. "I've just started a pot brewing."

"I'm so confused," I said wearily.

"That's understandable," Max said. "The situation is most perplexing."

Nelli lay down and started chewing on her bone.

"I gather that activity helps her think." Max added with a touch of resentment, "In any case, at least it keeps her from chewing on *my* belongings."

"Something's bugging me." Lucky rubbed his forehead. "The way these guys are dying ... in a sense, they're very ordinary hits. Shot through the heart in a restaurant. Hit on the head and dumped in the river. A shotgun in the face. It's work-a-day stuff."

"Oh, good grief," I said in disgust.

"No, let him continue, Esther," Max said.

"What I mean is," Lucky said, with an irritated glance at me, "the killer is either an ordinary wiseguy, or someone who wants us to *think* he's an ordinary wiseguy."

"Oh, well, that narrows it down."

"I really wish your cop boyfriend would do something to put you in a better mood," Lucky grumbled at me.

Before I could reply, Max said, "Let's not quarrel. What are you getting at, Lucky?"

"These hits are exactly how these things are done in our business. Except for ..."

"The mystical elements," Max said.

"Right," Lucky said. "And it's finally occurred to me to wonder why."

"Hmm." Max stroked his beard. "Interesting."

"A person or a thing that can make doppelgangsters and commit impossible murders without even being seen ..." Lucky frowned. "Why aren't the hits ... I dunno. More creative? More original? If you can spook Danny Dapezzo with a doppelgangster and slip unseen through a locked steel door, then why just blow him away with a shotgun, like any dim-witted foot soldier can do?"

"You mean," I said slowly, "why not make his death dramatic enough to match the mystical power behind it? Sort of an Edgar Allan Poe death?"

"A *what* kind of death?"

"The writer, Edgar All—"

"Yeah, I know who he is, I just don't know what you mean."

"He killed off his characters in bizarre, chilling ways," I said, remembering the times I'd left the light on all night after reading Poe. "So, for example, what if we had found Danny's corpse standing upright and staring in horror at the door, with no apparent cause of death? Or what if Charlie had suffocated after being buried alive, instead of getting shot over a plate of pasta?"

"Yeah, that would be scary," Lucky agreed. "That would be like nothing I ever seen before."

"Hmm. So in one sense," Max mused, "these murders are ordinary, mundane. Which is in direct contrast to the rare phenomenon of doppelgängerism—*and* to the unique way it's being employed here. In my reading so far, I have found nothing similar to our problem."

"Nothing at all?" I asked in despair.

He shook his head. "Even where doppelgängers invariably portend death, the demise which follows is relatively normal. There does not seem to be a known form of doppelgängerism whereby murder through seemingly impossible means is the cause of death." He stroked his beard again and nodded. "So while the murders are uncreative and unoriginal, the magic being employed here is *highly* creative and *quite* original. The contrast is striking, now that Lucky has brought it to my attention."

"Which brings us back to the question," I said, "of how someone actually committed Charlie's and Danny's murders. A bullet that went around a corner and hit Charlie right in the heart. There were lots of people present, but no one saw the killer. And then Danny . . ." I shook my head. *"How?"*

"I have a theory," Max said.

"Thank God," I said. "I'm wide open to anything at this point. What's your theory, Max?"

"Let's look at the problem from this perspective for a moment: Why was Danny killed today?" Max said. "Why not yesterday?"

Lucky shrugged. " 'Cuz the killer chose today."

"No, I mean to say, what was different about today?

Last night, after all, Danny found the idea of a doppel-gangster absurdly comical."

"Today," I said, "he saw the thing. And he was terrified."

"He was only terrified, I think," said Max, "because he knew what it meant. He knew because we had told him. Johnny saw his own doppelgangster, but he felt no fear, because he did *not* know what it meant."

"So, whether or not he knows what it means, the victim dies after seeing the doppelgangster. We'd already figured that out," Lucky said.

"But because of the way both Charlie and Danny died," Max said, "I now think there's more to it than that. When we said that upon seeing the doppelgangster, the victim is cursed with death, I think we failed to realize just how thorough the curse is."

"Oh." Lucky's eyes widened. "I think I see where you're goin' with this. These were guys who walked around with the threat of death all the time. An ordinary curse wouldn't really be a change of pace for them."

"Indeed," said Max. "As I understand it, a peaceful retirement is not the norm in your business. It's more common for a member of your profession to die violently and perhaps in his prime."

"Yeah." Lucky grinned. "But me, I been lucky."

"So these were men accustomed to taking precautions to safeguard their lives," Max said. "It was habitual for them. I'll wager that even Johnny Be Good, though he was careless in many ways, carried a firearm for self-protection."

"You bet he did," said Lucky.

"And Danny and Charlie had each reached an age and a rank that suggests they were good at staying alive."

"They were." Lucky nodded.

"This is why I believe the curse placed upon them was a powerful one," said Max. "Extraordinarily powerful. It didn't just sentence them to death. It ensured that *nothing* could prevent their deaths from that point onward. Not witnesses, not being hidden from view at a restaurant, not being in a locked cellar and well-armed. Once the victim was cursed, the killer could strike when and where he pleased."

"So you're saying the killer could stand at the window of Bella Stella's and fire his gun around a corner to kill Charlie, as long as he knew Charlie was in there?" I said. "He could walk right past witnesses like Bobby and Nathan at Vino Vincenzo, and just *will* them not to see him? Then simply open a locked vault to kill Danny, even though he didn't have the combination? And then leave again, still without Vinny and the others seeing him?"

"Yes, that's exactly how I believe this is being achieved," Max said. "The fatal curse imbued in the doppelgangsters made the victims utterly vulnerable to the murderer's deadly intent, no matter what precautions they took."

"Whoa," said Lucky, clearly impressed.

"But the killer is not *normally* invincible," Max said. "These doppelgangsters are quite sophisticated, so making them must cost him enormous energy. Therefore, I postulate that they are essential to his plan. Not to confuse the evidence trail, as we previously discussed. That's obviously useful, since the killer doesn't need an alibi for a murder if the time of death can't be established, but that's a ... a bonus, you might say. An example of how comprehensive our adversary's strategy is."

Max paused in thought for a moment, then continued, "Yes, I now believe each doppelgangster's *primary* function is to curse the victim by making him utterly defenseless against the intended murder. After that, whatever time, place, and method the killer chooses to employ, it is invariably successful. So successful that no obstacle can thwart him and no witness can identify him." Max concluded, "Therefore, once Doctor Dapezzo saw his own doppelgangster today, his death was virtually certain no matter what precautions he took."

"But if the killer is that powerful," I argued, "why go through this elaborate charade with the doppelgangsters? Why not just walk up to the victims, curse them to their faces, and kill them?"

"Well, there's one obvious reason," said Lucky. "He's already killed three people and no one's caught him, and no one can figure out who he is."

"And," I recalled, realizing the full significance of it now, "we got laughed off the stage last night when we tried to explain the danger to his next victim."

"Yes," Max agreed. "These are both excellent points. This method masks his identity, his activities, even his very existence. He calculated that no one would suspect doppelgängerism. And even if they did, he felt confident no one would listen to such a theory."

"He got that right," Lucky said morosely.

"Also," I said, thinking about it, "the whole idea of a doppelgänger is spooky. It creeps me out, it scared Charlie witless, and it terrified Danny. That fear gives the killer psychological power over his intended victims. Maybe inspiring such visceral fear even gives the killer a kick, some sadistic satisfaction."

"Hmm. Interesting point." Max frowned thoughtfully. "This is a subtle plan using innovative tactics, so we should not underestimate our adversary. I doubt that either his motives or his intentions are simplistic. There is something exceptionally . . . *devious* occurring here." Max sniffed the air. "I forgot about the coffee!" He rose to go get it.

When he came back with the pot, I said, "I just thought of something else, Max. We know now that Johnny's doppelgangster was telling us the truth about seeing Danny's doppelgangster."

"Ah, yes! Hmm. So they're not self-aware," Max mused as he poured the coffee. "That is to say, a doppelgangster evidently has no idea it isn't the real individual. Otherwise, why would Johnny's duplicate have told us about seeing another such creature?"

"It acted just like Johnny because it really believed it was Johnny," Lucky said.

"Exactly. Moreover," Max said, "there's an obvious corollary. The doppelgangsters cannot recognize each other."

I gasped. "That's right! When Johnny's double met Danny's double, he was as clueless about its true nature as the real Johnny would have been."

"Jesus, Mary, and Joseph," Lucky said. "Does this mean *I* could be a doppelgangster and not even know it? Or one of you?"

"That reminds me! Danny's death almost made me forget," said Max. "I continued my reading this morning, after a few hours of sleep, and I found the solution to one major aspect of our problem. It turns out that it is childishly simple to identify a doppelgangster!"

I blinked. "It is?"

"Do we need holy water?" Lucky asked. "I know where we can get all we need."

"No, not necessary," Max assured him.

I said, "I thought you were using Nelli to identify doppelgangsters?"

"Alas, until she actually exposes one, we have no way of being sure that she *can* identify these creatures. But according to my reading, we needn't worry."

"Under the circumstances, I'm probably going to keep worrying," I said. "But go ahead and explain. How can we identify a doppelgangster?"

"As we've learned, such a creature is made of ephemeral substances empowered through mystical means. One way in which the duplicates we've encountered fit the classic doppelgänger pattern is that their function is specific and limited. Therefore, all the effort invested in fashioning a doppelgangster goes to its outward appearance and its imitative behavior. For a brief period, it must *seem* to be the real thing, that's all."

"So?" I prodded.

"So its internal mass is undisguised ephemeral matter."

"I got no idea what you're talking about," Lucky said.

"In other words, they're not real people," Max said. "They're mystical in nature. So although you may hear a heartbeat if you get close enough—because this seems to be a very talented and thorough sorcerer who would not neglect such important details—there isn't actually a heart. Or a liver or bones or lungs or soft tissue or blood!" He looked at us triumphantly.

Lucky and I looked blankly at each other for a moment.

"So, Max, you're sayin' we gotta whack someone and open him up to see whether he's a person or a doppelgangster? That don't seem like much of a solution."

"No! No, nothing so extreme. Don't you see?" Max said. "Doppelgangsters don't have blood. They don't bleed!"

"So we gotta *stab* someone we suspect?" Lucky guessed.

"No," Max said. "We just need to, oh, prick him with a needle, for example."

"Oh! I get it now," I said. "We only need to do enough damage to see whether someone bleeds like a normal human being?"

"Exactly!" Max said. "If you prick someone's finger with suitable emphasis, and there's no sign whatsoever of blood, you've just found a doppelgangster."

"And once we find one," I said, "how do we, uh, neutralize it?"

"Oh, that's easy. We simply decapitate it."

"What?"

Max added, "From now on, we should keep large bladed weapons handy at all times for this purpose."

"Max!"

"It won't be like human decapitation, my dear," he said reassuringly. "Remember, doppelgangsters don't bleed or have any connective tissue."

"That's not the point!" I rubbed my hand over my face. "At least, it's not the *main* point. If we're going to cut off someone's head, we'd better be damn sure the individual in question really *is* a doppelgangster!"

"Oh, yes," Max agreed. "Yes, indeed."

"*Damn* sure, Max!"

He nodded and patted my hand. "That's why it's so important to prick someone and check for blood before you attempt decapitation, Esther."

"*I* can't decapitate someone!" I said, aghast.

"Strictly speaking, you won't be decapitating some-*one*," Max said, "but rather some*thing*."

"Either way, I can't do it," I insisted.

"Don't worry about it, kid. I'll take care of it. I'm used to it." Lucky added to Max, "It's not something a young lady should do."

"Perhaps you're right," Max said.

"But we're *all* gonna have to learn to identify doppel-gangsters," Lucky said firmly.

Feeling rather frazzled, I said, "Maybe we should get a test kit for diabetics. They have to prick themselves enough to bleed, don't they?"

"I've always got a couple of knives on me. For backup," Lucky said, reaching into one of his pockets. "I'll give you one. That'll do the job better than a needle."

"I don't think I want a knife," I said doubtfully.

"There's three guys dead, and we got no other way of identifying these creatures."

"Okay, I'll take a knife," I said. "You have a way of putting things into perspective."

"Here, have this one. It's small, a good size for a woman." He gave me a switchblade that seemed like some sort of stealth weapon. The curved blade was a dull gray color and barely two inches long. "You'd better start by using it on me."

"What?" I blurted.

"I feel perfectly normal," Lucky said. "But we've already figured out that every doppelgangster thinks it's for real. So before we do anything else, we better make sure nobody here is one of them things."

"Does that mean you're going to cut *me?*" I asked anxiously.

"Yep. Don't worry, I'm an expert, you won't feel a thing." He offered me his hand, palm up. "But since only wiseguys have been duplicated so far, I'm the most likely ringer in the room. So go ahead and make sure I really am who I think I am."

Grasping the little knife, I took Lucky's hand in mine, brought the sharp, dull-colored blade close to his flesh ... and then said, "I can't do it."

"Go on," he urged.

"I've never cut someone. I don't know how."

"It's just like cuttin' meat."

"Oh, God," I said, revolted. "That didn't help."

"Take the point of the knife and poke my finger."

I tried again, then shook my head. "I can't do it."

"I can see you really are gonna have trouble decapitating an ephemeral mystical creature," he said. "Come on, just do it, kid. Hey, I got an idea. Think about Salvatore Fatico."

That helped. I poked the blade into his finger.

"Ouch!" Lucky said. "Not so hard!"

"Oops! Sorry."

"I'll get a bandage," Max said.

While Max fetched something for the bleeding, Lucky looked at his wounded finger. "Well, at least we know I ain't a doppelgangster."

Since I obviously needed practice, the two men insisted I had to be the one to test Max, too. I didn't cut him hard enough the first time, which led to a tense moment among us all before I tried again and drew blood. Then Lucky tested me. Despite his guarantee, I felt the cut. But I only bled a little.

"Okay, so that's done," Lucky said matter-of-factly. "We're all the original versions of ourselves. Good to know."

As we sat sipping our coffee, I said, "Hey, I guess something else we know now is that the Corvinos were telling the truth. They didn't whack Charlie and Johnny. I mean, now one of their capos has been hit, too."

"And the Gambellos didn't do it," Lucky said.

"Will the Corvinos believe that?" I asked.

"It depends on whether Mikey Castrucci and Fast Sammy decide to believe what we told them last night," Lucky said. "And whether they can convince the guys upstairs."

"Upstairs?" Max asked with a frown.

"Their superiors," I explained.

"Ah."

I asked Lucky, "Can you make some calls and find out?"

He nodded and pulled out his cell phone.

Max offered me a cookie. I accepted. Nelli gnawed on her bone.

Lopez called my cell phone while Max was pouring another round of coffee and Lucky was trying to track down Fast Sammy by phone.

"I'm not going to make it tonight," Lopez told me apologetically.

Suspecting the reason, I asked, "Why not?"

"I'm in Brooklyn. We've got a dead Corvino capo here."

I wasn't surprised, but I felt genuine disappointment. "But maybe after you're done there . . ."

"I don't think so." He sighed. "We've just had a Gambello wannabe picked up after he boasted in a bar that he did the hit, but—"

"What?" I frowned, thinking I had heard wrong.

"—his claims aren't very credible, so this is going to be a mess. I'll be working late again."

"You're saying someone's *confessed?*"

Max and Lucky looked at me.

"Oh, he won't confess in the legal sense. But he's taking credit, you might say." Lopez sounded disgusted. "And he's probably lying. Which creates extra legwork for us."

A Gambello wannabe . . .

"Is it that busboy I work with? Angelo Falcone?"

"I can't answer that, Esther." He sighed again. "Even though it'll probably be all over the news by tonight."

"How about this? Just tell me if I'm wrong."

He didn't say anything. And since I doubted he could say anything else to me about the case right now, either, I said, "Call me tomorrow?"

Apart from wanting to finish our interrupted tryst, I knew it was time to come clean with him—though I wasn't yet sure just how much that meant telling him.

"I will," he promised. "And if there's a miracle and I'm wrong about working late tonight . . ."

"Let me know," I said.

After I hung up, I told Max and Lucky what had happened.

"Oh, dear," said Max.

"Angelo? That punk!" Lucky said in exasperation.

"How do you think he learned about the hit so quickly?" I wondered.

"Word travels fast in our business," Lucky said. "And that Falcone kid is always hangin' around and trying to soak up juice. He probably heard about the hit before your boyfriend did."

"So you agree with Detective Lopez's initial assessment that Angelo Falcone didn't commit the murder?" Max said. "But I don't understand. What does the young man get out of falsely claiming he did it?"

"He *thinks* he's getting the attention of the don," Lucky said. "What he'll *actually* get is an early grave. If the Corvinos don't whack him, the Gambellos will."

"Goodness! Why?"

"Because of all the trouble that putz is about to cause."

"Is it that bad?" I asked.

Lucky nodded. "Even with Vinny, Nathan, and Bobby telling the Corvinos the truth, it wasn't gonna be easy to convince the family that the Gambellos didn't whack Danny. But now, with that *babbo* boasting about the hit, they'll think he did it to get his button. They'll figure we ordered the hit. Or at least hinted that we wanted it done. What else *could* they think?"

"But if the cops don't think Angelo did it," I said hopefully, "then maybe the Cor—"

"It don't matter what the cops think." Lucky shook his head. "Angelo has stood up for the hit. In our business, there's no taking that back."

"Not even if we can find out who's really doing all this?"

"That won't help Angelo stay alive. It might calm down the two families, though," Lucky said. "But we ain't having much luck so far in figuring out this thing."

"We've got to do better," I said.

"Yes, we must," Max agreed.

Lucky nodded. "Or there's gonna be a full-scale mob war the likes of which ain't been seen in a long time."

I knew he was right. I also suspected that now that Danny was dead, everything Lucky had said to him last night might be interpreted by the Corvinos as a threat rather than an attempt to help him.

Whatever dark feelings I had about Lucky's murder of Elena Giacalona's second husband, I didn't want him to die. And I knew that what he wasn't saying was that he would be high on the Corvinos' list of targets now.

17

"Shelley, the English poet, saw his doppelgänger shortly before he drowned," I said wearily. "Fascinating."

"'He'? The guy's parents named him Shelley?" Lucky shook his head. "I guess they took one look at that baby and could tell he'd grow up to write poetry."

I looked up from the book I was perusing with fast-growing boredom. "Actually, they named him Percy," I said. "Percy Bysshe Shelley."

"*Percy.*" Lucky rolled his eyes. "What's with the English, anyhow?"

Sitting at the big table in Zadok's Rare and Used Books, I flipped impatiently through the pages of the volume in my hands. "According to this, a double or *doppio* may also be known as a 'beta body,' or a 'subtle body,' or—"

"Ain't nothing subtle about getting whacked," Lucky said gloomily.

"—a 'fluidic body.' In Irish and English folklore—"

"The English again," Lucky grumbled.

"—it's called a fetch."

I sighed and tossed the book aside. It hit a pile of other equally boring books sitting on the edge of the table. They fell over and crashed to the floor. Lucky, who was pacing around the shop, drew in a sharp breath and flinched. Nelli, who was napping, woke up and leaped to her feet with a sharp bark. Max, also sitting at the big table, looked up from his reading, blinked, then went back to reading.

"Sorry," I said to Nelli. "My fault. Go back to sleep."

She yawned, wagged her tail, then turned three times in a circle before lying down and returning to her slumbers. I gathered up the books and restacked them. "And in the *Tibetan Book of the Dead*," I said to Lucky, "a double is called a Bardo-body."

"Who cares?" he said.

"My point exactly. Who cares?" I sighed, folded my arms on the table we were sitting at, and rested my head on them. "We're not getting anywhere."

The shop's telephone rang. It startled me, but I didn't even lift my aching head. I heard Max rise and cross the floor to answer it.

"Zadok's Rare and Used Books. How may I help you? Yes, this is Max . . . Hello? Hello?"

I lifted my head in time to see Max putting the phone back into its cradle. There was a puzzled expression on his face.

"Who was it?" I asked.

"I don't know." Max frowned. "The caller said, 'Max?' When I said yes, he said, 'Shit' and hung up."

"The voice didn't sound familiar?" Lucky asked, also frowning.

"Does *anyone's* voice sound familiar on the telephone?" Max asked, glancing at the modern device with open distaste.

"But it was definitely a man?" I asked.

"Yes. I mean, I think so."

Lucky and I looked at each other. Then I gasped.

"Max! It . . . it couldn't have been *you*, could it?"

Lucky blinked. "You think his doppelgangster was phoning him?"

"Oh, dear," Max said. "I hope not."

"Don't jump to conclusions, kid," Lucky said to me. "This is a store. That call coulda been from anyone who likes dusty books. Or it coulda been the IRS."

"Oh, no!" Now Max was *really* alarmed.

"Ah, don't worry, Doc, I can take care of that little problem for you."

I said, "Lucky, I don't want you to—"

"My point is, let's not make ourselves crazy. That's exactly what the hitter wants, right?"

Max took a little breath and nodded. "You're absolutely right, Lucky. We must strive for rational thought at all times."

"You've got be kidding," I muttered, looking at my pile of literature on doppelgängers and etheric bodies.

"Let's get back to work," Lucky said.

"Work?" I said to him. "What work are *you* doing?"

"You been on my back since last night," he said irritably. "What's with you?"

I didn't want to talk about it in front of Max, since I was the one who had introduced Lucky to him. So I said, "*We're* studying stacks of books with long-winded print the size of subatomic particles, while *you're* pacing around and talking on the phone."

"*You're* the one who told me to try to find out what the Corvinos are saying about Danny's death," he pointed out. "And it was a good idea, so that's what I'm doing."

Obviously trying to prevent an argument, Max said, "Esther, perhaps some ice cream will help you keep your strength up? There's some Ben and Jerry's Chubby Hubby in the freezer."

I took a steadying breath. "An excellent idea." I rose to my feet to get sustenance, spoons, and bowls. "Who else wants some?"

We spent the rest of the evening studying. In between Lucky's phone calls, we exchanged ideas.

"If I'm correct in my theory that the victim's encounter with his own doppelgangster unleashes a powerfully fatal curse," Max said, wiping some Chubby Hubby from his beard, "then our short-term strategy should be to attempt to mitigate the effect of the curse."

"Huh?" Lucky said.

"To try to take the juice out of the doppelgangsters," I translated.

"Gotcha," Lucky said. "No curse, no hit."

"So how do we mitigate the curse?" I asked.

Lucky said, "By chopping off the doppelgangster's head before it meets the victim."

"That would be effective," Max agreed. "But only if we meet the doppelgangster before the victim does."

"Surely it would also only be a temporary solution?" I said. "I mean, if whoever's behind this can create a doppelgangster, then can't he create a replacement for it?"

"Possibly," Max said. "It depends on how the creatures are being created. Which we still don't know." Nelli came to the table to examine our empty ice cream bowls. Max petted her absently while he said, "And, unfortunately, the other potential means of blocking their power also relies largely on understanding how they're created."

"What means is that?" Lucky asked.

"If I knew more about their creation or how their power functions," Max said, "then I might feasibly be able to develop a potion or spell to help protect the victim— even if only temporarily—from their influence."

"Well, Charlie and Johnny would've gobbled up any drink we put in front of them," Lucky said. "But Danny was real careful about his diet. So whether or not that'll work will probably depend on the target."

"It will also depend on learning more," Max said. "Without sufficient information, such intervention could easily endanger the next victim more than help him."

"Yeah, my grandma—the *strega*—once accidentally gave someone a hernia when trying to get him to fall in love with her client." Lucky shook his head. "Potions and spells can be tricky."

"Indeed," Max said.

"Whether or not you can protect the next victim also depends on our knowing who it is," I said. "Which we don't. Maybe there's another doppelgangster wandering around out there right now, and we just haven't heard about it yet—or heard about the resultant death."

"I got my ear to the ground," Lucky said, tapping his cell phone. "I'll know if any more Gambello duplicates turn up at least."

"And our ultimate objective, of course," Max said, "is to unmask and stop our adversary. If the deadly effect of the curse can be eliminated or reduced, the sorcerer creating these entities would have to regroup and adapt. And that might give us time to find and expose him."

Looking at the problem from another angle, I said to Lucky, "So with Danny dead, too, do you see any link among the victims yet? Something they all had in common?"

"The only thing I can think of is that plenty of guys would've lined up around the block to whack any one of them." Lucky added, "If you think about it, it's amazing that Johnny lived *this* long."

"So we have no way of determining who the next victim might be," Max concluded.

"Each of these deaths has brought the city one step closer to a Corvino-Gambello war," I said. "Who would *want* that? Who would be crazy enough to engineer something that's so destructive and so potentially dangerous for innocent bystanders?"

Lucky shook his head, leaned back in his chair, and stared at the ceiling as he thought about it.

Max said to me, "While our friend ponders how and why the victims are being chosen, you and I should return to researching how they might be created or disempowered."

With a weary nod of agreement, I opened another book and said, "I'll leave the Middle High German tomes to you, Max."

We continued reading while Lucky continued talking a lot on his cell phone, trying to ward off a mob war. By that night, I knew more about doubles, apparitions, and bilocates than I had ever dreamed of learning or had any desire to know. And, as fatigue eventually made the small print of old books blur before my eyes, I didn't feel my newfound knowledge had accomplished anything more than giving me a splitting headache.

At a certain point, Max suddenly said, "Good heavens! How careless of me."

I was too punchy by then to take any interest as he rose from his seat and walked quickly to the back of the shop. I heard the cellar door open, and I assumed he was going down to his laboratory.

My eyes drifted shut, my head drooped, and I dozed for a few minutes while Lucky sat nearby talking on his cell phone. After a while, something cold and wet poked my cheek. Startled, I opened my eyes. Nelli's immense face was close to mine. She panted and stared at me meaningfully.

"Huh?" I pushed her away, wondering why Max couldn't have conjured a familiar with better breath.

I glanced at my watch and was surprised to see that it was only ten o'clock. It felt later. Much later. Time drags when you're reading about fetches and Bardo-bodies.

Nelli trotted to the front of the shop. I heard her whining faintly by the door.

"I think she wants her walk," I said wearily.

"I'll do it," Lucky said as he pocketed his cell phone. "You look beat. Maybe you should go home and get some shut-eye."

"Maybe you should, too."

"Nah, I'm waitin' for another call from the boss." The old hit man shrugged. "Might as well keep Max company while I wait."

"What news have you got so far?"

"It sounds like Vinny, Bobby, and Nathan came through and told the Corvinos what really happened. But, of course, it's such a crazy story, they're juggling theories now and arguing over what to do. We don't know exactly what they're saying within their family, of course, but it's easy to guess. And I can't repeat to a lady what they're saying to *us* tonight."

"What do you guess they're saying within their family?"

"Well, probably their least favorite theory is that we was tellin' the truth last night and Danny was cursed with death by a doppelgangster."

"Go figure." I rose to get Nelli's leash from the back of the shop, near the cellar door. Her whining was getting louder.

Lucky raised his voice so I could hear him. "They're probably saying maybe I had Angelo Falcone whack Danny for laughing at me last night. Or, alternate theory, maybe Angelo's a loose cannon who's bumping off made guys without permission, and we—the Gambellos I mean—are his victims just as much as they are."

As I removed Nelli's brand new pink leather leash from the wall hook where I'd seen it hanging earlier, I heard clanging and banging in the cellar. I opened the door and called down the stairs, "Max? Are you all right?"

"Ouch! What? Oh! Yes, Esther, everything's fine. I'm just . . ." I heard the clattering crash of metal objects hitting the cellar floor.

"Max?"

"I'll be up in a moment!" he called back.

I shrugged and closed the cellar door.

"The Corvinos are probably also wondering," Lucky

said, as I returned to where he was sitting and handed him the leash, "whether our family's using Angelo to do some fumigating and just making it look like he's a loose cannon, so we can whack one of their guys without retribution." He rose to his feet.

Thinking over what he'd said, I asked, "Do you suppose it's possible Angelo actually *is* mixed up in these murders?"

Lucky shrugged. "After the last few days, I think *anything's* possible. But I gotta say, Angelo sure don't strike me as the genius sorcerer Max is describing. If Angelo ain't really just a dumb punk trying too hard to get connected, then he's been doin' the best imitation I ever seen."

I nodded. It was hard to disagree with that impression. "But if the Corvinos think Angelo may be a loose cannon who's killing wiseguys from both families, then at least they won't start a war over Danny's death."

"Sure they will."

"What?" I blinked. "Why?

"'Cuz men in this line of work are cautious, kid. Short of seeing indisbootable evidence that the Gambello family had nothing to do with killing Danny—"

"Indisputable," I said automatically.

"—they gotta make the conservative judgment call and assume we knew exactly what was going on. And then whack as many Gambellos as they can." He shrugged philosophically. "This is business, after all."

"Business," I repeated, feeling dread settle into my stomach.

All things considered, I began to realize that Max and I had made a terrible mistake by attending the sit-down last night. Now that Danny Dapezzo was dead, the Corvinos might well decide to include us in their retribution. We had used our real names at the meeting, so it would be easy for a criminal organization to track us down now. Whatever their intellectual or educational

shortcomings, wiseguys were notoriously good at finding and killing their enemies.

I felt sick as I sank into a chair at the table.

Lopez was right. I had been naive.

Having summed up the situation, Lucky said cheerfully to Nelli, "Come on. Let's take a walk."

He rounded the tall bookcase that stood between us
and the door. I heard the soft clinking of metal as Lucky
clipped Nelli's leash to her collar, then the door chimes
rang merrily as they left the shop together.

I began rethinking my position on protective custody
again. And now Max, I realized, would have to go into
hiding with me.

I pressed my fingers against my pounding temples as
I acknowledged that I was going to have to tell Lopez
what we had done. And he'd be so angry once he found
out that I'd attended a Corvino-Gambello sit-down with
Max, he might not even *want* to put me in protective
custody anymore. He might decide to let the Corvinos
have me, and good riddance.

"This is a nightmare," I muttered.

There might be a Mafia contract on my head now!
And all because Chubby Charlie Chiccante had died
right in front of me. I was suddenly incensed at the fat,
vulgar, rude, overdressed mobster. Why did he come
to Bella Stella's that day if he knew he was marked for
death? And why sit in *my* section?

I was so angry now, if Charlie weren't already dead,
I would kill him myself for getting me involved in this
madness.

And why had *I* involved Max? What was I *thinking?* After surviving for some three hundred fifty years,
which couldn't have been easy even with the help of a
mysterious elixir, he might soon be sleeping with the
fishes because of me!

Wait a minute. I remembered why I had dragged Max
into this. Because Lucky had convinced me I might be in

danger from the killer, since Detective Napoli's interest in me was making it look like I knew something. And because Lucky had taken Charlie's talk of a "double" and the evil eye so seriously.

So this was all Lucky's fault! *And* Napoli's. Ah-hah!

It was good to have someone to blame.

I heard the cellar door open and close. Max's footsteps, accompanied by some metallic scraping and rattling, crossed the floor of the bookshop, moving toward me. As he came around a row of bookcases and I saw what was causing the noise, I rose to my feet and stared in surprise.

"Here we are!" he said a little breathlessly.

He was carrying two swords and a large, ornate ax.

He said, "Er, can you help me with . . ."

"Huh? Oh! Sure." I gingerly reached for the ax—which was even heavier than it looked and fell to the floor with a thud. I jumped in time to prevent it from taking off half my foot.

"Max! What are you doing with these things?" I demanded.

"As per our earlier discussion," he said, depositing the swords on the table, "we need to keep tools handy for the decapitation of doppelgangsters."

"My God." I looked at the items on the table while Max stooped down to pick up the ax. He gave a little grunt as he heaved it up, then set it on the table with a heavy thud, alongside the other menacing objects.

I tried to picture decapitating Johnny Be Good in the crypt of St. Monica's with one of these bladed weapons. I had found him repulsive even before knowing he was a doppelgangster. Knowing what I knew now, could I behead him?

After a long moment, I let out my breath in a rush. "I can't cut off their heads. They're too lifelike. I just can't do it, Max."

He patted my hand. "That's quite all right, my dear.

Lucky is no doubt correct when he says it's not a proper task for a young lady."

I lifted my gaze from the weapons on the table and said, "Max, I think you and I may be in danger."

"While Evil is afoot in New York," he said with heroic serenity, "we're always in danger, Esther."

"No, I mean a more, um, mundane kind of danger. Lucky says that the Corvino crime family—"

The chiming of the doorbells interrupted me as someone entered the shop. It was after ten o'clock now—too late, surely, for the newcomer to be a book shopper. I froze, caught in a moment of debilitating terror. I recalled the brief, anonymous phone call a few hours ago. Had that been the Corvinos, hunting us down?

As footsteps approached us, a hot rush of survival instinct flooded every capillary in my body. I snatched a sword from the table and turned to face the mortal danger bearing down on me.

Lopez came around the corner of the bookcase.

My jaw dropped as I gaped at him.

"Detective Lopez?" Max said. "What a pleasant surprise! How nice to see you again."

Lopez and I stared at each other. He didn't look at all surprised to see me here. In fact, he looked as if my presence confirmed his worst expectations, and his expression was grim and resigned.

Max looked at the weapon in my hand, then leaned closer to me to whisper, "Er, are you angry at him?"

"What? Oh." I put the sword back down on the table, uncomfortably aware that I must look crazy and dangerous.

Lopez was dressed in the same clothes he had worn this afternoon, jeans and a pale shirt. Since then, he had added a denim jacket to his ensemble.

"Hi," I said. "Why are you here?"

"Because of the note you gave him." Lopez's voice was tired, flat, and a little cold.

"The note?"

"I found it at the scene."

I just stared blankly for a few moments. Then my brain woke up, and I realized what he was talking about.

"That phone call a few hours ago!" I blurted. "The hang-up. That was you?"

Lopez nodded.

"I don't understand," Max said. "Why did you hang up?"

"Because I didn't call to talk," Lopez replied tersely.

Max asked, "What note have you found? What is its significance?"

"It was on Danny when he died?" I guessed.

"Danny," Lopez repeated. His voice got chillier. "You were on first-name terms?"

I said to Max, "He's talking about the piece of paper I gave Danny last night."

"It was near the body," Lopez said. "Probably fell out of the victim's hand—or maybe a pocket—when he died."

"Oh, dear," Max said.

Lopez said, "It's easy to see how it got missed. The scene was such a mess. And your note was stuck by dried blood to a broken bottle so that it almost looked like part of the torn wine label. It's just luck that I'm the one who noticed it." His expression didn't suggest that the luck was necessarily good. "No names. Just two phone numbers. I recognized one of them right away." He looked at me again. "Yours." His voice was still flat. "I had a bad feeling that I knew who the other number belonged to, but I was hoping I was wrong." He shifted his gaze to Max. "Until I dialed it and found out I was right."

This comment was followed by an awkward silence. My heart sank. I recalled thinking this afternoon, just before I left Lopez so I could try to help Danny, that I would tell him the truth tonight about where I'd gone today. But this wasn't how I had intended to break the news.

I asked, "Has this made things very bad with Detective Napoli?"

"Napoli doesn't know," he said.

My shoulders sagged with relief. "Oh, that's good."

"No, it's not good," Lopez snapped. "Today I concealed evidence in a murder investigation, Esther!"

"Oh!" I realized what he was saying. "*Oh.* You found that note with our numbers on it, and you . . . pocketed it? To protect me?"

"Yes." His voice was clipped, his expression dark.

"That was very thoughtful," Max said, beaming at Lopez.

Lopez gave him a look that scared me.

"Max," I said, "try not to talk."

"Hmm?"

"If they find out," I said anxiously to Lopez, "would you be suspended? Or . . ."

"Or *charged?*" He unleashed his anger now. "For stealing a note that connects my 'fiancée' to a brutal murder? *Yes*, Esther, I could be charged with obstructing justice. Probably, though, the department would rather keep it quiet and just kick me off the force. No one wants a scandal in the Organized Crime Control Bureau, after all, so the NYPD probably wouldn't like to *advertise*, by charging me, that one of their detectives concealed evidence in a murder to protect the mob girl he's been dating. The possibilities for tabloid headlines alone would be bloodcurdling, from my captain's point of view."

Feeling terrible about this, I said, "I never—"

"Merely *suspending* me, of course, is a possibility. That's the kind of pass that a superior officer gives to a detective he likes and who has a track record in his department. But guess what?"

"I know," I said, my heart pounding as I saw just how furious he was. "Napoli doesn't like you, and you've only been in OCCB a few days. But—"

"And that's not the point!"

Max said, "Perhaps we should all calm—"

"If you don't shut him up," Lopez said to me, "I swear to God I'm going to do something that they'll *have* to charge me for."

"Max," I said sharply, *"don't talk."*

"The point," Lopez said, "is that there's been a murder, and I concealed evidence and removed it from the scene, and I'm a cop, and that's *not* what I *do*."

And that was the bottom line, I realized. He was more appalled by what he had done to protect me than he would be by anything that could happen to his career because of me.

"Then we have to face the music," I said.

"What?" he snapped.

A sudden sense of fatalistic calm washed over me. "You've got to enter that evidence into the investigation. You didn't destroy it, did you? So take it to work and say that you found it at the scene and something happened that distracted you, so you pocketed it without realizing it, and now you're—"

"And as soon as Napoli finds out whose phone number is written on this note, he'll know I'm lying," Lopez said dismissively.

"Of course he will. But he'll also know that, after you took the note, you came to your senses and brought it right back." When Lopez didn't respond, I said, "Or if you don't like that plan, then go back to Vinny's wine vault and leave the note there for someone else to find. You're a cop, you must know how to plant evidence." After a moment, I said, "That came out wrong."

But his attention was suddenly on a different matter. "How do you know the hit happened in the vault? We haven't released that information."

I had seen enough episodes of *Crime and Punishment* to recognize the implication. *"We* didn't kill Danny!"

"Gracious, no!" Then Max remembered he wasn't supposed to speak. "My apologies."

Lopez blinked. "For not killing Danny Dapezzo?"

My cell phone rang, making us all jump.

"You *know* we're not killers," I said as I went over to the table where my purse was lying.

"Don't answer that," Lopez said.

"I have to. It could be my agent," I said. "At long last."

"This late?" he said doubtfully.

"Maybe," I said. "We've been having trouble connecting and this is important."

"This is *more* important, Esther."

"I'm trying to get an audition for something specific," I said, opening my purse. "There's very little time left." In fact, I was afraid Thack was calling me to say it was too late by now, the part had already been cast.

"We're talking about murder and concealing evidence," Lopez said sharply.

The ringing persisted.

"The only reason I'm involved in this mess in the first place," I said, searching my purse for the phone, "is because I was waiting tables when Charlie Chiccante died instead of working a real job. So I would think that you, of all people, would appreciate how important it is that I get this audition!"

The door bells chimed. I froze briefly as I thought about Corvino assassins again, then relaxed when I heard Lucky's voice.

"Hey, has the Doc got some plastic bags or something?" he called. "Our favorite familiar left her calling card on the sidewalk."

Nelli growled.

Lopez turned toward the sound of Lucky's voice. "Jesus, Esther, please tell me that's not who I think it is."

"Hey, don't growl at me," Lucky admonished the dog.

I heard the metallic click of him unhooking her leash. "*You're* the one who . . . Nelli?"

I found my ringing phone in my purse, pulled it out, and looked at the LCD panel. Not Thack. Damn. The readout said "Caller Unknown." I didn't recognize the number.

Nelli's toenails clicked on the floor as she trotted around the bookcase, still growling. She froze when she saw Lopez, her body tense, her floppy ears pricked alertly.

I flipped open my phone and raised it to my ear.

Nelli's lips peeled back in a snarl, exposing her big, sharp teeth, and she crouched down on her massive haunches, letting out a ferocious growl.

Shocked, I dropped my phone. It fell to the floor with a clatter. "Nelli!" I said. "Stop that!"

Lopez looked at Max. "You got a vicious dog the size of a taxi cab? You really are out of your mind."

Lucky appeared behind Nelli and said to her, "Hey! What's with you?"

"Lucky Battistuzzi," Lopez said with resignation. "Great. Just great."

"Nelli, no!" I said, as the dog crept menacingly toward Lopez, still growling, her fangs bared. "Max, make her stop that."

"That does it," Lopez said, holding very still. "I'm having this dog impounded."

"I don't get it," Lucky said to Lopez. "Kids in the street can walk right up to this dog, no problem. But one whiff of *you*, and . . ." He drew in a sharp breath.

I heard a man's voice calling my name through my cell phone. Keeping my eyes fixed on Nelli, I bent down and fumbled around until my fingers felt the phone, then I picked it up.

Max drew in a sharp breath, too. Then he seized one of the swords on the table.

"Max, what are you doing?" I grabbed his arm and hung on. "Just reprimand her! You don't have to *kill* her!"

Lucky reached into his pocket and shoved past the massive snarling dog. I heard the snap of metal, and I saw something glint beneath the overhead lights as Lucky made a slashing motion at Lopez's face.

I cried out. Lopez moved just as fast. His fist shot out, his weight shifted, and the knife in Lucky's hand flew past Nelli as the gangster went tumbling to the floor.

"Max," Lucky rasped, sounding like he'd had the wind knocked out of him. "Now!"

Lopez had already picked up a chair and was using it to ward off Nelli, who was stalking him, her growls terrifyingly loud, her fangs dripping, her eyes glowing with feral aggression. "Call off your dog, Max, or I'll shoot it!"

"Nelli, run!" Max cried, shaking off my slack grip. "It's armed!"

I saw that the skin of Lopez's cheek was gaping open from the wound Lucky had inflicted.

There was no blood.

"Oh, my God," I said in a strangled voice. "Max! *NO!*"

The old mage rushed forward with his sword.

Still keeping the chair between himself and Nelli, Lopez reached for his gun. But dealing with three adversaries and surprised by Max's attack, he wasn't quite fast enough. He was still drawing his weapon when Max cut off his head.

18

I screamed so shrilly, my ears rang. Nelli barked.

Lopez disappeared.

One moment he was there, his body falling as his head was separated violently from his shoulders by the mighty sweep of Max's blade. And the next moment he was gone as feathers, chunks of soil, pale little sticks, leaves, and pebbles flew through the air and rolled around the floor.

I sank to my knees. I wanted to scream again, but my vocal cords wouldn't work. All that came out was a strangled, squealing sound.

Lucky was trying to sit up, coughing as he brushed feathers and dust away from his face. "Eph ... ephem ... ephemeral substances," he mumbled.

Nelli was busily sniffing at all the detritus and debris, scrambling around the room in furious haste as she examined the bits and pieces of what had been, only moments ago ...

"Lopez?" I croaked.

Someone was screaming my name over the cell phone that sat next to me. I stared in numb shock at the ephemeral substances scattered all around me, while Max helped Lucky off the floor. Then I picked up the cell phone. Moving mechanically, I raised it to my face.

"Hello?"

"Esther? *Esther!*" Lopez shouted over the phone.

"Yes, I'm here."

"Are you all right?" He sounded frantic. "Esther? It's me! Can you hear me? Are you all right?"

"I'm fine."

Lucky looked at me. "You're talkin' on the phone? *Now?*"

I tried to say Lopez's name. Instead, I slid sideways and hit the floor.

Drops of cold water sprinkled across my face. I groaned irritably and turned my head away.

A giant, warm, wet *thing* brushed my face. I gasped and opened my eyes—and immediately shut them as Nelli licked my face again.

"She's coming around," Lucky said.

Nelli made a little crooning whine of pleasure.

I remembered that I had just watched Max behead Lopez, and I sat bolt upright. *"Nooooo!"*

The sudden movement was too much for me, and I nearly blacked out again.

"Take it easy," said Lucky, his arm supporting me so I could remain sitting.

"Lopez!" I wailed.

"That was not Detective Lopez," Max said firmly. "That was a doppelgangster."

I was panting with anxiety. "It's not him? We're sure it's not him?"

"Yes," Max said.

"You're *sure?*"

"Positive."

Lucky shifted position a little. "Take a good look, kid. No body. Just ephemeral substances."

"No body?"

"No," Lucky said. "Just feathers and dirt and bird bones and crap like that."

I looked around the room. It was a chaotic mess. And there was indeed no corpse. "Bird bones . . ." I said vaguely. I remembered thinking that I had seen pale little sticks when Lopez—*oh, God, Lopez!*—exploded all over the room. Those must have been bird bones.

Lucky said, "That thing wasn't real. It wasn't him."

I rubbed my hand over my face. "It seemed like him. *Just* like him. It seemed so real." I tried to banish the memory of the doppelgangster's expression right before Max cut off its head. I felt a surge of nausea. "It sounded just like him. It said exactly what he . . ."

"Of course," Max said gently, handing me a glass of water. "It was fashioned after him. It was created to be identical to him in all outward appearances."

I took a sip of water, then said, "But you knew."

"Nelli's keen senses alerted us," Max said.

Nelli gave a little *woof!* and wagged her tail.

"Yeah, that was damn good work," Lucky said to her.

The velocity of Nelli's tail increased until it could have seriously injured anyone in its path.

"Her objective at the sit-down, of course," Max said, "was to identify doppelgangsters. But until she encountered the creature posing as Lopez, we didn't know whether she could indeed do so. Tonight's incident, however, was conclusive. We now know we have an excellent means of detecting the presence of a doppelgangster."

"That's a relief," said Lucky.

I found it unnerving to hear Lopez's perfect double described as "the creature."

"But it was the first time I'd ever seen her react like that," Lucky added. "So I wasn't a hundred percent sure until I cut that thing and saw there was no blood."

"You ripped open his face, Lucky!" I shuddered in remembered horror. "If that had been the real man, you'd go to prison for assaulting a police officer with a deadly weapon."

"Well, let's say I was ninety-five percent sure. Nelli never acted like that before, after all. Not even at the sit-down, when Danny was disrespecting her and deserved to get his leg chewed off."

Nelli went back to snuffling at the piles of ephemeral matter that were scattered all over the floor.

"Yes, excellent notion, Nelli," Max said. "Continue studying our adversary's handiwork. We must learn all that we can from this encounter."

"How are you feeling now, kid?" Lucky asked.

"Like I still want to scream."

"It's most unfortunate," said Max, "that the doppel-gangster was armed and dangerous."

"Y'think?" said Lucky.

"Rather than destroying it," Max said, "I would have liked to capture and question it. That's why I hesitated, my dear fellow, to dispatch it after you exposed its true nature."

"Great, so now we gotta *capture* one of those things?" Lucky said.

"One that isn't as dangerous as this one was," Max said.

"This one was only dangerous," I said angrily, "because he was—"

"*It*, my dear," Max said. "*It*. You need to dissociate that mystical, ephemeral creation from the man it resembled."

"It didn't *resemble* him," I said in shaky voice. "It was absolutely identical to him! And it only became danger-ous because you all attacked it—which is exactly what would make Lopez dangerous, too!"

"That's a fair point," Max conceded. "The situation was fraught."

"You really think that gun woulda worked?" Lucky asked Max. "It was in that thing's hand when you lopped off its head, and—"

"Oh, God." I felt faint again.

"—I saw it explode into dirt and stuff, too."

Max frowned thoughtfully. "At the time, I was too agitated by the realization that the creature was armed with a deadly projectile weapon—as Detective Lopez himself would be—to consider this. But you bring up an interesting point, Lucky."

"That the gun might not have fired?" I asked.

"Yes. Or that it may only have *seemed* to fire. The killer is a very talented sorcerer, but his creations are illusions, after all. They're convincing, but they're nonetheless subject to practical limitations." Max added, "However, we're theorizing without enough information. It's also possible that a bullet which is part of such an elaborate duplicate may indeed be effective, as was the creature's physical blow when it knocked down Lucky. So we must treat any armed doppelgangster with extreme caution."

"Good point, Doc. And even if the gun didn't work," Lucky said, "I guess the doppelgangster coulda picked up a real weapon—one of them swords you got on the table, maybe—and killed Nelli that way."

"Speaking of Nelli," I said to Max, "you never mentioned that if she detected a doppelgangster, she'd try to tear it apart!"

"She did react quite strongly, didn't she?"

"So of course he—*it*—threatened to shoot her! Nelli shouldn't have done that!"

I glanced in her direction, but the familiar seemed fully absorbed in her examination of the scattered debris.

"We must keep in mind," Max said soothingly, "that Nelli entered this dimension to protect New York City from Evil. Therefore, she would naturally react with vehemence to encountering a mystical entity created by a killer for the specific purpose of cursing a human victim with certain death."

"Oh, my God!" The realization hit me like a bucket of cold water. "Lopez!"

"It wasn't Lopez," Lucky said patiently. "It—"

"No, *Lopez*," I choked out. "Duplicated! Cursed! In danger!"

"Madre di Dio!" Lucky said. "She's right! Now the killer's trying to whack the cop!"

Max said decisively, "We must warn Detective Lopez."

"Right away!" I said. "Now! Where's my phone?" I gasped, suddenly remembering. "He called me! He was on the phone when I passed out."

"That was he?" Max said. "Oh, dear. I thought you said it was your agent. So I told him you'd call him back and hung up."

"You did *what?*"

"Hey," Lucky said, "you were lyin' on the floor in a cold faint after seeing your boyfriend's head cut off. You weren't exactly in shape to talk business."

"But—"

"In any case," Max said soothingly, "this means we know that Detective Lopez was fine just a short while ago."

"Oh, my God," I said more slowly. "He was on the phone. He *heard*." He must have thought I was in the middle of a deadly riot. And then Max had spoken to him. "If he realized where I was when he called me . . ."

"His doppelgangster looked for you here," Lucky said, handing me my cell phone. "So the real McCoy might look for you here, too."

"Yes." My heart was pounding. I heard a siren in the distance, approaching fast.

Lucky heard it, too. He went still and listened intently. When it sounded as if the vehicle had turned onto Max's street, Lucky's eyes met mine. "Here comes the cavalry."

The wailing siren came to a stop right outside the bookshop, then went silent. I heard a car door slam.

"Lucky," I said faintly, "help me stand up. Max, go to the door and show him in."

Max trotted around the nearby bookcase and headed for the door while Lucky hauled me to my feet. I felt like a toddler learning to walk, sure I would topple over at any moment. But I took a couple of faltering steps away from Lucky and toward the bookshop's entrance.

The door crashed open. The bells rang wildly. Nelli gave a little bark and lunged in that direction.

Lucky grabbed her collar. "No, don't," he admonished. "This one might be the real thing."

I heard Max say in a rush, "Ah, Detec-yahhh! Esther's fine! She's right here! There's no need for a gu— *Agh!*"

The sound of scuffling feet moved rapidly toward me. Max came around the bookcase by stumbling backward. He was propelled by Lopez, whose left hand was on Max's throat. A gun was in his right hand. Lopez pointed it at Nelli and Lucky while his gaze went to me. Nelli growled.

I said, "No, Nelli! *No!*"

Max's knees sagged and he made a little choking sound, as if the grip on his throat was tightening. His distress agitated Nelli, who growled more vehemently.

"Are you all right?" Lopez said to me.

"You have to let him go, you're upsetting the dog," I said, terrified of what was about to happen.

"Maybe *that's* not what's making her growl," Lucky said in an ominous voice.

"No," I said to Lucky. And then to Nelli, "Stop that!" And then to Lopez, "Please let Max go."

"Are you all right?" he demanded.

"I'm fine, I'm fine, everything's fine," I babbled. "You called at a bad moment, that's all. I'm fine. Now please let him go."

Nelli's growls were getting louder.

Lucky's hand crept toward the pocket where he kept his knife.

Lopez wasn't looking at the gangster, but he saw the motion anyhow. *"Freeze!"*

Lucky froze. We *all* froze. Nelli even stopped growling.

Lopez said more calmly, "You're sure you're okay?"

I tried to sound calm, too. "Yes."

"What happened?"

I shook my head. "It's hard to explain, but..." I searched for something that would get him to let go of Max, so Nelli would calm down. "They were protecting me."

It worked. He released Max. Then he said, "Is there anyone else here?"

"Well, not anymore," Lucky said.

Max staggered toward me, wheezing for air. I caught him by the arm and patted his back.

As Lopez holstered his gun, he looked around at the unsanitary mess covering this portion of the shop. "What the hell is going on here?"

Realizing that Nelli was calmer now, Lucky released her collar. She looked uncertainly at Lopez for a moment, then crept forward and delicately sniffed his legs while Lucky said, "Oh, this mook came into the store a little while ago and got out of hand, that's all."

"Who?"

Lucky looked at me. I looked at Max.

Max said faintly, "We have not yet ascertained the name of the individual responsible for the mayhem here tonight."

Good answer.

Looking again at the mess surrounding us, Lopez asked, "What *is* all this crap?"

"It's ephemeral matter," Lucky said. "Makes a helluva mess, don't it?"

"What's it doing here?"

"It came with the mook," Lucky said.

Lopez stared at him. "Did the mook say *why* he had a load of feathers, dirt, and pebbles with him?"

"He didn't happen to say why," Lucky said. "Fortunately, it's over now and everyone is fine. It's good thing me and Nelli came back from our walk when we did."

"Nelli?" Lopez looked down at the dog. She paused in her olfactory examination of him to meet his gaze. After a moment, she wagged her tail hesitantly. "Max's new roommate, I take it?"

"Yeah."

"And why are there two swords and an ax on the table?"

"They're antiques," Lucky said. "Max was showin' us his collection."

Lopez studied the objects. I had a feeling he was looking for blood. My gaze went involuntarily to the blade which had beheaded his perfect double tonight. Fortunately, the weapons were so old, they really did look like collector's items. It occurred to me they were probably valuable.

"All right," Lopez said, "I'll need a statement from each of you—except Nelli—and a description of the guy who came in here."

"We didn't get a good look at him," Lucky said.

Lopez looked at Lucky, who looked at Max, who looked at me.

I said, "Um . . ."

There was a long, extremely uncomfortable moment of silence.

Lopez sighed and said, "Everyone who isn't Esther, take a walk."

Lucky bristled. "You got a warrant?"

"I don't need a warrant to talk to her." Lopez glanced at him. "And I'm sure I can come up with a reason for probable cause if I decide to search you right now for an unlicensed gun."

"Max, let's take a walk." Lucky clipped Nelli's leash back onto her collar.

"Er . . ." Max looked doubtful.

"It's all right." I squeezed Max's arm reassuringly. We

knew from Nelli's reaction that this was the real Detective Lopez. "Take Nelli for a walk."

Already halfway to the door with Nelli, Lucky added, "And bring some plastic bags, for the love of God. What do you feed this dog, anyhow?"

"Don't say 'dog.'" Max stumbled after them.

As soon as the doorbells chimed to hail their departure, I said to Lopez, "Have you seen your own perfect double?"

That caught him flat-footed. "Huh?"

"Have you seen anyone who looks just like you?"

He frowned. "You mean . . . *ever?*"

"No, I mean quite recently. Today. Maybe yesterday?"

"No," he said. "Now what the he—"

"Think hard," I said. "It might be someone who you think just looks a *little* like you."

"What are you talking about?" he said impatiently.

"We tend to think we look like the image we see in the mirror. But that's a reflection, so what we're seeing is actually in reverse. Actors have to know what others see when they look at us, but many people are surprised by their own appearance in photos and don't really know what they look like."

"Fascinating," he said. "Now let's talk about—"

"So have you seen anyone who looks even a little bit like you? Same height and build? Same age and coloring?"

"Probably dozens of people," he said. "So what?"

"He was wearing the same clothes you're wearing now," I said. "Blue jeans, pale shirt, denim jacket . . ."

"*He?* Who are we talking about?"

I froze as I realized what I had just said. "The same clothes . . ." Both versions of Charlie were wearing the same suit on the night that Lucky and I saw his doppelgangster at Bella Stella's. And Lopez's doppelgangster had been wearing what the real Lopez was wearing tonight.

"He *who*, Esther?"

Did this information mean anything?

"What was Johnny Gambello wearing when he was pulled out of the East River?" I asked.

"What?" Lopez was confused by the sudden change of topic.

"Was it a red shirt and white leisure suit with silver trim?"

Frowning at me, he shook his head. "No."

So was I on the wrong track? No, not necessarily. Johnny had gone home and talked to his wife after seeing his doppelgangster. So maybe he changed his clothes sometime after he was duplicated and before he died.

So maybe . . . "Yes!" I said, grasping it.

"Yes, what?" Lopez prodded.

Maybe the clothing the doppelgangsters wore could help us pinpoint *when* they had been created!

"I have to tell Max," I said, heading for the door.

Lopez grabbed my arm. His grip was hard. "Tell him what? No, wait, never mind. Whatever you think you have to tell Max, you and I have things we need to talk about first."

"You're right." My thoughts were scattered. I was still in shock from seeing him beheaded. I had to pull myself together. Focusing on the single most important thing we needed to discuss, I said, "You're in danger."

"Yeah, of getting suspended." He released my arm.

I looked at him in surprise. "Because of the note that I gave Danny?"

"The one with your phone number? And Max's land line? Yeah, I found it near the body."

I gazed at him in confusion. How could he and his double *both* have found it?

He continued, "At the time, I was . . . upset."

"Upset," I repeated faintly.

He rubbed a hand over his face, looking tired. "But you know, it's been such a hell of a day since then, I kind of forgot about it."

"What?" I didn't understand. The doppelgangster had been furious.

With a weary, resigned expression, he reached into his pocket and pulled out . . .

"Photos?" I said.

"Surveillance photos." His voice was flat, tired, a little cold. "We look at most of them digitally. These are just a few that I printed out for myself tonight. Call me sentimental."

They were four-by-six color prints with a matte finish. He laid them out slowly on the table for me to look at, one by one.

The photos had all been taken at night on a city street. The composition wasn't good, and neither was the lighting. There was a dark car outside what looked like the entrance to a church, a couple of men, a *gumata* with big hair and shiny clothes that were a little too small for . . .

"Oh, my, God!" I blurted. "I didn't realize how that blouse gapped when I moved."

Even with the bad lighting, you could see a glimpse of my bra in one of the shots. I looked up at Lopez to explain that I'd put together that costume on short notice.

Our eyes met, and I realized that probably wasn't important just now.

I gasped as another thought occurred to me.

"You've got me under surveillance?" I demanded.

"No," he said with forced patience. "We've got capos in the major crime families under surveillance, Esther."

"Oh. Right." And I was so naive, this hadn't occurred to me when I met with Danny "the Doctor" Dapezzo in Little Italy last night. "Of course."

He put another photo on the table. It showed me handing a small piece of paper to Danny. The next photo Lopez laid down was a shot of me, Max, and Nelli leaving St. Monica's together last night.

Lopez said, "What in the name God did you think you were doing?"

"Napoli's going to want to question me again, isn't he?" I said in resignation.

"No, he thinks these are pictures of Danny's daughter."

"What?"

Lopez shrugged. "There's definitely a resemblance. Well, when you're dressed like that, I mean." After a moment he added, "She hasn't got your cheekbones. And your shape's a little different. But since it was dark and the pictures aren't that good, Napoli didn't notice."

"But you did." Of course.

"I look at you a lot more than he does."

"You have to tell him," I said quietly.

"No, I don't think so."

I shook my head. "I don't want to be the cause of you doing something you think is wrong."

"Too late now," he muttered.

"You can still fix this."

"Well, I know this will sound unconvincing if I wind up having to explain it later to someone, so I hope I don't . . . but we're already wasting time on one dead end, thanks to the Falcone kid's story, and I don't think we should waste any time on another."

"So it *was* Angelo who claimed credit for the hit?"

"Yeah. And, like I figured, it's all over the news now. You haven't seen it?" When I shook my head, he continued, "Something like this makes it harder for the DA to prosecute a case after the cops find and arrest the real killer. So we can't afford *not* to treat Angelo seriously, even though he's full of shit. We have to take him apart so well that he can't be used to help a slick defense lawyer create reasonable doubt with a jury."

"Take him apart?"

"Prove he didn't kill Danny," Lopez said. "And prove he had his reasons—however dumb, warped, and shortsighted—for lying and saying that he did."

"I see."

"And that takes time. So I don't want to waste any more time or stretch the team any thinner by giving Napoli a crazy old bookseller and well-meaning actress to chew on."

"Oh."

"Did you have anything to do with killing Danny Dapezzo?"

"No!" Caught off guard, I was startled and indignant.

"But you knew him?" His voice was clipped.

"Briefly."

"*How* briefly?"

"I met him the night before he died." I added in surprise, "*Last* night, I mean." It already seemed like a long time ago.

"Did you see him today?"

"No. But you must know that, since you had him under surveillance."

"Surveillance isn't like what you see in the movies," he said. "We don't have the budget or the manpower to cover these guys nonstop. So we don't know where Danny was between leaving St. Monica's last night and winding up dead in his cousin Vinny's wine cellar this afternoon."

"I don't know where he was, either."

"So what were you and Max doing at St. Monica's with half a dozen wiseguys last night?" He added, "And why were dressed like that? Both of you?"

"We were trying to fit in. It was a sit-down. Max and I were Lucky's, um, guests."

"Why did Lucky bring you two to a sit-down?"

"He thought we could help prevent a mob war." Unnerved by Lopez's stony expression, I said in a rush, "That's why I'm involved in this. Max, too. To stop anyone else from getting killed. To prevent a mob war. All we've done is *talk* to people! Trying to get information and to convince them not to act rashly."

"Trying to get *what* information?"

"Trying to find out who's behind the killings. The Gambellos didn't hit Danny. Danny said the Corvinos didn't hit Charlie and Johnny—and Lucky believed him," I said. "Lucky and Danny couldn't stand each other, but neither of them wanted another mob war, and that's why they met last night."

"What did they say at the meeting?"

I thought about it. "Actually, I guess Max did most of the talking."

"Oh, good God." Lopez rubbed his forehead as if it suddenly ached. "We'll be lucky not to have corpses all over Mulberry Street by tomorrow."

"That's what we're trying to *prevent!* And as far as I can tell, the Corvinos want to avoid a war just as much as the Gambellos do. But these are jumpy, violent guys who don't trust each other, so every time someone else gets killed—"

"You have *got* to get out of this."

"And now it's gone beyond that! Now *you're*—"

"Esther, I'm taking you—"

"Listen to me!"

"No, *you* listen to *me*."

"You're in danger." I tried to keep my voice calm and rational, not to sound hysterical. It wasn't easy. "Whoever is behind these murders has targeted you. You're next. He's trying to kill you."

"These guys don't hit cops, Esther," he said. "They're not geniuses, but they're smarter than that."

"This one," I said, "is breaking the rules. He's trying to kill you. You must believe me. You're in terrible danger."

He frowned. "Who is it?"

"We don't know yet. That's what we're trying to find out! It's why we're involved in this."

"All right, *now* you're going to listen to me." He took my shoulders in his hands. "You're a civilian. Max is a loon. You ignored me after I told you to stay out of this, and now you've gotten yourself right in the middle of a very dangerous situation. I'm taking you into protective custody. Max, too, God help me."

A little while ago, I was ready to embrace protective custody with open arms, and to drag Max with me. But not now. "Not while this ... this ... this *person* is trying to kill you! I won't go! And Max won't go! He can help you! He's probably the only one who can help you!"

"What the hell are you talking about?"

"I want you to listen to me. Just listen." I took a steadying breath and tried to organize my thoughts. "Do you know anything about doppelgängers?"

19

"Me?" Lopez said, standing in the middle of the bookshop with his hands on his hips. "Me."

"Yes," I said. "Well, not *you* you. But your perfect double."

I had done my best to explain what we knew, and what the danger was. I thought I had been methodical and cogent despite my agitation about the mortal danger he was in now. But while I talked, his expression went from impatient, to skeptical, to—at the moment—appalled.

"This . . . this *crap*," he said, "that's all over the floor and the chairs and the bookcases and your hair—"

"It's in my hair?" Revolted by the thought of doppelgangster detritus in my hair, I started brushing at it with my hands.

"You're saying it was a supernatural creature that looked and sounded exactly like me?"

"Yes."

"And if I saw it, I'd be cursed with certain death?"

"Yes," I said, relieved he was getting the picture.

"And Max beheaded it to save my life."

"Yes."

"Esther . . ." He shook his head. "What the *fuck* is in the coffee that Max gives you here?"

I sighed. "I've seen these ... these *things*. With my own eyes. Lucky has seen them, too."

"Lucky drinks the coffee here, too, doesn't he?"

"Danny Dapezzo saw his doppelgangst—uh, doppelgänger before he died."

"And by amazing coincidence," Lopez said, "Danny shared food and drink with Max the night before."

I blinked. "How did you know that?"

"Wiseguys never do anything that doesn't involve a ton of food."

"Oh." I said, "But what about Charlie? And Johnny?"

"Charlie was mentally ill, you're obviously confused about when you saw Johnny, and Max has planted a lot of crazy ideas in your head."

"So you just think I'm a gullible idiot?"

He avoided answering that. "I don't know much about toxicology. I've never worked narcotics. But it sounds to me like Max must be slipping you a whole smorgasbord of hallucinogenics."

"Max isn't drugging anyone!" I said in exasperation.

He pulled his cell phone out of his jacket. "I'm going to have this place searched."

I thought of the laboratory downstairs. *"No!"*

"If there's nothing here, then they won't find anything." His voice was professionally soothing as he dialed a number on his phone.

I leaped forward and knocked the phone out of his hand, startling him. "I will not be the cause of you violating Max's privacy!" Or the cause of Max getting locked up after they found weird things in his lab that couldn't easily be explained away. Especially not with Lopez so suspicious of him already.

Angry now, Lopez said, "You just told me you watched Max cut off 'my' head tonight, and then 'I' exploded all over the room! Do you really want to go on *another* trip like that, Esther?"

"I wasn't tripping!"

"Do you want him doing this to someone else, too?"

"He's not drugging anyone! Why won't you believe me?"

"Do you hear how crazy you sound?"

"Yes, I do! Do you honestly think I'd even *talk* to you about this if your life weren't at stake?" Frustrated, I said, "Max wants to protect you! And me! Why are you trying to blame him?"

He bit off whatever he was about to say, got control of his temper, and closed his eyes for a moment. Then he let out his breath slowly and said, "Because Max creating these delusions by drugging you is better than the alternative."

"Which is?" I gasped as I realized what he meant. "Oh! You think I'm crazy?"

He didn't say anything.

"So either I'm a drugged-up dupe or I'm a nutbag?"

"I'm trying to think of a third alternative, but nothing's coming to me." He crossed the floor and stooped down to retrieve his phone. Examining it, he said, "It's dead. Great. That's the second phone I've run through today."

Trying to relieve the tension in the room, I said, "What happened to the first one?"

"I don't know." He shrugged. "It'll turn up. But after I saw those photos, I didn't want to call you from an OCCB phone, and I couldn't find my cell." He turned the broken phone over in his hands. "I keep this in my desk. It's prepaid. Anonymous. Useful for work, sometimes."

"Oh." That explained why his call to me a little while ago had shown up on my cell as "Caller Unknown." I said, "I'm sorry I broke it. But I don't want you bothering Max."

"I'm worried about you," he said. "Seriously worried."

"I'm a lot more worried about you."

"I want you to stay away from Max from now on."

"No, I won't do that."

He glanced at his watch. "Shit. I have to go."

"Back to work?"

"I'm following a lead. I've got to go meet someone."

"You're not safe," I said urgently. "Don't go."

"The city's on the verge of a mob war, Esther. That's a very messy thing, and people besides wiseguys will get hurt. I want to get you out of here—"

"And maybe into an insane asylum?" I said sourly.

"—but I don't have time to fight about it. I've got to leave." He started collecting the bladed weapons from the table.

"What are you doing?"

"You sound insane, you're talking about beheading people—"

"Not *people!*"

"—and chopping off heads is evidently Max's bright idea. All things considered, I don't think it's a great idea for me to leave two swords and an ax lying around here when I go."

"You can't just *take* those! Don't you have to have a warrant or something?"

"Let's agree that I'm not taking them as a cop, but as your concerned ... friend."

"Give that back!" I grabbed the ax and tugged. "You can't leave us defenseless!"

He used his free hand to grasp my wrist and torque it downward. A sharp jolt of pain made me let go of the ax and stumble. He twisted my arm behind my back and pulled me up against his chest. I was breathing hard and grimacing in pain. He looked angry, sad, and frustrated.

"Either you're leaving here right now, or else these weapons are leaving." His voice was quiet, his tone unyielding. "God knows what you might do with them, in your current state of mind."

"Where do you want me to go?" I was angry and frustrated, too. "A psych ward?"

"That's not a bad idea." He lifted his brows. "Well?"

I lowered my head and tried to get control of my breathing, aware of our bodies pressed together. Aware of how different things were now than they had been only this afternoon. Nothing about this embrace resembled the one we had shared then.

"If you take these weapons," I said, realizing there was a silver lining, "keep them with you. And if you see your perfect double—"

"No, Esther, I'm not cutting off someone's head." He released me. "But I will take the weapons."

Ax still in hand, he picked up the two swords. "Don't eat or drink or inhale anything else Max gives you—"

"Oh, for God's sake."

"—and I'll try to call you tomorrow. We'll talk about protective custody."

"Lopez!" I followed him as he headed for the door. "Will you at *least* promise to call me immediately if you see someone who looks just like you?"

"We'll also talk about you getting treatment."

"Listen to me! What's happening here is more complicated than just another mob war! The Gambellos—"

"Esther, I know you want to help." He paused on the threshold and looked over his shoulder at me. "And some of what you told me tonight *is* helpful. It's useful. Okay? But now you've got to stay out of this."

And he left.

Max and Nelli were alone when they returned to the shop.

"Where's Lucky?"

"He got a call while we were out. He has been summoned by the don of his *famiglia*."

It was nearly midnight. "Don't wiseguys ever sleep?"

Max's gaze fell on the table where I sat. "Where are our weapons?"

I told him what had happened.

When I finished, he patted my back. "Don't blame yourself, my dear. I'm sure you explained the danger with excellent clarity. But I've learned through long and difficult experience that most people respond to mystical events precisely the way Detective Lopez does. That is to say, by dismissing some of the evidence and interpreting the rest according to their existing beliefs." He added morosely, "Or else they respond the way Doctor Dapezzo did."

Recalling the capo's unbridled mirth, I said, "Well, at least Danny had a good time on the final night of his life."

"And you mustn't fret about the loss of the bladed weapons. I have more."

"Really?"

"I have no more swords, alas, but I do have a rather good machete in the laboratory that will serve our purpose," he said. "And it is somewhat comforting to know that Detective Lopez is now armed with suitable weapons for dispatching a doppelgangster."

"He says he won't use them."

"We can only hope that, if confronted by his own perfect double, he will change his mind."

"But then it'll be too late! Once he comes face-to-face with himself, he'll be a victim of the killer's curse, and nothing can save his life after that! So how can we prevent him from meeting his duplicate?"

"Well, first of all, keep in mind that we have dispatched his double and that it's entirely possible the killer is unaware of this. In which case, he won't even consider making another duplicate until he suspects that something has gone wrong."

"And then he *will* make another, and—"

"So far, the killer has only created one doppelgangster per victim," Max said. "Therefore, it is not unreasonable for us to hope that he *can* only make one for each target."

"But you're not sure."

"No. But logic suggests that, at least for the rest of tonight, Detective Lopez is out of danger."

"Logic," I repeated. "You must be kidding." Still, this soothed my panic enough for me to remember what I had wanted to tell Max. So I explained what I had realized when confronted by the real Lopez.

"Hmm. Yes, this is most interesting, Esther!" He stroked his beard. "So Detective Lopez's doppelgangster tonight was wearing exactly the same clothing that the real man wore at your apartment early this afternoon . . ."

"Plus the jacket," I said, "which he didn't have when he came to my place. So I guess he hadn't been duplicated yet?"

"But by tonight, he was."

"What I don't understand is, how did Lopez avoid meeting his double? It sounds to me like they were both at the scene of the crime this afternoon. They both found the note with our phone numbers . . . Wait! *Oh*."

"Ah!" Max nodded.

"He was duplicated *after* he found the note," I said.

"The doppelgangster shared his memories up to that point. It recalled finding the note at the scene of the crime, concealing the evidence, and phoning this number to verify that it was indeed mine."

"But it *didn't* know about anything that happened later," I said. "It wasn't affected by the things that took Lopez's mind off that discovery as the evening progressed. And it didn't know about the surveillance photos, either, which bothered the real Lopez more than the note did."

"The doppelgangster," Max mused, "gave in to the impulse to come here immediately and confront you about the note. An impulse that Detective Lopez presumably *felt* when he found our phone numbers with the deceased, but couldn't act upon at the time."

"Because he was on the job. He could place a phone

call, but he couldn't leave." I paused. "But, wait, the doppelgangster *didn't* come here immediately, Max. It came
here right before Lopez did."

"It didn't come here immediately after the discovery
of the note," Max agreed. "I postulate that it came here
immediately after it was *created*."

A chill went through me. "This is creeping me out."

"So we know the doppelgangster came into being
sometime after I received Detective Lopez's extremely
brief phone call and before the creature arrived here."

"That's a window of a few hours. Does this mean
that's how long it takes to make a doppelgangster?"

"Possibly. Or perhaps even much less time than that.
Alternately, however, the process could have begun well
before this afternoon and then been completed this
evening."

My shoulders slumped. "So we haven't really nar-
rowed down anything after all?"

"On the contrary!" Max said encouragingly. "While
we still don't know how it was done—nor precisely how
long the whole process took—we *have* discerned the
moment of Detective Lopez's life from which his doppelgangster was created: While he was angry about the note
and conscience stricken over concealing it, but before
his subsequent experiences began distracting his attention from this."

"All right," I said. "We know approximately *when* . . .
but we still have no idea *why*."

"Why he was duplicated?"

"The other three victims were all wiseguys. Why is
the murderer trying to kill a cop now?"

"Because Detective Lopez is his adversary," Max
suggested.

"Wiseguys don't target cops," I said with a frown. "So
are we looking for a wiseguy who's violating that custom? Or are we . . ." It occurred to me for the first time.
"Is it possible the killer isn't a wiseguy?"

"Hmm. That's a theory we've overlooked until now. The victims all had enemies in their own, er, profession, so we made the reasonable supposition that the killer is a colleague. However, you're quite right—that needn't necessarily be the case." He continued, "On the other hand, our adversary is creative, devious, ruthless, and clever. Given the unconventional nature of these murders, I find it difficult to believe he abides by popular custom, so to speak, when choosing his victims. Therefore, he may well be a member of Lucky's profession and yet entirely willing to target a police officer."

"But if a cop dies . . ." I felt sick at the thought of *which* cop we were talking about, but made myself continue, "There'll be hell to pay, and the killer must know that."

"If so, then he is indifferent to that eventuality." Max shrugged. "Perhaps he even courts it. It would certainly add to the violent chaos that is now imminent."

"Yes, it would. And why this *particular* cop?" I said desperately. "There's a whole team on the case!"

"Perhaps because the killer has identified him as a greater threat than his fellow officers are? As you are well aware, Detective Lopez is both astute and persistent."

"I should have conked him over the head and locked him up in the laboratory."

"No, he would get into mischief down there," Max said.

"Not if he was tied up," I said grimly.

There was a pause. Then Max said, "I don't wish to alarm you unnecessarily—"

"Why bother, when there's so much *necessary* alarm to be had?"

"—but before he left to see his superior, Lucky said that it's not entirely impossible that you and I are now in some danger from the Corvino family."

"Oh. Right. The thought had occurred to me." I said, "Also to Lopez. When he got here tonight, he wanted to

take us into protective custody. But now I think he wants
to put me in a loony bin and you in a maximum security
prison."

"That sounds most incommodious."

"Indeed."

"Lucky says that since you're a dame and I'm an old
guy, and we've never whacked anyone, we won't be high
on the hit list if the two families go to the mattresses—"

"You're learning his dialect, I see."

"—but we should nonetheless take reasonable precautions until he knows exactly what the Corvinos' intentions toward us are."

"Such as?"

"He recommends that I keep the bookstore closed
for the time being. And since I can ward this building
against mundane intruders—as well as their firearms—
you are to sleep here tonight."

Actually, that sounded fine by me. It had been an ex-
hausting day. The tense journey to Brooklyn, Danny's
murder and Vinny's strange story, followed by a mind-
numbing evening of doing more reading about apparitional bilocated doppelgängerism ... All capped off
by *two* awful confrontations with Lopez, during one of
which I had watched him get decapitated. All in all, I realized I'd have trouble just crawling as far as the nearest
bed now, never mind making it all the way home to be
murdered in my own apartment by Corvino hitters.

Max said, "Hieronymus' rooms on the third floor are
vacant, if you think you would be comfortable there."

"Hieronymus." I grimaced.

"The accommodations are modest, but adequate for
your temporary needs, I think."

I thought about it and gave an involuntary shudder.
"Oh, I don't think I want to sleep in a bedroom that was
recently inhabited by a demented young wizard who
would have wound up killing half the city if we hadn't,
er, sent him away." Remembering what we had done

to Hieronymus made me think of Lopez again, which made me feel anxious and weepy. "My nerves are frayed enough as it is, Max. I'll just sleep on your couch."

He nodded. "Nelli usually sleeps on the couch, but I feel certain that she would be pleased to relinquish her usual place to you, given the circumstances."

"I'm wiped out. I think I'll go straight to bed." I stood up. Nelli, who'd been sitting nearby, rose to her feet, too, and yawned. I asked Max, "Are you coming upstairs now?"

"In a little while," he said. "I need to meditate and focus my strength to ensure this building is well protected for the rest of the night."

I nodded, turned, and walked to the back of the shop. Nelli followed me. I opened the stairwell door so we could ascend to Max's sparsely furnished apartment on the second floor. I'd only been there once before, but I knew where the bathroom was. I went in there, turned on the light, and conducted a quick and very basic nighttime toilette. Then I poked gingerly around the apartment for a few minutes in search of a blanket. I found a worn but clean cotton quilt that was folded up and lying in a cedar chest in Max's monklike bedroom. I took it back into the living room, turned out the light, and lay down. I would sleep in my comfortable knit dress. The couch sagged a little, but was relatively comfortable. Unfortunately, though, only days after her arrival in this dimension, it was already redolent of Nelli. I would definitely need a shower in the morning.

Nelli didn't seem to mind my being in her usual sleeping place, but she mistakenly thought the couch was big enough for two. Without warning, she cheerfully climbed on top of me and started settling herself into the cushions with contented little snuffles, impervious to my attempts to shove her off. After a brief argument which didn't seem to faze her a bit, I decided that as long as I could breathe, I was too exhausted to care about retaining feeling in my legs. And although I thought at first that her snoring would keep me awake all night, it wasn't very long before my own fatigue overcame the noise. I sank into oblivion and slept like the dead until late the next morning. I didn't even hear Max come upstairs and go to bed, nor go back downstairs again to resume his work sometime after sunrise.

And as is so often the case, getting enough sleep for the human brain to function effectively made a tremendous difference. The following day, I woke up knowing who the killer was and why Lopez had been targeted.

20

"The Widow Giacalona?" Max said when I confronted him in his laboratory with my revelation.

"Yes! I was so exhausted and upset last night, I couldn't see it at the time." The truth had hit me within minutes of waking up. I had raced downstairs without a shower, my hair in a rat's nest and my clothes stinking of Nelli, to put the facts before Max. "And it's probably a good thing Lucky's not here. I don't think he would listen to reason. He's in love with her, you know."

"Oh, dear."

"Who hates the Corvinos and the Gambellos enough to kill men in *both* families? Elena Giacalona. Why? Because a Gambello killed her second husband, and a Corvino killed her third."

"I can see how that might stoke vengeance in her heart," Max said sadly.

I started pacing as I reviewed the next point. "Johnny Gambello was a useless *momzer* who was no threat to a rival family. Danny Dapezzo, a Corvino capo, even played cards with him, for goodness sake! The Corvinos had no reason to whack him. And Don Victor had forbidden any of the Gambellos to kill him. But who hated Johnny enough to want him dead? The woman

who'd lost her first husband because of Johnny!" I told
Max, "Anthony Gambello died horribly, leaving Elena a
widow, because Johnny masqueraded as Anthony while
having an affair with a violent drug lord's girlfriend."

"Good heavens!" Max said.

"The night before last, when I got to St. Monica's
a little early for the sit-down, I told Elena that Lucky
and I had encountered an apparition of Johnny after his
death. And *she* tried to convince me that's not what I
had seen, that I was mistaken about the timing."

"But isn't that what Detective Lopez thinks, too?"

"Yeah, but that's because he thinks I'm delusional."

"Might not the Widow Giacalona also think you're
delusional?"

"Might not the Widow Giacalona," I said, "be trying
to cover up the trail of her handiwork by insisting I saw
the real Johnny Be Good and not an apparition?"

"It does sound feasible."

I continued, "Elena wouldn't spare Johnny just because he was under the Shy Don's protection, the way
others have spared him. It's hard to believe she cares what
the old man wants, and easy to believe she'd like a chance
to make him grieve. After all, Victor Gambello not only
ordered the death of her second husband, he also tried to
strangle her for the sin of marrying a Corvino!"

"Zounds!"

I recalled thinking at one point during my conversation with her that Elena didn't look wholly sane. I had
thought it was excessive religious fervor. Could it instead have been homicidal mania?

"Who would be crazy enough to *want* to start a new
Corvino-Gambello war? Who would do something so
dangerous and destructive?" I concluded, "The widow
who hates both families so bitterly!"

"It is a most convincing theory," Max admitted. "Is
Detective Lopez investigating her? Is that why he has
been selected as the next victim?"

I sat down suddenly, feeling sick and guilt-ridden. "No, that's my fault."

He blinked. "How is that possible?"

"I told her about Lopez. That he was a smart, honest, hardworking detective who was investigating the case. And although I didn't mean to, I think I gave her the impression that he and Lucky were cooperating on the investigation."

"Oh."

"Lucky," I elaborated, "who murdered her second husband."

"And between her loathing of Lucky and her fear that Detective Lopez could pose a serious threat to her plans . . ."

"The following day—yesterday—Lopez's doppelgangster suddenly appeared."

Max frowned. "But not Lucky's."

"What?"

"Why did she duplicate Detective Lopez before Lucky?" Max mused. "Indeed, why did she kill Charlie Chiccante rather than Lucky? It sounds as if Charlie played no direct role in her sorrows, whereas we know that Lucky did."

"I assume she'll get around to Lucky," I said. "We've got to stop her before she does. Let alone before she duplicates Lopez again and curses him with certain death!"

"When I saw her at St. Monica's," Max said, "she did not strike me as a patient woman. To say the least. And her hatred of Lucky was, er, energetic. So I find it puzzling that he was not her first victim. Nor does he even seem to be her fourth intended victim."

I thought about this for a moment. "We talked yesterday about the killer gaining psychological power over his—*her*—victims with the weirdness of these murders. Maybe she's enjoying toying with Lucky, building up the anticipation. Maybe she has intended all along that he'll be her *final* victim, rather than her first. And that by the time he sees his doppelgangster, it'll terrify him witless."

"Hmm. Yes, I can easily believe that of the person behind these killings. As I've said before, this seems to be a subtle and devious individual." He frowned. "But I find it *less* easy to believe such patience and planning have been exercised by the emotional, volatile, direct woman whom we saw in that church."

"We hardly know her, Max. She could be acting, to conceal her true nature."

"Ah! Yes." He thought it over. "*Yes*. Certainly my sense of our adversary is that this is someone quite capable of concealing his—or *her*—nature from others."

"So what do we do now?"

"The sorcerer—or sorceress—creating these doppelgangsters must have a workshop or laboratory. At the very least, an elaborate altar of some sort. And finding this would give us conclusive evidence that the widow is indeed the killer. It would also enable us to destroy her means of creating any more of these deadly creatures. And such a discovery may also lead us to any remaining doppelgangsters roaming the city so that we can dispatch them." He nodded decisively. "Ergo, we must search the widow's abode."

"Her home?"

"Yes."

"I don't know where she lives," I said.

"It seems likely that Lucky would know." His gaze met mine. "And I don't think we should deceive him about our reasons for asking."

I sighed and said, "He won't like this." But I pulled out my cell phone and called the old gangster.

"Esther!" Lucky said when he answered his cell. "Are you at Max's?"

"Yes. Where are you?"

"With the boss."

"Still?"

"I'm about to leave. He's agreed to talk by phone today with the boss of our mutual acquaintances."

I frowned. "The boss of our mutual acquaint . . . Oh! You mean the don of the Corv—"

"No names on the phone, kid," Lucky admonished.

"Huh? Oh. And, er, the other boss? Has he also agreed to have this conversation?"

"I'm still workin' on that," he said. "But luckily, after what happened to the departed yesterday, there's a few boys in that camp—I think you know them—who are urgin' their boss to consider it."

I puzzled this over for a moment, then realized he meant that some or all of the Corvino soldiers whom I had recently met—Fast Sammy Salerno, Mikey Castrucci, Nathan, and Bobby, as well as Vinny Dapezzo—were telling the famously dapper Don Carmine Corvino that the Gambellos might not be responsible for Danny's bizarre death.

Lucky continued, "But it's a very delicate situation, and everyone's real jumpy. So if anyone else should happen to wind up dead, things are gonna go up in smoke around here."

"I see."

"I'm heading over to St. Monica's to talk to Father Gabriel about Charlie's and Johnny's funerals. Then I'll come back to the bookstore."

"The funerals?" I said. "I thought the cops didn't want to release the bodies?"

"Yeah, they're still draggin' their heels, but they can't hold the bodies forever," he said. "They must have strong stomachs at the police morgue. Do you know how much a corpse stinks after a few days if it ain't been embalmed?"

"No, and I don't want to know," I said firmly.

"So how we doin' at your end with solving our problem?"

"Better," I said, meeting Max's anxious gaze. "We have a suspect."

"Yeah?"

I threw caution to the winds and used her name.

As expected, Lucky was utterly appalled by my theory. He interrupted me with angry arguments and protests so often, it took me three times as long to explain my reasoning as it should have taken. After I had laid it all out for him, he remained adamant in his denials.

"No," he said. "*No*. You got it all wrong."

"Lucky," I said, sorry to be breaking his heart, despite everything he'd done. "She's got the motive to commit these murders. Now we need to find out if she's got the means."

"She ain't got the motive! She ain't like that! She's pure of heart."

"I think you're not seeing this cl—"

"You don't know her! I do! I've known her for thirty years," he insisted. "Ever since Anthony married her. I admit she's hotheaded, but she's not a killer."

"Look, I understand that you—"

"And can you *really* picture her blowing Danny away with a shotgun?" Lucky demanded.

"I'm trying not to picture *anyone* doing that," I said. "But maybe she can handle a shotgun, Lucky. It's an unusual method of murder for a woman, but it's certainly not unprecedented. And we're dealing with an unusual killer, after all."

"You're saying you think *she* bashed in Johnny's skull then dumped his body in the East River? Oh, come *on*."

I knew it wasn't impossible, but I had to admit it was hard to imagine. "Unless . . ." I looked at Max. "What if she has an accomplice?"

"Someone who does the dirty work?" Lucky said.

"An accomplice," Max said, rising to his feet. "Of course!"

"Yes," I said, realizing it would explain a number of the things that had puzzled us.

"Forget it," Lucky said. "She's not involved in this."

"This original, subtle, and inventive sorcery we've witnessed," Max said as he stroked his beard. "Contrasted to the violent, unimaginative nature of the actual killings."

I looked at Max and said, "*Two* killers!"

"She ain't a killer!" Lucky shouted over my phone.

"Two completely different styles of dispatching the same enemy!" Max was pacing around the room in his excitement. "Two drastically dissimilar personalities cooperating on the same murders!"

"One of them a woman," I said to Max.

"One of *what?*" Lucky said me.

"She had the power to create the doppelgangsters and the shrewdness to play on old enmities to generate a mob war between the two families she hates," I continued. "But she needed the assistance of someone who could actually commit the *physical* slayings. She had no experience at that. And probably no stomach for it, either."

"Will you *stop?*" Lucky said.

Max said, "So she found an accomplice who was willing to finish off her victims once she had ensured they would be defenseless!"

"Who?" I wondered. "Angelo Falcone?"

"You gotta be kidding me," Lucky said. "That putz?"

"She's a beautiful woman," Max said. "And we've seen for ourselves that at least two, er, experienced men of action are enthralled by her allure."

Our eyes met. We both knew that she wouldn't have invited Lucky to be her partner in crime; he would certainly be one of her intended victims.

"Don Michael 'No Relation' Buonarotti," I said slowly.

"No way is Elena in cahoots with *him!*" Lucky said, having heard this. "Are you nuts?"

"Buonarotti's infatuated with the widow," I said. "He's an experienced killer. And I'll bet he didn't become the don without having plenty of ambition. So maybe he thinks the Buonarotti crime family can take advantage of the situation and come out on top if the Corvinos and Gambellos tear each other apart in another mob war now."

"Yes." Max was nodding furiously and tugging at his beard. "Yes, this is an excellent theory, Esther!"

There was a leaden silence on my telephone.

"Lucky? We have to search the widow's place," I said. "We have to look for evidence that she's creating the doppelgangsters."

"She's *not*, I tell you." He sounded anxious now, uncertain. Worried. "She turned to the church in her grief, not to whacking people."

"All the same, we must search her home." Recalling Lopez's words last night, I said, "Look, if there's nothing there, then we won't find anything."

There was a tense pause. Then he said, "And if you don't find nothin', then you'll get off her back?"

No, we would try to figure out where else she might be conducting her mystical activities. But I said, "Yes." Because sometimes you just have to say whatever it takes to make progress on a problem.

Lucky let out puff of breath. "All right. After I'm done with my other business, I'll search her place today."

"You don't have to do that," I said, hearing how unhappy he sounded. "Max and I will search it."

I met Max's gaze again, and he nodded emphatically.

"You don't trust me?" Lucky said wearily. "You think I'm going to find some doppelgangsters hanging in the closet and not tell you?"

"I don't think you're going to find anything quite that obvious," I said patiently. "This is a mystical problem. You might not recognize something incriminating in Elena's apartment. That's why Max has to do this."

"All right, tell the Doc to meet me at Elena's place."
He gave me the address.

"What time should we be there?"

"You're not coming with him. While we search her
place, you're gonna keep an eye on Elena."

"What?"

"Relax, she ain't guilty. Anyhow, you'll be perfectly
safe. You'll be in church."

Since Lucky timed his own visits to St. Monica's specifically to see Elena, he knew her schedule for prayer
and church activities. She was a member of the women's
auxiliary club, and they were meeting at St. Monica's
that afternoon to discuss fundraising. The church was
over one hundred years old, and portions of it were in
dire need of update and repair.

The stairs to the bell tower and to the courtyard
were dangerous. There was faulty electrical wiring in the
church sanctuary. The floor in the choir gallery needed to
be renovated or replaced; the tiles were so chipped and
uneven, several choir members had tripped and fallen
lately. The church organ needed tuning and cleaning.
The old dormitories above this meeting room should be
renovated and put to good use. The bathrooms for the
congregation needed refurbishment. All of this necessary work would require a great deal of money.

I learned all this because I attended the women's auxiliary club meeting to keep an eye on the Widow Giacalona while Lucky and Max searched her apartment. She
lived on Mulberry Street, only three blocks away from
St. Monica's, in the opposite direction from Bella Stella's.
My job was to call Lucky when Elena left St. Monica's,
ensuring that he and Max had enough time to leave her
apartment before she got home.

Today's gathering, I realized after I got there, was
a social event as much as it was a business meeting.
There was plenty of coffee, food, and gossip, and no one

seemed in a hurry to call the meeting to order. This gave me plenty of time to read the secretary's report that summarized which renovation projects and fundraising efforts the group would be discussing today.

Elena had noticed me when I entered this meeting room in the east wing of St. Monica's, but it had obviously taken her a couple of additional glances to remember who I was. Then her expression grew cold and she didn't deign to meet my eyes again. Which was just as well. I was tense and afraid of arousing her suspicion.

Her outfit was even more austere than usual, just a simple dark dress with a modest V-neck. No scarf or jewelry, and her hair was scraped back severely from her face. Her settled expression of resigned unhappiness made her look mysterious and vaguely tragic, rather than sour and embittered even though, in reality, I believed it had turned her into a devious and demented killer.

The rest of the women here were well-dressed, well-coiffed, wearing makeup, and gaily accessorized . . . and yet it was Elena's stark, still beauty that attracted the eye in this chatting, giggling, fluttering throng. The good light in this meeting room made her true age—early to mid-fifties, I assumed—more readily apparent to me than it had been the first time I met her. The naked skin of her throat and the creased corners of her eyes revealed her years today. But she still wore time very well.

I checked my watch. Lucky and Max should be in her apartment right now. I counted on Max to convince Lucky that the evidence they found there was damning and the widow must be stopped.

"Esther?"

"Huh!" I jumped.

"Did I startle you?" Father Gabriel asked. "I'm sorry."

"Oh! Uh, no." I pulled myself together and met the priest's luminous brown gaze. "I was lost in thought, that's all. How are you, Father?"

"I'm delighted to welcome you to St. Monica's once again." He smiled warmly as he shook my hand.

I had showered and tidied up at Max's before coming to the church, but I was still wearing my black knit dress from yesterday, and it was the worse for wear by now. I saw the priest's nostrils quiver slightly as he got a good whiff of Nelli.

"Sorry," I said. "I was, uh, playing with a friend's dog before I came here."

"I'm more of a cat person." He smiled and added, "It's wonderful to see you taking such an interest in our crumbling old church! Is your interest in this meeting architectural? Or dare I hope that our congregation holds some spiritual attraction for you?"

"I . . ."

I thought my mother's soul would abandon her body in Wisconsin and fly to New York to tear my tongue out of my mouth if I claimed to be thinking about converting. But I was spared the need to pretend a passion for architecture. We were interrupted without apology by a middle-aged woman whose hair was a shade of blond that had no equivalent in nature. She grasped Father Gabriel's arm, cooed his name, and dragged him away from me as she flirted outrageously and invited him to Sunday dinner at her house. I wondered whether her husband would be present for the meal.

As I had noticed once before, many of the women here seemed to be dressed for a hot date rather than for church. Their eyes followed the handsome priest with enthralled interest, and a number of them were openly competing for his attention.

How ironic that a man with such sex appeal had chosen a celibate vocation. I was glad that Lopez hadn't done the same, even though his being a cop was, once again, proving to be very inconvenient. As well as dangerous.

As I watched Father Gabriel deflecting subtle and not so subtle advances from these women with courteous skill, I wondered at the level of spiritual commitment that had led him away from the temptations of the opposite sex and the pleasures of marriage to dedicate himself to a solitary life of worship and devotion.

Realizing I was hungry, I crossed the room to examine the selection of cakes and little sandwiches that had been provided for the attendees. I was perusing the food with interest when my cell phone rang. The caller was Lucky.

"Hello?"

"Hey, you was supposed to warn us if she left the church," he snapped at me. "What gives? Did she never show up there, or something?"

"Huh?"

"We were only in her place for maybe ten minutes when she walked in on us," Lucky said angrily.

"What?"

"Talk about embarrassing. Max did his best to talk our way out of it, but I won't be surprised if she calls the cops and files a complaint. She was real mad."

I felt my eyes grow wide with horror as I stared at the widow, who stood about fifteen feet away from me. "You . . . you . . . she . . ."

"Anyhow, the job is done. Her apartment is tiny. She ain't makin' any doppelgangsters there unless they're the size of mice. We were practically finished lookin' around anyhow, when Elena walked in on us."

"Lucky," I choked out.

"So you and Max better be satisfied now is all I'm sayin' about it."

I turned toward the corner and covered my mouth so I wouldn't be overheard. "Lucky, she's here."

"Who's where?"

"The widow," I said, keeping my voice lowered. "I'm at St. Monica's. She's *here.*"

There was a pause. "No, she's not. I just left her in her apartment about thirty seconds ago."

"She's here, I tell you!" I stiffened when I saw someone glance at me. I mustn't attract attention. In particular, I mustn't attract *her* attention.

I looked cautiously over my shoulder. I saw her pouring herself a cup of coffee. "I'm looking at her right
now." Trying to keep my voice steady, I repeated, "Right
now."

He sucked in a sharp gasp of breath. "Holy shit."

I heard him tell Max, and I heard Max's exclamation
of surprise. Then Max took the phone from Lucky and
spoke to me.

"You're still at St. Monica's?" he asked.

"Yes. Where are you?"

"Right outside the widow's apartment building."

"You *just* saw her?" I asked, wanting to be absolutely
sure. "Just now?"

"Only moments ago."

"Holy shit," I said.

An older lady standing nearby flinched at my language, then moved quickly away from me.

"You're looking at her right now?" Max asked. "This
moment?"

"Yep."

"Have you got your knife with you? The one that
Lucky gave you yesterday?"

I realized what he was about to suggest. I turned back
to the corner, covered my mouth, and said as quietly as
possible, "Max, I can't do that! There are lots of people
here."

Unfortunately, Max had left Nelli at home. Since we
thought Elena was the killer, it hadn't occurred to us
that we might have to identify her doppelgangster today.
And Nelli wasn't exactly an inconspicuous companion to
take along for the stealthy search of a city apartment.

"Given the widow's reaction to finding us in her home
after we had broken in," Max said, "I would rather not
return now and pierce her skin, if there's any possible

away of avoiding it. I fear that such a confrontation will unavoidably result in an unfortunate interview with the authorities."

"Well, there's probably also going to be an 'unfortunate interview' if I do this in front of thirty witnesses," I argued.

I heard the two men discussing it, then Lucky came back on the phone. "You're an actress. Make it look like an accident."

An accident. Right. I would just *accidentally* open a switchblade at a church meeting and cut Elena with it. "Great," I muttered. "Fine. All right. I'll call you back."

"We'll be right here."

I put my phone back in my purse. I felt around for Lucky's little knife and opened it inside the handbag. Keeping the short blade concealed with my hand, I took the knife out of the purse and lowered it to my side. My gaze sought the widow. She was walking in this direction. She stopped about five feet away from me to look at the selection of desserts, evidently wanting a snack to go with her cup of coffee.

If only Lopez could be right. If only this were all a delusion.

I approached the widow and stood alongside her, pretending to peruse the same selection of cakes and cookies.

"Hello," I said brightly. "We meet again."

"Yes," she said without enthusiasm. "Hello." She didn't lift her gaze from the food.

As she leaned forward and picked up a cannoli, I figured it was now or never.

"Oh, that looks good!" I leaned across her, reaching for a cookie. I pretended to lose my balance, toppled sideways, and grabbed for her, as if reflexively seeking rescue from my fall. I took the widow, her cannoli, and her coffee cup crashing to the hard floor with enough force to break her cup. Through her shrieks and our tangled limbs, I managed to slash her hand quickly with my knife. I was pulling on her hair at the same time, hoping this would distract her.

"Agh!"

"Oh, my gosh, I'm so sorry!" I cried, rising to my knees. "Are you hurt? Are you okay?

A dozen women descended on us to help us to our feet and inquire after our well-being. And I had evidently given a good performance. Everyone present seemed to assume I was just very clumsy.

Except for Elena, who snapped, "Are you drunk?"

"I'm so sorry." I concealed Lucky's small knife by pressing it against my midriff with my spread palm. "Are you all right?"

"*No*, I'm not all right."

She looked down at her hand. I looked, too.

There was blood.

I was torn between relief and a desire to blurt out a muddled confession. But I stayed in character. "You cut yourself on your coffee cup!" I exclaimed. "Here, let me see."

"Stay back," Elena said firmly, shying away from me.

"May I have a look?" Father Gabriel stepped through the women crowding around us. Smiling kindly, he took Elena's bleeding hand and examined it. "Oh, my, it *is* bleeding, isn't it? Nothing serious," he said reassuringly, "but you should get a bandage and some disinfectant. I believe Mrs. Campanello has some supplies in the office. Shall I come with you?"

"No, thank you, Father. It's just a cut. And I'd like to stop by the ladies room, anyhow." She glared at me. "I feel a bit disheveled now." She turned and left.

The priest asked, "Are you all right, Esther?"

"Just fine."

The women around us were already tidying up the cannoli, coffee, and broken ceramic cup that had scattered across the floor. I picked up my purse. Keeping the knife concealed, I dropped it in there under the pretext of fishing around for a comb to tidy my hair.

"I think I'd better go," I said to the priest.

"There's no need for that," he assured me.

"I feel self-conscious now," I said. "She didn't like me very much to begin with."

"Oh, I'm sure she'll come around. You don't need to—"

"And, actually, I banged up my knee when I fell. It's throbbing a bit now."

"Oh, well, in that case, yes. You should go home and rest. Be sure to put some ice on it."

"Yes, I will, Father. I'll see you again, I hope."

"Straight home now," he said with a kind smile. "No walking around on these cement sidewalks and uneven pavements with a sore knee. You'll regret it dearly tomorrow if you don't take care of it today."

"Yes, Father. Good-bye."

As soon as I was outside the church, I called Lucky.

"Well?" he said.

"This one's the real deal. She bled. What do we do now?"

"Max says now we gotta abduct the ringer and bring it back to the bookstore for questioning. So we'll see you back there, kid."

21

What we really wanted to avoid now, I thought, was another visit from Lopez.

We had Elena Giacalona's shrieking doppelgangster tied to a chair in Max's basement. Her hands were also bound together behind her back. And although we had initially left her legs free, Lucky had agreed to tie her ankles to the legs of the chair after she kicked Max in the groin.

It was not a scene I felt I'd ever be able to explain to Lopez's satisfaction. So I fervently hoped he didn't feel another urge to come to the bookstore tonight.

Abducting a grown woman in the middle of Little Italy in the middle of the day wasn't easy, but Lucky was an expert at this sort of thing. With a couple of quick phone calls, he had arranged for a large trunk, a small truck, and two sturdy Gambello soldiers to do the heavy lifting. And thus he had gotten Elena's perfect double from her apartment to Max's basement with no fuss, no mess, and no awkward questions asked.

The creature seemed to be dressed for Sunday Mass. Or possibly a dinner date. With Elena, it was hard to tell. She wore a dark blue knit dress, a silver wristwatch, cheap pantyhose, and plain black pumps. Her hair was styled in a simple but flattering twist, and around her neck hung the lovely cross she had inherited from her mother, made of silver, diamonds, and mother-of-pearl.

"Are you out of your *minds?*" she raged at us. "This is kidnapping! You'll go to prison for this! And *you'll* rot in hell, Lucky!"

She was every bit as convincing in her role as the other doppelgangsters we had encountered. But we had no doubt of her true nature. Apart from the blood I had seen oozing from Elena Giacalona's hand at St. Monica's today, Nelli's hostile reaction to this creature, upon meeting it, had confirmed that it was indeed a duplicate.

Nelli was now upstairs, since keeping her separate from the creature was easier on everyone's nerves.

Questioning the doppelgangster, which Max had been so eager to do, proved to be disappointing. As Max had previously postulated, they were not self-aware. Like the other ones we had met, this one was utterly convinced it was the real thing. Consequently, Max's probing questions revealed exactly what we would have learned from the real Elena Giacalona about the nature of the doppelgangsters, the method of their creation, and the identity of their maker: nothing.

"I gotta go," Lucky said after we'd spent about an hour with the infuriated perfect double.

"Go?" I repeated "Where?"

"Someone's trying to kill Elena," he said, his face strained. "I've got to tell her and convince her to get out of town until this all blows over."

"Good plan," I said. If I thought Lopez would agree to get out of town, I'd pack his bags and buy the plane ticket. "Go on."

After the old hit man left, I took Max aside and admitted to feeling discouraged. Instead of being the killer, Elena was the next victim.

"I went way down the wrong track on this one," I said.

"And we're still no closer to stopping the killer than we were yesterday."

"Don't lose heart," Max said. "Although you were mistaken about the widow, your suspicion of her did inadvertently lead to our saving her life by ensuring she and her perfect double don't meet. So some good has certainly come out of today's events. Moreover, my instinct is that we are getting very close to a solution. We may not be able to see it yet, but I feel as if it's *just* out of reach."

I, on the other hand, thought it seemed a million miles away. But I didn't think that saying so would help the situation, so I kept this opinion to myself.

The doppelgangster didn't want any dinner, but I was hungry by that evening, so Max ordered some Chinese food to be delivered. After it arrived, Max insisted I eat first, while he guarded the doppelgangster. Then I went back down to the lab to guard her while Max and Nelli took their evening meal.

I knew "the widow" wasn't the real thing, but she looked and acted so real, I didn't want to leave her alone and frightened in the subterranean laboratory tied to a chair.

I also knew that the situation was taking a heavy toll on Lucky. He wouldn't be able to behead this doppelgangster, nor to let Max behead it. It was too much like the woman he loved. On the other hand, we certainly couldn't release the creature. Left to its own devices, after all, the duplicate would sooner or later meet the real Elena Giacalona unless the widow went into hiding for the rest of her life.

I sat down on a spare chair in the laboratory, within a few feet of Elena's double, and wondered what to say to it. The doppelgangster didn't like me any better than the real woman did. Actually, since I was keeping it tied up in a cellar, it probably liked me even less.

After a few minutes of sullen silence, Elena frowned

as her gaze moved over me. "That wretched dog has shed all over your dress."

"Oh. Yes." I brushed self-consciously at the increasingly unhygienic black knit material. "I slept on Nelli's couch. In this dress. With Nelli on top of me."

"Perhaps it's time to change clothes," the widow suggested with fastidious distaste.

"I don't have any spare clothes here. And I don't really want to go home until Lucky knows whether the Corvinos are planning to k—"

"*Lucky*." She scowled. "So what's he going to do, now that he's kidnapped me? Rape me and then feed my body to a cement mixer?"

"*What?* Oh, good God, no!" I was shocked. Okay, yes, he had murdered her second husband. But *still*. "Look I know it sounds crazy," I said to the glaring doppelgangster, "but Lucky's trying to save your life." I blinked, realizing it wasn't *this* thing's life that he was trying to save. "I mean, um—"

"Oh, nonsense!" she snapped. "His obsession with me has sent him over the edge! I wish his wife had never died! None of this would be happening if he still had a woman at home to look after him."

"Did he love his wife?" I had never asked him.

"Yes. And he mourned her death. Then when he was done mourning . . ." She gave a disgusted sigh. "He decided he was in love with me."

"I guess he's lonely," I said.

She made an exasperated sound. "Michael Buonarotti says *he's* lonely, too! That was his excuse for his disgusting behavior last night!" She added with satisfaction, "I pushed him down the stairs of my building."

"Really? I thought you and Buonarotti seemed like you were starting to get along," I said.

"Not after last night. He's an animal!" She added with a dark scowl, "Well, I've had *enough*. I didn't press charges for the murders of any of my husbands, but I will have Michael arrested if he ever comes near me again, and I will *definitely* prosecute Lucky for kidnapping me!"

"None of the murders were prosecuted? I suppose that's because you were afraid for your life," I said.

"No," she said dismissively. "I stay out of the business."

"Pardon?"

She gave me an irritated glance. "Don Victor took care of Anthony Gambello's killers. I stayed out of that. And the deaths of Salvatore Fatico and Eddie Giacalona . . . It was business, and I stayed out of that, too."

"You think of Sally Fatico's death as *business?*" I said, stunned.

"That doesn't mean I don't hate Lucky for it," she said darkly. "But Sally . . . well, there's no denying he brought it on himself."

"By marrying you?"

"What? No." She glared again. "Being married to me was what kept him alive after they found out what he was doing."

I felt lost. "What was he doing?"

"He was cutting into the Gambellos' truck hijacking business." Her shoulders slumped for the first time since I had met her. "Sally was a bit of a fool. Dashing and handsome and romantic, and . . ." She sighed. "A bit of a fool."

"He was *stealing* from the *Gambellos?*" A fool indeed.

"Lucky liked Sally, so he warned him. And when that had no effect, Lucky warned me. Normally I would—"

"Stay out of the business?"

"Yes. But I realized how serious this was. How dangerous. So I told Sally to stop." She shook her head. "But Sally just didn't believe they'd kill him. Because he was married to me, and the don was fond of me."

"I thought the don had tried to strangle you?"

"Yes, well, he has a peculiar way of showing his fondness," she said coldly.

"So . . . Sally wasn't killed for marrying a Gambello widow?"

"You read too many tabloids," she said. "Oh, Don Victor threw a violent tantrum the night I told him I had married Sally. That part of the gossip is true. But Lucky calmed him down—"

"Lucky was there?"

"Lucky was *always* there. I think he's a workaholic," she said. "He told the don I was too young to remain a widow for the rest of my life. He pointed out that a priest had married me to Sally, so it couldn't be undone. And also that the two families weren't at war, after all. Well, not at the time, anyhow." She shrugged. "A week later, Don Victor sent me a wedding gift and his blessings."

"Well, *that's* a story that's become very garbled in the retelling."

"Truth is seldom as well known as gossip." She shook her head. "And Sally wound up dead, anyhow."

"So the don ordered Lucky to kill him because he kept stealing from the Gambellos? Even after two warnings?" It wasn't a clean slate, certainly, but it was much more in keeping with the man I had thought Lucky was.

"And ten years later, the Corvinos killed Eddie for ratting on them to the FBI." She sighed. "I haven't chosen my husbands as well as I might have done."

"Who exactly killed Eddie?"

"I don't know. And I don't want to know." The settled expression of resigned unhappiness came over her face again. "It's business. I stay out of it."

When I came upstairs to the bookstore, Max asked, "Should I go downstairs and guard the doppelgangster?"

I shook my head. "She says she wants some time

alone. I checked her bonds in case it was a trick. But they're secure."

Max was sitting at the table, reading Middle High German. The area all around us was still covered with doppelgangster detritus. There were several large piles of mingled feathers and dirt, scatterings of pebbles and bird bones, dust all over the place . . .

"We should clean this place," I said.

"Yes," Max said.

We looked at the mess for a moment longer.

Then he went back to reading, and I sat down at the table with him.

"Max," I said, "what will we do with her?"

"*It*, my dear." He looked up from his book. "It."

"We can't keep it tied up down there forever. In fact, if doppelgangsters need to sleep or, uh, use the facilities, we can't even keep it like this all night. And you know we can't, um . . ."

"Dispatch it? We'll have to, at some point, Esther."

"Lucky won't stand for it," I said with certainty.

"That mystical entity's existence endangers a human woman's life." Max closed his book and set it aside. "It must be destroyed."

"Oh, Max, I feel weird about this. I just had girl talk with her—*it*. I don't see how we can . . . you know."

"Girl talk?"

"We talked about men."

"Ah."

"It's disturbing how much that thing seems like the real Elena. It remembers her whole life."

Max nodded. "Right up until the moment of its creation. But it has no knowledge of what happened this afternoon, Esther. Of your encounter with the *real* Widow Giacalona."

I nodded. After a moment, I said, "I still think Buonarotti's involved in this. Everything we said earlier today about him as a likely accomplice still holds true."

"Yes," Max said thoughtfully. "That's a good point."

"And last night, he got fresh with the widow. *Very* fresh, from the sound of it. She's furious about it. I doubt a woman who's chosen to marry three times would be shocked by roving hands, so I think Buonarotti must've gotten pretty rough."

"You think he tried to force himself on her?"

"Yes. And she pushed him down the stairs."

"Having met him, I suspect he would be enraged rather than contrite," Max mused. "And today the widow's doppelgangster appeared."

"Dressed as Elena might have been dressed last night, if she was on a dinner date that went bad."

"My goodness! Do you realize, Esther, that we have learned something useful, after all, from interviewing the doppelgangster? Or, rather, *you* have. This 'girl talk' is most informative!"

"But Buonarotti ... Is he the doppelgangster-making type? Is he the subtle, inventive, devious sorcerer you've talked about?" I shook my head. "I just don't see that."

"No. Whereas he *is* well-suited to be the accomplice whose role is to finish the work, so to speak. And evidently he asked his partner in crime to duplicate the widow," Max said. "I suppose her violent death might contribute to the eruption of tribal warfare, considering that Lucky is so fond of her—"

"Apparently Don Victor is also fond of her." I shrugged. "And, who knows, perhaps Don Carmine Corvino is fond of her, too. She married two Corvinos, after all."

"So the mysterious partner might see a benefit in cooperating with Don Michael Buonarotti's demand, which would explain why he complied. The widow's murder might push the two families even further toward the war that our adversary is trying to bring about. Even though, for Don Michael, the duplication was inspired by personal motives." Max thought it over and nodded. "A rejected and humiliated suitor, a violent man with a short temper and the capacity for brutal, opportunistic murder . . . Yes, if Don Michael is in league with the sorcerer, then the temptation would be irresistible to ask his colleague to duplicate the widow."

"Maybe you were right, Max." My heart started pounding. "Maybe the solution *is* just around the corner. I mean, we're saying . . ."

"We're saying," Max said, "that we think Don Michael knows who's creating the doppelgangsters."

"So how do we make a Mafia killer tell us what we want to know?"

My phone rang, startling me. I pulled it out of my purse and looked at the LCD panel. "It's Thack," I said. It seemed as if I had been trying to talk to him since forever. "Probably calling to tell me the role on *The Dirty Thirty* that I wanted to audition for has already been filled by now." I flipped open the phone. "Hello?"

"I meant to call you earlier, Esther, but it's been another crazy day!" There was a lot of noise in the background.

"Uh-huh." I glanced at my watch and noticed it was past nine o'clock already.

"A vodka tonic, please!"

"What?"

"I'm talking to the bartender," Thack said. "It's intermission at *Long Day's Journey Into Night* on Long Island. My God, the things I do for my clients."

That explained the background noise. I knew that play. *Everyone* would be racing for the bar. And if Thack was there to watch a client's performance, he couldn't even leave early. He'd have to sit through the whole thing.

"I'm afraid I've got bad news," Thack said.

"I thought so," I said with resignation.

"But the *good* news," he said gleefully, "outweighs the bad!"

"There's good news?" It was about time.

"Absolutely! But bad news first. You didn't get the part of the grad student on *Dirty Thirty*."

"No surprise there," I muttered.

"They liked your audition, but they just didn't think you were right for the part."

"What?"

"Hey, I said they liked your audition. So don't obsess about the other half of what I said."

"But, Thack, I didn't au—"

"God, *actors*. You guys kill me. So insecure."

"But I—"

"Hold on, Esther." Evidently speaking to the bartender, he said, "Can I get ice and lime with that, please?" After a moment, he said to me, "Send help! I'm in a place where you have to *ask* for ice and lime with your vodka tonic."

"Thack, what are you—"

"Where was I? Oh, right, so you didn't get the part. But the *Crime and Punishment* casting director—oh, what's his name? You know who I mean? The one who liked you last year but didn't think you seemed like a killer? Anyhow—drumroll, please!—he wants you for a *different* guest role on *Dirty Thirty*."

I sat up straighter. "He does?"

"Yes! It's later in the season, an episode they haven't finished casting yet. My notes are back at the office, so I don't remember the exact shooting dates. I think it's in July. Anyhow, Geraldo will call you next week with that information when the contract arrives."

"The contract? I've been hired?" I looked at Max with a big smile. "I've got the job?"

"Yes! And it's a bigger part than the grad student role was!"

"Great!" I said, bouncing happily. A job! A real job!

I wasn't just a singing server anymore. I had a guest role lined up on a hit TV series! "What's the part?"

"You're playing a homeless bisexual junkie prostitute."

I blinked. "I am?"

"Yeah, they thought you were absolutely *perfect* for it!"

"They did?"

"I think it was the outfit."

"The outfit?"

"Yeah, the guy says you wore a tight, low-cut black dress with a ... oh, a little see-through jacket around your shoulders? Something like that."

"I *what?*"

"And, as it turns out, it's probably a good thing that when you called me yesterday to find out what time the audition was—"

"I did?"

"—you didn't tell me what you were planning to wear."

"Oh, my God." Cold horror washed through me.

"Because I would've said it was the wrong outfit, since you were reading for the grad student role. But as it turns out things worked out great!" He chuckled. "Never give a good actor too much advice, that's what I say. Trust their instincts."

"Thack! I ... *auditioned* yesterday?"

Max sat bolt upright. Our gazes met.

"Oh, for Christ's sake," Thack said. "I just got my drink, and they're already dimming the lights in the lobby for the next act! I've got to go back to my seat. I wonder if I can hide this glass in my pocket?"

"Thack—"

"Anyhow, congratulations, Esther! And Geraldo will call you next week after we get the contract." He hung up.

I sat there staring at the phone in my hand. I felt like icy ants were running all over me.

"Esther?" Max touched my hand. "*Esther*. Tell me what happened."

"Max . . ." I heard my voice break with fear. "Max, I've been duplicated! The killer's after *me* now!"

22

"Your double was wearing the same outfit that you wore the night we met Johnny Be Good in the church crypt?" Max said.

"That's what it sounds like, from Thack's secondhand description." It was the dress I had worn in doomed anticipation of a hot date with Lopez that night.

"That was three days ago," Max said. "If your double was created then, where has it been all this time?"

"Well, yesterday, while I was looking for Vino Vincenzo in Brooklyn, it was going to *my* audition," I said, feeling bitter. "Other than that, I don't know."

"Perhaps it wasn't created until yesterday," Max mused. "Perhaps that why it hasn't crossed your path yet."

"That . . . *imposter* managed to get my agent on the phone when I couldn't," I fumed. "And why on earth did it go to my audition in *that* dress?"

"The physical form of the doppelgangsters seems to be fixed at the moment of their creation," Max said. "It's part of their temporary nature. They're created be convincing, but not to last long, after all."

"And what kind of audition did my doppelgangster give that made them think I'm 'absolutely perfect' for the role of a homeless bisexual junkie prostitute?" I wondered.

"So for some reason, although your double evidently didn't start living your life until yesterday, its creation is derived from your life two days earlier. The day when you were wearing that outfit and first trying to contact your agent about that audition."

"Don't get me wrong," I said. "I've got the range. I can certainly play the role. But what did my doppel-gangster *do* that made them look at me and see 'junkie prostitute'? That's all I'm wondering."

"Unless your doppelgangster did start living your life sooner, and yet somehow has not encountered you. Is that at all likely, though?"

"*I* think I'm right for the role of a smart, fully clothed graduate student," I said. "So what happened? Did the doppelgangster screw up the line reading?"

"Esther, if we could focus on the problem at hand?" Max prodded.

"Oh. Right. Sorry."

"Overall, I suspect it's a very good thing you didn't go home last night."

"Oh, my God!" I gasped. "You think that thing was in my apartment last night? Maybe even sleeping in my *bed*?"

"If it was indeed carrying on your normal existence to the best of its abilities, then I think that is entirely possible."

I shuddered in revulsion. "That's just . . . *wrong*."

"You can't go home," he said decisively. "You can't go to any of the places that comprise your normal life. The risk of encountering your perfect double is too great!"

"Max, right now, *this* is the place that comprises my normal life. I've been here constantly lately. When I'm not in church, that is."

"Good heavens! You're right! And the impulses that

draw you here may well draw your doppelgangster here at any moment, too! I must find a way to keep it out!"

"I have an idea," I said suddenly.

"Yes?"

"Lopez wants to put me in protective custody. I'll call him and tell him I'm ready to agree. I'll tell him to send a squad car to my apartment to pick me up. They'll take my double away and put it someplace where I won't bump into it!"

"What if your doppelgangster won't go with them?"

"Lopez may tell them to take me anyhow. He thinks I'm crazy or under the influence, right?" I nodded. "It's worth a try." I opened my cell phone and called Lopez.

A split second after I heard his phone ringing, a phone in the bookstore started ringing.

It wasn't the usual heavy ring of the shop's old-fashioned phone that was sitting nearby. Max and I looked at each other, puzzled, as the ringing continued.

It seemed to be coming from one of the larger piles of debris on the floor. Max rose, crossed over to it, and stooped down to examine the feathery rubbish from which the ringing seemed to be emanating. He started brushing his hand through feathers, bird bones, and clumps of dirt. A few moments later, he grabbed something, then held up a ringing cell phone.

I thought I recognized it. "Answer it."

He did. "Hello?"

I heard his voice clearly on my own phone.

"That's Lopez's phone." I closed my cell phone and set it aside. "His usual one." I had called it without thinking, accustomed to reaching him at that number. "The phone he said last night that he couldn't find."

"Pardon?"

I explained. Then I said, "If it was buried in that pile of doppelgangster leftovers, it must have been . . ."

"On the doppelgangster when I beheaded it," Max said.

"I don't understand," I said. "Why didn't it disintegrate the way the gun did?"

Max turned it over and over in his hands, frowning. "Because this . . . this is Detective Lopez's cell phone. I mean to say, this is a real object that belongs to the real man."

"How did the doppelgangster get a hold of it?"

"It could have been . . ." Max suddenly gave a sharp, jerky start and his eyes widened. "When did Detective Lopez lose his phone?"

"Yesterday." When I broke his prepaid cell phone, he said it was the second phone he had run through that day.

"*When* yesterday? Did he say precisely?"

"No, but uh . . . Let's see." I could tell from Max's fierce frown of concentration that this was important. "Here, give me that." I took the phone from him, opened it, and looked at the readout of outgoing calls. "When he called me here late yesterday afternoon to say he was in Brooklyn to investigate Danny's death, I'm pretty sure he was calling me from this phone." I vaguely remembered seeing his name on my phone's LCD panel before I answered the call. "Yes, here it is. This was the phone he used."

I continued scrolling through the screen of outgoing calls that Lopez had made yesterday. "He called two other numbers during the next hour." I didn't recognize them, but they were presumably work-related, since he would still have been at the scene of the murder. "And here's his call to the bookstore, when he hung up right after you answered. That's the last call made from this phone." I added, "When he called me later, while we were confronting his doppelgangster, he was using another phone by then. A spare."

Max's chest started rising and falling rapidly. He took the phone back from me and stared intently at it. "He used this phone to call me. He was consumed with a desire to come here and confront us. Then he lost this phone . . ."

"And this phone was on his doppelgangster when *it* came here to confront us," I said.

"God's teeth!" Max said. "So *that's* how it's being done."

"How it's . . . Max!" I grabbed his arm. "This means something? You know what's going on now?"

"This is *very* creative," he said, clearly impressed. "I've been reading about doppelgängerism for days without coming across any suggestion whatsoever of such a thing! We are dealing with a most innovative and resourceful individual!" He shook his head, "You know, it's really quite a shame that he uses his talents for Evil."

"He, *who*, Max?"

"Whoever imbued this phone with mystical energy to create a perfect double of the detective—a duplicate of the man at the very moment that this object was taken from him."

"I don't under . . . Imbued this ph . . . Wait. You're saying that's how it's done?"

Max nodded slowly, thinking aloud. "He acquires a token from the victim. Something he associates with him—or her. Something the victim possessed at the moment of existence which is re-created within the perfect double."

"He acquires?" I said. "You mean he *steals*, right? Because Lopez didn't give someone his phone. He just couldn't find it."

"Yes. Stealing the tokens seems most likely."

"Stealing . . . Oh, my God, that's why *that* dress!" I said. "I left my black wrap—the little see-through jacket that went with my dress—at the church the evening that we met Johnny's doppelgangster. I forgot it when we left. So I went back to the sit-down early the next night to get it. But it wasn't in the crypt, and it wasn't in the lost-and-found box . . ."

"It was stolen!" Max looked excited.

"The Widow Giacalona was there when I was asking for it. She said that a number of things had been stolen at church lately! She blamed young thugs and *goombata* . . . but then I got duplicated."

"We must find out what was taken from the widow," he said, heading for the back of the shop.

"I think I know!" I followed him as I recalled Elena's appearance that afternoon at St. Monica's. "Her necklace! That big cross. This afternoon at the church was the first time I've seen her without it."

Max paused at the door to the cellar. "And now her doppelgangster is wearing it. Excellent! I think I know what to do."

He went down the stairs, moving swiftly. I followed him.

Elena's perfect double looked up when we entered the laboratory. "Is this your entire plan?" she said in exasperation. "To keep me tied up in a basement? Don't you think—"

"Did Don Michael take your cross?" Max demanded.

"What?"

"I beg your pardon." Max said. "I know this is a distasteful subject, but I gather he tried to force himself on you last night?"

"He's a pig," she said with disgust.

"He manhandled you? Was rough with you?"

"Yes. When I resisted him, he got angry."

"You struggled?"

She nodded. "And he pulled my hair, shoved me around, tried to unzip my dress."

"He *is* a pig," I said. And Lucky would kill him when he found out about this.

"And your necklace?" Max said. "Your cross?"

"It came off while I fought him." She scowled, looking furious. "He picked it up and wouldn't give it back. It was my *mother's*. It's a sacred symbol! And that *stronzo* wouldn't give it back to me."

"So you kicked him down the stairs."

"Yes," she said with dark satisfaction.

"And what do you remember after that?" Max asked.

She looked confused. "After that?"

"After you kicked him down the stairs, and he went away," Max said. "What happened next?"

"Next? Next, next . . ." She looked puzzled as she thought about it.

"Tell me the very next thing you can remember after that moment."

Elena seemed bewildered. "Next I . . . I came home today and found you in my apartment."

"Yes," Max said. "That is indeed what happened next. To *you*."

He reached around her neck, grasped the silver chain that hung there, and snapped the clasp.

"Max," I said as he removed the necklace from her throat. The ornate cross glinted in the lamplight as it swung in his hand. "What are you doing?"

Elena's eyeballs rolled back in their sockets. Her head fell backward. Her whole body quivered. There was a small explosion, and a tower of feathers, bird bones, pebbles, and clumps of dirt collapsed all over the chair where, only a moment ago, the doppelgangster had been tied up.

"The token used to create the doppelgangster is the only part of the creature that's real," Max explained. "Remove it, and the illusion disintegrates."

"Is there any more of that sherry?" I couldn't stand sherry, but I had felt the distinct need for a soothing beverage, and sherry was all that Max had. "Pour me another glass."

He did, saying, "Try to sip this one slowly."

"Lucky's going to be upset when he finds out we killed it."

"We didn't kill anything," Max said patiently. "We deconstructed a convincing illusion."

"Well, at least we didn't have to behead it." The second glass of sherry was helping my hands stop shaking. With a grimace, I sipped a little more of the revolting stuff. We were back upstairs, sitting at the big walnut table, still surrounded by the filth of Lopez's former doppelgangster. I added with some relief, "So I guess we don't need to carry a machete around the city."

"No, I think not," Max agreed. "From now on, when Nelli identifies a doppelgangster, we merely need to determine what mystically imbued personal token it possesses and remove the object. That will banish the illusion."

"You mean make it explode into messy crap," I said.

Max said thoughtfully, "My reading in recent days led me to ponder the possibilities of psychic transformation, soul possession, animation of physically altered corpses—"

"Animation of *what?*"

"There were some theories I felt it best not to share with you unless I found confirmation of them in our actual experiences," he admitted.

"Good call," I said faintly.

"But *this* . . ." He made a little sound of admiration. "This is unprecedented in the annals of doppelgängerism!"

"How thrilling."

"As is the use of doppelgängers to facilitate—nay, to ensure—the success of assassination!"

"Remarkable."

"And at the same time, it's so absurdly simple!'

"It is?"

"Our adversary combined vastly different traditions—competing schools of thought, you might say—to enact his plan. Doppelgängerism is an abstract, elusive, and isolated mystical phenomenon. But the use of personal tokens in the practice of magic is common and widespread among multiple disciplines—all of them entirely unrelated to the highly esoteric mystery of doppelgängerism!" He shook his head in wonder. "I am forced to congratulate our foe on his imaginative practice of his art."

"Max, if we could cease the thunderous applause for a moment, I'd like to point out that our imaginative foe is trying to kill *me*."

"Oh! Yes, of course. How thoughtless of me, Esther." He pulled himself together. "Do forgive me."

"Let's look at motive, means, and opportunity," I said, using *Crime and Punishment* as my tactical guide. "The motive is evidently to destroy—or at least severely damage—the Gambellos and Corvinos by manipulating them into a new mob war when both families would much rather avoid that."

"Agreed."

"The means is innovative, devious, and mystical. So the person behind this is someone who combines a shrewd intellect with the ability to conceal his true nature from others."

"I'm convinced of it."

"Which brings us to opportunity," I said.

"Indeed. We must determine who has had the opportunity to steal tokens from the known victims."

"Someone who's a good pickpocket, I suppose." A moment later I gasped as I realized what I had just said. "A *pickpocket*."

"Esther?"

My heart was pounding. "The day I saw Chubby Charlie's perfect double." My God, had it been a week ago? How time flies when you're fighting Evil. "Now I know!"

"Know what?"

"Which one was the duplicate!" I turned to Max. "Charlie thought of himself as a sharp dresser, and he paid special attention to accessorizing. He always wore matching socks, tie, and pocket handkerchief. The evening that *two* of him came to the restaurant, the first one had all his accessories. The second one, utterly identical in every other way, was missing the pocket handkerchief. I noticed it because I had just seen Charlie, and I had *just* straightened that thing for him."

"And the second one was missing it?"

"He said it had been stolen. And I remember wondering who'd be reckless enough to pick the pocket of a Gambello killer!"

"That was the token!" Max said. "The handkerchief was stolen and used to create the doppelgangster that you encountered at Bella Stella's that evening, shortly before the *real* Chubby Charlie came to dinner."

"Okay," I said. "We know that Michael Buonarotti took the widow's necklace. But I don't see how he could've have taken the handkerchief, too. Not without getting caught. I think Charlie would've noticed the don of a rival family getting that close to him."

"Don Michael took the widow's necklace in violence and without stealth or secrecy. So, no, he doesn't seem a likely prospect for subtly extracting a valued accessory from the pocket of an experienced Gambello captain." Max added, "I doubt that Chubby Charlie would have been an easy target for theft. Therefore, I propose that the thief was someone he felt comfortable with. Someone whom he trusted, in a sense."

"But who did Charlie trust that Danny Dapezzo trusted, too?"

"It might help if we had some idea what token Doctor Dapezzo . . ." His eyes widened. "Oh!"

I realized it at the same moment he did. "His reading glasses!" At the sit-down, Danny was using a new pair that he didn't like.

My old ones are missing, goddamn it. Those frames were real *gold, you know.*

Max said, "So we're hunting an adversary who was able to get close enough to steal Doctor Dapezzo's gold reading glasses as well as Charlie Chiccante's handkerchief."

"But *I* wasn't pickpocketed," I said. "I was just careless. I left my wrap in the church crypt. How did the killer know? Was I followed?"

"The widow told you there have been thefts at the church lately. Perhaps the killer lurks there and stole the wrap out of habit, upon seeing the opportunity." Max slapped his hand on the table, making me jump. "And now we know how the victims are chosen!"

I blinked. "How?"

"Opportunity."

"Oppor— Oh! I see! He didn't set out to kill Charlie. He found an opportunity to steal a token from Charlie, and that turned Charlie into a victim."

"Yes! Similarly, Doctor Dapezzo became a victim *because* of the loss of his glasses," Max said. "The killer's objective was to create murder victims in each *famiglia* and to do so without his accomplice, who actually committed the slayings, being identified. However, it didn't particularly matter to him *which* family members died violently."

"Just as long as long as their deaths led to a war."

Max said, "This is why even Lucky, who knew the victims well, was unable to see a basis for how they were being chosen. Because the basis was, in a sense, quite random. They were simply the individuals from whom it had been possible to steal a token."

"But why duplicate *me?* I'm not a Gambello or a Corvino."

"And, indeed, the killer may have originally intended to restrict his victims to Gambellos and Corvinos. But

then he realized you posed a threat to his plans. Just as
Detective Lopez did. And so, since he had already stolen your wrap, the killer then overcame any scruples he
may have had, and he duplicated you."

"Well, that certainly didn't take long," I said sourly.

"I don't believe there was ever any serious possibility
that the killer would remain selective about his victims,
even if he commenced his activities with that intention,"
Max said. "Evil is always voracious."

I thought of the widow and realized how right Max
was. She had been targeted for death just because she
rejected a rough pass. "This guy really *is* evil."

"I suggest that he is also fully aware of our investigation."

"Right. I didn't get duplicated just for hanging out
too much in a church lately." I felt icy insects all over
my skin again. "But why duplicate me, rather than you
or Lucky? Don't both of you pose a bigger threat to the
killer than I do?"

"Don't underestimate yourself, my dear!" Max added,
"In any case, I am not, to my knowledge, missing any of
my belongings. Nor has Lucky mentioned the loss of any
personal possessions."

"But I was careless with my wrap," I said grimly. "So
I became a target of opportunity."

"Opportunity," Max said again, dwelling on the
word. "Our adversary is an improviser. He thinks on his
feet and continually adapts his plan to new events and
information."

"And he's filching stuff from a *church*." I was annoyed. "I loved that outfit."

"You've spent more time at St. Monica's than I have,"
Max said. "Whom have you noticed lurking there?"

"The Widow Giacalona, certainly." I shrugged. "Other
women, I guess. They've got the hots for the priest."

"Ah, yes. Well, he is an appealing young man, and it's

amazing how often celibacy creates an aura of . . ." Max sat up straighter, looking stunned. "Good gracious! The *priest* lurks around the church."

"Yeah, but that's his job," I said dismissively.

"Which means his lurking would pass unnoticed!"

"Oh, but, Max, he's such a nice . . ." I went blank for a moment, and then a shower of recollections fell on me. "*That's* what the victims have in common!"

"The church! The *priest*."

I nodded. "Danny was a parishioner there. Lucky said that Charlie went to Mass and Confession every week. And Charlie certainly knew Father Gabriel. He mentioned him the night he died."

Max said, "We have seen Don Michael Buonarotti there ourselves, whom we believe is the accomplice. And he seems to be on congenial terms with the priest."

"Buonarotti even courted the widow at the church."

"Johnny Be Good occasionally went to the church to pray for positive results in his gambling exploits," Max said. "And by all accounts, he was a careless man from whom it would have been quite easy to collect a token."

"*So* easy, it's probably not even worth trying to figure what the token was." I recalled, "Johnny must have known Father Gabriel for years. The priest told me a little about Johnny's youth and said that he—Gabriel—grew up around the Gambellos." I brought my hands up to my cheeks as I realized what *else* the priest had told me "Oh, my God!"

"What?" Max rose halfway out of his chair. "What is it?"

"Father Gabriel was the one who planted the suspicions about Elena in my head. Mind you, her own comments made that easy. But he told me at length about her reasons for hating both the Gambellos and the Corvinos." Looking back at the conversation with a new perspective, I could see that he had incited my curiosity and made leading comments that encouraged me to ask him for more information. "And the information he gave me about her past was so incomplete that it misled me!"

He'd *certainly* neglected to mention that Don Victor had forgiven Elena for marrying a Corvino and gave her his blessings. After hearing Elena's version of the past from her doppelgangster earlier tonight, I had assumed that Father Gabriel had merely been misinformed, relaying the popular gossip to me. But now . . . now I saw that he had been deflecting the possibility of suspicion falling on him by directing it elsewhere: to the thrice-widowed Elena.

"Oh, Max," I said, feeling guilty. "He also . . ." I nodded. "Father Gabriel also tried to drive a wedge between me and Lucky, and it almost worked!"

"How?" Max asked.

"He, uh . . . he told me something bad about Lucky that wasn't true. But I believed him until tonight."

"Ah, of course he would try that, upon realizing you were working together. Divide and conquer." Max nodded. "I gather that Father Gabriel's lie is the reason for your irritability toward Lucky lately?"

"Yes." I frowned. My revulsion had intruded on our relationship, but it hadn't ended our work. "But if the priest intended me to stop cooperating with Lucky, why didn't he tell a bigger lie?"

"We're dealing with a subtle individual," Max said. "He chose a lie that would distract you and, as you say, create a wedge between you and Lucky. But he avoided the mistake of telling a lie so big that you would either disbelieve it or immediately confront Lucky with it."

"Crafty," I said.

"Father Gabriel no doubt also underestimated your commitment to confronting Evil. He may have hoped that telling you something disturbing was enough to make you abandon your quest. It would be a common reaction, after all."

"He pretended to help me look for my wrap after he had filched it, and he used his minutes alone with me to mislead me. And I fell for it." I folded my arms. "Lopez was right. I'm naive."

"But since we know that the Widow Giacalona is not the killer, you can rest assured now that your talking to her about Detective Lopez is not what led to *his* being duplicated."

"I still may be the cause of that, Max. The widow was being courted by Buonarotti. Maybe she told him what I said to her."

I remembered that Buonarotti recognized me easily the night of the sit-down despite my disguise as a mob girl. Had the widow told him about my presence in the church? Or had Father Gabriel told him after he left the crypt and I remained down there alone for a few minutes? Had the priest and the don been meeting somewhere in the church before I arrived? If they were conspirators, it seemed likely.

I also remembered how the priest had encouraged the Widow Giacalona to accept Buonarotti's company that evening. Perhaps he had done it to keep Buonarotti happy, but perhaps he also wanted Buonarotti to get a full account of what Elena and I had discussed. "Besides, she's a devout woman who's always at church. Father Gabriel has influence over her, and she no doubt confides in him."

"We confided in him, too." Max's expression was heavy with self-reproach.

I nodded. "At the sit-down." We hadn't questioned the priest's presence there as peacekeeper. "He found out exactly how much we knew."

"And, being well practiced at deceit, he convincingly pretended to find our theories absurd. He also encouraged Lucky to believe that, despite their denials, the Corvinos were indeed murdering Gambellos."

With a sinking heart, I recalled, "Today he urged me

to go straight home and rest my knee when I pretended that I had hurt myself as an excuse to leave quickly. At the time, he seemed so nice, so concerned. Now . . ."

"Now you're wondering if he was trying to arrange a meeting between you and your doppelgangster by directing you to go home?" Max said. "I think it very likely, my dear."

"I wonder if he knew I had deliberately cut Elena, that I was checking to see whether she was real?"

"If he suspected, then he will likely escalate his activities, realizing that we're getting closer to unmasking him."

I reviewed the encounter, then shook my head. "I don't know if he suspected. I just don't know. But it's certainly possible. Because if we're right about him, then he's a *very* good actor." I looked sadly at Max. "Damn. I really *liked* him."

"That's precisely why he has been so successful in his bold scheme. He is tremendously skilled at concealing his true nature and at presenting a likeable and trustworthy persona to the world."

"Well, *I* never would have suspected him," I admitted, recalling that I had previously thought Father Gabriel seemed like someone who'd be good to turn to in a crisis.

"I'm still puzzled, though, by how he came into possession of Detective Lopez's telephone."

"Oh, my God, I know how!" I said, realizing. "Father Gabriel went to the scene of the crime!"

Max's eyes widened. "Ah, yes. Lucky called him to Danny's side after the murder."

"Because that's what you do when a guy dies," I said slowly, "even a guy like Danny. You call his priest."

"And Detective Lopez, a normally efficient and alert young man, was distracted by the discovery that you and I were involved with the brutally murdered Corvino capo whose death he was investigating."

"So the lurking Father Gabriel," I said with a scowl, "found an opportunity to steal his phone." Maybe Lopez had set down the phone and turned his back on it. Or maybe he had put it in an outer pocket of his jacket and never realized the kindly priest at the scene of the crime was a skilled pickpocket.

Max met my gaze. *"Opportunity."*

"He's not just evil, he's *insanely* evil," I said. "He's trying to kill two women and a cop, as well as start a raging mob war."

"The appetite of Evil always expands rapidly," Max said.

"But considering how well the priest has concealed his true nature and his activities, why team up with an accomplice? Especially someone like Buonarotti, who doesn't come across as either trustworthy or discreet," I said. "Why would Father Gabriel take that risk? Why not just commit the murders himself, since the curse ensures that no one sees the killer anyway?"

"Hmm." Max frowned in concentration as he thought about it. "He's an educated young man, a parish priest, and a talented sorcerer who has invested himself deeply in the study and practice of his art. He may well have had no time and no occasion to learn the physical logistics of murder." He stroked his beard as he continued, "Above all, though, I suspect this is a question of individual temperament. It seems likely that Father Gabriel has no stomach for violence. In his public persona, he chose to become a cleric rather than a member of Lucky's profession. And in his secret life, he has also chosen an intellectual and spiritual path, albeit of a very different nature. So while he willfully victimizes people with his sorcery, I think it likely that physical confrontation is anathema to him."

"You mean he's a physical coward," I said scathingly. "It's fine to curse me with death, but he needs someone else to strike the fatal blow for him."

"Precisely. Therefore he developed a strategy that would incorporate an accomplice to do the physical slayings," Max said. "And he chose a man who takes pleasure in violence and who has something to gain if these murders lead to a war between the Gambellos and the Corvinos."

"What a team they make," I said grimly.

"Distressingly effective, to date."

"But, Max, what about motive? I still don't understand *why* Father Gabriel would do this."

"That's because we only know what he has told us about himself, which is virtually nothing. But if he was telling the truth about one key point—that he grew up around the Gambello *famiglia*—then Lucky may know enough about him to postulate a motive when we explain our theory to him."

"I'll tell Lucky we need him back here as soon as possible." I opened my cell phone.

"Excellent. We'll review with him what we have learned tonight about the nature of the doppelgangsters while we prepare to confront our adversary."

"If we're right this time, Max, how do we stop a homicidal priest and his violent accomplice?"

"We will begin by destroying his immediate means of creating more doppelgangsters." He added, "Before we go anywhere, though, we must protect ourselves. You summon Lucky while I commence preparations in the laboratory."

23

"Nah, Gabriel's family wasn't connected to the Gambellos." Lucky looked up at Max. "How long before this stuff washes off?"

"Several days."

Down in the laboratory, Max was painting protective symbols on Lucky's face, back, hands, and feet with a mixture of henna, wax, oil, and some unsavory looking ground-up ingredients that I had deliberately not asked about. My face, back, hands and feet were already covered with similar symbols. Nelli and Max were both also decorated accordingly. So we had been busy while waiting for Lucky to return from LaGuardia Airport.

Lucky had managed to convince Elena Giacalona that her life was in danger, and she should leave immediately—that very evening—for Seattle, where she could stay with her sister. Although Elena hated Lucky, apparently she was sensible enough to listen when a man in his profession told her she was marked for death and should get out of town. She had allowed him to escort her to the airport, and he had stayed there until her flight was safely gone.

Upon entering the laboratory, he was somewhat shaken to see the pile of rubbish that had previously been Elena's doppelgangster, but he adjusted better than I had expected. Probably because he had just come from seeing the real woman.

"So Gabriel was lying about growing up around Johnny Be Good and the Gambellos?" I asked.

"No, that's true. He and his mom lived in the same parish as most of the Gambellos."

"Just his mom?" I asked, "Were his parents divorced?"

"No way, his mother was a good Catholic. Nice lady. She died a few years ago." Lucky drew in a sharp breath and protested, "Ow, that stuff is hot, Doc."

"I apologize, my dear fellow." To keep the wax from solidifying before it was painted onto skin, Max was keeping the mysterious mixture heated over a low flame. He blew gently on his brush before he went back to painting interesting symbols on Lucky's feet.

With still no idea how to protect us from a doppelgänger, Max had instead come up with a means of protecting us from a curse based on using a personal token that created a link to the victim. The symbols, ingredients, and chanting involved in this protection should, he said, deflect the fatal effect of encountering one's own doppelgangster. Although I was the only one of us whose doppelgangster was definitely roaming around somewhere out there tonight, he thought it wise for all of us to take precautions.

Nelli—with her face, back, and four paws all covered in oily, waxy, lumpy protective symbols that were the rusty color of henna—was sniffing at the remains of Elena's doppelgangster, trying to learn more about our adversary's work before tonight's confrontation.

I asked Lucky, "So where was Gabriel's dad?"

"Dead. But even without a dad, the boy turned out okay." Lucky paused. "Uh, until now, I guess."

"I'll wager he was a quiet and studious youth," Max said.

"You're on the money, Doc."

"And we've certainly seen that he developed good people skills," I said.

"Yeah, he was polite even as a boy," Lucky said. "And his mother was so proud when he decided to become a priest. It's a darn shame he's turned out to be an evil sorcerer." The old gangster shook his head. "Kids. Whaddya gonna do?"

"How did his father die?" I asked.

"Turned up one day in a Jersey landfill with two bullets in his head."

"*What?* I thought you said he wasn't a Gambello?"

"He wasn't," Lucky said. "He worked for the Buonarottis."

"Really?" This surprised me. "The priest's father was a Buonarotti soldier?"

Lucky shrugged. "Priests gotta have fathers, too, don't they?"

"Why was he killed?"

Lucky shook his head. "No one ever said."

"Who did it?"

"No idea."

"Really?" I said.

"Swear to God."

"There weren't any rumors?"

"Oh, there was *lots* of rumors. But the cops found squat, no one ever took credit, and no one ever got punished for whackin' a made guy. No one knew nothin'." He shrugged. "For real, that time."

"Is it possible that a Gambello did it and just didn't tell anyone?"

"Sure, it's possible," Lucky said. "That was one of the rumors. It's also possible a Corvino did it, which was another rumor. Both families was havin' serious disputes with the Buonarottis at the time."

"That sounds promising," I said, thinking about possible motives for the current murders.

"On the other hand," Lucky said, "it's also possible

that the hit was a piece of Buonarotti housekeeping that got kept real quiet."

"Was that a rumor, too?"

"You bet." Lucky nodded. "And some people said he got popped by a crazy girlfriend, or a jealous husband, or a crooked cop, or a tough mugger." Lucky shook his head. "But me, I always thought the hit was too clean and professional for that." He paused and added, "Well, maybe a crooked cop."

"Good heavens," Max said.

Lucky said, "But I never heard of anyone who *knew* what happened. And it was more than twenty years ago. So whoever popped him might not even be alive anymore."

"The father's unsolved murder would obviously be very disturbing for his son," I said. "But, well, the death wasn't exactly a surprising way for a wiseguy to go, was it? And since no one even knows who's responsible for the murder, I don't understand why it would lead Gabriel to trying to start a new Corvino-Gambello war."

"That's because you're thinking rationally, my dear," said Max, setting aside his brush and wiping his hands as he finished his work on Lucky. "Our adversary has a well-developed mind, but certainly not a balanced one. Having lost his father in childhood, he became obsessed with the idea of punishing his father's killer."

"But he doesn't know who that is."

"Indeed," Max said. "Ergo, he blames everyone who *might* feasibly be among his father's killers."

"But, as Lucky just said, that description includes people who are dead by now."

"You're still assuming the priest thinks about this rationally, which I sincerely doubt is the case," Max said. "He has long since grown to blame an entire class of people for his father's death, and he has enacted a plan to wreak terrible vengeance on them."

"But why wait so long to enact it?" I said. "His father died more than twenty years ago."

"First he had to grow up," Lucky pointed out. "And he probably spent a few years trying to figure out who whacked his old man. Hey, that might even be why he became a priest! Some guys tell their priests *everything*, y'know."

Max said, "His practice of his art and his adaptation to changing circumstances have been resourceful. So I suspect Lucky is right in assuming the young man attempted various methods of solving his problem before choosing to access the dark arts. He would have been thorough in his quest for a guilty party, I believe. And then, of course, he would have needed some years of study and practice to prepare for what he's doing."

I said grumpily, "Well, I don't see why he had to do it *now*, while I was waiting tables at Bella Stella. I never would have witnessed his first hit or—"

"*Opportunity*," Max said, his eyes widening.

"Come again, Doc?"

"Mercury is in retrograde! *That's* why Father Gabriel chose now," Max said. "It's a time of maximum confusion!"

"*Right,*" Lucky said, catching on. "What did you tell us about it, Doc? Messages get lost, things get garbled."

"Communications get misinterpreted," I said, "and people have trouble connecting."

"Mercury Retrograde made Gabriel's plan more likely to succeed," Max said. "It made his victims more vulnerable and his various adversaries less effective."

"It certainly seems to have worked in his favor so far," I grumbled as I reviewed the events of recent days.

"We're up against one smart mook," Lucky said. "No doubt about it."

"But what about Buonarotti?" I asked.

"No, he ain't that smart," Lucky said dismissively. "And he's a hothead."

"No, I mean that one of the rumors you mentioned

is that the Buonarottis killed Gabriel's father. So why would Gabriel work with Michael Buonarotti now?"

"What if he *ain't* working with him?" Lucky suggested, putting his shoes and socks back on over his painted feet. "What if he's just using him?"

"But Gabriel duplicated the widow," I argued. "Which we're assuming was essentially a favor to Buonarotti."

"Well, sure," Lucky said. "If you're using someone expendable to do your dirty work, you keep him happy for as long as you need him. You give him little things now, and you promise him big things later on."

"I see!" Max said. "Don Michael's motive for working with Father Gabriel is to position the Buonarottis to gain power. But it doesn't necessarily follow that he'll get what he wants when the Corvinos and Gambellos descend into chaos."

"*Oh,*" I said, also seeing. "Gabriel will betray him, or expose him, or turn on him."

"Or get the Gambellos and the Corvinos to turn on the Buonarottis after we've already turned on each other," Lucky said. "A *three*-way war would make a hell of a mess."

"Yes," I said with a nod, realizing Lucky was right. "If he does indeed want to destroy all three families, that may well be his plan." I felt appalled as I realized the scope of the devious scheme. "But innocent people could get hurt, too! Even killed. Doesn't he realize that?"

"He's evidently so obsessed with revenge that he considers it acceptable," Max said grimly. "After all, he's trying to kill you, though you had nothing whatsoever to do with his father's murder."

"He's trying to whack Elena and your boyfriend, too, who aren't wiseguys, either," Lucky added. "But if Max is right, and Gabriel ain't willing to get physical—which sure sounds like how I remember him as a teenager—then he had to have a wiseguy help him get this thing started.

He couldn't do it alone. And Michael Buonarotti was the easiest one for him to recruit, since Gabriel's father was on his crew back when Michael was a young capo."

"Ah," Max said, nodding. "So that's how the accomplice was chosen. *Opportunity*. How fitting."

"Do you think it's possible Don Michael killed his father?" I asked.

"Of course, it's possible," Lucky said. "And you can bet it's occurred to Gabriel. But he's never found no evidence, no motive, nothing to convince him."

"How do you know?" I asked.

"Because if Gabriel thought he knew who done it, would he bother doin' all *this*?"

"Good point," I said.

"And even if Don Michael didn't do it," Max said, "then he and his organization must nonetheless suffer for failing to protect his employee and prevent the murder."

"And also for failing to find out who did it and punish him," I said.

"Hey, you know something?" Lucky said, looking pleased. "You two are finally startin' to understand how Our Thing works."

I would have preferred to search the big old echoing shadowy interior of St. Monica's during broad daylight and with lots of people around. Going there at midnight to confront Evil wasn't my favorite possible plan.

However, if Father Gabriel suspected we were getting close to the truth, he would be escalating his activities. So we couldn't wait until daylight. There might well be another victim by then—perhaps several. We had to find and destroy his workshop or altar *now*.

Since the church was where he acquired most of his tokens, as well as where he spent most of his time, we decided to start our search there. With our painted faces and our massive dog, we had trouble hailing a cab—go figure—so we wound up walking to St. Monica's. By the time we got to our destination, Lucky was complaining that his feet hurt.

The main entrance to the church was locked when we arrived. This didn't surprise us, and Lucky and Max were both adept at entering locked buildings—albeit via drastically different means—so we were able to open the door within moments.

Inside, the church was pitch black.

"Stay here, I'll hit a light," Lucky said.

A few moments later, I heard the click of a nearby switch, but the church remained cloaked in darkness.

"It's not working," Lucky said quietly. "Do you think the priest cut the power?"

"Maybe. Or maybe that switch is one of the gazillion things here that needs fixing." I now remembered that the women's auxiliary report had mentioned faulty electrical wiring in the sanctuary. I wished I had thought to bring a flashlight. "We'll have trouble confronting Evil if we can't even *see* it."

"There are candles here," Max said. "Let's make our way to some of those."

"I ain't got matches," Lucky said.

"Not to worry. I can generate an incendiary effect, but it's momentary and volatile. Ergo, the stabilizing medium of physical substance is exigent."

"He needs something to burn," I said to Lucky.

"Oh, okay. Here, take my hand, kid." A moment later, he said, "*That* ain't my hand."

"I'm sorry," I said. "I can't see anything."

After I found Lucky's hand with mine, I stretched out my other one. "Max?"

I felt the clasp of Max's fingers, and then the three of us made our way gingerly down the left aisle, followed by Nelli. We shuffled toward the altar of St. Monica and the candles we hoped to find there. After we had gone perhaps thirty feet, Nelli started growling.

The stained glass windows allowed a faint amount of light to stream in from the streetlamps, and as my eyes adjusted, I could start to make out general shapes in the dark. So when something man-shaped rose from one of the church pews, I screamed.

This startled Max, who stumbled. Still holding my hand, he inadvertently yanked me with him. We fell together into the well of one of the old church pews. Lucky had let go of my hand when my fall yanked it out of his grip, and I heard his exclamation as he now saw what I had seen. Nelli was barking and snarling.

A moment later, the beam of a flashlight shone into Lucky's face. He squinted, turned his head away, and then dived sideways into the darkness.

The person holding the flashlight called, "Max? Esther? I know you're there. I don't want to hurt you."

It was Lucky's voice.

I stopped breathing.

Oh, no, I thought. *No.*

The flashlight turned in our general direction. Since we were on the floor, the beam of light missed us and hit Nelli. From my prone position, I could see the snarling dog stiffen and freeze, evidently shocked by the sound of her friend's voice coming from the creature she instinctively wanted to attack.

From the darkness about ten feet to our left, Lucky demanded, "Who's there? Who's got that light?"

"Who d'you *think?*" Lucky's voice came from directly behind the flashlight, about fifteen feet in front of where Max and I lay in an awkward heap.

Nelli whined and backed away from the voice, unnerved by this turn of events. She stepped on my hair, immobilizing me. I could tell she was trembling.

"Who *is* that?" On our left, Lucky sounded confused and hostile.

"It's me, you putz," said the voice with the flashlight.

I started breathing again. In short little pants of panic. "Max," I whispered. "What do we do?"

Max cleared his throat and called, "Lucky?"

Two men answered at once. "Yeah?"

"Oh, dear," Max said.

"Shit," said Lucky.

"Lucky," Max said, "I want you to think about what token you may have lost recently."

"What?" said the creature with the flashlight.

"Token?" said Lucky on our left.

"Think *hard*," I said.

"Right! What the hell that did that pickpocket priest filch from me?" Lucky said to himself. "What am I missing?"

I tugged at Nelli's leg, trying to get her to take her foot off my hair. She was making confused little whining noises and still shaking.

"Doc? Get Nelli to calm down," said the flashlight voice. "Look, I'm not gonna hurt you. I'm gonna behead that *thing*."

"Thing? Oh, you gotta be *kidding* me," said Lucky, outraged. I could tell that he was on the move, changing his location.

The doppelgangster could tell, too. The beam of its flashlight was searching the church, using its target's voice as a guide. While searching, it called to us, "Doc, I just want to give you and Esther a quick poke with my knife and make sure you are who I think you are."

"Poke?" Lucky said. "I think ... hang on ... yeah! One of my knives is missing, Doc! It's not in my pocket. That demented priest stole a knife from me!"

"Then you know what to do, Lucky!" Max called.

"I was here to talk about *funerals*," Lucky said an grily. "And he stole from me! In *church*."

"*Focus*, Lucky!" I shouted.

"It turns out that the two of you was here talkin' to

Father Gabriel the other day when *I* thought you was in Brooklyn with me," the doppelgangster said. "So now we're gonna have to figure out who's real and who ain't."

"The priest is lying to you!" I shouted at the doppelgangster. "He's the one who's behind all of this! And, anyhow, *you're* the one who's not real!"

The doppelgangster's footsteps started approaching us. "Oh? Fine. Convince me."

Nelli's shaking got worse, and a horrible sound came out of her throat. She shifted position, evidently intending to protect us, but obviously reluctant to attack something that sounded like just Lucky. Fortunately, the uncertain shuffling of her paws allowed me to free my hair and sit up.

"Hey, you!" Lucky shouted from another part of the dark church. "Over here, schmuck!"

"Hold still and face the music like a man!" the doppelgangster snapped at Lucky. The beam of the flashlight roved around in search of its quarry. "I promise you won't feel a thing."

While the doppelgangster's attention was distracted, I nudged Max, and we started hauling ourselves off the floor and out of the pew as quietly as we could. I grabbed Nelli's leash, which Max had dropped when he fell, and tugged. She resisted, still swamped with indecision about the doppelgangster.

"Doc, an evil wizard made this thing," Lucky called out to Max in the dark. "So I'm thinking it ain't such a good idea to let it get near you and Esther with a knife!"

"He's right," I whispered to Max.

"Indeed."

Lucky would never hurt us. But that creature wasn't Lucky, and we didn't know enough about doppelgangsters to be sure *it* would never hurt us. Under duress, Gabriel might be fiddling with the recipe, so to speak.

When Lucky spoke again, his location had changed once more. He shouted to us, "I'll deal with this mook! You two, go. *Go!*"

"Nelli, *come!*" Max commanded sharply.

Max grabbed my hand and dragged me through the dark. Nelli came with us, her feet stepping on ours, her whining giving away our location. Perhaps the next time we confronted Evil, I thought, we should leave Nelli at home. We slipped past shadowy pews and a hulking shape that was probably St. Monica. Behind us, I heard the sounds of clattering wooden pews, cursing in Italian, and then a crash of glass—candleholders I guessed—as Lucky and his doppelgangster chased each other through the dark church.

When we reached the end of the aisle, we walked into a staircase. We didn't know where it led, but we followed it blindly, ascending above the vast, dark area where Lucky and his doppelgangster were engaged in deadly stalking.

"Max, we can't just leave Lucky," I whispered urgently as we crept upward on the spiral staircase.

"We must! This is a delaying tactic," Max whispered back.

"It's a *deadly* tactic." I was panting as I dragged Nelli behind me. She had decided she didn't like climbing unfamiliar spiral stairs in the dark to an unknown destination. "That thing is armed with a knife! A *real* one."

"The preparations we made before we left the lab will protect Lucky from the fatal curse."

"What's going to protect him from that thing stabbing him in a struggle?" I said.

"If Lucky gets the knife away from it—"

"That's a big *if*, Max!"

"—it will disintegrate. Lucky knows that. The creature doesn't."

"That seems like an awfully slim advantage!"

"That doppelgangster is a trap, a distraction!" Max

was climbing the curving staircase rapidly, just ahead of me, dragging me as I dragged Nelli. "The priest *wants* us to stay there and remain ensnared in dealing with that problem, rather than proceed. We *must* find Father Gabriel's—*oof!*"

I froze when I heard him go *splat.* "Max? Max!"

He said faintly, "The stairs end here."

I carefully climbed the remaining couple of steps, then felt around in the darkness. I found Max's arm and helped him rise. Nelli shoved past me, then she stumbled a few feet later, too. As I made my way across the uneven floor, my heel caught on a broken tile.

"We're in the choir gallery," I said. "Be careful. The floor is need of repair."

"Yes, I've noticed that." Max still sounded winded. "We must find a means of illumination!"

I moved through the darkness with my hands up, palms outward, hoping to find a wall and then to move along it in search of a light switch. Somewhere below us, there was a terrible clatter of pews and some shouting. I glanced over my shoulder and saw, in the church below us, the flashlight flying through the dark. It went out when it hit the floor, leaving the church in complete darkness again. So Lucky had at least gotten the flashlight away from the doppelgangster.

An ear-splitting shriek of organ music made me jump out of my skin. Nelli barked. I bumped into something tall and hard, but not very stable. It fell over with a crash.

As the jarring wail of the organ faded, Max said, "I do apologize."

"Ow." Realizing what I must have bumped into, I bent over and felt it. "Max, I've found a candelabra." I hauled it upright and felt my way along its branches. "I think it's got—*yes!* Candles!"

"Excellent!" Max stumbled over to the sound of my voice. He took one of the thick candles between his hands, chanted in another language for about thirty seconds, and then blew.

Nothing happened.

"I, uh ... I'm feeling rather stressed and distracted." He sounded embarrassed.

"It's all right. Don't rush." My heart was pounding. "Take your time."

I flinched when I heard the crash of something heavy downstairs.

Max tried again and this time it worked. He blew a mystical flame onto the wick of the candle in his hands. It flickered uncertainly for a moment, then stabilized and burned steadily. I squinted as my eyes adjusted to this point of light. Max used the burning candle to light the others. Then we lifted the candelabra and brought it closer to the balcony railing. We looked out over the dark church, trying to see what was happening.

In the dim glow cast by the burning candles on the scene below us, it was easy to tell Lucky apart from his doppelgangster since he was the one with the weirdly painted face. That's how I knew he was the one lying on the floor, while his perfect double was the one standing over him with a knife.

"Lucky!" I screamed.

Lucky twisted and drove his heel into the doppelgangster's knee. It cried out and fell sideways, rolling away. The creature retained its grip on the knife.

Lucky looked up at the choir gallery and shouted, "I got this covered! Go stop the priest!"

Max and I each held a burning candle. I asked, "Where should we look first?"

"Normally, I'd say the crypt. But that room obviously gets too much use in this church to be a sorcerer's secret lair."

"And all those pink bunny costumes ..." I shook my head. "It just doesn't say 'lair' to me."

Deciding where to look first became easy when we heard a woman's piercing scream.

It came from somewhere beyond the east side of the choir gallery. Max, Nelli, and I dashed toward the door there. It was locked. Max gathered his focus and made a circular gesture with his arms, then a flicking motion with his wrists, as he spoke in rhythmic Latin. A moment later, the lock clicked, the doorknob turned, and the door opened to let us through. On the other side of it was a dark hallway. There was a light switch right next to the door. I flipped it. Nothing happened.

"He must have killed the lights for the whole building," I said.

"He knows the church intimately. We're strangers here. He counted on this to disorient us."

The hallway was eerie in the candlelight, but probably ordinary by day. This part of the church didn't seem to be in use. The floor sagged, the paint was chipped, and the overhead lights looked older than Lucky. There were a number of doors, both to our right and our left. They were all closed. I turned to my right and tried the first door I came to. It was locked.

"These must be the old dormitory rooms," I said, recalling the secretary's report from today's meeting. "I don't think anyone comes up here."

"No one but our quarry," Max murmured.

Nelli's ear pricked alertly and she trotted to the very end of the hall. She stopped when she reached a door that had, I noticed, shiny new hinges and a new lock instead of the rusting, decades-old hardware that was on the other doors up here. She started growling.

We approached the door. I could hear voices on the other side of it. One of the voices, which obviously belonged to a woman, was agitated and angry. The other voice was lower. Possibly a man. It sounded as if he was chanting.

Both voices ceased abruptly when Nelli scratched at

the door, growling louder, wholly focused on whatever was on the other side of it.

Max's eyes met mine in the dim light of our flickering candles. "It's time to confront our adversary."

My heartbeat was deafening. I realized I was breathing like a runner. I swallowed and nodded. "Let's do it."

Max put his hand on the doorknob and turned it.

"Don't move," said a male voice.

In the dark hallway behind us, I heard the sound, familiar to me from many episodes of *Crime and Punishment,* of someone cocking a semiautomatic gun to fire it.

On the other side of the door, the woman screamed again.

24

Max and I turned our heads to look over our shoulders at the newcomer. He was a shadowy figure at the other end of the hall.

"Jesus, what the fuck is that on your faces?" he said.

Max and I looked at each other. The elaborate face paint, I had to admit, gave us a rather disturbing appearance, particularly in this dim, flickering light.

Soft footsteps brought the man closer to us, into the pool of the golden glow cast by our candles. My gaze went first to the subtly gleaming barrel of the gun, then to the face of the killer pointing it at us.

"Buonarotti," I said without surprise. "Wonderful."

"Holy shit! *You?*" He frowned at me. "Which one *are* you?"

Nelli ignored Buonarotti and continued scratching at the door and growling.

I was about to suggest Max turn the gangster's gun into a winged bat. But then the door Nelli was pawing suddenly cracked open. Startled, I looked Max. I had a feeling, from the expression of concentration on his face, that he was the one causing it to open.

I glanced at Buonarotti. He looked uncertain, his gaze shifting from me to the door then back again. Then he saw Nelli move, and he pointed his weapon at her.

Without thinking, I stepped sideways to shield the dog.

"I'll blow you away, bitch!" Buonarotti warned.

I wasn't sure which one of us he was talking to.

Nelli took three fast steps into the room, then froze, her hair standing on end, her body stiff with surprise.

Directly in front of us was an elaborate altar that dominated an entire wall of the sparsely furnished room. A dozen or so candles illuminated it. The altar was decorated with a strange assortment of devotional objects, including piles of animal bones, three human skulls, numerous mirrors that were arranged to face other mirrors, symbols that were painted in what I had a feeling was blood, a collection of items that appeared to be the harvest of Father Gabriel's thieving habits, and several large terra cotta urns full of soil and pebbles. There were feathers all over the place. There was also a butcher's block, a bloody hand ax, and a headless, still-twitching chicken corpse.

Father Gabriel was kneeling before the altar, chanting. He held his arms high and spread wide. His sleeves were rolled up, and his hands and forearms were bathed in blood. If he was aware of our presence, he evidently chose to ignore it.

He was also ignoring the other inhabitant of the room. It was her presence, rather than the weird altar or dark ritual, that had caused Nelli to freeze. I felt frozen, too.

Sitting tied to a chair, wearing a low-cut black dress with a beaded bodice and a matching transparent wrap, was . . . *me*.

Or rather my perfect double.

It had been berating Father Gabriel when the door opened. Now it was staring at me in shock.

"Oh, my God!" I said.

That's who we had heard screaming?

The priest continued chanting. Nelli turned her head to look at me, then whined. I felt Buonarotti poke me in the back with his gun.

"Oh, my God!" I repeated, staring at myself in horror, and seeing myself stare back at me with an equal level of appalled shock. "Max!"

"I see it," he said.

"What *is* that on your faces?" my stunned duplicate asked.

"Inside," Buonarotti said, poking me harder with the gun.

"What? No!"

"*Inside*, bitch," Buonarotti ordered.

Nelli turned and started snarling at him.

Afraid the mobster would kill the dog, I said firmly, "*I'll* deal with this, Nelli."

"Max!" my doppelgangster shouted. "Max! Do something!"

The priest's chanting grew louder, as if trying to drown us all out.

My doppelgangster said to Father Gabriel, "And you! Will you shut *up*, for God's sake?"

"I am *not* going into that revolting room with that disgusting altar," I said to Buonarotti, "and that demented priest and a fresh chicken corpse and that . . . that . . . that *thing* tied to the chair!"

"Oh, for the love of God!" the priest blurted out, giving up on his chanting. "I can't do this with *both* of them talking!"

Buonarotti said, "Father, do you see this? What do I do? Which one is real?"

The priest rose to his feet and turned around to face us. Apart from the blood on his arms, his appearance looked so normal I felt disoriented. He was well-groomed and wearing his usual clerical suit. I had expected him to look evil and insane. Instead, he looked ordinary—apart from the blood—and exasperated.

As our adversary faced us, Nelli shifted her weight and recommenced growling.

The priest's expression changed from exasperation to alarm. He took a step back. "Michael?"

Buonarotti shoved me aside so he could shoot Nelli. I flung my full weight against him, unbalancing him. We fell against the doorway together and struggled. I heard Nelli barking. Buonarotti backhanded me across the face. I spun around, staggered into the room, and fell down. I heard Max shout something in another language.

My doppelgangster cried, "Nelli! Watch out!"

I looked up to see Max pointing at Buonarotti's gun. His expression was disconcerted. It was still a gun, it was still in Buonarotti's hand, and it looked fully functional. Max's gaze flew to the priest. I looked at Gabriel, too. He was holding the bloodied hand ax and eyeing Nelli. She was crouched down, snarling, and looking for an opening to attack him.

"What happened?" my doppelgangster said, looking at Max and then at the gun which was now pointed at him.

"*Nelli!* No! Don't!" I was winded from my fall. My voice was weak. The priest looked more scared than menacing. But the ax looked deadly. And since it was covered in chicken blood, he evidently didn't balk at killing animals with his own two hands, even if he was fastidious about whacking people.

"Nelli," my doppelgangster said, attempting to sound calm. "Come here. *Nelli*."

The familiar starting shaking with confusion and nerves. She looked at me and made distressed sounds in her throat.

"Call off your dog!" Gabriel ordered.

"Don't say 'dog,'" Max said tersely, poised to jump Buonarotti if the gangster moved the gun off him to shoot Nelli.

"Call it off!"

"Nelli," Max said. "Down."

With obvious reluctance, Nelli backed away slowly from the ax-wielding priest. Now we were spread out well enough that Buonarotti couldn't cover us all with the gun. We needed to keep it that way.

Still holding the ax, Father Gabriel looked at Max's painted face, then mine, then Nelli's. He frowned thoughtfully. "Interesting solution. But not one, I think, that will catch on among wiseguys."

Max look at the gun again. "You anticipated me."

"Transformations? Of course." The priest added, as if this were a great compliment, "You're not just a crazy old man."

"I'm afraid," Max said to me, "I can do nothing about the firearm. Father Gabriel has taken precautions in that respect."

"So I gathered," I said.

"Well, that's just great," said my perfect double. "Now what?"

I said to it, "What are you doing here?"

"What do you think I'm doing here? I was *kidnapped*." It looked at Max. "What's going on?"

I said to Gabriel, "Why the hell did you kidnap it? You *created* it."

"It?" my doppelgangster repeated.

"I didn't kidnap her," Gabriel said with renewed exasperation.

"You told me to grab the actress!" Buonarotti snapped at him. "I did what you wanted!"

"Grab me?" I said. "I thought you were trying to *kill* me."

"Yes, well, after your little stunt with the widow today, I realized you weren't likely to go down as easily as the others," said the priest.

"So you did suspect!" I said.

"Suspect what?" said my duplicate.

"Of course," said Gabriel. "And so I thought of a better use for you."

"You adapted," Max said. "Excellent."

"Max," my doppelgangster and I said in unison.

Buonarotti said, "She's leverage against the cop."

"We believe your young man is getting rather close to us," Father Gabriel said to me. "It seemed a good idea to create circumstances that would distract him."

"Kidnapping *me* would distract him," I said. "He won't miss that *thing*."

"Excuse me?" said the doppelgangster.

"Oh, I don't think the good detective knows what you know, Esther," said the priest. "So either one of you could be useful in that respect. That's why I kept her when I saw that Michael had brought me the wrong one."

"I did?" Buonarotti looked stunned. "So which one is the real one?"

Gabriel sighed and looked at Max. "Take my advice, don't ever get a partner. It's really more trouble than it's worth."

Buonarotti scowled. "Oh, really? So who'd whack the targets if I didn't have a piece of this action? *You*, you little pansy?"

Max said, "I gather this was a partnership of convenience, rather than one of mutual respect and esteem?"

"Get me out of this chair!" said the doppelgangster. "I've had *enough* of this!"

The priest glared at me. "You are the noisiest woman. You've barely been here an hour, and I swear I've got my first ever migraine now."

"No, *I've* barely been here fifteen minutes!" I said.

"Indeed." Still holding his ax, the priest crossed the room to stand behind my doppelgangster. "I heard you arrive. Half the city probably heard you arrive." He raised the ax. "You're not precisely the stealthiest enemies a man could have."

My heart thudded. I got off the floor and sprang to my feet. "What are you—"

"Don't move." Buonarotti pointed the gun at me.

"Untie me!" The doppelgangster looked over its shoulder and saw the raised ax. "Whoa! What are you doing?"

Max made a dive for the gun. Buonarotti slugged him so hard he bounced off the wall and slid down it. Nelli lunged, snarling, then came to a tense halt as she confronted the gun.

"No!" cried my perfect double. *"Don't!"*

The ax came down swiftly, cutting off the doppelgangster's scream of horror in mid-wail. I screamed, too, and covered my eyes with my hands. Nelli barked hysterically. Buonarotti laughed. He really was a pig.

My heart was pounding, my head reeling. I thought I might be sick. Then I realized that in another moment, I might be *dead*. I gasped and lowered my hands, blinking rapidly as I looked around the room. But the priest was back at the altar now, wiping chicken blood off his hands. Max was struggling to rise to his feet. Buonarotti was eyeing both him and Nelli, his gun moving uncertainly between them.

I forced myself to look at the spot where my perfect double had just been beheaded.

There was nothing there, of course, except a pile of by now familiar substances: feathers, dirt, bird bones, pebbles. And my transparent black wrap.

I made a horrible sound. All the men in the room looked at me.

"That is the single most disturbing thing I've ever seen," I said with feeling. I looked back at the three men. "And lately, that's saying a *lot*."

"Come on, come *on*," said Buonarotti. "We're wasting time."

"For once," said Father Gabriel, "I'm forced to agree with you, Michael." He bent over and examined the chicken. "It's not cold yet. I think I can proceed."

Max's gaze moved to a short marble pedestal on the altar. A gold cigarette lighter sat on top of it. "Who are you duplicating now?"

"Someone whose death will ensure this war finally gets started and goes all the way, until both families are destroyed." The priest said, "This morning, I paid a condolence call on Danny Dapezzo's boss."

I drew in a sharp breath. "You stole Don Carmine Corvino's lighter?"

"And when the Corvino boss dies," Buonarotti said, gloating, "the family will go apeshit."

"The war will commence," Max said grimly.

"Nothing can stop it," Father Gabriel said with satisfaction. "Not if the don is murdered. The family will blame the Gambellos, and they'll do anything to destroy them then, even if it leads to their own destruction." He shrugged. "That's just how these people are."

"No!" I said. "You've got to stop! You've got to stop *now!*"

"Be quiet!" the priest said.

"So far, only wiseguys have died," said. "But if you go through with this, innocent people will die, too."

"Shut the fuck up," Buonarotti said.

"Sooner or later, it'll happen! Gabriel, listen to me!" I cried. "How can you do this?"

"I'm entitled," he said.

"Entitled?"

"Yes," he said reasonably. "I lost my father in childhood and no one ever punished his killer."

"He should have chosen a different profession!" I snapped. "You *demented*, warped, bloodthirsty, craven—"

Buonarotti hit Max. Max fell on the floor, and the mobster kicked him. Max groaned and lay there in a daze.

"What are you doing?" I shouted.

"I told you to shut up. You keep talking," Buonarotti said, "and I'll break the old guy's ribs."

I stared at him in mute horror.

Buonarotti said to the priest, "*That's* how you make a broad shut up, genius."

Father Gabriel looked distressed. He said to Buonarotti, "That was unnecessary."

"*You're* the one bitching about how all her yapping gives you a headache." The mobster grimaced. "Now I'm getting one, too."

Gabriel gave himself a shake. "I've got to finish my work." He nodded at Max's prone body. "Get him out of here."

"What should I do with him?"

"Kill him, of course," the priest said dismissively.

"*What?*" I blurted. "No!"

Buonarotti pointed the gun at Max. My throat constricted. Nelli crouched low on her haunches, growling.

"Not *here*," Gabriel said irritably. "You know how I feel about violence. Take him somewhere to do it. The dog, too."

"How am I gonna take a vicious dog somewhere?"

"Oh, all right," said the priest, as if dealing with an annoying administrative problem. "You can shoot the dog here, but then you've got to remove its body."

"Are you kidding me?" Buonarotti said. "This dog weighs more than the old guy does!"

"These kinds of problems are your department, not mine," said Father Gabriel in exasperation. "So think of something."

"What do we do about the broad?"

"We keep her alive for now. Leverage against the cop."

"Oh. Right."

"Tie her up before you go," Gabriel said.

"*No,*" I said automatically, backing away as Buonarotti took a step toward me.

Nelli barked and moved toward him. He pointed the gun at her. A shot went off, the sound exploding through the room. I screamed Nelli's name . . . and was surprised to see Buonarotti flinch and whirl to point his gun at the door—just as Lucky came flying into the room, gun in

hand, his painted face contorted in a snarl of predatory
rage as he launched himself at Buonarotti.

There was a cloud of feathers in Lucky's short gray
hair and a dusting of dirt on his clothes. Souvenirs, I
figured, of his recently decapitated doppelgangster. He
flew across the room and hit Buonarotti with such force
that their bodies careened into Nelli, who got knocked
into the altar.

"No!" the priest cried, as feathers, dirt, and chicken
blood flew all over the place. A candle toppled over and
went out. Two facing mirrors fell against each other with
a crashing sound and broke. Rising to her feet, Nelli cut
her paw severely on a piece of broken glass and yelped
as Lucky and Buonarotti, locked in mortal combat,
rolled on the floor nearby, trying to kill each other.

Nelli limped over to me, trailing blood, and I looked
at her paw. Lucky and Buonarotti rolled into us. Lucky's
foot shot out and inadvertently kicked my arm.

"Ow!"

On the other side of the men's tangled, writhing fight,
Max dragged himself across the floor to the altar. He
pulled a large silver amulet out of his pocket, and laid it
at the base of the altar.

"No!" Father Gabriel cried.

I saw the priest reach for his ax. "Watch out, Max!"

Max looked up and rolled away just in time to avoid
the blade of the ax, which Gabriel brought down with
enough force to suggest that he was learning to over-
come his aversion to killing his victims with his own two
hands.

Buonarotti and Lucky were kicking and flailing, rolling all over the floor between me and Gabriel. Nelli and
I were trying to get around them, but they were moving
too fast and violently. Nelli was hampered by her injured
foot, and I was hampered by not being able to levitate.

Gabriel raised the ax again. I screamed. Max raised
a hand and uttered a hoarse command, better prepared

for this blow than the first one. The ax froze in mid-strike, and Gabriel cried out in pain, dropping it.

Buonarotti kicked Lucky in the face. The old hit man fell backward and his gun flew out of his hand. Buonarotti climbed to his feet, nose bleeding, and pointed his gun at his foe.

"No!" I screamed. Everything in the room came to an abrupt standstill.

"Good-bye, Lucky." Buonarotti pulled the trigger.

The gun jammed.

Buonarotti looked down at his weapon in appalled surprise, then back at Lucky.

Lucky grinned. "Didn't you know? I'm too lucky to die."

"But you were duplicated!" Buonarotti said. "You were cursed with death!"

"What, you think I paint my face like this because it's a good look for me?" Lucky dived for his own gun.

Buonarotti turned and fled the room.

25

Lucky said to me, "That gun is jammed, not dead. You stay here until I tell you it's safe." He ran after Buonarotti.

I crossed the room to where Gabriel was bending down to retrieve his ax. I grabbed him before he could seize the weapon.

"Let's see how you do with someone who isn't tied up or lying on the floor half unconscious!" I said.

Gripping his black shirt, I bashed my forehead against his nose and stomped on his foot.

He shrieked like a girl, and his nose sprouted blood.

"Nelli!" Max called. "Your assistance, please!"

I punched Gabriel as hard as I could, really mad now. Somewhere else in the church, I heard shots fired.

Nelli hobbled across the room on three legs to join Max at the altar. He started chanting.

"Noooo!" Gabriel lunged toward them.

I tripped him, knocked him down, and kicked him in the ribs. He cried out and curled up in a fetal position.

"Get up!" I kicked him again. "Get up you *evil*, murdering, self-righteous lunatic!"

He rolled over and crawled away from me. Somewhere else in the building, there was a lengthy exchange of gunfire.

Nelli started destroying the remaining objects on the altar, knocking down the candles, tipping over the urns of dirt and pebbles, scattering the animal bones. She took the dead chicken between her jaws and started shaking it furiously as if it were a chew toy.

This was a little too much for me. "Nelli, give me that," I insisted. I took it away from her.

Hobbling along with her bad leg, she rose up to knock the human skulls off the altar, then did her best to destroy them.

"No, no, no!" Father Gabriel was practically weeping now.

I swung the dead, mangled chicken and walloped the priest with it as hard as I could. He cried out and backed away. Stomping toward him, I hit him with the deceased bird again.

"Do you know how terrified Charlie and Danny were when they died? Did you get a kick out of that, you malicious bastard?" I hit him again. "You were going to kill Elena? A *woman?* Because she resisted being raped by your murdering, gloating, disgusting partner in crime?" I tossed the chicken aside and kneed Gabriel in the groin. He doubled over in pain.

Max's chanting grew louder. I was sweating. I thought it was because of my rage and exertion. But it dawned on me that, actually, the room was suddenly hot. *Very* hot. Unnaturally so.

"And you were going to have Buonarotti kill *me?*" I shouted. "ME? What did I ever do to you?"

Gabriel moaned pathetically. "You were going to find out. You were going to stop me."

"And you *should* be stopped, you warped, twisted, pathetic, homicidal asshole!" I grabbed him by the shirt shook him really hard. His head thudded against the wall. "You were *killing* people! You were going to get lots more people killed! Even innocent people! People who aren't wiseguys! Like Lopez!"

I clamped my fingers around his jaw and squeezed until he made a strangled sound of pain. "And you nearly blew my audition for *The Dirty Thirty!* You *JERK!*"

There was an explosion so strong it shook the whole room. I staggered backward, releasing my hold on the weeping, whining, disheveled priest. A blaze of fiery heat washed over my back. Nelli howled. I heard more gunshots somewhere in the belly of the church.

I turned around and raised an arm to shield my eyes from the intense glow emanating from the sacked altar. Squinting and looking through my fingers, I could see that Nelli and Max were enveloped in a bright golden light. Max was on his knees now, his arms raised overhead and spread wide, as Gabriel's had been when we first entered this room. Nelli sat next to him, her muzzle turned skyward as she continued howling. Max was bellowing words I didn't understand, and the intensity of light and heat increased until flames were rippling all around him and his familiar.

"Max!" I cried, afraid they wouldn't survive. "Nelli!"

Shapes started developing in the glowing flames, struggling to coalesce into coherent forms within the undulating white fire that consumed the whole altar. I thought I saw arms, legs, faces . . . Something huge and rotund emerged from the tangled fray of writhing, twisting, hideously suggestive shapes in the fire. It looked like . . .

"Charlie?" I said.

The figure resembling Chubby Charlie Chiccante seemed to fold into itself, tumbling over into more molten white heat and fire, and then another figure emerged, then another.

I saw the graceful curves of Elena Giacalona's figure moving through the flames, as well as Lopez's clean profile and taut body, Danny Dapezzo's tidy form, and Johnny Be Good's disturbingly Elvis-like image. Something that looked like Lucky floated through the flames and then dissolved, followed by a writhing entity that looked like my own perfect double, glowing in the liquid heat of this mystical cleansing. As the flames began receding and the glow faded, one final shape passed through my vision. I frowned, thinking I must be wrong about who it was.

And then the heat faded, dissipating almost as quickly as it had gathered. The flames vanished, leaving just one feeble candle on the altar to illuminate this old, forgotten room.

Breathing hard, Max slumped and started to keel over sideways.

"Max!" I rushed toward him and caught him before he hit the floor.

He was damp with sweat and panting with exhaustion. Nelli rose, staggering as she discovered that her foot was too tender to hold any weight, and hobbled a couple of steps closer to investigate Max's condition, her black nose wiggling as she sniffed his head. I saw that the intense heat had melted the wax in the painted symbols on both their faces, so that they were now covered with runny, rust-colored streaks and splotches.

I petted Nelli with one hand as I held Max in my arms. "Good work. Very good work."

Her tail wagged wearily.

"Max? Are you okay?"

"Fine. Just a little . . . fatigued."

We heard another gunshot.

I stiffened. "Lucky!"

"We must assist him," Max said faintly. "Help me up."

"He said to stay here until he told us it was safe to come out."

"We can't, Esther. There's one more doppelgangster."

"I thought so." I looked over my shoulder to demand the priest tell us who it was, even though I thought I knew.

But Gabriel had escaped while Max was destroying

the altar where the priest had cursed his victims with certain death.

"He's gone," I said in dismay. "I didn't beat him up enough."

"But you certainly gave it your best effort." Max stumbled toward the door. "We must go to Lucky's aid." I followed him as he added, "He will be outnumbered and taken by surprise."

Nelli was limping heavily behind me. Max turned in the dark doorway and said to me, "Oh, bring the candle."

Nelli suddenly growled. I turned away from Max to look at her. I heard a dull thud behind me and whirled around. Buonarotti was standing in the doorway holding the gun with which he had just pistol-whipped Max. Max fell to the floor, unconscious. Buonarotti seized my throat, pulled me against him, and pressed the gun to my cheek. Holding me between himself and Nelli, who was snarling and barking, he backed out of the room, ordering me, "Shut the door."

I couldn't speak, couldn't breathe, couldn't shake my head. I hung by my throat from Buonarotti's squeezing fingers. His fingernails dug into my skin. The pain was mind-fogging. I thought I would pass out in another second.

"Shut the door," he repeated, "or I'll shoot the dog. *Now*."

My hand fumbled for the door handle. I found it and pulled. Max's body was in the way. Buonarotti kicked Max with his foot, rolling him over. My eyes watering with pain and my vision blackening, I pulled the door shut.

"Good." Buonarotti pressed up against me in the pitch dark hallway. "Now tell me where he is."

I made a strangling sound.

"Huh? Oh." He loosened his grip enough to let me talk. "Where is he? Tell me, bitch, or I'll blow your head off."

"Where's who?" I choked out.

"Gabriel."

"I don't know."

He slapped me so hard I reeled away, then he yanked my hair to pull me close again. No wonder Elena had called him an animal.

"He ran off," I gasped out.

"Why?"

"He's a coward."

"What the hell is going on here?"

"Huh?" And then the truth dawned on me. *This* Buonarotti's face wasn't bloodied. "Oh, my God. It *was* you."

Another gunshot rang out. Then two more. My captor stiffened. "Who is that?"

"You don't know?" I rasped.

I was right about the final figure I had seen in the dying flames of the altar.

Buonarotti's doppelgangster grabbed my throat again. "You and I are getting out of here."

Well, Gabriel had *said* his partner was proving to be more trouble than he was worth. Apparently the priest had decided it was time to help him shuffle off this mortal coil. Once Buonarotti came face to face with his own perfect double, he'd be easy pickings. Perhaps the priest intended to bring about the three-way war by giving up Don Michael to the other two families now that he was vulnerable.

Holding me by the throat, his gun pressed to my head, the doppelgangster hauled me down the pitch dark hallway. We paused at the doorway leading to the choir gallery, and my captor leaned against it, listening. We heard voices shouting on the other side of it.

"No, not that way," he muttered.

"There's another way?"

"Stairway to the courtyard." He dragged me to the end of the hall. "It's how I came up."

"No, those stairs aren't safe," I protested as he dragged me toward them.

"That's just what he tells people to keep them out of here," Buonarotti said dismissively.

He took his hand off my neck long enough to open a door. Despite his comment, I was still anxious about descending a staircase in complete darkness with a gun pressed to my head. I was equally anxious about going anywhere with a murderous doppelgangster.

So it was a relief when I heard a man's voice coming from somewhere beyond the bottom of the stairs.

Buonarotti went still and covered my mouth with his hand, pressing the gun harder against my head. Along with the voice, we heard a gurgling electrical noise, like someone switching channels on a radio. This was followed by a metallic sounding voice. I couldn't make out the words, but I gave a reflexive start when I realized what the sound was: a walkie-talkie.

And then I realized what the voices were talking about. I could make out a man saying, "Shots fired," and giving this address.

Someone was talking on a police radio. There was a cop at the other end of these stairs!

I tried to cry out. Buonarotti squeezed my throat so hard I nearly blacked out. He shut the door and then dragged me back to the other door, the one that led to the choir gallery.

"One sound," he whispered, "and I'll kill you."

I was coughing helplessly from the abuse to my throat, so this seemed like a pretty stupid threat. He opened the door a crack and listened.

We both heard Gabriel whispering, "No, there's a cop in the courtyard! We need to leave *this* way."

Buonarotti—the real one—whispered back, "How do you think we're gonna get past Lucky? He's between us and the door."

The doppelgangster's body, which was pressed up against mine, stiffened. "Who the fuck is that?" When I didn't respond, he prodded, "Who's with Gabriel?"

"You are," I said.

"Huh?" He made an irritated sound. "Dumb broad." He opened the door and dragged me through it.

The gallery was pitch dark, too. Buonarotti and Gabriel weren't giving Lucky a target by illuminating themselves.

"You and your bright ideas," Buonarotti said to the priest. "I can't see a fucking thing."

"Then neither can Lucky," Gabriel said. "We'll slip past him."

And then a familiar voice at the far end of the church shouted, "*Police!* Weapons down! Police! *Drop your weapons!* I'm a cop!"

Lopez! Every cell in my body got a flood of renewed energy as I recognized the voice.

"Hey, I'm not armed!" Lucky shouted. "Don't shoot! I am not armed!"

"That *liar*," Buonarotti muttered.

"Lopez!" I cried.

"Esther! Stay down!" He didn't even sound surprised to hear my voice. "Lucky, is that you?" he called.

"Yeah. Watch out! Buonarotti's the killer! He's so off his rocker, he'll whack a cop!"

"Where is he?" Lopez's voice was coming from a new position. He was getting closer to us.

"I think he's up in the gallery," Lucky called.

The doppelgangster drew in a sharp breath through its nostrils, thinking this meant itself.

"What's wrong with the lights?" Lopez shouted.

"Not sure," Lucky replied.

"*Shit!* I don't have a flashlight."

"Listen, cop!" the doppelgangster shouted, its mouth so close to my ear that I flinched. "I've got your girlfriend!"

"Who the fuck is *that?*" said Buonarotti in the darkness.

In the dormitory hallway behind us, on the other side of the door we had come through, I heard a man shout, "*Police!* Weapons down! NYPD! Drop your weapons! This is the police!"

The doppelgangster shouted down to Lopez, his voice carrying through the darkness, "I've got her right here, and I'll blow her head off!"

"He's lying! His gun's empty!" Lucky said.

To clarify the situation, the doppelgangster fired a shot.

"Holy shit!" said Lucky.

"Who the fuck *is* that?" said Buonarotti.

"Lucky," I shouted, "there's a dopp—*agh!*" The hand on my throat tightened.

"Esther?" Lopez shouted. "Esther!"

At our backs, on the other side of the door, the cop again called, "Police! Drop your weapons *now!*"

"Esther!" Lopez shouted, his voice coming closer. Something crashed to the floor. "Goddamn it! Don't *any* of these lights work?"

The doppelgangster ordered, "Throw down your gun and get on the floor facedown, cop! I'm getting out of here! I've got your woman! You get in my way, and I swear to God, I *will* kill her!"

"Esther!" Lopez shouted.

"Answer him," the doppelgangster said. "Tell him to let us pass."

I was coughing, unable to speak. In the hallway behind me, I heard a scuffle, a faint thud, and then a groan. The door behind us opened.

"Esther! Goddamn it, where are you? *Esther!*" And then Lopez screamed, *"I want LIGHTS!"*

The lights came on, blazing throughout the church. The sudden brightness made my captor and me both flinch. I squeezed my eyes shut as they stung and watered.

The creature dragged me closer to the door behind us, ensuring that we remained shielded from Lopez's sight by the dramatic velvet curtains that framed the broad balcony.

"*Freeze!*" Lopez shouted, presumably at Buonarotti, who now stood exposed on the balcony with light blazing gloriously down upon him.

"What the *fuck* . . ." Buonarotti said.

As my eyes adjusted, I saw the mobster staring at me with an expression of appalled amazement. Then I realized he wasn't staring at *me*.

The doppelgangster sucked in its breath. "What the *fuck* . . ."

Buonarotti's gaze flashed to the disheveled priest who stood blinking and shielding his eyes, only an arm's length away from him. The snarl of murderous hatred on Buonarotti's face revealed that he knew his partner had betrayed him. He screamed—an inarticulate bellow of rage—and started beating Gabriel.

"Freeze!" Lopez shouted somewhere below the two men on the balcony. "*Freeze!*"

The gangster knocked down Father Gabriel, then reached for the candelabra I had knocked over earlier tonight.

"*I'll shoot!*" Lopez warned.

"I'll kill you, you bastard!"

"Don't do it!" Lopez shouted.

Buonarotti picked up the candelabra and screamed at the cowering priest. "*I'll kill you!*"

A gunshot went off.

Buonarotti cried out and staggered back, and blood rolled down his arm. I didn't understand what was happening for a moment. Then I realized that Lopez had shot him.

Undeterred by his bullet wound, Buonarotti stumbled back toward the priest, screaming, "I'll kill you, you bastard! I'll kill you!"

"Stop!" Lopez warned. "Don't make me shoot you twice!"

The priest turned to run this way, apparently forgetting there was a doppelgangster in his path. Not to mention a woman who had just beaten the shit out of him.

He stopped suddenly in his tracks, staring in sorrowful defeat. But he wasn't looking at us. He was looking past us.

"I was good, wasn't I?" he said, his voice flat.

I stared at him blankly.

Then from behind me, Max answered, "You were very talented."

The priest turned and dove over the balcony railing.

I choked on a startled scream and lunged forward reflexively as the body crashed into the wooden pews below the balcony. The doppelgangster was startled enough to release its grip on me.

I got to the railing and looked down. It was a long drop, but survivable. The priest, however, had thrown himself head first into a bank of pews. He lay at a horrid angle, his neck evidently broken and blood pouring from his shattered skull.

Lopez ran to the body and then leaned over to press his fingers against the neck, checking for a pulse.

"Is he dead?" Lucky called from the other side of the church.

"Yes," Lopez said after a moment. "Dead." His voice was grim.

I made a choked sound. Lopez looked up and saw me.

"Esther! Get out of there!" He quickly raised his gun to aim it at something on my left.

I realized that the wounded Buonarotti, standing to my left, was also looking over the railing and that I was much closer to him than was wise. I turned to flee, then stumbled and halted. The doppelgangster was in my path. But only for a moment. Max swung the bloody hand ax—the one that Gabriel had used this evening to kill a chicken—and decapitated it.

Buonarotti starting laughing as if the funniest thing in the world had just occurred to him. Within moments, he fell clumsily to the floor and just sat there, rocking back and forth, laughing, and saying over and over, "I'm a dead man! I'm a dead man!" His bleeding arm didn't seem to bother him.

Behind Max, I saw an unconscious cop in uniform.

Max followed my gaze, then said, "I was afraid the doppelgangster would harm him. It seemed best to remove him from the equation."

Nelli stood over the cop, holding her injured foot gingerly in the air. She snuffled the fallen man with concern. When the policeman groaned, her tail wagged with relief.

Lopez's running footsteps carried him up to the choir gallery via the long spiral staircase we had climbed in the dark earlier tonight. When he reached us, instead of covering the hysterically laughing Buonarotti with his gun, he pointed it at Max.

"Put the ax *down*, Max," he said.

"Pardon? Oh!" Realizing that his holding a bloody ax had been misinterpreted as a hostile gesture, Max set it down. "I hope I didn't alarm you."

"What the hell happened to McDevitt?" Lopez snapped.

"Who?" I said.

"The cop lying on the floor behind Max!"

"Oh! That's my fault entirely, I'm afraid," Max said. "I hit him with the ax handle."

"*Why*, Max?"

"I believed him to be Don Michael. Who was threatening to kill Esther." Max added helpfully, "It was very dark, you know."

"Yes, I know," Lopez said. "And the *blood* on the ax would be from what, exactly?"

"A chicken," I blurted.

"A what?"

"A chicken. Um, I guess that's where all these feathers came from." I kicked a pile of doppelgangster detritus with my foot. "The chicken."

"Father Gabriel killed it with the ax." Max shook his head sadly. "He also threatened *us* with the ax. I'm afraid he was involved in some most unsavory activities. The Church wouldn't approve at all."

"He was in league with Buonarotti!" I said.

"I know." Lopez glanced at the wounded mobster. The arm had only been nicked; it was bleeding, but didn't look serious.

I said, "Buonarotti's been committing these murders!"

"I know," Lopez said.

"You *do?*"

"Are you all right?" Lopez asked me.

"Yes."

"Are you sure?"

"Yes."

"What are you doing here?" he asked me.

"Don't you know?"

"How would I know?" he said in exasperation.

"Well, what are *you* doing here then?"

"I asked the local patrolman to keep an eye on the church and let me know if anything unusual happened. So when he saw a woman, two men, and a huge dog entering furtively around midnight tonight, he called me. And since I had a feeling I knew who he was describing, I told him to stand by, and I came here. By the time I arrived, he thought he'd heard shots fired."

"Oh." I frowned. "Wait a minute. It's just the two of you?"

"At the moment, thanks to Max assaulting a police officer," Lopez said, "it's just the one of me."

"Who turned on the lights?"

"What?"

"Who got the lights working again?" I asked.

Lopez shrugged and looked at me and Max. We looked at each other.

"Well, whatever brought the power back on," Lopez said to me, "I'm just glad it happened. I thought you'd be dead in two more seconds."

Max was staring at him.

Lopez noticed. "What?"

I stared, too, remembering the fierceness in his voice at that moment: *I want LIGHTS!* And suddenly there had been light, in answer to his command . . .

I blinked. Oh, good grief, what was I thinking?

Don't be ridiculous. It was just . . . coincidence.

Max kept staring hard at Lopez, his posture erect, his gaze intent and speculative. Lopez stared back, probably thinking again about having Max's place searched for drugs.

"Max?" I prodded, feeling uneasy.

"Pardon? Oh!" Max smiled. "Er, you were saying, detective?"

"I'm all *done* saying. Now it's your turn." Lopez said to me, "What the hell are you doing here?"

"We, uh . . ." I looked at Max.

Max looked at Nelli, who had by now limped to his side. Nelli looked at Lucky, who came up the staircase at a slow, painful pace, grimacing as he reached the top step. She wagged her tail.

Lucky said, "I'm gettin' too old for my work."

"What 'work' was going on here tonight?" Lopez said, keeping an eye on Buonarotti, who was still sitting on the floor, rocking back and forth as he laughed hysterically and occasionally shouted, "I'm a dead man!"

"Ah, forget it," Lucky said genially. "You can take all the credit. We was never even here."

Lopez look at all three of us for a long, tense moment.

Then he sighed. "Well, my backup will be here in about two minutes. So if you were never here, then you need to be gone before then."

"Really?" I said. "You'll let us leave? We don't have to talk to Napoli or anyone?"

"Esther," Lopez said wearily, "the very last thing in the world that I want right now is to spend the rest of the night ... No, the rest of the week ... No, the rest of my career trying to explain to Napoli and my captain what you were doing here tonight with them." His glance encompassed Max, Lucky, and Buonarotti.

"Oh."

"We've got tainted physical evidence and conflicting witness statements. The, er, chicken-slaughtering priest who's just committed suicide may be an accessory to murder. We recorded a phone conversation today in which Buonarotti brags about whacking Chubby Charlie, Johnny Be Good, and Danny the Doctor—"

"He talked about it on the *phone?*" Lucky looked appalled.

"—but he sounded so crazy in that conversation that I thought he seemed well on his way to making a credible insanity plea ..." Lopez took another look at Buonarotti, who was now shrieking with laughter. "Even before now." He shook his head. "Overall, I don't think either side is going to want to take this case to trial."

Lucky said, "So Buonarotti will go to a prison for head cases. The priest will get buried. This mess will go away quietly. Sounds good to me."

I looked at Max, who looked much the worse for wear. "Yes," I said slowly. "I guess that is for the best."

We heard sirens approaching.

"Go," Lopez said. "I won't cover for you if you're still hanging around when they get here."

"Thank you," I said.

"But someday, Esther ..."

"Yes?"

"Someday you're going to explain to me what the hell that crap is that's all over your face and hands. You look like you've had the worst tattoo accident in history." His gaze swept our group. "All three of you, actually. And your little dog, too."

26

"I was wrong about your boyfriend," Lucky said. "He may be a cop, but he watched our backs when it counted. He's a stand-up guy."

"I don't think he's my boyfriend," I said morosely.

"You ain't sure?"

"I haven't talked to him since that night."

We stood outside St. Monica's on the day of Father Gabriel's funeral, watching the mourners leave. I had initially resisted attending the funeral Mass of the demented killer who'd tried to manipulate three crime families into a war as well as kill me, Elena Giacalona, and Connor Lopez. But Max and Lucky had convinced me that we had to wrap up this one last piece of business.

So now we were loitering outside the front door of St. Monica's with Nelli, keeping an eye on the mourners—to see if a doppelgangster attended the service.

Buonarotti was the final deadly duplicate that Father Gabriel had made, as far as we knew from what we had witnessed upon destroying the demented sorcerer's altar. But I agreed that we'd rest easier if we made absolutely sure.

Nelli, with her injured paw wrapped in a fresh bandage and healing nicely, observed everyone leaving the church as the service ended, just as she had observed them entering.

The priest's funeral was heavily attended by members of all three of the crime families with which Father Gabriel's life and evil works had been connected. Many non-felonious parish members were also in attendance. In particular, there were lots of tearful women mourners.

Lucky said, "So your boyfriend figured out—"

"Can you just call him Lopez?" I asked.

"So Lopez figured out that the Gambellos and Corvinos wasn't hitting each other, huh? Not bad for a cop."

"I told you not to underestimate him," I said.

According to the newspapers—which was how I was learning about this, since Lopez hadn't called me—the Organized Crime Control Bureau had initially believed Charlie's death might be the commencement of a new Corvino-Gambello war. But after Johnny Be Good was hit, an unnamed "new recruit" to the bureau had pointed out that the Corvinos had nothing to gain by killing a useless *momzer* like Johnny and that the murder of Don Victor's own nephew would certainly incite a mob war at a time when the Corvinos and Gambellos each had far more to lose from such a conflict than either side could hope to gain from it. So the "bright young detective" had proposed the investigators consider who would actually benefit from such a war.

"Cui bono," Lucky said.

"Huh?" I said.

"Whom does it benefit?" Max translated. "Who stands to gain?"

"Oh."

"Betcha never thought I knew some Latin."

Following this principle, the OCCB had stepped up its electronic surveillance of the Buonarotti family, and continued this scrutiny even after Danny "the Doctor" Dapezzo's murder seemed to confirm a more obvious theory of events. Before long, circumstantial evidence pointed to Michael Buonarotti (quoted in a press release two days ago as assuring the media that he was "no relation" to Michelangelo). These suspicions were confirmed when the don was recorded on the phone admitting to the murders. That same night, Buonarotti was arrested at St. Monica's.

A leaked excerpt of a transcript of the incriminating phone call certainly seemed to suggest Buonarotti was out of his mind. He claimed godlike qualities, including invisibility, the ability to pass through locked doors and to shoot around corners, and inviolable immunity from counterattack. He declared his victims were helpless against him, and he insisted he couldn't be caught.

"Giving names and details on the *phone*," Lucky said. "He really was going off his rocker."

"I guess it all went to his head," I said. "The power that Gabriel's sorcery made available to him, the sense of supernatural omnipotence that Buonarotti felt when he—"

"There is no such thing as 'supernatural' phenomena," Max said, watching the mourners exit the church. "There is only—"

"Esther's right," Lucky interrupted. "The power went to his oversized head. He shoulda never got those hair plugs. They probably affected his brain."

"He wears hair plugs? Really?" I shook my head. "I never would have guessed."

So when I had told Lopez that night at the bookshop that the Corvinos and Gambellos didn't want a war, I had confirmed his theory that someone else was engineering all this. And he presumably had the church watched the following night because Buonarotti had alluded, in his recorded phone call that day, to having a "little bit" of help from a priest. OCCB hadn't expected violence at the church Buonarotti attended, but "an alert patrolman" had called for backup upon hearing shots fired there after midnight.

Rumors were running rampant, in the media and in the congregation of St. Monica's, about Father Gabriel's activities. Perhaps because he was Catholic, it was his death, rather than his possible involvement in three Mafia hits, that was causing the most controversy. Had the priest fallen off the balcony or had he deliberately *jumped?* I knew what I had seen, but apparently Lopez wasn't pressing the point. I supposed I could understand why not—Lopez was Catholic, too, after all, and suicide was a mortal sin.

"I hope Buonarotti goes away for the rest of his life," I said, thinking about Elena as I rubbed my throat. It was three days since Buonarotti's doppelgangster had grabbed me there. It didn't hurt much anymore, but the bruises hadn't faded yet.

"He will, for sure," said Lucky. "Because he ain't gonna live long."

Max and I both looked at Lucky.

The old hit man shrugged. "He stood up—on the *phone*—for whacking made guys in two families. What did you think would happen?"

"But how?" I argued. "He'll be in prison."

"Guys are easy to whack in prison. Nowhere to hide." Lucky shrugged. "And *this* guy has been cursed with certain death. Piece of cake."

"True," Max said thoughtfully. "Encountering a doppelgangster doomed the victim rather than empowering a particular killer. Anyone with murderous intent could have done what Don Michael did once the victim was cursed. But Don Michael happened to be the killer whom Father Gabriel chose to take into his confidence."

"So even without the Corvinos and Gambellos after him now . . ." I said.

"He wouldn't be long for this world, anyhow," Lucky said. "With his personality? The very first guy who has to share a breakfast table with him in the joint will probably whack him."

"Speaking of guys who aren't long for this world," I said, "what's going to happen to Angelo Falcone? The papers said he disappeared as soon as the cops released him."

"He sure did," Lucky said. "And good riddance."

"So the young man has left New York City?" Max asked.

"Yep. And probably even Angelo ain't dumb enough ever to come back."

We fell silent as Don Carmine Corvino and his wife left the church and walked past us. The flashily dressed mobster ignored Lucky. Behind him, though, Fast Sammy Salerno gave Lucky a little nod. Mikey Castrucci gave him the finger.

"What a putz," Lucky muttered. "We're at *church*."

After Buonarotti's arrest was announced, the Corvino family had accepted that the Gambellos weren't responsible for Danny Dapezzo's murder. There would be no mob war, they wouldn't target Lucky for a hit, and Max and I were completely safe from them. Like the Gambellos, though, the Corvinos were casting hostile glances at the Buonarottis who were in attendance today. Don Michael's organization, however, denied all knowledge of his recent activities. In any case, his high-profile arrest had weakened his crime family considerably, and the other families didn't seem to consider the Buonarottis a serious threat now.

Stella Butera came out of the church, dressed all in black and wearing a dramatically veiled hat. She clasped Lucky's hand and said he was looking well. She clasped my hand and asked if she'd see me at work tonight. I said yes. The restaurant had reopened two days ago. Although I couldn't sing for a few more days, thanks to the doppelgangster's brutal assault on my throat, I could certainly wait tables and earn money.

Jimmy Legs also paused on his way out of the church to greet us. Nelli recognized him and wagged her tail, and he patted her head. Ronnie Romano talked to Lucky for a few minutes, but he snubbed me; he still disapproved of my dating a cop.

"I'm not sure I'm still dating him," I said gloomily to Lucky when he explained why Ronnie had refused to acknowledge my greeting.

Lucky said, "Oh, come on, I seen the way that guy looks at you, and how mad he gets when he thinks someone's tryin' to hurt you."

"Then perhaps you also noticed how dangerously insane he thinks I am, and how fed up he gets with finding me involved in his investigations and with having to lie to his superiors to protect me?"

"You really think he'd dump you over a little thing like insanity and lying and concealing evidence and getting involved in ... Uh, I mean ..." Someone caught Lucky's eye, and he looked relieved to have an excuse to abandon the subject. "Hello, boss! Hey, you're looking great!"

Actually, Don Victor Gambello looked so close to death's door that I thought we should summon an ambulance, but I didn't contradict Lucky. The octogenarian boss of the most powerful crime family in New York might be skeletally thin, a sickly gray-yellow color, wheezing with the effort of walking down the steps of the church, and trying to control a tremor, but there was still a chillingly cold, ruthless shrewdness in the elderly gaze that assessed me, Max, and Nelli.

"So these," he said in a breathy, rasping, very soft voice, "are our friends?"

Lucky drew in a sharp breath of pleased surprise. "Yes, boss. This is Esther Diamond, Dr. Maximillian Zadok, and Nelli. *Our friends.*" Lucky added to us, "I told him what you three done for us."

I said, "Well, we didn't exactly do it for—" Lucky elbowed me, and I shut up.

Don Victor looked at us without saying anything. Max

acknowledged Lucky's introduction with polite phrases. Nelli wagged her tail, causing a passerby to give a startled exclamation of pain. The old mobster continued to stare hard at us for a long moment. I could tell that a lot of people around us were staring, too, aware of this marked attention and wondering what would happen.

At last, the Shy Don said, "Thank you." He gave Max a friendly handshake, patted Nelli's head, and raised my hand to his lips. Then he turned and left.

"Gosh," I said, aware of the puzzled and impressed scrutiny of dozens of people around us.

"Brief," Max said, "but gracious."

"You're *friends* of the Gambello family now," Lucky said. "So if you ever need anything . . ."

"Which reminds me, my dear fellow! I must thank you for your help with the Internal Revenue Service!"

My eyes flew wide. "Lucky! What did you *do*?"

"Relax, will you? I just gave those IRS letters Max has been getting to the boss' accountant, that's all. He cleared it up with one phone call."

"*How* did he clear it up?"

"It was all just a dumb mistake. So calm down," Lucky said. "The letters was intended for a business with a tax ID that's one digit different than Max's, is what the accountant says."

"They were dunning Max with letters on the basis of a typo?"

Max nodded. "Mercury Retrograde. Such things happen."

"So you can close your jaw," Lucky said. "I didn't break any legs."

"By the way," I said hesitantly. "I know I got a little snappish with you this past week, Lucky. I'm really sorry."

"Ah, forget it kid. Doppelgangsters, panicky wiseguys cursed with death, seeing Charlie whacked right in front of you, an evil sorcerer trying to screw up your audition, problems with your boy—with Lopez . . ." He shrugged. "Who *wouldn't* get a little cranky?" After a moment, he added, "Speaking of Lopez, here he comes."

I caught my breath and followed Lucky's gaze. Lopez was emerging from a car that was parked down the street. He was wearing a pale gray suit with a dark coal gray shirt and tie, and his black hair was neatly combed. His blue eyes looked alert and serious as he approached the church.

"Max," I said suddenly, "what do you think happened in the church that night? When the lights came on?"

Max's head turned sharply, his expression surprised as he met my gaze. "Oh! I didn't know you realized . . ."

"Realized what?" I prodded.

"Realized that one possible explanation for the sudden illumination was the unconscious imposition of his will on matter and energy at a moment when he feared for your life."

"But Max, you don't really think . . . I mean . . ."

"Think what?" Lucky said, his intent gaze fixed on the approaching cop. "What does Max not really think?"

"I think," Max said, "that we should keep our minds open to the possibility that Detective Lopez has talents of which he is unaware."

"Madre di Dio!" Lucky said.

Which was more or less my reaction, too.

"No," I said. "I don't believe it. No way. And Lopez *certainly* wouldn't believe it."

Max said nothing as he watched Lopez approach.

"Max and me will be inside," Lucky said to me, "paying our respects to the departed."

Max said, "Perhaps if I spoke with Det—"

"Leave Nelli with Esther." Lucky took her leash from Max and handed it to me. "Just in case."

I frowned at Lucky. "Lopez is *not* a dopp—"

"We'll be lightin' a candle to St. Monica while you talk to the cop."

Lopez's gaze followed them briefly as they retreated,

then moved back to me. My heart was thudding as he walked up to me. He looked so handsome, and Lucky was right, he *was* looking at me like he . . .

But if he really did feel that way, he sure didn't look happy about it.

"Hi," he said.

"Hi."

Nelli sniffed his hand, then gave a little wag of her tail.

Lopez looked at my throat and frowned with concern. He reached out as if intending to touch me, but then stopped himself and lowered his hand. "How'd you get those bruises?"

I told a semi-truth. "Buonarotti."

His expression darkened. "Does it hurt much?"

"Not so much now. I can't sing, of course, but that'll come back in a few more days."

"So you're okay?"

I nodded. He didn't say anything else.

"So . . ." I shrugged. "You didn't attend the service."

"Well, I've suggested the deceased was an accessory to murder, and I've refused to swear that his death wasn't suicide. So I thought he might climb out of his coffin if I showed up." He added, "But it seemed like a good idea to keep an eye on who did come."

"Oh."

After an awkward silence, he said, "I see the Shy Don is quite taken with you."

"He was just being polite." I reached into my purse and pulled out Lopez's cell phone. I had brought it along, thinking he might come today. "Here."

"Hey!" He was obviously pleased to get it back. "Thanks! Where did you find it?"

"The priest stole it from you. At Vino Vincenzo."

"Son of a bitch. So he was a pickpocket?"

"Yes."

He looked at me. "How did *you* get ahold of it?"

"Dumb luck, you might say."

He evidently decided not to ask any more about it. He put the phone in his pocket.

We gazed at each other.

I thought again about that moment in the church: *I want LIGHTS!* And then . . .

I said suddenly, "Have you ever . . ."

When I didn't continue, he prodded, "What?"

I wasn't sure what I wanted to ask. "Have you ever felt strange?"

"All the time, since I met you."

"Oh!" I blinked, and hoped that maybe . . . but then I saw how sad he looked, and I knew for sure where this was going.

"Esther . . ." He frowned and looked down.

I gathered from the subsequent silence that he had decided not to ask what I was doing at St. Monica's the night the priest had killed himself and Buonarotti had lost his marbles. Or why I had given my phone number to a Corvino capo, who dropped that piece of evidence when he was brutally murdered at Vino Vincenzo. Or whether I still believed I had seen Max decapitate Lopez's perfect double.

I could see him filtering through all the things he couldn't *not* think about when he looked at me now, and my heart sank. He was standing within a foot of me, but he was way out of reach.

Finally, he said, "It's not just your friendship with Max."

"I know."

"And it's not just the crazy things you said the other night."

"Uh-huh."

"Or even just the crazy things you keep *doing*."

"Oh?"

His expression was so unhappy, it made me want to put my arms around him.

In a low voice, he said, "I concealed evidence. I withheld information. I lied to my sergeant and to my captain. I let you and your friends leave a crime scene, and half my report about that night is fiction."

I nodded. I hadn't asked him to do any of that. It didn't matter. He'd done it to protect me. He was afraid he'd do it again.

"The priest is dead, Buonarotti's going to prison, no innocent people got hurt . . ." He let out his breath and shook his head. "But we got lucky, that's all. I can't . . ." He tried again. "You and I . . ."

"This went badly for us, huh?"

"Yeah."

"And you like me and wish things were different."

"Uh-huh."

"But things being what they are, you're not going to call me anymore or ask me out again."

He took a deep breath. "Yeah."

"And since you're the one breaking up with me," I said, "why do *I* have to write all your dialogue?"

That surprised him into a smile. "Sorry."

I folded my arms. "I wish . . ."

Well, mostly I wished he didn't think I was crazy and possibly felonious. He'd gotten past my bizarre involvement in the disappearances that had started with Golly Gee. It was too much, I could see, to ask him to get past this, too.

He cleared his throat. "Keep my phone number. If you need anything. I mean, if you need help or—"

"As in, psychiatric help?"

"As in, *my* help."

"Oh."

"If you do, I want you to call me."

"Seriously?"

"Yes. Seriously. Okay?"

"Okay."

"Yo, Esther!" Tommy Two Toes said as he passed me. "Are you gonna be singing at Stella's tonight?"

I shook my head and pointed to my bruised throat.

"Jesus! Well, don't you worry! That's *stronzo*'s gonna pay for what he done," Tommy said cheerfully. Then he noticed Lopez and flinched.

Lopez gave him a bland stare.

After Tommy was gone, I said, "I get the impression Buonarotti may not be safe in prison."

"Probably he should have picked a different profession," Lopez said.

Inside the church, Max was talking with a child who, it turned out, was Don Victor's youngest granddaughter. They were engaged, Max said, in a fascinating dialectical discussion of traditional Catholicism.

Lucky was kneeling before the statue of St. Monica, but I guess he wasn't deeply absorbed in praying. When he noticed me nearby, handing Nelli over to Max, he said to me, "Well?"

I came over to join him. "He broke up with me."

"The bum!"

"Maybe he's right, Lucky. He doesn't even know it, but he was cursed with death because of me." My longing for Lopez was swamped by my horrified guilt over having nearly gotten him killed. "He probably would have been just another cop on the case if I hadn't drawn Gabriel's attention to him by talking about him and by my involvement with him."

"Yeah, but—"

"No, Lucky. Lopez could be right about this. Maybe I'm bad for him."

Without having realized I was on the verge of it, I started to cry. I turned my face away from the church pews where Max was deflecting the child's energetic assertion of an omnipotent benevolent deity. I didn't want him to see how upset I was, since he'd probably blame himself for this.

"Come on, kneel down," Lucky said. "St. Monica comforts the afflicted, even if they ain't Catholic."

I knelt next to Lucky and tried not to think about Lopez's sad blue eyes and dark face as he told me he wouldn't see me anymore. I wiped my tears and sought a distraction as I stared at the berobed statue poised above the flickering candles.

Thinking of St. Monica's most devoted parishioner, I said, "I didn't see the Widow Giacalona at the funeral. When is she coming back?"

"She ain't." Lucky gave a heavy sigh. "She likes it out there in Seattle. Says she's staying. She's done with this life. She ain't never coming back. And she don't ever wanna speak to me again. *Ever*."

"Oh, Lucky. I'm so sorry to hear that." And after he had saved her life, too.

"Yeah. Well." The old hit man shrugged. "Love. Whaddya gonna do?"

We gazed up at St. Monica together, two broken-hearted souls seeking comfort ... And a single tear rolled down the plaster saint's cheek.

"*Lucky!* Do you ..."

"Yeah. I see it!" His gruff voice was filled with awe.

I watched the tear roll all the way down the saint's face, and I continued staring in silent wonder, until the tender trickle of moisture had dried and evaporated.

"Your saint really does weep for the brokenhearted," I said. "I thought it was just ..." I shook my head. "You know."

"Hey, kid, there's miracles everywhere," Lucky said. "You just gotta let your eyes be open to 'em."

"Wow." I was still brokenhearted about Lopez, but ... "I feel a little better."

"Me, too," Lucky said. "Ain't life something?"

My cell phone rang, startling me. "Sorry." I pulled it out of my purse and glanced at the LCD panel. "Oh, *no*."

"What is it?" Lucky asked in alarm.

"My mother!" How did she always do this? "How does she know I'm in a church, kneeling before a Catholic saint, and crying because my would-be boyfriend just dumped me? How does she always *know?*"

I considered not answering, but I'd just have to call her back later. "Might as well get it over with," I muttered. I rose to my feet and flipped open the phone. "Hello?"

My mother's first words were, "'Singing Server Sees Slaying'?"

"*You* read the tabloids?" I blurted.

"No, dear. But people love to share good news with a proud mother."

I sighed and started walking down the aisle. "It's all over now. They caught the killer."

As I guiltily headed for the exit before she could ask where I was, she said, "Please tell me you're not still waiting tables at the restaurant where this happened."

"Actually, I am. But things are looking up, Mom. I just got cast as a homeless bisexual junkie prostitute."

"How nice," she said.

"On a TV show," I said.

"Oh, good. This way a maximum number of people nationwide can see my daughter in that persona."

Outside in the sunlight, New York City greeted me with robust noise and color and life. Sometimes besieged by Evil, and sometimes full of heartbreak, but always full of wonders.

Acknowledgments

Blame my friend Mary Jo Putney for putting the idea of Mercury Retrograde into my head, though any misstatements about it in the text are strictly my own error. Apart from that, I once again owe MJP many thanks for her practical help and moral support.

I also extend my gratitude to Naomi Wiener and the Israeli science/fiction fantasy community, Karin Laub in Jerusalem, Denise Little and my friends at Tekno Books, Hilary and Tim Warmoth, Linda Howard, Valerie Taylor, Zell Schulman, Pat McLaughlin, Jerry Spradlin, Betsy Wollheim, Marsha Jones, Elaine English, and my parents, who all made it possible, in their various ways, for me to write this book and to see it published, after some hairpin turns in fate, while juggling many commitments and crossing the ocean twice.

Seanan McGuire

The October Daye Novels

"...will surely appeal to readers who enjoy my books, or those of Patrica Briggs." —*Charlaine Harris*

"Well researched, sharply told, highly atmospheric and as brutal as any pulp detective tale, this promising start to a new urban fantasy series is sure to appeal to fans of Jim Butcher or Kim Harrison."—*Publishers Weekly*

ROSEMARY AND RUE
978-0-7564-0571-7

A LOCAL HABITATION
978-0-7564-0596-0

(Available March 2010)

To Order Call: 1-800-788-6262
www.dawbooks.com

DAW 142

Once upon a time...

Cinderella—real name Danielle Whiteshore—did marry Prince Armand. And their wedding was a dream come true.

But not long after the "happily ever after," Danielle is attacked by her stepsister Charlotte, who suddenly has all sorts of magic to call upon. And though Talia the martial arts master—otherwise known as Sleeping Beauty—comes to the rescue, Charlotte gets away.

That's when Danielle discovers a number of disturbing facts: Armand has been kidnapped; Daniellie is pregnant; and the Queen has her own Secret Service that consists of Talia and Snow (White, of course). Snow is an expert at mirror magic and heavy-duty flirting. Can the princesses track down Armand and rescue him from the clutches of some of Fantasyland's most nefarious villains?

The Stepsister Scheme
by Jim C. Hines
978-0-7564-0532-8

"Do we *look* like we need to be rescued?"

DAW 130

There is an old story...

...you might have heard it—about a
young mermaid, the daughter of a king, who
saved the life of a human prince
and fell in love.

So innocent was her love, so pure her
devotion, that she would pay any price for the
chance to be with her prince. She gave up her
voice, her family, and the sea, and became
human. But the prince had fallen in love with
another woman.

The tales say the little mermaid sacrificed her
own life so that her beloved prince could find
happiness with his bride.

The tales lie.

Danielle, Talia, and Snow from
The Stepsister Scheme return in

The Mermaid's Madness
by Jim C. Hines
978-0-7564-0583-0

"Do we *look* like we need to be rescued?"

DAW 109

Tanya Huff
The *Smoke* Series

Tony Foster—familiar to Tanya Huff fans from her *Blood* series—has relocated to Vancouver with Henry Fitzroy, vampire son of Henry VIII. Tony landed a job as a production assistant at CB Productions, ironically working on a syndicated TV series, "Darkest Night," about a vampire detective. Tony was pretty content with his new life—until wizards, demons, and haunted houses became more than just episodes on his TV series...

"An exciting, creepy adventure"—*Booklist*

SMOKE AND SHADOWS
0-7564-0263-8
SMOKE AND MIRRORS
0-7564-0348-0
SMOKE AND ASHES
0-7564-0415-4

To Order Call: 1-800-788-6262
www.dawbooks.com

DAW 46